Praise for *A Darker Reality*

"Anne Perry's lush descriptions of the magnificent home and luxurious setting help settle readers into a comfortable niche to observe and listen in on Elena's conversations with the well-connected, distinguished guests, which lead her to question her grandparents' political beliefs. . . . Anne Perry leads readers on a steady march, keenly analyzing suspects, subjecting readers to palm-sweating confrontations with Agent Elena in disguise and deep, emotional delving into grief."

—Historical Novel Society

"A good historical mystery is like a balancing act—too little period detail and the story feels fuzzy, too much and it gets bogged down—and Perry, who has also written the Charlotte and Thomas Pitt and the William Monk series, gets the balance just right. It would be easy to believe that Elena Standish really did exist, and that the books are actual biographical stories. Perry proves once again why she is among the top writers of historical mysteries."

—*Booklist*

"Another sharply and well-written story focusing on the great character of Elena Standish and her secret work. The story keeps the reader engaged throughout the novel, with twists and turns and with Toby the dog back again for his third novel."

—Red Carpet Crash

"*A Darker Reality* is full of Anne Perry's trademark moral quandaries and historical detail that instantly brings credibility to the story but also makes it feel like an actual slice of world history."

—*Bookreporter*

"*A Darker Reality* is a terrific installment and offers details and insights into the character and history of Elena Standish, the victorious British M16 agent. . . . *A Darker Reality* is an absorbing and calculating thriller/mystery that grabs the reader from the first page. Readers will look forward to more Elena Standish adventures as she continues her passage through intrigue and adventure."

—Great Mysteries and Thrillers

"There can be little denying that Anne Perry is a prolific storyteller and mystery writer. She has written a number of beloved mystery series and Elena Standish is just the latest series of hers which has quickly gained in popularity. . . . If you are a fan of Perry then you will no doubt find lots to love in this one."

—The Lit Bitch

BY ANNE PERRY

FEATURING ELENA STANDISH

Death in Focus
A Question of Betrayal

A Darker Reality
A Truth to Lie For

FEATURING WILLIAM MONK

The Face of a Stranger
A Dangerous Mourning
Defend and Betray
A Sudden, Fearful Death
The Sins of the Wolf
Cain His Brother
Weighed in the Balance
The Silent Cry
A Breach of Promise
The Twisted Root
Slaves of Obsession
Funeral in Blue

Death of a Stranger
The Shifting Tide
Dark Assassin
Execution Dock
Acceptable Loss
A Sunless Sea
Blind Justice
Blood on the Water
Corridors of the Night
Revenge in a Cold River
An Echo of Murder
Dark Tide Rising

FEATURING CHARLOTTE AND THOMAS PITT

The Cater Street Hangman
Callander Square
Paragon Walk
Resurrection Row
Bluegate Fields
Rutland Place
Death in the Devil's Acre
Cardington Crescent
Silence in Hanover Close
Bethlehem Road
Highgate Rise
Belgrave Square
Farriers' Lane
The Hyde Park Headsman
Traitors Gate
Pentecost Alley

Ashworth Hall
Brunswick Gardens
Bedford Square
Half Moon Street
The Whitechapel Conspiracy
Southampton Row
Seven Dials
Long Spoon Lane
Buckingham Palace Gardens
Treason at Lisson Grove
Dorchester Terrace
Midnight at Marble Arch
Death on Blackheath
The Angel Court Affair
Treachery at Lancaster Gate
Murder on the Serpentine

FEATURING DANIEL PITT

Twenty-One Days
Triple Jeopardy
One Fatal Flaw

Death with a Double Edge
Three Debts Paid

A Darker Reality

ANNE PERRY

A Darker Reality

An Elena Standish Novel

BALLANTINE BOOKS

NEW YORK

2022 Ballantine Books Trade Paperback Edition

Copyright © 2021 by Anne Perry
Excerpt from *A Truth to Lie For* by Anne Perry copyright © 2022 by Anne Perry

Published in the United States by Ballantine Books, an imprint of Random House, a division of Penguin Random House LLC, New York.

BALLANTINE is a registered trademark and the colophon is a trademark of Penguin Random House LLC.

Originally published in hardcover in the United States by Ballantine Books, an imprint of Random House, a division of Penguin Random House LLC, in 2021.

Originally published in hardcover in the United Kingdom by Headline Publishing Group, London, in 2021.

This book contains an excerpt from the forthcoming book *A Truth to Lie For* by Anne Perry. This excerpt has been set for this edition only and may not reflect the final content of the forthcoming edition.

ISBN 978-0-593-15938-5
Ebook ISBN 978-0-593-15937-8

Printed in the United States of America on acid-free paper

randomhousebooks.com

1st Printing

To Victoria Zackheim, with gratitude

A Darker Reality

CHAPTER

1

The car came round the curve in the gravel drive and in front of them stood the house, magnificent in the sunlight. Katherine drew in her breath with a gasp of pleasure. This was the house in which she had been born and had grown up, long before she had fallen in love with and married Charles Standish and moved to England, and then to various capitals of Europe. Now, in the late spring of 1934, after so many years away, Katherine was coming home. And she was bringing with her Charles and their younger daughter, Elena.

Charles sat in the front seat of the limousine that had collected them at the Washington, DC, train station. He looked back at Katherine, who was next to Elena in the rear seat, and smiled at her obvious pleasure. She had not seen her parents for many years, and now, on the occasion of their sixtieth wedding anniversary, she was bringing her family here to celebrate with them. They knew Charles, of course; Margot, the elder daughter, they had met years ago, but Elena they had seen only as a small child, and she herself had no memory of it.

"It's beautiful, Mother, really gorgeous." Elena did not have to pretend anything. The house was huge but so graceful in its lines, pale against the dark trees towering around it, including slender, exquisite dogwoods in bloom. She had not seen them before, and all along the drive from the station to this outer suburb, she was bewitched by their exotic, pale grace.

The car reached the front portico. The house looked full of space and sunlight, with a sense of timelessness, as if the troubles of the world beyond could not touch this place.

Elena felt a great sense of peace as she opened the car door and stepped out. It had been a long journey by train from London to Southampton, then the trip across the ocean, the excitement of New York, a little shopping, a little sightseeing, and finally the train to Washington, the nation's capital. Now, at last, they were here.

The massive oak door opened. It was not a butler or a maid, but an elderly woman elegantly dressed in the palest green, with a cream-colored lace collar. Her silver hair looked casually pinned up, but Elena knew how difficult that was to do gracefully. She herself had given up attempting the look that suggested a very skilled lady's maid.

Elena drew in breath to speak, but her grandmother, Dorothy Baylor, spoke first. "You must be Elena. Welcome to Washington." Dorothy smiled, but her eyes went to Katherine, now stepping out of the car on the other side, assisted by Charles. The women moved toward each other and reached for a hug. They were the same height, with the same lean effortless grace, even the same high cheekbones. Katherine's hair, however, was brown with soft auburn lights in it.

Charles approached them, smiling. "Hello, Mother-in-law." He stood back a little. It was a long time since they had seen each other, and theirs had been an uncertain relationship at best. He was English and had taken their only daughter to live in Europe, as he rose in his career until he was a full ambassador.

Katherine turned in a single, graceful movement to include him. Elena saw the light in his face, and the tiny knot inside her eased.

A moment later, Wyatt Baylor was there, behind his wife. He was tall, imposing, his hair thick and iron gray in color. His face was hawkish, redeemed of harshness only by the charm of his smile. Now he strode forward and hugged Katherine, quickly and hard, then turned to Charles, grasping his hand with both of his own. "Welcome! Welcome to Washington." He turned to Elena and, quite frankly, looked her up and down, his smile growing wider. "I'm delighted to see you, my dear."

Elena was aware of the power of his personality, almost as if she had touched a live electric wire. It was exciting, invigorating, demanding her attention. Utterly different from her other grandfather, who was probably the person with whom she felt most at ease.

"How do you do, Grandfather?" she answered. She smiled back tentatively. "Thank you for inviting us to your sixtieth anniversary. We're delighted to be here."

"Then come in!" He stood back and waved his arm in invitation. "Leave your cases there. They'll be taken to your rooms for you. Come in, come in."

Katherine was the first to follow her mother, and then Charles, and Elena behind him.

Elena could not help gazing around at the magnificence of the hall, with its glittering chandeliers and arched ceiling, and the staircases, which went in twin curves up to the balcony of the first floor, a sort of musicians' gallery, with delicately carved banisters and railings. Of course, she had seen marvelous houses before, but not as a family home. Not her family anyway. It was not the wealth of it that held her; it was the beauty: the soft, pale colors that complemented each other, the cream of the walls and the pale gold of natural wood. She saw it in upholstered chairs, and in the curtains of soft greens, and the occasional flash of coral in a cushion, rich and bright. All the photographs she would be taking would be black-and-white, but even then, the intensity of these colors would be evident.

She followed the others across the hall and up the staircase, then along a passage to the bedroom that her parents were to share. The open door showed cream again, but this time with a soft coffee color and blues. Then on to the one for her, with twin beds. One of them would have been for Margot, had she been able to come. She had wanted very much to join them, but she had sprained her ankle quite badly, and the long sea journey from London, on crutches, would have been no pleasure for her. Elena was missing her sister and sharing all of this with her. Left alone in her room, she admired the bedcovers of blue, aquamarine, and white, piled with pillows, many of them satin. Yet what seemed strange to her was home to her mother, as familiar to Katherine as Grandfather Lucas and Grandmother Josephine's house was to Elena. In truth, theirs was more home to her than the different embassies across Europe her family had lived in, culminating in Paris, Berlin, and Madrid.

There was a knock on the door, and she answered it to find a manservant holding her suitcases. She stood aside as he carried them in and put them on the luggage stand nearest to the wall. "Thank you," she said. "Thank you very much." She smiled at him with sudden intensity. "I appreciate it."

He smiled back. "You're welcome, miss."

Elena and her father spent the first few hours following Katherine as she showed them through the house, pointing out the places she particularly remembered, where special events in her life had taken place. It was all graceful, pleasing; nothing looked scuffed or mended. The furniture was antique, yet none of it appeared well used. Perhaps there was a room like that somewhere else?

Elena watched with changing emotions. She was twenty-nine now, and by that time in her mother's life, Katherine was married and had three children: Mike, who had been killed in the last week of the war and was buried somewhere in France; Margot, only a year younger than Mike; and Elena. But the war had changed everything for Elena's generation of women: a generation of young men had been lost.

For Elena—having been joined by her American grandmother, a woman who was in ways so like Elena's mother, and yet also different—the house tour was exciting, a sweet experience. She saw her mother in a new way, belonging here. She watched the light and shadow in her mother's face as memories came to her. A view of the lounge, across the way from the stairs, the angle of the picture above the mantelpiece, sunlight on the curtains—all would bring back memories. They were good memories; Elena could see that. Katherine glanced at her father and caught his eye as he was watching her. He smiled, sharing her pleasure.

Elena was filled with happiness that she had come, that she had been given this opportunity. She had taken her mother's quiet courage for granted. Margot knew her better than Elena did. Elena had always been closer to her English grandmother, Josephine. And, of course, Lucas. Was it usual for your grandfather to be your best friend? The person who always had time for you? Who treated you like an adult, who told you wonderful stories about history, and the nature of the stars, and really funny jokes? The one who could recite absurd rhymes that made you laugh?

She smiled as she thought of her grandfather, and it was the same smile that touched her mother's face as she looked through the arch at the sitting room, where so many of her early memories lay.

Dinner was delicious. They ate slowly, seated in the dining room, which looked out through trees and onto the lawn, talking all the time about many things, moving from one subject to another in excited sentences: "Do you remember . . . ?" followed by places, incidents, and people. Elena was happy to listen.

She was taken by surprise when Wyatt Baylor asked her what she did for work. He was staring at her, smiling. "Didn't you have a really good job at the Foreign Office? Interesting?" It was a polite question, expressed with regard.

Elena could understand why Katherine had not written and told him of her disgrace. Falling in love with someone unsuitable might be considered a failing of her parents, but sleeping with anyone she was not married to would mark her as a fallen woman to her grandfather's generation. And the fact that her lover, Aiden, had also turned out to be a traitor to England, and to all who were against the violence and atrocities of rising Nazism, would be unforgivable. Only now, years later, and after a whole episode in Italy that had so nearly taken her life, did she feel able to leave it behind.

She looked around the table. Everyone was staring at her. Her parents looked as if they were trying to think of something to answer, but they said nothing. Even now, only Grandfather Lucas knew the whole truth about what she had done in Italy, and at what cost.

Elena forced herself to meet her grandfather's eyes, even to smile. "I do something quite different now, but it's confidential."

His eyebrows went up. "From your own family?" For an instant he looked at Katherine, then back to Elena. He was still smiling, but there was a chill in it.

The answer was on her tongue immediately. "It's for their protection, too. Then, if anything goes wrong, they can't be blamed." Did that sound like an excuse, an evasion? "But most of the time," she went on, "I'm learning to be a news photographer. Filling in with appropriate words. And, of course, covering society parties." She smiled. "That's another reason I find the prospect of your party so exciting. And this beautiful house will be a perfect backdrop for all sorts of gorgeous pictures. Enough to fill a book." Now she was gushing. She hated that.

Charles relaxed and leaned back a few inches, as if he had changed his mind about interrupting to defend her.

"She's really very good," Katherine said quickly. "She's had many of her photographs published in the most fashionable magazines. I imagine a lot of people would be interested," she smiled, "and envious of those who came to your party. And she is right about the house. I'd forgotten how lovely it is. I'm sure some of it is new, since I was last here." She gave a rueful little smile. "But the colors are the same." She turned to her father and then looked at Elena. "Don't you think so? That coral shade in the lounge and in the hall is so . . . so flattering to the complexion. And anyone could look elegant against the stairway."

"Yes, it is," Elena agreed. "Actually, all the colors I've seen here are lovely. And the staircase is wonderful . . . that long curving line that breaks the vertical lines of the hall. It begs to be stared at!"

Elena relaxed as the conversation moved along. They all left the table in a pleasant mood. Charles and Elena excused themselves to go to bed early, after their journey from New York, while Katherine stayed up with her parents. Wyatt and Dorothy were excited about their party, a celebration of sixty years together, and an evening never to be forgotten.

CHAPTER

2

The following day was the sixtieth anniversary party. Elena woke up to a bright sunny morning and for an instant wondered where she was. Then she recalled with pleasure the previous evening and lay back again to watch the sunlight shining through the trees outside her window, making patterns on the ceiling.

She had a late breakfast, as did everyone else. They had a big day ahead. Before she left England she had already decided what to wear to the party, with Margot's approval. Margot knew better what suited Elena and had more courage to be original. Elena had been conservative—translation: boring—whereas Margot was outrageous, but never vulgar. She wore crimson and looked wonderful, and she drew gasps of admiration with her avant-garde tastes. Margot had very dark hair, which she wore sleeked back in a loose knot at the nape of her neck. Elena was blond, her hair fairer now than Nature had given her, since her necessary disguise the previous year in Germany. That was, in a sense, when she had been reborn. She had been hiding in a scarlet silk dress! Everybody noticed the dress, she learned, and no one would remember her face when she dressed so daringly.

For the party this evening, she would wear her wavy blond hair loose, and her slender, beaded black dress that was not exactly tight, but made to fit in a highly flattering way. Katherine had not seen it yet, but Margot had thoroughly approved, and that was enough.

Elena had the gown out and ready, with new silk stockings and stylish, lacy underwear.

The hours seemed to fly by, and it was suddenly time to go downstairs to have afternoon tea with her mother and Grandmother Dorothy. There was a buzz of excitement in the air. Her grandparents had household servants—a cook, two housemaids, and a butler—but the party was going to be catered. Slender men in black were bringing in trays of food, linen cloths, crystal glasses, and silver trays. And flowers: vases of gold and white blossoms.

The first guests were due to arrive at six. Well before that time, Elena was dressed, pacing the floor, uncertain whether to go down early or not. Should she see how her mother was doing? No. She would be giving a final touch to the wrapping of the family gift, not something Elena was good at. Odd, since she had such a sense of proportion in photographs, and the balance, drama, and meaning of light and darkness were second nature to her. But the tying of ribbons, particularly the technique that made them stay as they should, defeated her.

She took a last look in the mirror. Was she satisfied? Not quite. But perhaps she never would be. She took her smallest camera and a notebook and pencil to record names and addresses. She went out the door, closing it behind her, and headed for the stairs.

From the top landing, she looked down into the massive hallway. There was more than a score of people there talking, laughing, greeting new arrivals as they joined them. The men were all in formal black, but the women were a kaleidoscope of colors. One woman with auburn hair wore a gown of rich pink, with a plunging back almost to her waist. She was willowy enough for it to be perfectly decent. She made Elena think of a budding rose on a slender stem. Immediately, she pulled the camera out of her bag and took a picture of the woman. This could be a terrific evening.

Something about her abrupt stillness must have caught her mother's eye. She was directly below where Elena stood, and she looked up suddenly. Elena noted that Katherine was wearing a lavender-blue gown with a sweeping skirt, almost regal, as elegant as she always was. She did not know how to be clumsy. Margot had inherited her grace. She, too, moved like a dancer, and was slender, with only just enough shape to be feminine.

Elena expected a frown from her mother at the use of the camera when the subject was unaware of it, but Katherine gave her a dazzling smile. Elena raised her camera and captured it on film.

More people arrived. One couple caught Elena's attention. The man looked like any other in a beautifully tailored black suit; it was the woman who was quite breathtaking. She was exquisitely feminine in a shimmering, perfectly cut gown of dazzling white. There must have been thousands of tiny beads on it, and each one caught and reflected the light as she moved. Her hair was a soft, dark cloud around her head, but it was her face that most held Elena's attention. It was a brave face, fine-boned, even delicate, but full of life.

Others noticed her, too. Elena, now halfway down the stairs, could see people turning, both men and women. Grandmother Dorothy was one of them, and she came forward. She wore a high-necked gown of the same rich coral shade she had used in the house: warm, softer than red, vibrant, and definitely flattering. Her silver hair gleamed as she passed under the chandeliers and welcomed her new guests.

Elena took a picture of this also. She was too close to them to get the whole panorama. It would not do to sell to any magazine, but it caught the spirit of the evening.

She put her camera back in her bag and continued down to the hall to meet whoever her mother wanted to introduce to her, and be charming and say just enough to look interested, yet not command the attention that should be her grandmother's on this occasion.

"You'll get some wonderful pictures," Katherine said to her softly, as she took her arm to lead her toward the first people to whom she would be introduced. "But please be discreet. Be a guest here, part of the family, and only secondarily a photographer."

Elena hid her smile at the irony of it. She thought at least half the women were there to be seen, as would be the case at any party they went to. They may have dressed for the fun of it, but above all they dressed to be remembered. She had shot enough social pictures to know that this was universal. But now was not the occasion to say so. "Yes, Mother," she said obediently, and before Katherine could comment on her tone, they were next to Dorothy and facing the woman in beaded white.

To Elena she was as perfect close up as she had been from the top of the stairs. What had not been observable from above, however, was the glint of humor in her eyes.

"Mr. and Mrs. Harmon Worth," Katherine said with a smile. "I would like you to meet my daughter Elena, and please excuse her enthusiasm for photographing everyone. She is very good at it but seldom gets the opportunity to see such an occasion, where every direction you look is another memorable scene."

"I'm delighted to meet you, Miss Standish." Harmon Worth bowed very slightly and offered his hand.

"How do you do, Mr. Worth?" Elena replied.

He smiled, and it lit his face with warmth. "I think I'm doing better all the time," he replied. "A marvelous party, to celebrate much happiness."

Elena's first thought was that he must be a diplomat, but Katherine corrected her. "Harmon is a distinguished scientist. He and Grandfather Wyatt have worked together quite often, but Grandfather's role has to do with the finance—that's where he is brilliant."

"I'm afraid science can be expensive." Harmon smiled apologetically. "Endless experiment is necessary, and some of it costs a fortune."

Elena was listening with more than polite interest now, but Katherine did not elaborate any further, and the conversation moved to a more mundane subject. After a few moments, Elena found herself alone with Mrs. Worth. It seemed odd to address this woman beside her as plain Mrs. Worth. She stood out even in this glamorous society. More and more people were arriving, the women's gowns a parade of the latest, most expensive, and most daring style.

"They say so much about a person, don't they?" Mrs. Worth commented quietly, but with amusement. Her European accent was faint but quite distinct. It added to her charm.

Elena looked at her.

"Austrian," she answered the unspoken question. "Please, call me Lila."

"Thank you," Elena responded. "I hope you don't mind, but I took a photograph of you as you came in. I was standing on the stair . . ."

Lila laughed. "Are you going to photograph many of us? People expect it at an event like this, and how they are dressed, the way they walk, whom they speak to, it's all so fascinating!"

Elena looked at this woman more closely. She was beautiful, certainly, but there was far more than perfect features to her: there was intelligence, curiosity, and humor in her face, as well as a certain daring. "Do I need to ask their permission, do you think?"

"Not at all," Lila said vehemently. "That would rob it of half the meaning. You would still have their choice of gown, of course, and that would tell you a lot—the color, the fabric, and most of all the cut." She waved a dismissive hand. "But if they do not know they are posing for the camera . . ." She looked very directly at Elena. "Are you a good photographer?"

Elena did not even consider lying. "I have failures, and I can't always tell which they are going to be, but I have successes also. And yes, I think some of them are very good."

"Your best?" Lila asked.

One came to Elena's mind immediately. "My sister, Margot, who is quite a lot like my mother to look at, lean and dark and terribly self-controlled, and elegant. Very early one morning in Amalfi, I was on the slope of the hill, quite a long way above her. She was alone in the square, in a red dress, dancing. I took a few photographs. One of them was so beautiful—not just the tones, but the angle, the shadows, and the courage in—"

Lila waved her hand, cutting her off. "You don't need to explain. A scarlet dress for courage, dancing alone in the rising sunlight. Yes, I would guess you are a very good photographer, even great at times." She glanced around the room. "You will find surface glamour here, but you will find reality underneath the artifice, if you look. You will see the courage to be yourself, the loneliness of a pose when the reality hurts, when you are far more alone than you want anyone else to know. That woman to your left—no, don't look at her now!—but that dress with the simplicity of a Greek statue, do you see it?"

"Yes. It's really classic."

"It's her husband she's trying to please, not any of us," Lila said.

"How do you know?" Elena asked.

"Do you dress to please yourself?" Lila looked her up and down so frankly that Elena felt herself blush. "Of course you do," Lila replied to her own question. "At least, this time. Don't tell me your mother chose this gown. Your sister perhaps, for you, but not one she would wear herself. You say she is lean? A dancer at heart? That dress says more about you than you think!"

Elena could feel her face burn.

Lila took her arm so lightly that Elena could see it rather than feel it. "It's the dress I would wear myself, if I had your figure. It's a 'to hell with everybody else, I am me, take it or leave it' dress."

In spite of herself, Elena laughed. "I don't know whether that is a compliment or not, but I like it."

"Oh, it's a compliment," Lila said lightly. "Now, let's go and see what else there is to notice."

Elena agreed immediately. She liked this woman, with her honesty and acute perception.

She was still with Lila, talking as easily as if they had known each other for years, when the guests of honor arrived. Everyone in the sitting room fell silent due to a noise in the entrance hall. Clearly, something was happening.

Lila looked at Elena questioningly.

"I don't know," Elena replied.

Two footmen—or perhaps waiters—one on either side, opened the double doors to the hall, and all conversation stopped. As a man in a wheelchair came in, one or two people sitting in chairs or on the sofa rose to their feet.

"Oh, my goodness," Lila whispered. "Now I am impressed. That's our President, Franklin Roosevelt. I underestimated your grandfather as an occasional consultant."

Elena was left speechless. She stared at the woman who came after the President. Eleanor Roosevelt was unattractive by usual standards, but fascinating. Her intelligence was an aura around her such that Elena did not notice what she wore, only that it was dark. It could have been any shape at all.

The crowd closed around them, as close as was permitted within the bounds of respect. Katherine had said nothing about her father knowing Roosevelt, and certainly not enough to have invited him to their home.

"You didn't know, did you?" Lila said softly.

"No."

"So much we don't know, even about those closest to us."

Elena did not answer, though she was aware of Lila's eyes on her: gently, but with acute observation. She thought about her grandfather Lucas, her father's father. It was only one year ago that she had discovered the truth: that during the war, Lucas Standish had been head of MI6, the foreign intelligence service of Britain. Spymaster Lucas! Everyone thought he had been a civil servant of some sort, shuffling papers in the safety of an office. Charles, his own son, had been deeply disappointed in him for that. He would never have used that word, but it was the truth. Elena had discovered her grandfather's true role as head of MI6 one dreadful, violent night, and she had been horrified. Now she had joined him in the intelligence service. Inadvertently at first, and then later with a whole heart.

She was a novice compared to her grandfather, but she was learning. And she cared. She cared even more deeply about the work she and Lucas were doing because the rest of the world, even her own mother, was completely unaware of the part she was playing. Only Grandmother Josephine knew, and had always known. Not that Lucas had told her, but because she had been a decoder during the war and had worked it out for herself.

"Of course, we don't know, and yet we assume all kinds of things," Elena replied. "Some assumptions are wildly wrong. And if we have any respect for our families, we will let them keep their secrets. There are things I don't want to know. Everyone is fallible, but kindness allows mistakes to sink beyond sight." She smiled at Lila. "I would like mine to be forgotten. I've certainly made an ass of myself more than a few times."

"It's one of the great arts in life," Lila said with a moment's profound feeling. "When to look, and when not to."

Elena hesitated to reply, because she felt the woman's comment warranted something more than a simple agreement, but any intended reply was prevented by a buxom woman who was dressed in green, which was surprisingly attractive on her. She had interrupted them to introduce a tall man with a charming smile.

"James, my dear, let me introduce you to Mrs. Worth, and Wyatt's English granddaughter, Miss Standish." She indicated Elena with a questioning face, as if she were not quite sure of her identity.

Elena responded immediately. "How do you do, Mr. . . . ?"

"Allenby, James Allenby, Miss Standish." His voice was soft, courteous, with a definite, almost English, precision. Anglo-American, perhaps?

He turned immediately to Lila. "A pleasure to see you again, Mrs. Worth."

Lila hesitated a moment, possibly searching for a memory. Then she smiled. "Captain Allenby. I half expected to see you here. I hope you are well?"

An odd question, Elena thought, but he answered as if he had expected it. "Very well, thank you. Your advice was . . . better than I expected."

And an odd answer. Then Elena chided herself for being ridiculous. She was seeing double meanings where there were none.

The woman in green looked a little puzzled, opened her mouth to say something, then said nothing.

"May I bring you a drink?" Allenby asked Lila. "Champagne?"

"Thank you, that would be very nice," she accepted.

Allenby turned to leave, perhaps to escape?

"Is this your first visit here, Miss Standish?" the woman asked.

"Yes, it is," Elena replied, and started to tell them both all the things she could think of that she had admired and enjoyed. The awkwardness passed. Allenby returned with a waiter close behind him bearing a tray of drinks.

A few minutes later, Lila took the woman in green by the arm, eager to introduce her to someone else.

Allenby gave a smile and a sigh.

Elena smiled back. "I'm sure somebody enjoys it," she said quietly. As soon as the words were out of her mouth, she thought perhaps they were unwise.

"It's the price one pays for meeting the people you will actually like," he said with a smile.

"Then I agree," she answered immediately. "Cheap at the price. I will learn to talk polite nonsense and look as if I am hypnotized with fascination, rather than concentrating on not falling asleep."

"Are you falling asleep? There's a five-hour gap between here and London. You can hardly be blamed."

"We had several days on the ship, and then we came via New York, so that's not an excuse anyone would buy," she told him.

"You don't lie easily or well, do you?" he said with quiet amusement.

"No, but I am quite good at evasion. I am so candid that when I do lie, you won't notice it."

He stared at her soberly for a moment, then gave a wide, beautiful smile. "You win. I have no idea. I saw you with a camera earlier—are you going to photograph these people for fun, or a more sober reason? They'll be flattered either way."

"A more sober reason," she answered. "It's what I do. One really good picture, either of somebody everyone's interested in or of someone anonymous that catches an instant and a momentary candor, can be more powerful than a hundred written words."

"Have you taken any like that?" He suddenly seemed completely serious.

Elena found herself answering honestly. "One. It was in Berlin, about this time last year. It was of students at the book burning on the tenth of May. It was in the firelight, and they personified madness. Minds beyond human reach. It still terrifies me to look at it."

"You took that?" he asked, almost urgently.

"I took one like that. Why?"

"I saw one like that. The firelight was reflected in their eyes. It frightened me as nothing else has."

She looked at him steadily and saw the emotion in his face. Then, as suddenly, it was gone.

"For God's sake, don't show us so honestly," he said so quietly she only just caught the words.

"There's nothing here like that," she answered.

"High society, politicians, the rich and ambitious. You don't think they could be as dangerous?" His tone was light, but his eyes were perfectly serious and questioning.

She wanted to be as honest, but she knew she could so easily say something she should not. Based on her work for MI6, she must be careful, but not look it. Where was the line between too much knowledge and not enough? "Perhaps I should look a little more carefully," she said, on the edge between gravity and ease.

His eyes widened in surprise. "Really? You disappoint me. I thought you would want to catch 'the great and the good,' as they say, in an unguarded moment. Show both their glamour and their humanity."

"That is exactly what I shall try to do," she replied. "You put it very well. Thank you, Captain Allenby." She smiled at him, and for a moment there was complete honesty between them.

"With her permission, you might get a good one of Mrs. Roosevelt," he went on. "She has the most interesting face in the room, I think."

"I agree with you. Thank you for the advice." And with another smile, Elena excused herself and walked over toward a group of people that included her mother and grandmother. She was welcomed immediately in a conversation already under way and full of emotion.

"What will our grandchildren know of it, if we let it slip out of our hands?" one woman demanded, her mouth pulled tight with anger. Elena saw it was the person who had introduced her to Captain Allenby.

Elena had no idea what they were talking about. She glanced at her grandmother, but Dorothy only nodded in agreement, and put her hand lightly on the woman's arm. "Don't worry, Mabel. We've never been beaten yet, and we won't be now."

"Thank you, dear," Mabel replied. "We have a lot to hope for. I think Europe is fighting hard, and they at least have their values in the right place."

"You are right to be prepared, of course," Dorothy said quietly.

"I hope Mr. Roosevelt turns out to be as good as—" Mabel began.

"Have I introduced you to my granddaughter?" Dorothy interrupted, her hand tightening almost imperceptibly on Mabel's satin-clad arm. "Mrs. Mabel Cartwright, may I introduce my granddaughter, Miss Elena Standish."

"We met earlier," said the woman. "With Lila Worth."

"We did," Elena responded.

This time, Mabel Cartwright looked Elena up and down, a shadow crossing her strong-boned face.

Elena had known the black dress would have that effect on some people, possibly including her grandmother. She gave Mabel a radiant smile and could feel her mother relax.

Katherine turned and looked at them both. "Elena, perhaps Mrs. Cartwright will allow you to photograph her. She is definitely one of the celebrities here that a society magazine would find impressive."

"Oh, now, you are too kind," Mabel said, the shadows softer on the outline of her jaw.

Elena took the cue. "Would you mind?" she asked as humbly as she could manage. She did not want to embarrass her mother, or her grandmother.

"Of course not, my dear," Mabel said with a smile. "I'd be happy to. I know an excellent place. Lighting and background, and all that sort of thing."

Elena tried not to flinch. Mabel was taking over already. "By all means," she said. "I see you know a good deal about it."

"Oh, I've been photographed a few times," Mabel said lightly.

Elena glanced at her mother's face and read it perfectly. The moment was saved.

Mabel was leading the way across the crowded hall, bustling past people with an airy wave of her hand, diamond rings sparkling in the light. Elena followed. She guessed the spot that Mabel was heading toward, just halfway between the lights. There was nothing to do but follow.

Mabel reached the point she was looking for and turned around with a swirl of her green dress. "Here?" she asked.

Elena looked at the light. It was bright and hard, not in the least flattering to a woman of a certain age. She looked around for a better place. The camera can certainly lie, but not all of those lies are kind. She saw the stairway by which she had entered. The light was softer, shadowed in some places.

"There," she said firmly. "That's where the light is best."

Mabel frowned. "It's shadowed," she said flatly.

"It's dramatic," Elena replied. "You have strong bones. It could be commanding, if I do it well. Highlight the cheekbones." She touched her own cheek quickly. "But if you prefer, I can do both, and then you keep the one you like."

Mabel's eyebrows rose but her expression did not change. "Really?"

"If you stand where you feel comfortable." She waited while Mabel stood one way, and then another, and then a third.

"Chin down a little," Elena suggested.

Mabel jerked her chin up. It was arrogant, but a striking appearance.

Elena took the photograph.

Mabel froze. For a long instant, neither of them moved, and then Mabel relaxed. "Good girl," she said, with slight surprise at her own words. "You see?"

"Would you stand on the stairs, just to please me?" Elena asked. "I think you'd make a marvelous picture." Please heaven it would be good. She'd have to eat a whole crow in front of Mabel if it was not. "Please go up a few steps," she requested. "And then come down a step and stand, and then another."

"If you insist," Mabel acquiesced. She walked across the floor. One or two people moved aside, smiling. She climbed three or four steps, and then another three. She turned and very slowly came down two steps and stopped for a moment. Then she started down again, descending two more. Someone laughed. Mabel turned. Elena caught the exact moment the light touched her cheeks and softened the harder lines of her face. She took a second, another step farther down, but only as a stopgap.

Mabel reached the floor and walked over to Elena. "Thank you, my dear. You have an air of confidence, even of command, about what you do. I look forward to seeing your pictures."

"I shall develop them tomorrow," Elena said.

"Will you? I should appreciate it so much." Mabel's face was alight with anticipation. "You know, I have a feeling you could be right, and the stairs were the perfect frame after all." She leaned a little closer to Elena. "Did you know that Herr Hitler's lady friend is a photographer? It's a very important thing to be."

Elena froze. Had she really heard that? "Yes," she said awkwardly. "Yes, I had heard that. I . . ." She stopped, overwhelmed by her memory of the distress and horror during her time in Berlin: the violence, the hatred and fear breaking through from beneath the surface of calm and order. Had Mabel really said that so easily, so naturally, comparing Elena with Hitler's girlfriend? It made Berlin seem suddenly so close.

Mabel was staring at her. "Are you all right, my dear? You look . . . a little pale."

"Oh, I'm sorry." What excuse should she make? "I'm a bit overwhelmed, so many important people . . ." That sounded pathetic! "I . . ."

"Don't mind us, dear. We are all friends, you know. We all like and admire your grandfather. And Dorothy, too, of course." She leaned closer. "We all mean to keep this country safe from communists, left-wingers, Jews, and, of course, the blacks. Herr Hitler will stop them sweeping across Europe. The British will help, of course. You have some great people who can see ahead and do the right thing, don't worry!" She gave Elena's arm a pat, then walked away.

Elena felt the room sway around her and then right itself. Had Mabel really said that Hitler would show the Americans how to solve their problems? And if the woman believed this, what did her grandparents believe? Where did their sympathies lie?

CHAPTER

3

The party continued, a swirling mass of color punctuated by elegant black. Elena took note of her parents and grandparents, but she mostly moved from one circle to another, asking permission to photograph certain of the guests: the men because they were prominent and the women for the high fashion of their gowns. Everyone seemed delighted and not in the least surprised when she took notes of their names, addresses, and—where appropriate—their occupations. They were scientists, bankers, entrepreneurs, editors of newspapers, and diplomats. There were several congressmen and at least one senator. And, of course, the President of the United States. It was natural she should want to caption any picture she sold to a magazine and offer to send a copy to the subjects, if they wished. For herself, she was curious to know who her grandparents' friends were and, increasingly, as she listened to scraps of conversation, what their opinions were.

She saw Grandfather Wyatt every so often, moving among his guests, accepting their congratulations and well wishes, offering them more wine, and more of the excellent food that the waiters were serving.

"Are you enjoying yourself, my dear?" he asked her.

"Yes, thank you very much, Grandfather," she replied. "And I appreciate you allowing me to photograph your friends. It's very gracious of you. I think I have some striking pictures."

"You haven't yet got one of me!" he said with a smile. "I'll speak to some of the most outstanding guests, and you can take us together."

"Thank you, I'll do that."

She went with him as he moved about the main rooms, greeting people, always introducing her, and often requesting to be photographed with his guests. Most of them were delighted to oblige him.

As she passed, Elena caught several comments that disturbed her, even if she had not heard the whole conversation. "She's going to marry who?" asked one of the guests. "Ghastly little man. But of course, he has lots of money."

"But he's a Jew, for heaven's sake!"

"Really? Are you sure?"

"Of course I'm sure."

Raised eyebrows, uncertainty, then indignation.

Elena shivered. Her trip to Berlin a year ago came vividly to her mind. She had seen things she had wanted to forget, but neither conscience nor emotion would allow that. Old men humiliated in the street, made to stand in the gutter while young Brownshirts swaggered along the pavement. That was the presentable side of it. The other side was the young man flayed of the largest part of the skin on his body because he was a Jew, lying semiconscious on the kitchen table, oozing blood everywhere. Were they still alive, those people who had sheltered Elena when she was being hunted for a murder she did not commit?

And now here, tonight: How could these people stand in their gorgeous clothes and speak casually, as if they were discussing a rainy day or who won the last horse race? The Germany she had seen was a world away from the Germany they were talking about: the trains running on time again, the currency worth something, and food in the shops.

She must hold her tongue. They were friends of her grandfather. Perhaps he had not seen that side of them?

She took more photographs, including several of her mother. Katherine was noticeable for her vitality, the graceful angle of her head when she was listening to someone, the way she looked straight at people, and her quick, bright laughter. She seemed to feel at home here, as if the years between this visit and the last had slipped away unnoticed. Had she missed this life? Or was it just nice to be reminded of a place that had equipped her so well to be an ambassador's wife? She had played that role with such skill in Berlin, Paris, and Madrid. Wherever Katherine Standish went, she was still remembered with admiration.

Elena looked around for her father. She would like a picture of him, but he seemed to have disappeared. As she peered into various rooms, a door briefly swung open to her grandfather's study, and Charles was sitting in an armchair, leaning forward earnestly and listening to President Roosevelt speaking. She could see no one else. Then the door closed.

He did not know the President, did he? He had said nothing to her, or as far as she knew, to Katherine, about any business with the American government. But then, of course, he wouldn't. He knew about discretion as well as she did.

She turned around to find James Allenby standing behind her. There was nothing on his face to show whether he had seen Roosevelt in the room with Charles or not.

"Get some good photos?" he asked.

"I think so," she replied with a smile. "It's a wonderful house for finding places to pose. The light and shadows are flattering to almost everyone."

"Is it a photographer's job to flatter people?"

She could not read his face. "If that's the sort of photo with which you make your living. Most of us like to think we look better than we do, but . . ."

"But?"

"But . . . in between those, I like to take pictures that reveal something about the person that is not so easily observable. Possibly something they don't know about themselves, or would rather keep hidden."

"Then I had better not pose for you." He smiled.

"You have . . ." She stopped.

"What?"

"I was going to say that you have a nice face."

He pulled it into an expression of disgust. "What a damnable thing to say! It sounds so . . . bland!"

"That's why I didn't say it. Sorry about *nice;* it's a silly word. Unless you say it with its old meaning, not as in merely pleasant, but as in a refined degree, a *nice* distinction."

His eyes lit with humor. "You got out of that very nicely, Miss Standish."

She winced. "I deserve that."

"You do," he agreed. "Seen any good gowns lately?"

"None as good as Lila's. But then, anyone else in the same gown would look ridiculous."

He looked her up and down, openly appreciative. "I could say the same of yours. Black suits you very well. But I imagine a lot of colors do."

"I used to wear a lot of blue, and it was very ordinary," she responded. "I could easily be mistaken for anyone else." That was true, but that was also before Berlin. She had changed since then.

"I thought blue would be . . ."

". . . nice," she finished for him.

He laughed outright. "Fine, you win that one. How about purple? Dark, regal purple, silk or something else floaty?"

She wondered why he had such interest in her clothing. Or was he just teasing her to see how she would respond?

"Actually, that would be a lovely idea. Ever thought of going into fashion designing?"

"Never," he responded. "But I do believe that color is only a last-moment thing; it's the cut that matters. Don't you think that's the case with so many things? That it's the design that makes the difference?"

It was a light question to ask, but she had the feeling that he was talking about far more than the effect of a dramatic dress.

However, there was no time to pursue it. They were joined by the senator, who wished to have his picture taken with his wife. She was a striking woman, her slender figure swathed in a dress of ice-blue silk, her hair ash blond, and her perfect skin barely touched with color.

Elena glanced at Allenby to excuse herself and saw the amusement in his face. She thought she knew what he was thinking: Would this be a fashion-plate picture or a portrait showing freezing regality, like a solitary bare tree beside a frozen lake, beautiful and frightening? Should it evoke admiration or fear . . . or pity?

They were waiting for her. Elena smiled her thanks and began to consider light, tone, and background, where they should stand and how. She had to be courteous, suggest rather than direct, give reasons for why she asked them to move this way or that. But in the end, it was well worth her care. She got a picture of the senator and his wife together that she knew would flatter both of them. And then she took one of the woman alone, which she thought was startlingly revealing of the beauty of her icy nature, both inside and out. Elena took their information, noted the time, thanked them, and moved on.

Over the next hour, she took another photograph of her grandfather Wyatt and someone whose name she forgot. Pushing aside her discomfort, she asked the man to repeat his name and jotted it down for later.

Her next shot was one of Lila Worth, close up and laughing, vivid and uniquely beautiful. Then came a picture of Katherine and Dorothy together, daughter and mother, followed by another of her grandfather smiling at everyone, being charming and slightly imperious.

It was getting late. Elena looked forward to being able to excuse herself and go upstairs to bed. She had spent hours in intense focus. But she hoped to speak with Lila before she went home, to see if there was a time when they could meet. She had liked her immediately and looked forward to seeing her in a more leisurely way, perhaps over lunch.

She saw the gleam of the white dress across the room. But when she made her way there, Lila had moved.

"Elena!" It was her grandfather at her elbow, with two more friends. They were a silver-haired man and a handsome, middle-aged woman, both of them smiling. He introduced them and assured them that Elena was a very gifted photographer. He had a definite place in mind and shepherded them out through the big hall, down a corridor, and into a smaller room classically furnished in the French style. There was a beautiful ormolu clock on the mantelpiece.

"Here," Wyatt said enthusiastically. "Stand next to me." He beckoned to the man, who came nearer with a wide smile. The woman stood next to him and took his arm. Wyatt stepped away from them, turned, and studied the group. "Move that way." He waved his hand sideways a bit. "No, no! You've got that clock growing out of your head."

"Should we move left?" the man asked.

"No, you stay there! You move, that's right!" Wyatt smiled. "I'll just stand here," he said, joining them and putting his hand on the man's arm. "Now!" He flashed a smile at Elena.

She took the picture, then moved a step back and took another, and then a third. She stood farther back and took a fourth.

"Thank you, my dear." Her grandfather put his arm around her in a quick hug. "You are going to immortalize this evening. I'm so happy you came."

"So am I, Grandfather," Elena replied, and she meant it.

Elena went back into the main hallway. Guests had drifted into groups and were talking animatedly. Waiters were serving brandy from a half dozen carved crystal decanters. She looked around for Lila but did not see her, so she walked over to where her mother was standing alone. Her mother asked her nothing, but Elena saw the question in her face and smiled. "Yes," she answered. "I've got some pictures that I think are very good." She gave a slight shrug and looked around the room. "I hope they think so, too."

"They will," Katherine assured her. "You'll be surprised by what will come out of this. Washington is a beautiful city. I'd love to show you some of my many favorite places."

"I'd love that," Elena said sincerely. "And you can tell me what happened there, and how you felt, whom you knew, everything."

"Certainly not!" Katherine said for the laugh. "Unless, of course, you will do the same for me when we're back in Europe?"

"What? Tell you . . ." Elena was shaken. "I can't . . ." She thought of all the things she could never tell anyone, nearly everything about her job in MI6.

Katherine could not keep a straight face. "Of course, darling, I wouldn't want to peer into your secrets, private or professional. Just be careful . . . in both. I don't want to see you hurt again." Her voice was soft. The people even a few feet away could not have heard her.

Elena looked at her mother and saw that her face was gentle. This was not a light conversation they were having, she was certain of that. Her mother was making a promise. It was an understanding that came to Elena with a wave of emotion, too deep and sudden to allow her to find words.

Before she could summon an acknowledgment, the front door flew open, then the inner door. A young man in a chauffeur's uniform stood just inside the hall, his face white, fingers red with blood. "It's Mrs. Worth . . ." He was forcing the words out. "Someone ran over her in the parking lot. She's . . . dead!"

CHAPTER

4

Elena froze. Lila . . . dead? It was impossible to grasp. Half an hour ago they had been talking, laughing, feeling as if they had known each other for years. What could have happened?

She turned to her mother. Katherine was as horrified as she was. Someone in the vast hallway gave a cry of denial.

Wyatt came forward from the back of the room. He patted the shoulder of the young man who had just announced the terrible news. When he spoke to him, it was as if he was speaking to all of them. "Thank you. Now take me and show me what you saw." He turned to someone and instructed him to call the police.

"We'll have to deal with the situation, no matter what it is." He looked at all the people in the room. "Please stay here. It appears there might have been a terrible accident. The police may wish to speak to us. Allenby . . ." He looked around. "Where are you, Allenby?" Wyatt caught sight of him. "Be a good fellow and come with me. I may need a hand. Charles," he said, turning to his son-in-law, "please see that everyone keeps calm." As if taking for granted they would do as he directed, he spoke quietly to a servant who had hurried forward, and then turned to follow the young man who had brought the news. Together, they went out the front door, pulling it shut behind them.

Elena realized that no one had mentioned Harmon Worth, Lila's husband. She turned to her mother. "Where's her husband? Somebody's got to tell him."

"I will," Katherine said immediately. "You stay here." And without adding anything further, she turned, looked around, then headed across the hall, excusing herself as she went.

No one else moved, except to talk to those closest to them.

Elena also stood still. Did everyone feel the same sense of loss as she did? It was as if somebody had dimmed all the lights. This morning, she had not even heard of Lila Worth. Her biggest anxiety had been about whether the party was going to go smoothly, or if her grandmother would disapprove of her dress. Were these people, in their gorgeous clothes, with their power and wealth, as used to death as she was? America had lost soldiers in the Great War, too, but nowhere near as many as European countries had. Still, when it's your own family, it's devastating no matter how many or how few other people have lost. Most of them learned that the world went on, while others tried to pretend that somehow things would stay the same for them.

There was a light touch on her shoulder and she flinched.

"Where is your mother?" It was her father asking, his face filled with concern.

Elena was intensely pleased to see him. "She's gone to look for Harmon Worth," she answered. "Someone has to tell the poor man."

"Can you help me?" Charles asked urgently. "If there really is a death, we need to get President and Mrs. Roosevelt out of here quickly. His presence here would divert attention and give the newspapers a story that could result in a problem."

"They'll have to be taken through the kitchen door," she replied. "That way, their exit will be round to the back."

Charles nodded. "Will you organize that? The faster we do this, and with the least fuss, the better. They were about to leave anyway."

"Yes," she replied, "of course. But . . . Father?"

"What?"

"Are you doing this because you know the Roosevelts, or because—"

"I'm doing it because it needs to be done," he replied. "I don't know what happened, but Wyatt is going to have to deal with it. He'll be busy, and getting the Roosevelts safely away is what he would most want done. None of us knows yet exactly what's happened. Now, go and find his driver and tell him to bring the car round to the side door." And without waiting for her acknowledgment, he turned and left.

Half a dozen heads swiveled to watch him. Everyone was still suffering from shock and a confusion that, for the moment, was paralyzing.

Elena went along the passage to the kitchen and then into the servants' quarters. She assumed that the Roosevelts' chauffeur would be there somewhere, awaiting summons when he was needed.

A man was walking toward her. "You lost, miss?" he asked, reproof in his voice.

"I need to speak to President Roosevelt's chauffeur," she said stiffly. "It's something of an emergency. Would you fetch him right away, please?"

"Is Mr. Roosevelt ill?" The man's face paled.

"No," said Elena. "Just get him, please. Don't argue the point!"

He hesitated only a moment, then turned on his heel and went back the way he had come. Less than a minute later, a man in a chauffeur's uniform appeared. He looked anxious.

"I am Mr. Baylor's granddaughter," Elena introduced herself. "There's been a very bad accident in front of the house. A guest is dead. I think it would be advisable to give President and Mrs. Roosevelt the opportunity to leave by the side door. There is nothing they can do to help, only draw unnecessary attention to this tragedy."

"They're not hurt?" he asked immediately. "No, of course they're not. I'm sorry. I'll get the car." He looked around furtively, fear in his eyes.

"My father, Ambassador Standish, will take them to the side door, where you're to bring the car."

"Yes, ma'am," he said. As fast as he could move with any dignity at all, he bolted back the way he had come. Elena went to the side room off the hall, where she had last seen the Roosevelts. She knocked on the door. As soon as she heard a voice, she went in.

Franklin Roosevelt was sitting in his wheelchair by the fireside, although the fire itself was not lit. He was a striking-looking man with gray hair and patrician features. He regarded her with interest. "Yes?" he inquired.

"Mr. President, I'm Elena Standish," she answered quietly. "My father asked me to have your car brought round to the side so you could leave quickly. There's a situation, and it could become ugly. With the police arriving, you might find you'd have to stay here much longer than you wish to."

"What has happened?" His voice was perfectly level. He could have been requesting another glass of wine.

"Someone has had an accident in the car park," she replied. "I think it was fatal. My grandfather has gone out to see. But the police will be called, and an ambulance as well. My grandfather has taken charge of that." She didn't mention her nagging suspicion that this might not have been an accident, and all the ugly possibilities following from that.

"I see. Who is hurt?"

"Lila Worth." She heard her voice crack and a sudden sense of loss enveloped her. It was ridiculous! Yesterday she had never heard of the woman.

"I'm so sorry," Roosevelt said quietly. "Yes, thank you, let's not turn this into a circus. Can you please find Mrs. Roosevelt and tell her what has happened?"

"I'll make sure she knows." She turned away so he would not see the tears on her face.

"Did you know her?" he asked.

"No. And . . . yes, I think I did." She left before he could ask her to explain. She was thinking about how they might have had so much in common, believed but not yet explored. And now that would never happen.

The next twenty minutes went by very quickly. Katherine took Mrs. Roosevelt to the garden room and out through the side door. Elena saw the President and his wife get into their car and pull silently away, taking the back route, which meant avoiding the circular gravel area in the front of the house, used for guest parking. They missed the police's arrival by less than two minutes.

Elena watched the lead policeman take his position before the guests. He was an average-looking man, medium height and build, neither dark nor fair, but he had an unmistakable air of authority. Almost immediately, he had their full attention.

"Ladies and gentlemen," he announced, "my name is Captain Miller, and I will be taking command of the situation. As soon as possible, we will let you all go home, but not just yet."

"What!" a man with a thatch of white hair demanded loudly. "I—"

"I know, sir," Captain Miller said, cutting across him. "There has been a very serious accident in the parking lot. I'm afraid a woman is dead. Apparently, she has been run over by one of the cars. We have to ascertain how that happened, and who was involved. The more you all cooperate, the more quickly that can be done."

"You can't think any of us had anything to do with it!" someone called out heatedly.

"I don't *think* anything, sir," Captain Miller said calmly. "I look at the facts and see what they tell me. We shall have to question everyone—residents, guests, servants, the temporary staff. The sooner you allow us to do that, the sooner you can all go home."

Wyatt Baylor came up beside him. "Captain Miller, we have several rooms that could be made available, so you can question people as quickly as possible."

"Thank you, sir," Miller replied. "If you show me the rooms, we'll set them up for interviews. We will have more men here as soon as possible, so we can find out without too much delay everything your guests can tell us."

"Thank you." Wyatt said nothing more.

The next fifteen minutes were spent organizing fresh tea and coffee, finding empty rooms where the policemen already in the house could begin their questioning and the others could set up when they arrived. People milled around restlessly, some taking a nervous seat in any room where there were sofas or chairs, even hard-backed dining-table ones. Dorothy and Katherine helped by pouring tea and offering words of condolence.

Elena saw that her father had found Harmon Worth and was urging him to take a stiff whiskey, then a cup of sweet tea. Worth looked to be shaken to the core, his hands trembling as he tried to sip from the cup. His whole body seemed drained of energy, as if the life had slipped out of him, too.

Elena felt as if she had lost a friend, so how must he feel? She was familiar with loss. Almost everyone in Britain had lost someone in the war. She had lost her brother and her brother-in-law, Margot's husband of one week. Both of them were killed just before the end of the war, when they were beginning to think it was over at last. But in war, at least you half expected death. Lila's was out of the blue, like a lightning strike when there's a clear sky above you. What on earth could have happened?

Elena was standing in the middle of the hall, dazed and feeling useless, when she heard a footstep behind her. She turned and saw Captain Allenby. He looked as grieved as she felt.

"Why don't you come and sit down?" he suggested. "There's a seat over there." He pointed to a padded and elegant love seat at the far side of the hall. At this moment, it was not occupied.

Elena thought this a good idea. Without answering, she went over and sat down, a little heavily, as if her legs refused to support her anymore.

"Can I get you anything?" he offered.

She heard the strain in his voice and saw the slight pallor of his face. "No. No, thank you." She tried a weak smile. "I . . . I liked her very much, although I only met her today. Sounds silly, doesn't it? Did you know her well?"

"Pretty well," he replied. "She's someone you either hit it off with straightaway, or else you never do. It will take a little getting used to . . ." His voice cracked for a second. ". . . her not being here," he finished.

Elena suddenly realized how selfish she was being. She had lost a friend she might have grown close to, but Allenby had lost a friend he already knew. And Harmon Worth had lost his wife. She swallowed hard. "Forgive me, I'm acting uselessly. I must be overtired. Everyone put such a lot of work into this party. It's . . . it's all wiped out, devastated. It seems faintly ridiculous that we were celebrating, thinking of what we wore and who we were introduced to . . . as if it mattered."

"That's healthy," Allenby replied. "We can't live on the brink of tragedy all the time. You lose your grip that way. Sorry, I'm sure you know that." A look of both compassion and understanding crossed his face, and then was gone again.

"I'm sorry, I'm being feeble." She gave him a little smile. "The police should be able to let some of the guests leave in an hour or so. Do you know what they are saying happened?"

"An accident," he replied, watching her as he said it. "She tripped and fell, and must have knocked herself out, and then someone drove into her. That's what killed her."

"What?" She was confused. "She tripped on the flat ground in the parking place? Did you ever see anyone who moved more gracefully, who was less likely to fall over her own feet?"

"Shhh," he said softly.

"I won't! I—"

Allenby put his hand on her arm; his grip was hard. "Hush, Elena. Don't say anything yet. These waters may be deeper than you think."

She was about to protest, then caught the gravity of his expression and fell silent. Why did he speak to her with this level of understanding, almost as if he was trying to convey some other message? Who was he? He had approached her casually at first, but as if he knew her. But then, everyone knew she was Wyatt's granddaughter. Did he know more than that?

After the traveling and all the excitement of meeting new relations at a strange place . . . and now this . . . it was just the sort of situation Peter Howard had warned her against. She could remember his exact words. "You are never off duty, Elena, remember that. You may know your friends and your enemies. Some people are exactly what they seem. Probably most. But there are always those who are not. Be careful!"

"Right," she agreed quietly. "I suppose they have to ask everyone where they were, what they saw."

"Yes, and it may take a lot of piecing together," he agreed. "Can I get you a cup of coffee? Or would you prefer tea?" He stood up.

"Thank you. I had better stay awake, and not wander around looking as if I'm the one who needs help."

"Stay here. I'll get you something." And without waiting for her response, he turned and walked away with surprising grace for such a tall man, almost as if he were a dancer.

The night dragged on. The police spoke to more than half the guests in the first couple of hours and allowed them to leave. The guests walked out quietly, with heads down, as if uncertain where they were going.

Elena's grandfather was everywhere, comforting people, reassuring them, being especially gentle with the women. She saw him walk a couple to their car and then return, pausing at the front door. He looked tired, but when he saw Elena, he smiled.

"How are you doing, honey?" He put his arm around her lightly, gently. "Sorry about all this. Some damn fool must have had too much to drink and wasn't looking where he was going, I suppose."

"Does it have to have been someone from the party?" she asked.

He looked at her curiously. "Trying to make me feel better?"

"No, I thought perhaps it could be someone coming off the street."

"To steal a car?" he asked. "Yes, of course, why not? Well thought, girl." He tried to smile. "But with all the President's extra security looking?" He peered around. "Have you seen your mother? Is she all right? I've been so busy trying to calm everyone and keep an eye on Dorothy, I've hardly seen her." He smiled bleakly. "Kate was always the brave one."

Elena had never heard her mother referred to as Kate, but it sounded warm, familiar. She smiled back. "I'll go and find her."

He gave her a quick squeeze of the arm, then moved over to a congressman and his wife, who were looking very shaken. She heard how he spoke to them reassuringly, calmly, and even made a mild joke. They laughed bravely.

She went to look for her mother and found her pouring wine for a man who was holding out his glass. He thanked her and she smiled at him. He would never have known how much that cost her, but Elena could tell. She had seen her mother's concentrated attention before, her steadiness of hand so not a drop was spilled.

The man looked at Elena. "I don't suppose you've any idea when they're going to let us go, have you? I saw Wyatt talking to you."

"No, I'm sorry," Elena answered. "But there seem to be far fewer people here than earlier, so maybe it will be soon."

"Don't know what things are coming to," he said with disgust, "when men like Wyatt Baylor can't have a party in his own home

without some riff-raff coming onto the property and assaulting people. Not that the woman was American, of course. Some sort of a
foreigner from Europe . . ." He left the rest of his sentence unfinished, assuming they knew what he was going to say.

Elena felt a chill inside herself. She looked to see if her mother
would object. Katherine looked uncomfortable, but she said nothing.
At another time, Elena might well have challenged him. The words
were on the edge of her tongue, but this was not the moment.

She heard other conversations around her, snatches of comfort,
and of irritation at what seemed like an unnecessary delay over of-
ficiousness by the police.

"For God's sake, why can't they get on with it? It's practically
dawn!" one woman demanded, smoothing down her crumpled dress.
"Speak to them, George. This is ridiculous. One Austrian tart? Forgive me, but she was, and then she falls over in the parking lot, and
we're all stuck here half the night! What was she doing out there
anyway?"

"Meeting someone, no doubt," George said sourly. "But there's
nothing I can do about it, Constance. Just . . . put up with it!"

Elena opened her mouth to speak up for Lila, then swallowed the
words she had been about to say. This was the time to support her
grandparents, not to voice her social opinions. "I think it's better the
police question us all tonight," Elena said calmly. "Then they won't
have to bother us any more after this. Is there anything I can get
you?" She couldn't think of their names. "Fresh coffee, or perhaps—"

"Thank you, dear," Constance interrupted. "But no, we only want
to leave. Perhaps you can fetch my coat?"

Elena froze. "I'll ask one of the maids. I'm afraid I don't know
your name."

Constance drew in a quick breath, then let it out again without
speaking.

Elena gave her a dazzling smile and held out her hand. "Elena
Standish. Wyatt Baylor is my grandfather."

Constance was saved from having to reply by the police captain coming in through the front door of the hallway. Gradually, all conversation stopped and the dozen or so people remaining turned expectantly toward him.

"Ladies, gentlemen, I'm afraid we have more questions to ask you," the captain said.

"Why the hell couldn't you have done that earlier? What's your name? Miller? Muller?" George demanded.

"Captain Miller, sir."

"You've already kept us here all the damn night for no good reason? I'll be speaking to your superior. He'll have something to say about this."

"I'm sure he will," Miller said quietly, but his voice carried throughout the entire room. "Especially because this is now a case of murder."

CHAPTER

5

For what seemed like endless minutes, Elena stood frozen. Nothing around her moved, until someone gasped.

"Murder?" a man said incredulously. "Don't be ridiculous!"

"I'm sorry, sir, but there is no doubt," Miller replied.

Someone blasphemed hoarsely, and then there was silence.

Elena turned to Katherine, who was nearest, and saw the complete bewilderment in her face. Elena moved closer and put her arm around her shoulder. "It'll be all right, Mother. The police will clear it up. It must have been someone who came to steal a car, and Lila caught them. They panicked . . ."

Katherine blinked, as if doing so would make the roomful of dazed, horrified guests disappear.

"We had better find Grandmother," Elena went on. "She will be terribly upset. Let's see what we can do to help. Have they got more whiskey or brandy, do you think? One stiff drink might do her good." She could hear the buzz of voices around her. There were now nearly twenty people in the room, and the import of what Captain

Miller had said was beginning to sink in. It was not an accident. Lila had been murdered, deliberately run over by a car.

What had the police found in the dawn light that they had not seen in the dark? How did they know it was not an accident? Beautiful, exotic Lila, so very alive. Elena could still hear her laughter, if she tried, if she shut out the voices in the room. Suddenly, her eyes filled with tears. She was so tired that she could easily have given in, curled up somewhere alone . . . and wept.

How much worse could Grandmother Dorothy be feeling? This was her sixtieth wedding anniversary! Elena turned to her mother. "You go and look after Grandmother, and I'll help Father see about the guests."

"Yes," Katherine said, standing up straighter. "I'll find her, and then make breakfast for people. It's not necessary, but it's something to do, and that is necessary." She looked around. "Where is Charles?"

"There." Elena indicated a small cluster of men, including her father and grandfather. They were talking to the senator and Captain Miller, and the senator seemed calmer than he had been earlier.

More police were coming in through the front door and were being directed around the hall and into the various rooms set aside for them.

Wyatt Baylor turned from Captain Miller and addressed the room. "Ladies, gentlemen!" Voices all around fell silent. "The police need to ask us more questions, different ones from before. Now that it seems to have been a crime rather than an accident, they need to view it differently. Have patience and answer them as you can. We need to get this over with."

"Nonsense!" one porky man said loudly. "Someone came and tried to steal a car. Mrs. Worth got in the way, for whatever reason . . . and God knows what she was doing out there—"

His wife cut him off. "Well, dear, we must try to find out!" Her tone was sharp and challenging. "For heaven's sake, that can't be too difficult. Where was everybody? I spent most of the evening talking with Mrs. Hunter. She'll say so. And I—"

Captain Miller cut across her. "Yes, ma'am. As soon as you've told us what you know, what you saw, heard, or can swear to, then you can sign a statement to that effect and go home."

"But—" she began.

"Thank you, ma'am," Miller interrupted again. "Now, if all of you will please wait here until we call you."

"What on earth do you expect to find?" demanded a lean, dark man in a perfectly cut dinner suit. "If we had seen anything, we would have stopped it, or at the very least told you without being herded around like a flock of sheep."

"The more you argue, sir, the longer it will take," Miller said wearily.

The man took a step back, but he made his displeasure obvious.

Elena raised her voice. "My mother and grandmother are going to make breakfast, for anyone who would like it," she told the crowd.

"Breakfast? Are you out of your mind?" the man demanded. "The house is full of police discussing murder, and you're talking about breakfast? As if—"

"Not eating isn't going to help," Elena said calmly. "If you are calm, it will help everyone. I'm sure you're composed in a crisis." That was a total lie, but she knew flattery would win, where orders would give him something to fight over.

"Well, yes, there is that . . . of course," he conceded.

Wyatt came over from the other side of the room, where he had been talking to another of the policemen. He put his arm around Elena. "Thank you, my dear. Excellent idea." He looked at the man who had been complaining. "I count on you, Patterson, to help keep everyone steady. Perhaps if you lead the way to the kitchen, you could tell Katherine and Dorothy what you'd like to eat."

Patterson gave in reluctantly.

"Elena, come with me," Wyatt said. "You obviously have a gift for seizing an opportunity, or reading a situation and taking control."

She felt a sudden chill. Had someone told him about her work in

MI6? That could only be her father, couldn't it? Even he knew so little. And he also understood what an appalling betrayal that would be, to reveal information about her. She looked at her grandfather. No matter how they were related, Wyatt was American, and so his loyalty must be different from hers. He had already made it plain that he was an adviser to Roosevelt. He was proud of it, justifiably.

She walked with him, almost keeping step. "I don't know these people, Grandfather," she began, "so—"

"No," he agreed, cutting across her. "But you're steady. It doesn't take long to see that. This place is strange to you, and you must be so tired—you're running on empty! And yet you aren't panicking, weeping, or blaming anyone." He turned to her with a smile. "You're like your mother, God bless her. I'd like to think you got something of that from me." He hesitated a second, and then whatever he had been going to say, he left it. "Come on. We mustn't keep these people waiting. If we see their panic, they'll never forgive us."

"I'll pretend not to have noticed," she promised.

They moved from one group to another. Wyatt was always courteous, but very firm that there was no cause for any of them to be concerned.

"No one would imagine for a moment that you were involved, Benjamin," he said to one man, who was trying to comfort his wife, Mary, and looked very frazzled. "It's just that you might have noticed something."

"Like what?" Benjamin demanded.

"I don't know." Wyatt shook his head. "Perhaps the last time you saw poor Lila in the room? It would help the police to pin down the time she left. Who you were talking to, things like that?"

"Oh, yes, of course. What an appalling thing to happen." Benjamin shook his head. "It's a nightmare for poor Harmon. But hear that, Mary? The police will get it sorted, and there's really nothing we can do."

Elena smiled at him, then turned to Mary. "That's a beautiful gown," she said. "But you look cold." Indeed, the woman was shivering. "Can I find a wrap for you to borrow? I'm sure Grandmother would be happy to lend you something."

"Thank you, dear, that would be kind," Mary responded.

Elena excused herself and went to the kitchen, where she asked her grandmother, who seemed pleased to help. She disappeared immediately to find the best, warmest wrap she could.

"Are you all right, Elena?" Katherine asked with concern. "You look exhausted."

"Aren't we all?" Elena said lightly. "But I'm getting to know Grandfather better. He's quite impressive."

Katherine smiled genuinely, not bravely or politely, but from real pleasure. She did not need to answer, but the way her shoulders relaxed said a great deal.

Elena went back into the main room and found her grandfather talking to his guests, reassuring them, swapping memories, talking about the future. No one spoke of Lila, but she was as present as if she stood on the edge of every conversation, silently.

Elena found her father offering his help, too, occasionally sitting in while people were being interviewed, at their request. Clearly, this man from England had quickly gained their trust.

"Can I do anything?" she offered. "What are the police asking, Father? Did anybody see anything?"

"Not much," he replied with a rueful expression. There was a shadow in his eyes and his hair was rumpled. "But some feel better if there's somebody on their side, so to speak. Miller looks like a competent man, and he's not going to let anything slip."

"What on earth does he think any of us can tell him, other than when Lila Worth was last seen?"

"Rather more than that," Charles replied. "I think the police are ruling some people out as suspects."

"Suspects?" Elena demanded. "He thinks one of us could have followed her out and . . . and then run her over? That's . . . absurd!"

"Come on, sweetheart," he said gently. "You know as well as I do that anyone can have an affair, be blackmailed, jealous, desperate, and still think themselves above the law. Of all the people I counseled, fought for as ambassador, half of them were people you'd never suspect. Most of them were guilty of something, even if it was stupidity, or the arrogance of people who think another country's laws don't apply to them."

"But these are all Americans, in Washington," she argued. "Do you really think that someone here either killed Lila, or knows who did?" She thought it was unbelievable, and her voice carried this conviction.

"No, not likely," he replied, touching her cheek gently. "But the police have to consider the possibility. If anyone went outside, for any reason . . ."

"Such as what?"

"Such as speaking to someone privately, business of any sort, and got into a quarrel. Or two people in love . . . any reason," he replied. "Come on. I don't know what you do at work, and I don't want to, but you can't really be as naïve as you seem now."

He was right, she didn't have an argument. "I'm trying to help," she said, "but I need to keep what I do a secret." Her voice was sharper than she meant it to be. "I'm just family, nothing else."

"Family is the best," her father said, with both certainty and a rather wry smile. "It's sad that this anniversary party should end like this. But the police will soon be finished and a good night's sleep will make a difference."

"I liked her."

"Who? Lila?" There was suspicion in his voice. "You only met her tonight."

"I still liked her," Elena insisted.

"You like people too easily, sweetheart. I regret to say it, but Lila Worth was of a very dubious reputation. I think you're going to find a domestic tragedy at the back of this. Be prepared for it."

Captain Miller came up to Charles, glanced at Elena, then turned back to Charles. "Mr. Standish, I appreciate that you've been a lot of help with these people. This is your in-laws' house? Do you know many of the guests?"

"No, I don't," Charles replied. "We only arrived from New York last night, and from London about a week ago."

"We?"

"My wife, my daughter, and myself."

"May I ask you what you observed this evening?"

"Of course," Charles agreed.

"And then you, Miss Standish," Miller added, turning to Elena.

It was clear to Elena that he preferred to speak to her father alone. "Right." She glanced at Charles, then walked away and waited in the hall. It was nearly empty now, perhaps half a dozen people there. One of them was James Allenby.

As soon as he saw her, he excused himself from the man he had been talking to and came over. "How are you holding up?" he asked. "I see they're talking to your father. Are you next?"

"Yes." She gave a bleak smile. "But I'm all right. They have to learn what they can. They might leave us alone then and we can all get some sleep. Haven't they spoken to you yet?"

"Yes. Not that I could tell them anything useful."

"Then why haven't you gone home?" As soon as the words were out of her mouth, she realized how rude she sounded.

He smiled candidly. He was really very charming, she thought. "What do you think I'm doing?" he asked quietly. "Trying to prop you up? I wouldn't dare!"

She was taken aback. "Now you're treating me as if I'm sagging."

"No, just exhausted, and hurt by what seems like a senseless trag-edy. But I'm afraid it's worse than that. Maybe a lot worse."

"What could be worse than murder, and in my grandparents' house on their sixtieth anniversary?" She meant to sound incredu-lous, but she merely sounded angry and afraid.

"Do you mind coming over here, by the window? In fact," he added quickly, "let's go outside and admire the dawn over the gar-den." He started to take her arm.

She snatched it away. "The police will soon be looking for me. And I can't think of anything I care about less than looking at dawn over anything!"

"Peter said you could be awkward," he remarked, quite casually, as if the words were to be expected.

She froze. "Peter . . . who?"

"Peter Howard, of course." He leaned closer and bent to speak softly. "Now come out into the garden, and let me tell you what else he said."

She refused to move, trying to take in what he had just revealed.

"Come on!" he said more sharply. "Don't make a scene. That's the last thing we need now." He took her arm this time, but he held it lightly and pulled her gently toward the side door. "You just need a little air," he said, loudly enough for a young man in a waiter's jacket, still standing around, to spring to life and open the door for them.

"You'll feel better, miss," the waiter said encouragingly.

Allenby's grip tightened ever so slightly on Elena's arm.

"Thank you," she said to the waiter, and went outside, having no choice but to remain in step with Allenby. As soon as they were out of anyone's sight, she pulled her arm away, and he didn't resist.

"Listen to me," he said grimly. "We haven't much time. The police will be coming for you any moment. You must be very careful what you say, but you must appear frightened, protective of your family—that would be natural. But none of them must know what you really do."

She stared at him, ice-cold fear gripping her, twisting her stomach.

"Lila worked for MI6, too," he went on very quietly. A yard farther away she would hardly have heard him. "So do I. We didn't work together often, but I've been here for a couple of years. Lila was all the good things you think of her. Her work for MI6 entailed stopping valuable information from leaving America and ending up in Germany. She did this by substituting false information in its place, or partially false." His face looked sad and grim. "I'm sorry, but scaring the hell out of you seems to be the only way to make you take me seriously. And there is no time to waste. I don't know who killed Lila, or why, but it was someone at this party, and we can't think that it was chance. That stuff about a car thief is rubbish."

"How do you know?" she demanded.

He was patient, only now it seemed to be an effort. "You mean apart from the President's security people practically sealing the place off? These are all high-quality cars, belonging to rich and well-known people. The police would be on to a theft in moments. The thieves couldn't sell the car as it is, and who's going to take a Rolls or a Cadillac to break it up for parts? People who drive cars like that can easily afford spare parts from the dealer, in the unlikely case that they need them. My uncle has a Rolls that's gone for fifteen years without a hitch."

"You're saying Lila was murdered by one of the guests, who knew who she was?" Her voice was catching in her throat.

"Yes, I am. I'm sorry. But she was on to something pretty big. She didn't tell me much, but this I knew. Her murder may look very personal, but it's not. It's professional."

Now Elena was cold right through to the bone, as if exhaustion had overtaken her and left her shuddering. "You mean she was killed by someone my grandparents know."

Allenby's face was surprisingly gentle. "As you must have noticed, they are more than a little right wing. Some of them actually admire Hitler's efficiency, and don't yet mind the cost of it. If you launder your clothes and get rid of the dirt, it's considered a good thing. Some people find it's a good thing if you launder your population, and get rid of what you consider to be the polluting elements. Like Jews or people whose skin is a different color."

"Do you mean some sort of extermination, by race?"

"Some see it as preserving their own race."

"The biggest danger to their race is poison from the inside," she said savagely. "Have you been to Germany lately? Have you seen them beating Jews in the street? I saw one young man who had the skin flayed off his body."

"Yes, I have," he said sharply. "Keep your voice down!"

She almost choked on her anger. Then she realized he was right: they were not necessarily among friends here.

"It only takes one person," he said softly. "When people are frightened, and believe they are protecting their own, a whisper is as good as a shout. They won't ask if you agree, they'll just assume that you do. You're Wyatt's granddaughter."

She said nothing.

"If you don't care about yourself, think about your parents, and about Lucas and Josephine. And incidentally, you're in MI6 to fight the enemy, not to indulge your own anger."

He was right, of course. She was behaving like a child because it was her own family. It was her mother, coming here after all these years, seeing her parents for the first time since Elena was a small child. If Katherine's parents had changed, she had not had time to see it, to come to terms or look for reasons. Elena was sure her mother must be full of the memories of her youth: precious, wrapped around hopes and dreams. Time blurs the sharp edges: you see things the way you wish they had been.

"I'm sorry," she said sincerely. "I'm too tired to make a proper judgment. I so much wanted it to go well for my mother." She glanced down, away from him "That's no excuse, I know that. The enemy is not a fool. These are just the moments they search for." She looked back at him gravely. She meant it. "How do I know you're not one of them?"

"I work for Peter Howard, just as you do," he answered. "And as Lila did, at least some of the time. But I know Lucas. And more to the point, he knows me. I even met Toby once."

"Did you like him?" she asked quickly. "Toby, I mean."

"What kind of a twisted man doesn't like a dog?" he replied. "Especially a golden retriever? I threw sticks for him, out in the field near the bluebell woods, although it wasn't bluebell time."

"Did he fetch them back?"

Allenby laughed very softly. "No, he gave them to Lucas; he knows whose dog he is." And then he quoted, " 'I am His Highness's dog at Kew; Pray tell me, sir, whose dog are you?' "

"I suppose I'm Lucas's dog as well," Elena answered.

"Good. Then be innocent for the police, but not stupid. We'd better go back inside; they'll be looking for you." He put his hand on her arm, but gently this time, and then removed it.

She went inside and almost immediately was met by a policeman who took her to Captain Miller, in one of the rooms off the hall.

He stood up from behind the desk and then, as she sat down, he did also. "Thank you, Miss Standish."

He was polite, which she appreciated, even if she'd had no choice whether she came or not. She bore in mind Allenby's words. But regardless of that guidance, she knew she must do all she could to protect her mother and grandparents. She must not volunteer anything, just answer what they asked. She waited for him to continue.

"Had you met Mrs. Worth before this evening, Miss Standish?" he began.

"No."

"Heard of her, from anyone?"

What was he asking? Was it possible he knew something more about her? "No," she replied. "My grandfather may have mentioned her, but without a face, that would mean nothing."

"Nobody told you anything about her? Or about Mr. Worth?"

What did he know? He was just a regular homicide policeman, wasn't he? What had Allenby said about her? She must not seem to hesitate, to have to think of the answer. "Not that I can remember. Someone mentioned that Mr. Worth is a scientist, but I don't remember if they said in which field."

"You're not interested?"

"To be honest, I was more concerned with making sure everybody was made welcome, had something to eat, wine, or coffee. That no one was standing alone and feeling neglected. Until we knew of Mrs. Worth's death, it was a party, and the hostess was my grandmother."

"Yes, of course. So, you made Mrs. Worth welcome? Talked to her? Asked all the usual questions one does of a stranger?"

"I suppose so. She was very easy to talk to. I liked her immediately." That was the truth. It was difficult to say this using the past tense.

"Did it strike you that she was afraid of anything? Nervous? Watching anyone else? In hindsight, Miss Standish?"

"I'm afraid I didn't notice anybody taking more interest in her than was understandable. She was very beautiful, very alive, and she was wearing a fabulous dress. People did look at her. I did."

"What do you know about her, Miss Standish?" Captain Miller's expression was bland, mildly curious, no more. There was no indication that this was a leading question. Had someone told him Allenby had taken her outside?

"Not much, if you mean facts. I knew she had a sense of humor, that she was very frank in some things," she said. "I'm sorry. We talked about other women's gowns. I can't think that had anything to do with her death."

He waited a moment or two, watching her.

She watched him in return, waiting him out. The temptation to break the silence was intense, but she managed to resist it.

"What do you do, Miss Standish? Your profession?"

"I'm a photographer."

"Yes, I heard you took a considerable number of pictures."

"Yes, I did. Not all of them will be good. Do you want to see them?"

"If you please. If you could hand the film to us."

"Why don't I develop it and give it to you? They won't all be good, but I promised to give copies to the subjects, and perhaps Mr. Worth would like the ones of Lila."

"Asking you was a formality, Miss Standish. We can confiscate the film, if you make it necessary." His voice barely changed, but his eyes looked harder, colder.

"Please let me develop the photographs," she said. "You can have one of your men stand there and watch me, if you like. But they are my work, and I promised these people I would provide them with copies of their pictures. It's my livelihood, and my reputation." It was the one thing in which she could have some control. It mattered.

He hesitated, obviously considering her suggestion. "Please hand over your camera, Miss Standish. We will let you develop the film, under our supervision. I recognize that this is your living."

And that my grandfather is an adviser to the President, she thought. "Thank you," she said. "I'll give it to you tomorrow morning. I mean, later on this morning, when I've had an hour to—"

"No, Miss Standish, you will hand it over now." He held up his hand to stop her from interrupting. "We will not remove the film, just keep it safely in the camera. I'm sure you understand that the contents of your film now represent evidence in a murder case."

"I suppose so," she said reluctantly, but her head was spinning. Could her father have let something slip, even as simple as saying she worked for the government? Or had Allenby been trying to protect her by suggesting she was important? An ambassador's daughter? An ex-ambassador's? Was that good, or bad? Was there any way for him to know that Lucas was former head of MI6?

"It's not much use if it's been out of our control," he pointed out.

"Sorry," she said. "Of course it isn't."

He smiled and held out his hand.

Reluctantly, she took the camera out of her bag and gave it to him.

"Thank you," he said gravely.

"I'm coming with you. I'll develop them now."

"If you insist. But you must be exhausted."

"That can't be helped . . ."

He rose to his feet, and she stood also, but before she could turn and leave, there was an abrupt knock on the door. It opened to admit a young policeman.

"Sir," he began, apparently not seeing Elena. "We found blood on the front grille of one of the cars. A lot of blood—" He saw Elena and stopped.

"Whose car?" Miller asked.

The young man's face flooded with color.

"Whose car, Finch?" Miller demanded.

"Mr.—Mr. Baylor's, sir. Mr. Wyatt Baylor."

"It can't be!" Elena said impulsively. "That's ridiculous."

Miller held up his hand to silence her. He swallowed as if he were choking. "Are you sure?"

"Yes, sir. The keys were not in it. Whoever drove it took the keys with them. The chauffeur identified it. He'd know it, without doubt. He didn't know why we were asking, of course."

"Arrest him."

"You can't do that!" Elena said furiously. "He's an adviser to President Roosevelt!"

Miller froze.

"On . . . on what charge, sir?" the policeman asked, his face white.

"Murder, of course," Miller replied. He turned to Elena. "I'm sorry, Miss Standish. Do you still wish to come in and develop your film? We can do it for you, but perhaps not as you would do."

She had trouble finding her voice and speaking steadily. "I would like to watch the development, at least."

He nodded. "Finch."

"Sir?"

"You will remain here with Miss Standish while I go and arrest Mr. Baylor."

Elena swung around. "You can't do that! He can't possibly have killed Lila. It's absurd. Why on earth would he?"

"I don't know that, Miss Standish. I don't know why anyone would kill Mrs. Worth, but undeniably, someone did. And Mr. Baylor was also the only one who could not account for his time."

"Of course he can!" she tried not to raise her voice. "You've just . . . miscalculated. He wouldn't kill anyone!" She took a breath. "He barely knew Mrs. Worth."

"You arrived in Washington only yesterday, Miss Standish. Look after your mother and your grandmother. Don't make it harder for them." His voice had finality in it.

There was nothing she could do.

Elena was half asleep on her feet. A wave of exhaustion almost over-balanced her, and for a moment she missed her step as she followed Captain Miller outside across the gravel and into the police car.

"Are you all right, Miss Standish?" he asked her with what sounded like concern. He grasped her arm to steady her.

"Thank you." She forced the words out. She could not afford to offend him. In the police car, sitting in the back while it made its way through the very early traffic, she did actually drop off into a hazy dream, and then woke up with a start to find Miller grasping her shoulder. The car was stopped and the back door was open. Miller was bending forward to help her out. It took an effort, but she stepped out and stood up.

He led the way into the police station and she followed half a step behind him. She had no idea where she was going, passing through several doors and along passages until she finally sat down in a small, very bare room, and somebody gave her a large mug of coffee. It tasted foul, bitter and strong, but it jolted her awake.

She had barely finished and put the mug down when Miller re-appeared and conducted her to the darkroom, where her film would be developed.

She hesitated.

"You can watch. See that nothing is destroyed?" he offered.

She started to answer, and then stopped.

"It needs a steady hand," Miller said more gently.

"Yes . . . yes," she agreed, grateful for the offer. One mistake, one clumsy movement could destroy a picture. "Thank you," she added.

It seemed a long, slow process, but she watched carefully. The man assigned to the task was young, but very keen to do the job well. In spite of her feelings about the whole subject, Elena found herself liking not only his skill, but the courtesy in showing her what he had, each time he took a further step, all the way from developing the negatives through to making a print for each one that was good. He also showed her the negatives that were too out of focus, exposed to light, or blurred by movement.

"These are very good, Miss Standish," he said respectfully. "I love the way you play with light and shadows. That's really beautiful. Do you do this professionally?"

Elena found herself smiling. "Thank you. Yes, I do. I . . . I had no idea anything was going to happen to make them . . . evidence."

"I don't know if they'll make any difference," he said seriously. "But they're very clear. Do you want them in the order in which they were taken?"

"Yes, please. And we'll need the bad ones, too. They might tell us something."

"Oh, I'll give them all to Captain Miller. But a copy of all the good ones will be for you to give to your grandparents, or to send to whomever they wish. Do you want another cup of coffee, while I make up all the ones you want?"

"Yes, please. It will help me stay upright a little longer. But I would really like to look at the bad ones, too. There might be something that matters in them."

"Yes, ma'am." He smiled at her. "I'll get Captain Miller to find a car to take you home."

"Thank you," she said sincerely.

She was asleep in the chair when he came back.

CHAPTER

6

"Peter Howard," he announced, answering the phone on his desk.

It was used primarily for overseas calls, many of which were highly confidential. Europe was one hour ahead of London, and the east coast of the United States five hours behind. What could Washington want at seven o'clock in the morning, their time?

His fingers were stiff when he held the instrument to his ear. "Yes, what is it?"

"Cadogan here, sir. I have someone who wishes to speak to you. Are you alone in the room, sir?"

"Cadogan, from the Washington Embassy? Yes, put him on." He felt only a slight twinge of alarm.

"Good morning, sir."

He recognized the voice immediately. It was James Allenby. "Good morning, Jim. What's happened that you're at the embassy at this time of day?"

"Rather worrying event last night, sir."

Peter kept his temper out of his voice with difficulty. Elena was in Washington. "What was it?"

"Lila Worth was murdered," Allenby replied. His voice sounded strained. "At first, it looked like an accident, then murder by a possible car thief. But by dawn, they had arrested Wyatt Baylor."

"Lila? But who . . . ?"

"Sorry, sir. But Wyatt Baylor is Charles Standish's father-in-law and Elena's grandfather. Standish and his family are here now. Sixtieth wedding anniversary."

"I know that!" Peter's hand gripped the telephone so tightly that its hard edges dug into his flesh. "How is Elena?"

"She's worried for her family. I gather she didn't know her grandfather until she arrived here the day before yesterday. They put on one hell of a party. She actually met Lila. They got along immediately." Now there was a sharp sorrow in his voice.

"What the hell happened?" Peter demanded. "Have you any idea? What's the situation now? Where is Baylor? In police custody, or haven't they got that far? Does Roosevelt know?"

"He'll know within an hour or two," Allenby answered. "He was there, at the party. Spoke to quite a few people, Charles Standish among them. But I don't think he'll interfere in this."

Peter thought for a few moments. "Any ideas? Is this what we feared?" He did not want to be any more specific than that, even on this line, which, as far as he knew, was absolutely safe. Lila had been working on a project concerning the leaking of vital scientific information, but it had not yet been played out—or so he had thought. Now it looked as if he could have been wrong.

"Possibly," Allenby replied quietly. "Too soon to tell. It only turned that way just over an hour ago. First, it looked like an accident, and then it seemed she was murdered by an intruder, a thief of some sort. Finally, they knew there was no intruder. With President Roosevelt here, security was absolutely watertight. So, it had to be someone at the party. Someone who couldn't account for where they were, or with whom, at the time she was killed. It was Baylor's car that killed her. He was arrested around dawn."

"Is Elena all right?" Peter asked again. Perhaps it was not the question he should have been asking, but it was at the front of his mind. It had always been a risk, employing someone he cared for, even if it could never be more than a rather one-sided friendship. Perhaps he should not have employed her. She was not recruited the usual way. It was not even her choice. She had been plunged into it by circumstance, but she had shown courage and imagination and the instinct, the speed of thought, to succeed. Still, she needed more experience, more training before she was deliberately put in dangerous situations. Her recent trip to Trieste had turned out to be unforeseeably dangerous. That must not happen again.

He had thought this time Elena would be out of danger, on a family trip to America. Now it seemed she was right in the middle of the worst kind of family crisis, which was inevitably going to involve MI6. Lila Worth was a complex character, far deeper than she appeared at first, beyond doubt a woman of unusual intelligence and courage, with a passionate hatred of Hitler and all things Nazi. She had offered her considerable services to MI6 several years ago, and she had never let them down. At least, not so far as Peter knew. Some of the most important information she supplied had yet to be proven. But wasn't that the way a good spy worked? Peter had done it himself—sought and provided valuable information—sometimes directly, but now he did it more usually through others who worked for him. The procedure sounded simple enough, but it could be complicated. First, have his MI6 spy pass on lesser pieces of information that were probably true, and then add to that information, build trust with those who served their purposes, and then manipulate these people so they would feed the adversaries the really large pieces of information that were partly true, or even entirely lies, whatever worked to thwart the plans of the enemy.

Lila had given them elements of discovery, slowly piecing together information about the American scientific effort. It concerned splitting the atom, and it could result in an almost incalculable power being unleashed. The British were working on the same thing, ever since New Zealander Ernest Rutherford had first succeeded in splitting the atom. Now it was being studied and pursued by people of ill will.

Peter knew that Lila had gained this information through her husband, Harmon Worth. Was this actually why she had married him? There were stranger and less honorable reasons why a woman would marry a particular man, or for that matter, why he would marry her. Before the marriage, she had lived and studied in Austria. How much of her studies had been mathematical, or in connection with atomic physics? Information about her was sketchy. What was the depth of her knowledge? It was she who had told them about the most recent work the Germans were doing, trying to develop atomic power, ostensibly for industrial use. But if they succeeded, how much longer before they turned it into weaponry, into bombs of devastating power?

Peter asked himself the questions that sent a chill up his back. Was she a double agent? Even triple?

Allenby was talking to him, and he had not been listening. "Sorry," he said. "What did you say?"

On the other end of the line, three thousand miles away, he could hear Allenby's bitter amusement. "I was telling you about the investigation. Last time I saw Elena, she was practically asleep on her feet, and trying to comfort her mother and grandmother. Then she went with the police to develop all the photographs she had taken. They could be evidence."

"Of course. I . . ." Peter was not sure whether to tell Allenby to use her excellent position in the case, taking advantage of being part of the family . . . or to try to keep her out of it.

Allenby interrupted his thoughts. "I told her who I was, or at least that I worked for you, and that Lila did, too." His voice became sharper. "Damn! This is a bad thing. I suppose we need to know whether Lila's murder was personal or professional, though we have to suppose it was professional. We can't afford not to. And how did they get on to her? I find it difficult to believe she was careless. In all the time I've known her, she was always meticulous."

"If she weren't, she wouldn't have lasted this long," Peter replied. He'd known Lila's reputation before he had ever worked with her himself.

"I want to find out who betrayed her, what happened," Allenby went on.

Peter listened, thinking how much emotion one could detect from a voice alone. Allenby's tone was more than sad; it was overwhelmed, even a little bitter.

"Yes," Peter agreed. "But be careful!" he added, somewhat reluctantly. He knew Elena, and he could easily imagine how these torn loyalties would hurt her. Perhaps the truth could save her grandfather's life. But there could be a lot discovered that was painful, exposing an all-too-vulnerable man. Not many people could stand being so emotionally naked. And that knowledge could never be taken back.

Allenby's voice was insistent in his ear. "Peter, it's important . . ."

"Yes," Peter repeated, answering the question he knew was behind Allenby's persistence. The subject was one they could not ignore. The danger was real. The Germans were using their best scientists in their own study of the atom and the possibilities of a bomb that could annihilate an entire city with one stroke. "Use her, if you have to. But remember, she'll have divided loyalties between her job and her mother, where Baylor is concerned. Elena's . . ." he went on. He wanted to say she was very emotional, but that sounded like a harsh criticism, as if she were unstable, which was not at all what he meant.

"Unreliable?" Allenby asked, saying exactly what Peter had feared.

"No!" Peter said sharply. She had been tested on that account, but he had no intention of telling Allenby about that. "No," he said again, "but it will hurt."

"I know that, sir," Allenby said quietly. "If we didn't care enough to pay the cost, we should stay at home, preferably under the bed!"

Peter had forgotten how forthright Allenby could be, how emotionally involved, beneath his urbane exterior. "All right, Jim, I take your point," he replied a little testily. "Use her as you have to. But she's not expendable. And remember that she's Lucas Standish's granddaughter."

"Thank you. I'd worked that out myself. I'll keep you posted."

"Do that! I don't want to have to send someone out there to rescue you both!" And before Allenby could reply, he hung up the receiver.

Peter sat still at the desk, thinking, marshaling all the facts in his head. This news touched so many facets of his work. Lila was a great loss. He had met her only twice and still he could not work out how far he trusted her. But he had liked her and, perhaps more important than that, he had respected her. Now, hearing of her death, it was as if someone had turned out all the lights, leaving him in a single pool of illumination in which to work out what the darkness held. He hated losing people. He had had the crazy illusion, for a little while, that the end of the war meant the end of sudden, violent, and unforeseen deaths. Ridiculous, really, as if all greed, fear of the different, hunger for power disappeared with the laying down of arms. There were so many other weapons, some of them as yet only half imagined. And other information told him of the Germans pouring money they could ill afford into expensive equipment, directing the top scientists to secret projects.

It had taken two or three years to realize that the hidden war was always there. The stakes were a little different, but just as high. Or were they perhaps even higher? He was acutely aware of the darkness on the horizon that presaged more, and possibly worse, storms to come.

On her visit to Berlin a year ago, Elena had seen that storm. Remembrance of it was in her face sometimes, when she was not aware that he was watching her. He must not let her catch him. Emotion had no place in the game they were playing. It was a piece of self-indulgence that in the end could too easily lead to distraction, a moment's loss of concentration, and a mistake that could not be corrected. And that mistake could be deadly.

He picked up the telephone again and called Lucas. When he answered, Peter said only a few words: "This evening. Seven or so. Usual place. It's very important."

"Right," Lucas said in reply.

"Thank you." Peter replaced the receiver gently. He meant it. Lucas's advice was always sound, the best he could find amidst the uncertainty of secrets and lies that was counterespionage. But more than that, confiding in Lucas was the one emotional release open to him, and he was fully aware of how much he needed that.

Peter left the office a little early. It was in central London, so he took the underground train home. It was quicker and more reliable than any surface transport. When he met Lucas later, he would not explain to Pamela where he was going. He never did. She had long grown accustomed to his unexplained absences. He had tried not to do it with frequency, out of loyalty to her, but he had so often failed that she had learned to expect it of him. Of course, she did not know what he did. MI6's existence was not even acknowledged to the public, and its exact nature was hidden from family members. For the most part, even wives did not know. It was in a great measure for their own protection. It never gave them the opportunity to let something slip. No error, no accidental betrayal could ever be traced back to them.

All of this meant that he could not tell her where he was going, even in his sudden, unplanned walks, and she had never asked. He did not know if she was even interested.

He arrived home just as she came in from the back garden. She was holding flowers. How often had he seen her like that? Gardening was a suitable occupation that could be taken up or interrupted at any time, and she did it extremely well. He should be more appreciative of it. There was peace in it, and certainty. In these days, all of this was of great value.

"The first?" he asked, looking at the yellow roses in her hands.

She smiled. "Yes. I debated whether to pick them or not, but I knew you would have little daylight time to see them." She held them out.

He took them and looked at the delicate golden blooms. The yellow climber—he forgot its name; something gold, marigold, perhaps—was always the first to bloom. For a few moments, he forgot Allenby's news. He smiled at her. "I like the spring flowers. The snowdrops mean the birth of the new year. But for all the glory of the wildflowers, the rose still means the promise of summer."

Pamela looked surprised. "I didn't know you noticed them," she said with obvious pleasure. "I'll put them in a vase. Sitting room or dining-room table?"

"Sitting room," he said immediately. "I . . ." he began, then hesitated.

Her smile faded. "I know; you have to go out."

"How do you know?"

She pushed back a lock of her fair hair, the color of honey. "Peter, I've known you for twenty years! You think you're very hard to read, but you aren't."

He could not think of anything useful to say. Did he want to be hard to read? Even to her? Or was it a comfort that she knew, without the difficulty of words?

She walked past him, holding the roses carefully, and he went upstairs to change into something more appropriate for walking in a country lane. In a dark city suit, he would be about as discreet as a black fly on a white ceiling.

Peter pulled the car into the usual parking place, locked it, and then walked up the slight rise toward the woods. He knew this stretch of

land so well he could place every copse of trees, the streams running
through them, and every turn of the path. Over the sixteen years
since the war ended, he had met Lucas here in all seasons, from
snowdrops on the sheltered banks under the bare trees to clumps of
daffodils, sheets of bluebells that covered the ground, the wild irises
through full summer . . . and to the leaves turning and falling again
to strip the magnificent trees bare: beech trees, smooth and elegant,
their trunks like the legs of dancers—strong, disciplined, and ach-
ingly beautiful.

He saw Lucas standing by the usual tree where they met. He was
over seventy-five now, tall and lean, a little bent, the wind tugging at
his gray hair. He looked mild and thoughtful, an elderly gentleman
walking his dog. The dog, Toby, must have heard something. His
head came up from the smell he had been investigating and he
looked straight at Peter. Then he recognized him and came charging
through the bluebells that carpeted the ground in a haze of color
like a fallen sky. He leaped at Peter, about waist high, and had Peter
not been braced for the charge, it would have sent him flying.

"Toby!" Lucas shouted, and was completely ignored. Toby was
wagging his whole body with delight as he jumped up and down.

Peter smiled and hugged him. When Toby wriggled free, he
launched himself again. Peter patted his head and straightened up as
Lucas approached. "I needed that," he said, cutting off Lucas's apology. "There's nothing quite as wholehearted as a dog's welcome."

Lucas smiled his apology. It happened every time, and he was not
really sorry. It was just a formality.

Toby danced around them in excitement. He knew they loved
him, both of them, and that sooner or later they would throw sticks
for him to fetch.

"What's happened?" Lucas asked, looking at Peter's face. Then he
began to walk slowly down the well-worn path between the trees,
branches of new leaves vivid against the sky, and with the few high,
sparse wild pear trees sprinkled with white blossoms.

Peter was used to telling people all kinds of news. Tragedy was never easy; it was best not to string it out. "Lila Worth was murdered last night. Knocked down and run over in a car park outside a private house."

Lucas said nothing for several moments. They walked a little further, their footsteps silent on the damp earth of the path. "Definitely murder?" he asked finally.

"Police think so. They've made an arrest."

Lucas stopped and faced him. "Who?"

"Wyatt Baylor."

"Wyatt Baylor?" Lucas repeated. "Are you sure? That's . . . that's absurd!"

"Yes, I'm sure. My informant is reliable. One of our people I've known for many years. There's no mistake."

"Not Elena . . . ?" The question held more than just a simple yes or no.

"No, James Allenby. It was the Baylors' sixtieth wedding anniversary. Of course, Elena was there, and so was Allenby. I'm afraid there's no doubt. They took Wyatt away this morning. Allenby telephoned me from the embassy."

Lucas stared at him as if he could hardly grasp what he had said. And yet the beginning of understanding was there in his eyes. "What else? What evidence is there?" he asked. "Do you know?"

"Allenby said the police found rather a lot of blood on the front of Baylor's car," Peter replied. "It's partly the blood, the amount of it. There were people in and out of the car park earlier in the evening. No one saw the blood earlier. Some of them will swear to it. It stretches credulity that Wyatt took a drive in the countryside halfway through his party, hit an animal—quite a large one—and then drove back without anyone missing him. Especially since Franklin Roosevelt was there. You can imagine how tight the security was."

"But could somebody else, other than Baylor, have driven the car?" Lucas said quickly.

"They're working on it. But they wouldn't have taken him in un-less they'd explored the obvious alternatives," Peter replied. "I'm sorry." It was an expression of regret, not an apology.

"What have you done?" Lucas asked. "Are you giving our investi-gation to Allenby?" His face did not express either approval or dis-approval.

"Yes. He's a good man, and he's got a head start in that he knew Lila. And thought highly of her. And now he also knows Elena."

Lucas remained motionless, staring along the path between the tide of flowers.

Peter remained silent, turning over in his mind all the possibili-ties he could think of.

"Two possibilities seem likely," Lucas said, as if speaking to him-self. "Either Baylor's involved somehow, or he isn't. People have conspired to make him look guilty, or else he actually is." He turned to Peter. "I know you don't know, or you would have said. What do you think? And Allenby, he's on the scene. What does he think?"

Peter considered for several moments before answering. "I think Baylor is involved. But if somebody framed him, they did it very well. Which means someone very clever, well organized, and lucky is working against him."

"Why?" Lucas was perfectly serious. "What will change irrevoca-bly if he is removed from the scene? Could it be a diversionary tac-tic? If so, what is he hiding?"

Peter hesitated. "Diversionary from what? Something we're working on, or something we might discover? Something to do with the atomic experiment? They must be close to cracking it, in order to take such a drastic measure."

Lucas bent down and picked up a stick. He threw it for Toby, who went tearing through the bluebells after it, tail high. "Who is the intended victim?" he asked, not looking for an answer. "Was this to get rid of Lila, because she was becoming dangerous? Too close to an answer? And poor Wyatt Baylor was incidental damage? Or was

Baylor the intended target, and Lila simply the means to strike it? If that's it, what did he know? He's heavy industry, so was it about money to finance more experiments? Technical equipment? Steel? Or ..."

". . . or killing two birds with one stone," Peter finished for him. "But why implicate Baylor? He's pretty right wing. Or is he? Is that what you're suggesting? That someone else is using him? Or is he on his own, a loose cannon?"

"God knows," Lucas said wearily. "It's like Russian dolls, something inside something else, which in turn is inside something else again." He bent down and took the stick from Toby, patted him gently on the head, then threw it again. "Best way to fool a spymaster is to wrap everything up inside something else until there's paper all over the floor and you've forgotten what you were looking for in the first place."

Peter ignored him. "Lila is still dead, and Wyatt Baylor is still in custody. Possibly for some reason we don't know, but also, very possibly, because they think he's guilty."

"Could he be?" Lucas said with perfect gravity. "Either for personal reasons or professional?"

"He's your son's father-in-law, Lucas. Don't you know anything at all about the man more than the obvious apparent right-wing leanings?"

"People change," Lucas replied, watching Toby running around in circles looking for the stick. "Beliefs, needs, pressures ..."

"So, we shouldn't try?" Peter asked.

"I'm sorry." Lucas shook his head. "This is too close to home. I don't know the man, and I should. Was Allenby working on him, or was he just there by chance? Can you keep Elena out of it?"

For Peter, there was no point in being anything less than honest. And apart from that, Peter had never lied to Lucas, even in the blackest of times. That was the one relationship in his life he trusted. It was necessary to him. It replaced what he should have felt for his parents, and for his brother. But his brother had died in the war, like so many others, a hero whose image would never be tarnished with the inevitable failures that touch everyone's lives.

And he couldn't keep Elena out of it.

"I can't tell Elena not to support her other grandparents, whatever she thinks of them," he told Lucas. "She won't obey that. I'll instruct Allenby not to use her, but I'm not sure that will make any difference, if she's determined to be a part of this. Of course, if he uses her, at least he'll have some idea of what she's doing, and some control over what happens."

Lucas was silent for several minutes.

Peter did not interrupt.

Toby wandered off to follow a smell, tail in the air.

Lucas looked up at last. "Do you really think it's as bad as you imply? Or are you simply thinking ahead to possibilities?"

"I suppose both," Peter answered. "Maybe it will turn out to be a domestic murder with a motive we don't yet know, inconvenient, a bad loss for us."

"Was she so important?" Lucas asked. "Apart from being a useful source of some of what her husband was doing?"

"Yes, she was," Peter said, feeling a sudden chill as he did so. A gust of wind rattled the branches of the silver birch above him. "Lila understood quite a lot about the work they're doing on atomic fission. She had a good idea of how far America's got, and more important than that, how far the Germans are. If she said there is something to worry about, then there is."

Lucas shivered. "I was afraid you would say that."

After Peter had gone, Lucas walked slowly in the opposite direction, through the trees to where he had left his car. They had met in these woods, or in the open fields that lay beyond them, for years. The world had changed radically since the first time, which was after Lucas left MI6, at least officially. Some of the scars of war had healed over. That is, the visible ones. The undying beauty of the land, the certainty of the returning seasons, healed much. The snowdrops under the trees, then the primroses on the south-facing banks of the streams, the bleating of lambs in the distant fields, and the high piercing sound of the skylarks, those tiny birds that flew so high they were invisible, though their song seemed to fill the air. If you stood still, you could hear them above the sigh of the wind in the grass.

Then blackbirds, clouds of cherry blossoms, hedges white with hawthorn and loud with bees. Late summer, when the scarlet poppies filled in the corners at the edges of the fields. One for every soldier lost in that blood-soaked war. That was behind them, but still

in the hearts of those who had lost friends, family . . . which was almost everyone.

Could they possibly be lurching toward another war? Some of the
men who had fought in the first one and survived it would still be
young enough to fight again. Would England survive another? It was
spring. The air was sparkling, the light clear and sharp. New leaves
were barely tender green. The whole year lay before them, yet it felt
like autumn. Gold in the air and fading, the richness of harvest nearly
over, ripe plums, hedges full of berries, leaves golden, falling. But that
was in his imagination, his own mind. It was hard growing old.

Lucas did not want even to consider another war, but what Peter
Howard had told him was forcing him to face that possibility, really
face it, as more than a blur in the border of his mind.

"Come on," he said quietly to Toby. "Let's go home."

Josephine was in the kitchen chopping vegetables. Behind her, on
the huge kitchen range, a kettle was beginning to whistle. She smiled
at him. "Tea?" She did not wait for an answer. She turned and took
the kettle off the hub, poured a little water into the pot to warm it,
then tipped it out and put in several spoonsful of tea from the caddy,
and poured in the hot water.

He waited for her to set the tray, then he carried it into the sitting
room and returned to watch her cut into a cake, rich with fruit. It
was indulgent, and he loved it. She waited a few more minutes for
the tea to brew, then poured it. It was nearly sixty years since she
had needed to ask what he would like. Nearly sixty! They had married in 1876. Victoria had been on the throne. Women wore floor-
length gowns. None of them imagined voting. The nightmare of
Jack the Ripper was still in the future, never mind the sinking of the
Titanic, then the Great War.

They walked into the sitting room, where Josephine passed Lucas
his cup, exactly as he liked it. "What's upsetting Peter?" she asked.
"He sounded really urgent."

A few years ago, she would not have asked him. His work was secret and they both respected that. But since Elena's trip to Berlin, much that was possibly known but unspoken had been dramatically revealed, between them and, of necessity, to Peter Howard. Charles at last had learned of his father's role in intelligence during the war, and for some time since then. It had changed everything between them. The old condescension, even shame that Charles had felt for his father's anonymous and apparent pacifism had been replaced by a pride that Lucas was afraid was unearned. That pride was based on exploits that required enormous courage, more often of the mind than physical achievements, although there had been some of those. He could tell Charles nothing. And now Elena was following him, albeit only just beginning. He was prouder of her than anyone else could be, because he knew what she was doing, and even better than she, the chance of loss. He might have stopped her, had that been possible. But it was not.

It took a little time for him to find the right words, but Josephine waited him out, not asking, not pursuing or hurrying him. He must search for them, and they did not come easily.

He was seated in his favorite chair. Outside, the spring light was clear, pale on the long-familiar furniture and the new rug. They had had to replace the old one a year ago. But that was history now.

He looked across at Josephine, where she sat waiting. They had been married a long time, but she was still the same curious, quietly clever woman, patient, funny, and of the most tremendous courage. Her hair was still beautiful, but it was mostly white now, still long. At his insistence, when so many women had moved to shorter skirts, slender silhouettes, and above all, bobbed cuts, the one thing she did not change was her hair. He was happy with that.

"Lucas!"

"Yes," he answered. He must tell her, naturally. There was no need to leave anything out. She had kept his secrets, and her own, for so many years. "One of our agents, one of the best, has been murdered. Peter heard by telephone from the British Embassy in Washington."

He saw the surprise in her face, and then her immediate connection with Katherine and Charles. And Elena. He should not keep her in suspense, and yet if he told it in the wrong order, it would make little sense.

But Josephine circumvented all his intentions, which he should have foreseen. She asked the one question he had not thought of. "Did you send Elena over there to deal with this?" she asked.

"No! It happened the second night they were there . . . right out of the blue!" He sounded indignant. "Peter only heard about it by telephone from the embassy. Our man nearest to the case called him directly."

"Do you know him?" she asked.

"Allenby? Yes, and he's pretty good." That was true, but so incomplete an answer would not do. "Peter has confidence in him," he added, knowing that Peter Howard was one of the few men of MI6 that Josephine had actually met, and liked.

"Do you know what he was working on?" she asked, going straight to the point, as usual.

He knew she meant the agent who had been killed. He had already committed to telling her the whole truth, or as much of it as he knew, in mentioning it at all.

"She," he corrected. "The agent was a woman." He smiled bleakly. "The sort you would put into a film. She was beautiful. Not just attractive—you couldn't take your eyes off her."

She frowned. "Why did you choose someone . . . so conspicuous?" she asked quietly.

"Partly for her beauty. It opened many doors. And it did not occur to most people that she was also extremely bright, especially in the field of science. And she was Austrian by birth. Very out of sympathy with the new German leadership. But she understood it, and she had the sense to be afraid." He found himself surprisingly emotional about the death of someone he had met only briefly. He felt as if some bright light far away had been turned off. Half the reflections had gone; the distance was dark.

"Lucas?" Josephine's tone was suddenly very gentle.

"What? Oh. I'm sorry. She was a bit like Elena. Both so very alive. Nothing like her in interests or appearance, though. Lila was dark and very slender, with a background in science. We are not even certain that her death had anything to do with what she was working on for us." He stopped. He was going into territory he could not share.

"You mean it could be personal? Do you want to have the police think it was?"

Again, she had gone straight to the point. Lucas smiled in spite of himself. It was funny in a bitterly oblique way. "We can't afford anything but the truth. It may be nothing very much, little more than a shadow in the sky—"

"Don't you dare say 'no bigger than a man's hand,'" she cut across him. Her face betrayed her anxiety. "So, in Washington . . . Has Katherine's father something to do with that? Is he involved?"

"I don't know," he said honestly. "He's deeply into politics, of the rather more conservative kind than Roosevelt. At least that is what we thought. But he's been newly appointed as an adviser to the President."

"Advising on what?" she asked, frowning now.

"Heavy industry. Banking. Possibly business in general. Probably what the right-wing isolationists are thinking. He could certainly tell Roosevelt a few things about what his main adversaries are thinking."

"Because he knows them, and would betray them?" she asked, her eyebrows raised. "In that case, I hope Roosevelt has more sense than to trust him." There was a look of disgust in her face.

"It may not be as bad as that. He could be trying to keep Roosevelt in the middle of the road. You can't blame America for not wanting to be involved in another European war."

"I can, if they invest in Hitler," she said sharply. "Poor Katherine."

"There's no reason to suppose he's as far to the right as that!"

She raised her eyebrows, her gray eyes full of anxiety. "So what does Peter want you to do?"

He looked at her face. He knew that what she was really concerned about was Elena. Their granddaughter was over there, in Washington, and her family loyalty would be toward her mother, and therefore, naturally, toward Wyatt as well.

"I think he just wanted a sounding board," Lucas answered.

"And to warn you that Elena is there, right in the middle of it." Her eyes dared him to deny it.

He hesitated. Neither the truth, nor any lie, would do.

"This cloud?" she brought the conversation back to the beginning of the discussion. "How big is it? This shadow in the sky."

"About that size," he replied, looking at her steadily.

"A man's hand? And all that it means? If you remember your Bible, it portends torrential storms."

"Yes, but we need to be sure."

"And what may this cloud turn into?" she persisted.

Lucas paused before responding. "Splitting the atom," he finally said. "I know Ernest Rutherford did that years ago, and here, not in America or Germany. It's a matter of following it up, finding a way to create a chain reaction and freeing the unimaginable power it would generate."

"To do what?" Her face was almost expressionless, waiting.

"Any number of things," he said. "Starting with industrial use, machinery, electricity. But what alarms us most in the present political climate is explosives, bombs. Atomic bombs. With unimaginable destruction."

Josephine's eyes widened slightly. "And the Germans, Lucas, they're working on this?"

"We're pretty sure they are. It's far in the future, ten years at least, but we need to know what they're doing. And it wouldn't hurt to know what the Americans are doing, either. They tell us, but we would like to know for certain that what they're saying is actually the truth, or close to it."

"And this woman, this Lila, she could have helped you?"

"Yes, and her husband. Lila's husband is involved as a scientist."

Josephine thought about this for a moment. "Could he have found out she was a spy? What a terrible thing for him!"

"She was a spy for us, Jo. I doubt he would have felt betrayed. According to Peter, her death was violent. She was hit in the head and then run over by a car." He saw her face filled with pain at the thought of it. "That isn't the worst of it."

"What?" she said sharply. "What could be worse than that?"

"It was at a party. Specifically, the sixtieth wedding anniversary of Wyatt and Dorothy Baylor."

The color drained from her cheeks. "Katherine . . ."

"Peter didn't know specifically how Katherine is. But she has Charles."

"And Elena. You say Peter was concerned . . ." She did not finish the thought aloud.

"She'll have to do what she can," said Lucas. "I'm afraid they arrested Wyatt this morning."

"For what? Lucas! You don't mean they think Wyatt could have killed this woman?" Her face was very pale.

"Apparently, they do. They've taken him into custody."

Josephine sat still for several minutes. Lucas did not interrupt because he could think of nothing to say. He did not really know Wyatt Baylor at all. But then, few people knew Lucas. Many knew him as an acquaintance, even a friend, a quiet man who loved his home and family, his dog, who read a lot and was good at telling jokes, especially the long-winded ones known as "shaggy dog stories." Too many of those who knew the things he cared passionately about were dead now. Some of them were lost in the war. Others were growing old quietly, somewhere in the countryside, anonymously, remembered with affection by those who thought they knew them. But it was only on the surface, as the wind troubles the surface of the sea, blowing this way and that, but never changing the great currents beneath.

CHAPTER

8

Charles lay awake in bed. It was long past dawn, but then it had been the early hours of the morning before they even went upstairs, dizzy with exhaustion and grief, too numb to think anymore. They had been here only two nights; it felt much longer.

He and Katherine had taken Dorothy upstairs, leaving her alone in the huge master bedroom, reminders of Wyatt all over the place. There were the empty hangers on which his dress suit had hung. The police had not given him the option of changing clothes before they took him away.

God! What was happening? In a matter of minutes, the whole world had caved in on them. The calm and cheerful host, who had seemed so much in control of everything, had been replaced by a white-faced elderly man seemingly stunned by circumstances he could not possibly have imagined, let alone foreseen. Happiness had turned to tragedy, and then to horror. The laughter, the noise of chatter, the engines of cars had all fallen silent. The hired staff had packed up and gone away, taking dishes, glasses, and leftover food with them. The residual domestic staff had superficially tidied things, then disappeared.

The family had gone to bed, all except Charles, who snoozed on and off in the armchair downstairs, waiting for Elena to come back from the police station, where they were going to develop her photographs. Katherine had offered to stay with her mother, but Dorothy had taken a sleeping draft of some sort and she had at last fallen asleep.

Katherine had returned to the bedroom and was there when Charles finally came to bed. Several times she had begun to speak, and then said nothing, as if she realized she had nothing new to say. Everything had already been said.

Charles lay silently beside her and eventually he, too, had fallen into an uneasy sleep. He had never felt so utterly alone. During the worst of times, like when they'd learned the news of Mike's death, they had clung to each other, consoling in a silence of understanding. And they had shared Margot's grief, too, over not only the loss of her brother, but her husband of one week.

They had commiserated with each other over Elena's disgrace and dismissal from the Foreign Office, the career she had studied so hard to qualify for, and then thrown away for the love of a traitor. Of course, she had not known that then. It was poor judgment on her part, not treason.

This was different. Wyatt Baylor was Katherine's father, not Charles's. He had met the man only half a dozen times, if that. Charles had shown him his professional face, the ambassador who was charming to everyone. It was his job, and he was good at it. And usually he enjoyed it.

But then, he had thought he knew his own father, too, and he could not have been more utterly mistaken. He grew hot with shame even now as he remembered some of the dismissive, even disdainful remarks he had made about Lucas, comparing him unfavorably with Mike, who had gone to war, uncomplaining, as had millions of young men like him, and never come home. He had no idea where Lucas had fought his war, sometimes going on missions into Europe himself, even though he was not supposed to. How many friends, comrades, had he lost? He had never said.

What had Wyatt Baylor never told anyone, that he was now paying such a high price for? Was it possible he, too, had a life he could not share with his family?

At last he drifted to sleep beside Katherine. She was breathing evenly, not moving, but he had no idea whether she was actually asleep, or just pretending to be. Either way, he did not touch her. He had nothing helpful, nothing comforting, to say.

They both woke up well after ten o'clock in the morning. Another sunny day, but somehow even the bright light coming through the curtains seemed hard-edged, without warmth in it.

Katherine climbed out of bed and stood in the middle of the bedroom floor. She looked tired and rumpled, and very alone.

"Did you sleep?" she asked Charles.

"Yes, for a while. Did you?"

"I think I must have." She pushed her fingers through her tousled hair. It was not a real bob, but it was naturally curly and always looked right to him. "Charles, what are we going to do?" she asked. "How can we help? I don't know anything anymore."

He thought rapidly. "Find out all we can. The answer lies in a truth we don't know yet. I don't know whether Miller is going to go on looking. He may, but we must. There's an easy answer to this somewhere."

"Not unless . . . perhaps the President will step in."

"He may," Charles agreed. "He's probably only hearing about it now." He gave her as much of a smile as he could. "No one would have woken him in the middle of the night to tell him, and this afternoon it may all be over." He nearly added "with an apology," but that seemed a bit optimistic.

She attempted an answering smile and did not succeed. "I'll get dressed and go see if Mother is awake. She's going to be . . ."

"You don't need to look for a word," he said. "I know."

She walked over to where he was sitting on the edge of the bed and kissed his cheek quickly. "I'm sorry. I never foresaw this."

He stood up and put his arms around her. She felt thin, and stiff to his touch, as if holding herself together with difficulty. "Of course you didn't," he said softly. "How could anybody? But we'll get through it. Now, go and see if Dorothy is all right. We'll let Elena sleep as long as she can."

Katherine frowned. "Do you understand her, Charles?"

"Dorothy or Elena?"

"Elena. Why did she spend so much time with that fellow Allenby? I can see that he's charming, and handsome in a way, but . . ."

"She also spent a long time with Wyatt, taking photos of his friends, as he directed," Charles pointed out.

"I mean after that."

"I don't know. Does it matter?"

"No, not really, I guess." She pushed him away gently.

He watched her walk toward the door, her head upright and her shoulders squared. He realized that his mother, Josephine, walked like that, too.

He washed and shaved meticulously. Nobody was going to notice, but it was a matter of self-discipline. Even if banks were failing, people jumping out of windows, or there was gunfire in the streets, he would go on looking as if he were perfectly in control.

He went downstairs and into the kitchen, seeing if the servants were all well and in charge of things. He was very relieved that they were. He requested breakfast, not because he really wanted it, but because it gave an appearance of normality. He went to the dining room and found Elena there, looking tired and worried, but fully dressed. He went back immediately to the kitchen and requested breakfast for her also.

"Thank you," she said when he returned. "Did you sleep?"

"Some," he replied, sitting opposite her. It was a time for courage, but a degree of honesty as well. "I've been thinking." He ignored her smile. "Wyatt may come home today. They could realize they've made a mistake, or the President might intervene. I'm not quite sure how, or what power he has, or at what cost." He saw the shadow across her face. "If he appears to abuse his power, then he loses it. This could turn out to be a high-profile case. Don't say that to your mother—at least for now. She needs to believe that he can help." Charles did not know how to go on.

"We can't rely on that," Elena said. "And apart from Grandfather Wyatt, somebody did kill her." Her face pinched with misery. "I want them to suffer for that."

He looked at her. She was close to tears. He could remember her so clearly, the moment she was born. A tiny, perfect body, except for her broad little red nose. She had fought her way into the world, nose first! Then, an inquisitive toddler, who was always asking questions. "How?" "Why?" "What does it do?" "What for?" It had been Lucas who had had the patience to answer her. Charles thought that, in some ways, she was like Josephine, too. Perhaps it was her coloring, her hair.

He jerked his mind back to the present, reminding himself that she was an MI6 agent now, even if a very new one, and barely trained. He did not know that officially, of course. No one did. But he could work it out, not so much from what Lucas said, but from the pride he showed in her, and what he did not say.

"We have to find out as much as we can of what actually happened," he said. "It may be something the police won't even look for."

Elena didn't argue.

"And for the time being, at least, set aside your interest in Allenby. He's a nice young man, or not so very young, but right now your mother needs you, and your grandmother."

She looked incredulous, about to laugh, then puzzled, as if she couldn't find the way to answer.

"Elena, I know you . . ." He trailed off, wordless. When she remained silent, he asked, "What? If he really does like you, maybe there'll be a time later. What man worthy of you would expect you to leave your family in this tragedy and—"

"Father!" she cut across him. She leaned over the table and spoke very softly. "He's MI6. He works for Peter, just as I do. And if you breathe a word to anyone about it, even Mother, it could cost him his life. Not to mention mine, too."

He was momentarily robbed of words. She had admitted it to him. She was caught in a trap of loyalties. "Are you sure?"

"As sure as I can be. He knows Peter Howard, and he's met Grandfather Lucas. And Toby."

"Who's Toby?"

"Father! He's the dog."

"I suppose if the dog approves of him, he must be all right." He let a sarcastic note creep into his voice, but he didn't mean it. It eased out some of the knots in his chest. "Just be careful. I don't know how good you are. I know what Lucas thinks, but he's hopelessly biased."

"I will," she promised. "I'm here. You couldn't bring in someone else and place them as brilliantly. In fact, you couldn't put them in this house at all."

"Did he tell you that?" he asked.

"Who? Allenby or Grandfather Lucas?"

"Don't play games with me," he said, his voice sharpened, betraying his emotions. "This is pretty desperate."

"I'm sorry." Elena looked down at the tablecloth. "It's the only way to deal with some things, and still carry on. And we have to do that. I haven't spoken to Grandfather Lucas at all, but I believe Captain Allenby will call Peter this morning. From the British Embassy, here in Washington. No doubt Peter will be in touch with Grandfather."

"What on earth could my father do?" Charles asked. "He has little authority in Britain now, and none at all here. In fact, they might very well resent it if he tries."

"Not officially, Father," she said.

Charles could see that she was keeping the sharpness out of her own voice with an effort.

She bit her lip, a habit she had had since she was about three, when trying to put complicated questions into words. "Someone killed Lila," she went on. "And intentionally, that's what the police say. And they used Grandfather Wyatt, making it appear he did it. It's hard to believe that was coincidental."

Charles knew that was true, and it had been at the back of his mind. "Of course not," he conceded. "But does Allenby know anything about it?"

"I don't know. I'm not sure if he will tell me, and I have no direct way of contacting Grandfather Lucas." A look of dismay crossed her face at that realization, and she made an effort to mask it.

"So, you have only Allenby's word for it?" The moment the words escaped him, he wished he had not said them, but Elena had a record of believing in the wrong man. He had not said as much, but she was quick to understand and drew in breath to bite back. But she did not say it, and instead breathed out a sigh.

He put his hand out and touched her arm gently. "Be careful, Elena. Whoever is behind this, they're dangerous. They didn't hesitate to murder a woman and blame an innocent man for it. Either they meant to destroy both of them, or one, and the other was just incidental damage along the way."

Her face paled and she swallowed hard, all but choking on her own breath. "I know, but whoever it is, they are not going to paralyze us with fear so we just sit by and let him—or her . . ."

Charles was prevented from responding when his wife entered the room. She was elegant—it was part of her being—but she looked tired, and she seemed to have aged. He could see it in her movement, the shadow of the old woman she would become. He knew this was largely from worry, and having slept little. But, above all, she was frightened.

He stood up, almost without thinking. It was the good manners he had been taught from childhood. He did not get round the table in time to pull out her chair, next to Elena, but he held it for her, and then saw to it that it was pushed back in as far as she wished.

"Just tea," she said, shaking her head, and cutting off his movement to go to the door and call the maid.

"Are you sure?" He did not tell her she needed more, as if somehow that would diminish her fear, or make it seem as if it were not real. He sat down again and poured a cup.

"Thank you," she said, accepting it, and finding it not too hot to sip immediately. Then she looked at Elena. "Are you all right? Did you manage to sleep?"

"Yes, thank you, I'm fine." She began to say more, then changed her mind. "How's Grandmother?" she asked instead.

"She's still asleep," Katherine answered. Then she turned back to Charles. "We have to do something, since Mother is not able to. Although I'm not certain what that is. She's a wonderful hostess. She remembers everybody's names, and who likes whom, and who doesn't. She never puts a foot wrong. She's funny and gracious and kind. But Father is her world. He's never let her down, and she can't handle this. I think she'd do anything at all to help him, but none of us knows what we can do! Apart from not getting hysterical."

"Would you know who Wyatt's lawyer is?" Charles asked. "Or, at least, who would be the best person to call?"

"I have no idea," said Katherine. "But I'll look through Father's desk, if Mother doesn't know. We've got to get professional help. God knows what that policeman thinks he's doing."

"Given the assumption that Wyatt is innocent."

Katherine's face froze.

Charles realized his mistake. "We believe he is, but they don't. Katherine, darling, everybody has enemies, for whatever reason: envy, some grudge or other, or just different political beliefs. We've only been here a couple of days, but already it's painfully clear that feelings are running high. Some are pro-British, and some are very isolationist, which by extension means not very much in favor of the British."

"Can you blame them?" she countered. "We lost a lot of men, too, and it wasn't even our war!" Her face was pale and tight with fear.

"*We* being America, I take it?" he retorted. It was on the tip of his tongue to point out that it was a small fraction of the men Britain had lost, including their own son, but he bit it back. He ached to be able to comfort her, to tell her this was a terrible mistake that would be over in a matter of hours. But he did not know that.

He glanced at Elena, who met his eyes and shook her head so slightly it was scarcely visible. She put one hand over her mother's, gently.

"I'm sorry," Katherine said so quietly it was barely audible. "I so wanted this to be a happy occasion for them, and for you. A sort of reunion, when my parents would get to know my family, and you would see the house I grew up in." She bent her head into her hands and gave a silent sob. Then, after a matter of seconds, she mastered herself and looked up, ignoring the tears that ran down her cheeks.

As much as he wanted to put his arms around her and hold her tightly, defending her from the pain, Charles knew her pain was inside her, beyond his reach. "It would seem that your father has some very serious enemies," he said quietly, controlling his own feelings with an effort. "We need to organize ourselves and think what we can do. Someone will know who his lawyer is. And if the police don't realize their mistake within a matter of hours, we should go and see him, tell him what has happened, and put him to work. We'll need your mother's agreement, of course, but we don't need to bother her with the details. Might she know who his enemies are?"

Katherine shook her head. "I doubt it. I can ask her a little later, when it has sunk in that it isn't all a terrible mistake. But you don't think it is, do you?" There was a faint lift of hope in her face as she looked first at Charles, and then Elena.

"Possibly," said Charles. "But what felt like a mistake is now growing dangerous."

Katherine blinked, looking bewildered. "Who would hate him this much?"

"That's what we need to find out. And whether it's personal . . . or political."

Elena interrupted for the first time. "Do you think it's possible Grandfather knows who actually did it? And that they're making sure he's blamed, so his testimony against them won't be believed if he tries to tell the police?"

Katherine's face came alive with sudden hope. "That would make sense!"

Elena had come up with an idea that, on the surface at least, held weight, but Charles was suddenly certain that she did not believe it at all. She was trying to give her mother hope, and so give herself and Charles time to look deeply into everything they could . . . and find the truth.

"Good idea," he said. "We need to find out all we can." He turned back to Katherine. "You look after your mother. Reassure her we are working hard. And if she can remember anything useful, make a note of it." He had been through grief himself, and had helped all kinds of other people through it. It was the waiting that was hardest, when the imagination causes them to hope, then despair, and back again. Having something to do did not solve much, but it was the only palliative that worked at all.

He watched Katherine sip her tea and then pick up a slice of toast. She knew the discipline of taking care of herself, before becoming a burden to others. She knew all the words of comfort and could repeat them like the alphabet.

She gave Charles a rueful smile, and then reached for his hand and held it tightly, just for a moment.

*   *   *

Charles collected a letter of authority from Dorothy, who looked like a ghost of the woman she had been only the evening before. Her eyes were hollow and she had pinned her hair back, but not in any style, mainly to keep it off her face. She handed the note to Charles and made an effort to smile. "Please let me know what he says. I . . . I hope . . ." She stopped, as if uncertain what she meant. She had given him the name of their personal attorney, Max Borrodale.

"I will," he promised, knowing that he had no intention of telling her anything but the best possibilities at present. He knew nothing about this Max Borrodale, except that he had a reputation for high skill, and was apparently Wyatt's own choice. There was no time to find out any more, and no point, since Borrodale was on a retainer with Wyatt, which meant theirs was an established relationship with a financial agreement already in place.

"I'm coming with you," Elena stated, and Charles could see from the look in her face that she was not going to be excluded. Actually, he was pleased to have her, both for the company and, oddly enough, for her opinion. Thinking back on the little he knew of her exploits in Berlin, and afterward, she was a lot braver, and perhaps more agile in thought, than he was used to believing. What other assumptions had he made about his daughter that needed revising? "Thank you," he said simply, to her clear surprise.

Max Borrodale turned out to be a comfortably assured man of indeterminate middle age. His hair was beautifully cut, his shirt looked like Egyptian cotton, and his tie was of woven silk. He looked appropriately grave, but he exuded confidence as he invited Charles and Elena into his huge office lined with bookcases full of leather-bound volumes, titles on the spines in gold letters. He invited them to be seated in the leather-covered chairs, then sat behind the huge, highly polished desk and smiled solemnly, showing the slight gap between his very white front teeth.

"I can only presume you are here about the highly regrettable event that occurred last night," he said. "I have made a few inquiries, but I have not done anything about it yet. I assume Wyatt would wish me to, but I need the authority, you understand."

Charles took the letter from his inside pocket and passed it across the desk.

"Thank you, sir," Borrodale said. He opened it, read it, and then left it on the desk surface, one lone document on the leather-bound blotter. "I think this is all I need. Obviously, I should see Wyatt as soon as possible. I have not been able to determine anything, except that he is in police custody. But I am assured that he is in good health, and comporting himself with the dignity and courage I would expect." He shook his head slowly. "But I have to tell you the truth: this is a nasty situation."

Charles felt a sinking sensation. He had hoped Borrodale would be positive, feeling this must be some kind of mistake—evidence wrongly identified, someone lying, intentionally or not.

It was Elena who spoke first, before Charles could sort out his thoughts.

"Are you saying that you believe he might be guilty, Mr. Borrodale?" she asked. "That he left his sixtieth wedding anniversary party, met this woman in the parking area, hit her over the head, then got into his own car and drove over her body and killed her? In fact, that he murdered her, then re-parked his car, came inside, and carried on entertaining his guests? Is that the man you know? You see, he's my grandfather, but I don't really know him. I don't live in America." She managed to look halfway between naïve and sarcastic.

"Good heavens, my dear!" Borrodale looked taken aback. "Of course I'm not! No, not at all. I have known Wyatt Baylor most of my life! As have dozens of the best men I know. I do not want to give you false answers that this will be over very quickly. We may have a battle on our hands. Powerful men have powerful enemies."

"We want to save my grandfather from being executed for a crime he did not commit!" declared Elena. "But you do not sound very hopeful. Perhaps we should . . ." She made as if to stand up.

"Sit down, my dear," Borrodale said, this time with urgency. "I was just trying to prepare you for . . . for a more difficult battle than you may have expected. But we will win! I assure you, we will win!"

"If we can't prove he didn't kill Lila, then we must find out who did," she said.

Charles was about to interrupt her, but she was saying what he was actually thinking.

"The police—" Borrodale began.

"Think he did it," Elena finished. "Or they wouldn't have arrested him."

"Miss . . ."

"Standish," she told him, leaning forward as if to press home her point. "Tell me what we can do to help. And what you are going to do, so that we can tell my grandmother. She needs to believe you have got this well in hand, and that you are . . . committed."

Charles nearly spoke, but then he realized that Elena had already wrong-footed Borrodale, and she had no intention of letting him regain his balance.

Borrodale looked uncomfortable. "My dear, it only happened early this morning. I have already contacted Captain Miller of the police and he assures me that Wyatt is well, but naturally deeply shocked. Who on earth could have foreseen such an appalling situation? You cannot prepare for such things, but we will prevail, eventually. Just . . . just keep your head."

Charles could almost feel Elena's body tense. The one thing guaranteed to scrape her temper was to be condescended to. He reached across and put his hand over hers. "What message can we take back to Mrs. Baylor? And what can we do to help?" he asked, facing Borrodale.

"I don't know yet," Borrodale admitted. "Keep up her spirits. Wyatt has plenty of friends out there, but . . . I have to say, there are powerful feelings involved. Wyatt is a man of strength, conviction, and considerable influence. There are those who disagree with him, and might possibly take this opportunity to . . . rob him of some of his influence."

Charles's throat was dry. "You mean . . . frame him for a murder he did not commit, in order to silence him?"

"Sounds a bit melodramatic," the attorney said with distaste. "But I suppose that is roughly what it amounts to. However, that's far ahead of us. It may still prove to be an exceedingly unfortunate, even stupid mistake of the police."

"You will keep us updated." Charles made it a statement, not a question.

"Of course. But you understand, I report to Wyatt."

Charles stood up. "Yes, of course."

Elena stood as well, followed by Borrodale, who moved toward the door.

"I should give you a message for Mrs. Baylor," Borrodale said. "Please assure her, it will be fine . . . in a little while." He nodded. It wasn't a bow, even a slight one, but it was a form of finishing the interview.

Elena followed Charles out of the door. They had walked some distance from the building before she spoke. "Is that what they're going to say?" she asked very quietly. "Framed by a political enemy? Because of the President, and Grandfather's influence?"

"Not quite," Charles responded. "More likely there will be a price for suddenly finding a different solution. Wyatt is cleared. Apologies all around. He emerges a hero, and then does as he's told."

"That . . ." Elena seemed lost for a word powerful enough for the revulsion she obviously felt.

"I know," Charles said quietly. "But I'm not sure if there's anything we can do about it."

When they were being driven home, Charles and Elena did not discuss what Borrodale had said. The matter was private and, in the car, Wyatt Baylor's chauffeur would be unable to help overhearing.

Charles was going to find it difficult enough to tell Dorothy the things she had a right to know, but also to work out what he needed to keep from her. He hoped that everything would change, please heaven, within a day or two, or even hours, yet he must not give her false hope. That would be unnecessarily cruel.

It was not until they were standing at the front door, and the chauffeur had driven away to park the car, that Charles spoke. "We'll see your mother first," he said. "I think she should be the one to tell your grandmother. At least, make the choice of how much to tell her now."

He did not get to finish his thought because the maid, who had clearly been listening for the car, opened the door for them.

"Thank you," Charles said. "Is Mrs. Standish . . . ?"

Before he finished, Katherine came into the hall. She was dressed in plain linen of a neutral blue, the kind of color Elena used to wear. On Katherine, it looked elegant, but somehow unfinished. Perhaps it was the lack of color in her face. The question she wanted to ask was evident in her expression, even before she spoke.

Charles had decided how he would tell her, and yet now the words eluded him. His hesitation frightened her; he saw it in her eyes.

"Charles! You did see Borrodale, didn't you?" she asked urgently.

"Yes," he assured her. "And he's spoken to the police, who say Wyatt is well, and very composed. The problem is that it's hard to know what to do until the evidence is much clearer."

"It was clear enough to arrest him!" she protested, her voice sharp.

"Can we discuss this somewhere other than standing in the hall?" he asked quietly.

She looked as if he had slapped her. But it wasn't anger, it was fear.

He had to be able to tell her something that would help, but a lie now would break the trust that she needed, in order to keep control—not only for herself but for her mother, who was already frightened and confused.

Elena stepped forward, touching Katherine's arm. "Mother, it's complicated. You know how lawyers speak. You have to disentangle it before you know what they mean, which is usually some version of 'I don't know, but it's not my fault anyway.'"

Against her will, Katherine was forced to smile. "All right, I'll listen to you. A cup of tea?"

"Yes, please," said Elena. "But first, I must go and change my shoes. These are killing my feet."

Katherine turned to Charles, but she had a slight smile. "Is she being tactful, and leaving you to tell me the news?"

He led the way toward the sitting room. "I think so. And trying hard not to do it for me."

"She always did interrupt," Katherine said, but it was with affection, remembrance of the little girl just discovering words, who couldn't get enough of them.

He led the way to the sitting room and waited till she sat down, then sat opposite her. He did not let the silence hang between them. "Borrodale is Wyatt's choice, and he seems to be competent enough," he began. "But if I sound unenthusiastic, put it down to the fact that I didn't like being condescended to, or treated like a novice. He has your father's well-being at heart, not mine. And he's right to be careful."

"About what?" she asked. "Does he doubt his innocence?" Her voice was shaking and she seemed ready to slide from fear to anger.

"No," Charles said quickly, although he had wondered the same thing at the time. "He's just preparing us for a possible battle, covering himself. Lawyers do that."

"But it's absurd," Katherine protested. "It's impossible that Father could have had anything to do with Lila Worth! Why is he supposed to have done it?" Her voice was slipping out of control. "They couldn't think he was having an affair with her. For heaven's sake, she's half his age, if that! She's not much older than his granddaughter!"

Charles did not bother to argue that this was not a reason to dismiss the idea. Katherine was keeping a very tight control on her fear, but it could tip over into anger so easily. And then she would be embarrassed and ashamed. He had seen it before, not only in her, but in other proud and brave people who had suffered unbearable loss. It was much of an ambassador's job: stepping in when sudden tragedy overtook people far from home. It was the very worst part, so he had worked at it, thought about it, and even in his own fashion prayed about it. Not to God, specifically—he was not on any personal footing with such a being, if there was one—but to the universe, to all the men before him, anywhere, who had sought to share another person's anguish.

"Charles!" Katherine's voice cut across his thoughts. She was beginning to get angry. "Didn't you tell him that Father couldn't possibly be guilty?"

He brought himself sharply back to the present. "He knows Wyatt far better than I do, Katherine, and he takes for granted that he's innocent. But he pointed out that someone has gone to a lot of trouble to implicate him. The police would never have dared arrest him otherwise."

"No, you're right," Katherine said. "And the more powerful the man, the more powerful the enemies. For heaven's sake, Father's one of Mr. Roosevelt's advisers in finance. He knows more about money than most actual bankers. And Roosevelt's brilliant; he could be exactly what the country needs. But he's controversial. He's bound to raise opposition, even if it's based in fear of all sorts of things, not merely sliding back into the Depression again. It was a slow, terrible death to so many people. We have to hope.

"Father is for change, courage, a new start," she went on. "It's going to take strength to do that. Fear can paralyze. Some people are afraid of change, or they have a vested interest in things as they are, but we can't face another depression." She took a deep breath. "He's told me more about it than you know, in his letters. It's been . . ." She stopped, mastering her feelings with difficulty.

She had never spoken of this before. He had not realized how often Wyatt must have written to her. His own father had not confided in him, but then his work was secret, and he did not confide in anybody. Wyatt's observations were different. The hardship of the Depression was public knowledge, to anyone who cared. Maybe he shared with Katherine things he could not with Dorothy. Would Charles share with Elena the things he could not with Katherine? Yes, he could imagine it.

Katherine was speaking again. "I believe Roosevelt is struggling to create a new economy, a new way, fairer, stronger than before, built on ideals that won't break so easily under pressure. And if even half the news is right, there's going to be pressure. How could anybody be so willfully blind as not to see that? Charles, all these people here at the party were his friends!"

"I know," he began. "And I—"

"Do you?" she interrupted. "Friends or family, these are the people we trust most in the world. Some can disagree with our ideas, and there are those who might, but we don't attack! Who would do that?"

Charles could feel Katherine's fear, and he understood that she felt attacked. Wyatt Baylor, the parent she loved, who had protected her as a child, was now being threatened. And threatened by those he trusted the most.

"Katherine!" He put out his hand to take hers, but she pulled away. "Katherine!" he repeated, his voice insisting. "It's about proving that Wyatt didn't kill Lila, for any reason, personal or professional, and that someone else almost certainly made it look as if he had. We've got to know why. It's the only way we can find out who."

"How can you do that, Charles?" Katherine asked. "You're in the Foreign Office. I don't know exactly what you do, but you're not a detective, and you are not even a citizen here. Please, don't get yourself in trouble with the authorities. That would just be . . ." her voice cracked, and then she got control of it again, ". . . unbearable."

It was a fear he had not even considered, but it was quite rational. Hardly any country looked kindly on a foreigner questioning their legal system, let alone interfering in it.

"Please," she added, "don't risk making it worse."

Charles glanced toward Elena, who had entered the room and was listening carefully. He silently wished her to speak, but she said nothing. "I haven't spoken to anyone except Borrodale," he said. "I had to take that chance, to make sure Wyatt is represented. No one would expect Dorothy to be up to that. She's nearly eighty years old!"

"So is Lucas," Katherine replied with a rueful smile. "That doesn't stop him from interfering in anything he can manage."

Charles was startled. Then he saw her amusement.

"You always imagine women don't know things," Katherine said. "And we let you do that. It's so much easier that way." Then she was serious again. "But I know Mother is completely devastated by this. On the surface she's refusing to accept that it's anything more than an idiotic procedural mistake of some sort, but part of her knows it's real. It's there in her eyes, and I don't know whether she wants me to ignore it or not. I think she's afraid of losing the kind of life that she finds so sweet . . . so safe. And she's afraid of being alone, and of the disgrace." She turned her head, as if trying to hide her tears from him.

Charles saw pain and confusion in her face because she realized Dorothy would not look at what she could not bear, and then she would protect herself by building a wall against reality.

"First, we have to find the truth, before we judge how to deal with it," he said quietly. "Your mother may be right, and it will unravel itself without our needing to do much more than keep up our courage and look after each other."

Katherine searched his face, his eyes. Was she looking for condescension? If so, she would not find it. If she saw a shadow, it was fear that he was not up to dealing with it. That is, if Wyatt were somehow involved in this tragedy.

"We'll find out as much as we can, Mother, and without interfering," Elena said, giving her mother a smile; there was a thread of humor in it. "I used to be pretty easy to read, but I'm getting better at being clever. It's part of my trade now. That is, to look innocent and unaware of what's really happening."

Katherine was clearly confused.

"I'm learning tact," Elena explained quickly. "We'll find a way to prove Grandfather innocent, and we won't stop until we do."

Katherine's face was soft, as if she were smiling at a child. Then, she looked longer at Elena, possibly remembering how much she had changed since Berlin. Elena had not told her all about it, but she knew at least how Charles's view of his father had changed completely from ill-concealed contempt to a dazed respect, which was deepening as the months went by. "Be careful, please," was all she said, and then stood and walked slowly out of the room.

"Father," said Elena, "the authorities are not going to appreciate our interfering."

"I can't sit by and do nothing," Charles protested. "Do you trust Borrodale? Either his ability or his commitment? It seems Wyatt has real enemies, not just people who don't like him very much. I mean, serious people who consider him dangerous, and believe it's their duty to stop him."

"Stop him from what?" she asked. "What could he do that would justify murdering him?"

He saw right away what she meant. If Wyatt Baylor was convicted of killing Lila, for whatever reason, it would not only ruin him and all he stood for, it could eventually send him to the electric chair.

The warm colors of the room melted and became invisible. Its grace felt artificial; only the coldness inside him felt real. Where was the shelf of books that one kept because one loved them, not because they looked smart? The half-finished knitting? The pillow out of place because it was the most comfortable one, mismatched in color and fabric because each pillow was a memory of a different place and time in their lives? He felt far from home. He was a man of the world, multicultural, multilingual, and yet he felt it all slipping out of his grasp.

When he and Elena stood, she slipped her arm through his. "Captain Allenby will help us," she said.

He focused on what she was saying, and what she had left unsaid. She had barely met Allenby. How could she trust him so soon?

She saw his hesitation. "Father," she said, her voice softer, "we need all the help we can find . . . please?"

"Yes, all right," he agreed reluctantly. "Your mother has more than enough to deal with. She's not weak, Elena. Really, she isn't. She held it all together when we lost Mike. And when Paul died. She moved from place to place, taking care of us, and then we moved to each new assignment and she started again. New house, new friends, new language, she never complained. It's just that this, what's happening now, this is family. I mean, her family of birth, the people she grew up with. These are her roots."

He was not sure what he was saying, only that as he grew older, he turned more and more to his own roots. He had learned that, before we reached our best in anything, found our strength, we had to know who we were and believe it. Learning the truth about Lucas had been core to rediscovering his own strengths.

Now it was his loyal, brave, and so independent Katherine who was seeing the crumbling of her roots. She saw Dorothy's terror, and the way she was clinging to dreams that were all too close to being shattered, towers of glass, not steel. And she saw Wyatt's integrity dissolved, his beliefs exposed as questionable, even his basic morality in doubt. It had all happened in one evening. The whole edifice of the past, built on years of belief, was threatened. Charles must help his wife and her family. Either they must prove Wyatt innocent or, if that could not be done, stand loyally by him in the storm.

He turned to Elena. She was watching him. "We must form a plan," he said firmly. "We've got to know the truth about Wyatt, whatever it is. But think hard before you tell your mother, and harder still before you let Dorothy know anything."

"You don't think that he did it, do you?" Elena asked, searching his face. "Murdered Lila?"

"No, of course not, but he may know who did, and why. I don't entirely trust Borrodale to be fully on Wyatt's side. I don't even know what the sides are, let alone who's on which."

"And we haven't much time," Elena added with a bleak smile. "But we have to start somewhere. We've *got* to save him, however difficult it is."

"We will," Charles said with feeling. "Now, let's get started."

"Yes, of course. I would be delighted to see you," Katherine said into the telephone. "I'll tell Mother, and if she is up to it, I'm sure she would be, too. It is most kind of you." She replaced the receiver in its cradle.

"Who was that?" Elena asked anxiously. They were sitting in what was known as the afternoon room, because the sun lingered there almost until twilight. It was not uncomfortably hot, and the room was more casually furnished than the formal drawing room, so one felt more able to relax. They were alone. Dorothy had come down for lunch, and then had decided to go back upstairs. Possibly, it was to avoid callers such as this.

"Mabel Cartwright," Katherine answered, her face a little pinched. "She wants to come by and express her concern, and her loyalty. I think that was how she said it. I was caught off guard, I admit."

"And you said she could?" Elena was surprised. "Grandma will—"

"I want to see her," Katherine interrupted. "At least, I don't . . . the truth is, she's just about the last person I would like to see, but we need to start doing something. Horace Cartwright is pretty close to Grandpa, at least in some of his political opinions. He might be able to help." Katherine shook her head. "Don't look like that. I don't like them either, but we have to try all that we can."

"Yes," Elena said, smiling slightly for the touch of pride she felt, because her mother believed that she could put on a good face and receive anyone who came, to try to find a thread, any thread, to follow. "So, you want me to stay with you?" she asked. "It might help."

"If you promise to remember that this is about Grandpa, not anything else. Not your own opinions, for instance."

"I can say or do anything necessary," Elena replied. She saw her mother's doubtful look, and wished she could tell her how much she had truly learned when her life had depended on it. But like Lucas, she must keep silent. She looked at her mother, white-faced and controlling herself with much effort, and ached to comfort her. But it would be a moment's reprieve to pay for with a lifetime's regret.

Katherine was still looking at her doubtfully.

"I'll stay silent, if you like," Elena offered, with a promise she never intended to keep. "But it's natural for me to be with you, by your side. She'd think it odd that I would abandon you."

There was a shadow of a smile on Katherine's face; then it was gone again.

It was only half an hour later when the maid announced that Mrs. Horace Cartwright was here to visit. She carried a glorious bunch of early summer flowers in her arms. "Shall I put them in water, ma'am?" she asked. "And would you like tea? Iced or hot? And sandwiches, or cakes, ma'am?"

"A little of each, please," Katherine answered. She would normally have used the maid's name, but Elena knew it had temporarily slipped from her mind.

The maid left to escort the guest into the room.

A moment later, Mabel Cartwright entered. Today she was wearing black and white. It made her look entirely different. It was smart, individual, and actually quite flattering.

Elena stood up. As a woman a generation younger, it was a necessary and expected politeness.

"Thank you for the flowers," Katherine said. "I'll be sure Mother sees them."

The maid quietly excused herself to take care of the flowers and refreshments.

Mabel appeared startled for a moment, then she collected herself. "How are you, my dear?" she said to Katherine. "I feel dreadful for you, but I am so glad you are here." She sat down in the chair opposite Katherine, gave a nod and a smile to Elena, and then carried on speaking. "Poor Dorothy must be beside herself, but you will give her our love and support, won't you?" She looked at Elena. "And you, dear, how long are you going to be here? Had things been different, we would have loved to have had a party for all of you. But it would be hardly . . . appropriate."

Elena forced herself to smile. "How kind of you," she said, as if it were something she would have enjoyed. "Those are marvelous flowers you brought. We will all appreciate them, and I'm sure feel . . . the warmth of your friendship." She nearly choked on the words.

Mabel took it for emotion and smiled back. "We are all very fond of your grandfather, my dear. And your mother, of course. But Wyatt and Dorothy have been the strongest and most loyal of our little group for years." She turned back to Katherine. "Assure your mother of our deepest appreciation."

"Appreciation" was a curious word to use, as if Dorothy had given them something. Elena saw Katherine's eyes widen a little.

"I will," Katherine said quietly. "I'm sure she will . . . value that."

"You will be the greatest strength possible," Mabel went on, her voice gentle. "And I promise you, your father's work will not be in vain."

A look of incomprehension filled Katherine's face.

"The cause," Mabel said softly. "Free America. We must never let this chaos happen again. There are elements that must be rendered . . . ineffective, shall we say?" Her smile was brief, warm, one of confidentiality. "It won't be long, dear. And you are playing your part perfectly, if I may say so."

Elena longed to ask her what on earth she meant, but she knew better. Any interruption would break the spell of unreality that seemed to hang over them, perhaps remind Mabel that they were strangers, even though she seemed to think she knew them well.

Katherine drew a deep breath. "My husband and I only just got here. I'm afraid I'm struggling to understand it all. My father mentioned certain things, of course. Beliefs, values, and so on. But he was wiser than to put too much of it on paper in his letters to me."

Elena realized with deep satisfaction that her mother grasped perfectly how she could use this situation to their advantage.

Mabel smiled. "Of course. Some things are easy to misunderstand. But it has to be this way. Even letters can fall into the wrong hands. People forget that."

"As you say," Katherine agreed. "It's too late to be sorry afterward."

That would be true of anything. Katherine was struggling and Elena was aware of it.

For a moment, the silence lay heavy in the room, like an intruder.

Mabel moved position uneasily. She looked roughly Katherine's age, but the years sat far more heavily upon her.

Elena smiled at Katherine. "Mother, I'm sure Mrs. Cartwright has things she would like to say to you privately, memories to share, more pleasant things to catch up with now." She leaned forward, as if she were about to rise to her feet.

"How thoughtful of you," Mabel said appreciatively. She looked at Katherine. "Lovely girl."

Did Katherine understand that Elena was leaving her in the hope that she would inquire further into this group that Mabel referred to as Free America? Or, at least, that Mabel would feel comfortable referring to it more directly?

But Katherine went the other way. "No need to leave us, dear. It is time you learned a little more about how the world really is. I'm sure Mabel can tell you things I only see from the outside. At least, that is how it has been lately. I never know what to believe in the newspapers."

"Not a great deal," Mabel said, with a touch of bitterness. "You have no idea how left wing they are!"

Katherine was apparently lost for an answer.

Elena remembered the tone of most of the comments she had heard at the party. She had tried not to take them seriously at the time, but they returned to her now. Words about resurgence of heavy industry, trade with Hitler's rising Germany, a few anti-Semitic comments, recollection of times past that were good. Keep America free. Now she realized what she had heard was Free America, and she had heard it more than once during the evening. No words were added. Those who heard it were expected to understand. She tried to remember who those people were. Wyatt certainly. And Mabel and Horace. There were several others.

She drew a deep breath. Katherine and Mabel were still talking about mutual acquaintances, it seemed. The look on Katherine's face was one of deep concentration. They seemed to have forgotten Elena. Was her mother trying to learn something? Was she as aware as Elena was of the intensity of the conversation, the repetition of the new ideas, the sentence that seemed to have a surface meaning, and a deeper one underneath that surface?

Elena felt forgotten, and she sat unnaturally still so as not to remind Mabel that she was there. She was far from feeling lost and ignored. Instead, she was listening, and trying to remember everything, what was said and what was implied.

When Mabel finally rose, she glanced at Elena, who smiled as sweetly as she could, but she said nothing. She did not want to break the illusion that she had neither understood nor questioned anything.

Katherine thanked Mabel again for her friendship, and for the flowers, and walked with her as far as the front door.

When she came back, she looked straight at Elena, searching her eyes. She sat down next to her, where she had been before. She was waiting, her face full of questions.

Elena said exactly what she was thinking. "Free America?"

Katherine drew in a deep breath. "I think it's a society, a brotherhood, that my father belongs to. Mabel talked about sacrifice . . . and nobility. The cause. And it not being in vain." She took another breath, almost a gasp. "I don't know whether the members will help Father or not." She touched Elena gently on the arm, not a grip at all. "Elena, I'm frightened."

CHAPTER

10

The next day, the fourth of their visit, dawned clear and warm. The sun streamed in through the breakfast-room windows, as if there were nothing wrong, nothing different. Katherine stood in front of them and stared out at the garden, her gaze on birds hopping across the grass, picking at seeds or worms. The sun on her face was harsh, searching out the minor flaws accentuated by time. She looked as if she had slept far too little, which was hardly surprising. After Mabel Cartwright had gone, she and Charles had sat talking quietly, trying to understand the deeper implication behind the visit.

What had Mabel come for? To reassure Katherine and, indirectly, Dorothy? Or to find out if they were loyal to Wyatt? If they knew anything about Free America, whatever that was? Apparently, Wyatt was a member, but did that mean that they were going to fight to prove his innocence? Or did Mabel mean that taking the blame for Lila's death was a sacrifice Wyatt was expected to make?

They had both gone to bed disturbed, unable to understand.

Now it was morning, and Elena was standing silently, and as yet unnoticed, just inside the door at the far side of the breakfast room. Her presence meant interrupting her mother's quiet thoughts in a way she had not intended. And yet, it was time she spoke. "Good morning, Mother. Did you sleep?"

Katherine tensed, then turned slowly. "Good morning, darling. I'm so sorry about all this. It was going to be such fun." She blushed hard, refusing to acknowledge the tears on her cheeks.

"It may still be, after we get this mess sorted out," Elena responded, coming fully into the room. "But that has to come first. How is Grandma? Did she get any sleep?"

"Not a great deal," Katherine replied. "I don't think she's going to, until we bring Grandpa home. And I don't know what to say to her. Your father said Borrodale didn't reassure him very much. Do you suppose Borrodale knows about this Free America?"

"I'm not sure," Elena said. "But we have to assume he might. In any case, he's Grandpa's choice, so we have to go with him. We need a lawyer who really knows what he's doing, and believes that Grandpa can't possibly be guilty. And he understands how complicated it is. There's far too much that we don't know. What is this Free America? And is Grandpa part of it? Or are they warning him?"

"I think he's part of it," Katherine said slowly. She spoke the words as if they were dragged out of her. It was, in a way, a confession.

"Do you think he knows their plan?" Elena asked. "Or are they using him? And is Borrodale part of it?"

Katherine took a deep breath and let it out slowly. "Your father didn't tell me very much. I think he's trying to protect me, but I find it only makes me wonder what it is that he's holding back. Or it's possible that he doesn't understand it any more than we do."

"Isn't politics always complicated?" Elena said. "You never know what a person's private agenda is. I'm certain Father wants to bring Grandpa back as soon as possible, with his name cleared of any suspicion at all, and—"

"Of course he does!" Katherine cut across her.

"And it will only work if his name is completely cleared," Elena repeated grimly. "If it looks like someone's influence was used, or any political power exerted, that might get him out of jail, but it won't give him back his good name, his reputation."

Katherine turned slightly, so she was completely facing Elena. "I admit, I hadn't thought of it like that. It's so preposterous. I thought no one would believe it. But I was wrong, wasn't I? Why is he supposed to have done it? Do they think he had an affair with this . . . Lila?"

"No, I don't think so at all," Elena said sharply. "And neither do you! This is political."

"I do know that. I'm not sure it's any comfort . . ." She stopped, glancing briefly at the sunlight on the garden, and then faced Elena again. "But I mean to get to the bottom of it all. We have no choice."

Elena was suddenly overwhelmed with love for her mother, a desire above all things to protect her from pain, though she knew she could not. Especially if the truth proved her grandfather guilty of murder, or even supporting a group like Free America. Katherine was afraid; Elena knew that. They both were. "I'm trying to find out more," Elena said quietly. "That's why I'm in touch with Allenby. He's from the embassy, and I think he can help."

"Thank you," said Katherine. "I can't get Mabel Cartwright out of my mind. The things she said may be significant."

"I know, which is why we've got to think carefully," Elena agreed. Mabel's words had dug deep into her, too. "Police are not usually quick to admit their mistakes," she went on. "It's very difficult to prove you didn't do something, if you could have done it. We have to prove he couldn't have. Or better still, find out who did. And why."

"Why can't it be just as it seems?" Katherine asked. "Some car thief saw all the beautiful cars in front of the house and picked one, which happened to be Grandpa's. Maybe it was an accident, and the thief didn't mean to hit Lila Worth. Then he saw what he had done, and panicked. Of course, he didn't take the car then, because it had blood on it, and he'd be caught straightaway."

Elena drew breath in, then let it out without speaking.

"Isn't that the best answer?" Katherine asked.

"Yes," Elena said reluctantly. "So, why did Captain Miller not believe that? Grandpa was talking to people, pretty much in full view of everyone, and for most of the evening. I was with him myself, so I know that."

"Did you tell Miller so?"

"Yes. And so did lots of other people. He has to have something else," Elena pointed out.

"Fingerprints?" Katherine gave a little downward-curving smile. "It's Grandpa's car. Of course his fingerprints are on it. Do you think Captain Miller could be doing this for a political reason of his own?" Her body was rigid now, her shoulders stiff under the silk of her dress. "Elena, what do you know that you're not telling me?"

Elena looked steadily at her mother. So much of the past came sweeping in like a tide, strong, taking the sand from around her feet and threatening her balance. Her own mistakes. The news of other people's losses, and Katherine comforting them, doing small practical jobs to see that they ate, had somewhere to sleep, were not left alone. And then their own terrible news just as the war was all going to be over.

Elena wanted to hug her, but it seemed too much a reversal of their roles. It was Katherine who consoled her. Would such a gesture signify that she thought there was an ultimate disaster ahead of them?

"Elena!" Katherine said sharply. "What are you holding back?"

"Nothing, really. I didn't like Borrodale, but that might be because he talked to Father over my head, as if I weren't there. That always irritates me. What does Grandmother know that could help? She might know a lot, without realizing it's relevant. We don't even know whether killing Lila—" She still found that difficult to say.

Katherine shivered. "If it *was* meant to implicate Grandpa, then it was probably one of the guests."

"Can it be anything else, if whoever killed her meant to do it?" Elena asked. "And can you believe any of it was an accident, really?"

"No," Katherine admitted.

"Then it's to do with this . . ." Elena tried to find the right word. ". . . this society, or whatever they are, that Grandpa seems to belong to. This Free America. Will they save him?" She swallowed hard. "Or is Grandpa some kind of sacrifice for whatever their cause might be? And does he know that?"

Katherine's face was ashen. "You mean all this is happening and perhaps he doesn't understand, let alone agree to it? That's terrifying!"

"We'll fight it," Elena said, mainly because she could not bear the silence. She physically ached to comfort her mother, to promise that it would be all right, that they had weapons they would use. "We have to know the truth, whatever it is."

"*Whatever it is?*" Katherine repeated. "You mean even if we find something about Grandpa that is ugly? He didn't kill Lila—of course he didn't—but perhaps he knows who did, and even why."

"Yes," Elena answered.

Katherine smiled for a moment, quite genuinely. "Thank you, darling. You've put it back in proportion for me. Now, do you want to go upstairs and take Grandma a tray of tea, and see if she'll eat a little breakfast? We've got to keep her spirits up."

Elena agreed.

She went to the kitchen hoping she might learn something more about her grandfather. She realized now how little she knew about him, and this seemed the best opportunity. Perhaps she could ask something that might show her more of this Free America society. She wanted to think it did not matter: just a club for people to air their opinions. She wanted to think it was no darker than that. After all, there were several such societies in England, just loyalists who wanted there never to be another war like the last.

The kitchen staff was there, standing idly. When they saw her, they looked embarrassed to be caught doing nothing. Elena smiled at them, as if she had not noticed. "Smells good in here," she said, looking around the huge room, every surface clean, all the cooking equipment gleaming. "Has Mrs. Baylor sent for anything to eat lately?"

"No, ma'am," said one of the maids. "You think she might like something?"

"I think she ought to," Elena answered. "I'll take it up to her and see if I can persuade her to eat a little."

The cook was clearly relieved to have something to do, and walked about making light, delicate sandwiches with a variety of fillings. She set them out on a tray that was covered with a lace cloth, and added a clean napkin.

Elena entered the hall carrying the tray and went up the wide, elegant staircase and across the landing to the passage leading to the family bedrooms.

Her grandmother was propped up in bed looking fragile, almost haunted, an old lady in a room that was familiar to her, though to Elena it was new and gorgeous. The bed was huge, piled with pillows, some satin, many edged with lace, all in pastel tones of creams and golds. There were ornaments everywhere, but lovely ones, things of beauty and grace, and probably many of them expensive. But there were also homemade ones, some by Katherine when she was a child or a young girl. And there were far more photographs on the walls than good taste would allow, but they were the moments in Dorothy's life most important to her. One of them was Katherine and Charles on their wedding day, both very formal and trying unsuccessfully to look well in control. Their happiness shined through.

Another silver-framed image was simpler: Dorothy and Wyatt, her wedding gown very old-fashioned, mid-Victorian. Dorothy had been truly beautiful then.

"You like it?" Dorothy's voice came from the bed. Elena turned to place the tray gently across her grandmother's lap.

"I'm sorry," she said. "You looked so lovely, I had to stare. My mother taught me better manners, but it wiped all that away for a moment." She smiled. "Shall I pour the tea? Or would you rather do it yourself?"

Dorothy looked at the tray. There was no milk on it. "It's all right, you pour it, dear. You can't spoil it with milk, because there isn't any. You could squeeze the quarter-lemon for me."

The sandwiches were very thin and lightly buttered, wrapped in a napkin to keep them fresh.

"May I look around your room?" Elena asked with a smile. "It is so beautiful, and it says so much about you."

Dorothy hesitated a brief moment. "Of course you may," she answered. "Did you sleep, dear?"

"I must have," Elena lied. Actually, she had slept very little, too grieved and too worried to relax. "Did you?" She looked directly at the old lady and saw the confusion in her eyes. "I'm concerned about you," she said gently. "We'll find out who really did this. There's been a ridiculous mistake somewhere, or—"

"Or what?" Dorothy asked, fear in her voice.

Elena knew that she must weigh what she said very carefully, with Katherine not in the room to aid her. At the same time, she could not miss the chance to seek the information they needed.

"You have so many beautiful things, but they're all individual. Does each bring thoughts of a place, events, people?" she said, hoping to lead the direction of the conversation.

Dorothy smiled. "Yes, and so many happy memories." She blinked away tears again. "Oh, this can't be happening! I just don't believe it. Who would do this to us?"

"That's a very important question." Elena sat on the edge of the luxurious bed. "Somebody must be very jealous of you. I can understand that. You have a lot of friends . . . and influence. People can't help but envy you."

"I suppose so," Dorothy replied. "But doing this isn't going to change their lives. It's so . . . hateful. I can't help wondering which of my friends—and we didn't invite anyone except friends—which of them . . . ?" She stared at Elena, as if she expected an answer.

Elena knew that she must not let this conversation escape her. She needed to ask questions before her grandmother could decide what to say, or not to say. Or what to conceal out of pride, or because she feared saying anything that could be considered disloyal.

"Someone you thought was your friend," Elena went on slowly. "And Lila must have thought they were her friend, too."

Dorothy winced. "Oh, my dear, I didn't like Lila much. I thought she was too easy in her morals. But I wouldn't have had this happen to her. It's dreadful. Do you suppose she got involved with someone of . . . ?" She spread her hands helplessly. The right word eluded her—or else it was one she did not wish to use.

Elena wanted to argue, to say the judgment was harsh and cruel and did not justify anyone attacking Lila. But this wasn't the time to say so, and it probably never would be. "Do you think it was because of Lila?" she asked. "Her dress, or whatever?"

"Don't you?" Dorothy asked curiously, her brow wrinkling. "If you knew her a little better, dear, you would change your mind."

"I was thinking that maybe something else went wrong," Elena said thoughtfully. "More like a plan to hurt Grandpa, damage his reputation. Perhaps even bring the President into disrepute."

"Oh, my goodness!" Dorothy looked stunned. "Oh, I hope not. But you could be right. There are some dangerous and unscrupulous people these days."

"Well, it makes more sense," Elena said, wondering if she had gone too far, but she must follow it now. "Even the scandal alone might change other things, mightn't it?" She wrinkled her face into a frown of confusion. "Is that possible?"

"I suppose it is. But it's very frightening. How could you hate someone so much that you would stoop to . . . ?" Dorothy let her breath out in a sigh. "What have we come to?" She looked helpless. "We have changed, I'm afraid. Nothing is the way it used to be!"

Elena shifted on the edge of the bed and leaned a bit closer to her grandmother. "Grandmother, we must find out who really killed Lila. Maybe it had nothing to do with Grandfather, and if we could prove that, they would let him go. Maybe it was because of some affair Lila had with somebody, or didn't have. But if it was a deliberate move to take Grandfather out of political power, or influence the power he has, we have got to know the truth."

Dorothy looked startled. "You think it could be? But why?"

Elena considered for a moment. Was this the time to introduce Free America?

Dorothy looked at her anxiously. "I don't wish you to be frightened, dear. Your father is doing his best, and Wyatt has a fine lawyer. It's bound to be a mistake, and they'll find that out soon."

Elena realized the conversation was slipping away from her. She could not afford to lose this chance. She did not know America in general, or Washington, DC, in particular. Even though her mother had grown up here, that was nearly forty years ago. The whole world had changed utterly since then. And she must not let her eagerness lead her into betraying who she worked for. Dorothy was an old lady, innocent of a lot of the changes that had happened, but she was far from foolish.

"Of course you're right, Grandmother," she said ruefully. "I just want so badly to help."

"Oh, I know you do, dear," Dorothy said fervently. "We all do. And I feel helpless, too. Wyatt is a good man! He spent his whole life fighting for what he believes in. A lot of people haven't agreed with him, but he always sticks to his guns, whether it's fashionable or not. That's the kind of courage he has." She looked beyond Elena, at a watercolor painting of trees and flowers around another large, graceful house, and into a past only she could see.

"What sort of things does he believe in?" Elena asked. Was her heart starting to beat faster, knowing she was finally getting somewhere?

"Oh, fighting to preserve what we value." Dorothy shook her

head slowly, dislodging a long strand of silky hair. "The same sort of things we all believe in, dear. I know you're British, but underneath it, apart from the king, and all that, you still have the same values. The right to be ourselves, freedom of speech, freedom of worship, of assembly. And never having another war." She hesitated a moment, then went on. "I'm sorry, dear, but we can't do that again, even if we are with you in heart. And we can't afford another depression, like the one we're not really out of yet. That also killed so many people. Such heartache. We've got to stop these Bolsheviks from coming here with their crazy values. We've got to protect our identity, all that we sacrificed to build." She gave a little smile of both sadness and pride.

Elena hesitated a moment and then asked, "And who would be fighting against that, Grandmother?" She felt as if someone had opened a door somewhere and let in a breath of cold air; memories of the horror she had felt in Berlin, watching students dancing around a fire that burned books, adventures of the mind that hovered on the edge of possibility.

Dorothy was smiling and Elena had missed something altogether.

". . . such happy memories," Dorothy finished, watching Elena's face to see if she was listening, if she was moved. Was that to impress? Or just the loneliness of an old woman whose whole identity was bound up in memories? They were infinitely precious, and they were threatened with destruction, violent and ugly, by the accusation the police were leveling at her husband. The newspapers were already reporting it. And everyone Dorothy knew would definitely read about it.

Elena's mind wandered for a moment and then was pulled back by something Dorothy said. Was it possible? Had she just mentioned that Hitler was good for America? She pushed the thought away; she must have misheard. "I'm sorry," she said contritely, trying to shake off that thought, "I was daydreaming, thinking of other things I've seen." She wondered how much of our identity is created by what we believe of the past, whether in the end it is true or not. Impulsively, she put both her hands, very gently, over Dorothy's. "Don't worry, Grandmother, we'll find the truth, I promise. If you don't see me very much, it's because I'm trying to learn that truth. I'm afraid it's the only possible conclusion, that someone else killed Lila and meant to implicate Grandfather."

"Thank you, dear. That is very sweet of you. But what can you do? You don't know anybody here, least of all those who have no understanding of our values. The danger is far more than most people think."

"What danger?" Elena asked, nearly holding her breath.

"Why, the danger to our freedom, dear. We have fought for it, and some have died for it. Wyatt has always been passionately brave, and he always will be. You're very loyal, and I love you for it. But please, listen by all means, but don't run any risks. The enemies of freedom are stronger. You know that yourself!"

"I'll be very careful," Elena promised. "But I have to do something: I'm family."

"Yes, you are, dear; you're very much one of us," Dorothy said gently, and smiling.

Elena had to wait for her father to come home before she could speak to him, and it was midafternoon when she at last caught him alone. Katherine had gone up to be with Dorothy, who was still in her bedroom.

"Did you manage to learn anything this morning?" she asked, the moment the door closed, leaving them alone in the sitting room, now mellow in the afternoon sun.

"I went to see the people Dorothy suggested." He looked tired already. He sank into one of the soft seats. "Everyone is stunned, of course. But if they weren't, they wouldn't admit it to me. They're very polite, very supportive. But no one admits to knowing anything useful. I got a lot of good wishes, but no help."

Elena took the chair opposite him and spoke softly. "I think it was too carefully planned to fall apart at the first inquiries," she said. It was meant to be comforting, so he would not blame himself. Looking at his face, she knew she had failed, at least at that.

"We aren't achieving anything," he said bleakly. Perhaps she was the only person to whom he could admit that.

"I spoke to Grandmother today." She struggled for a way to express the thoughts that were beginning to take shape in her mind. "You have to make the police let you see Grandfather. You're the closest relative who can. You can't expect Grandmother to go. She's badly shocked by all this, and she's not well. And what can Mother do? She's looking after Grandmother, trying to keep up her spirits, and taking care of letters, bills, anything that has to be done. Would they let me see him?"

"Wyatt? No, but I'll go. I . . ." He shook his head as if to deny it. "I'll go tomorrow. I hoped I could take him good news, but there isn't any . . . yet."

"He must have some idea," she pointed out. "He has to be thinking about what really happened, and how to prove it. And, at the very least, that it wasn't him!" She took a breath. "Father, you've got to push him on a subject he may not want to talk about."

"Elena, I hardly know the man! Your mother—"

"Mother won't press him," she cut across the argument. "We haven't got time to be tactful with each other, or go gently around things that are almost certainly going to hurt, and even to offend. There's no time to tell lies, and hope you can avoid whatever it is because it could be embarrassing. What is this group, Free America? Are they friends . . . or enemies?"

"We all need some illusions, Elena," he said quietly. "Even you."

"Yes, I did! And believe me, having to recognize them was one of the hardest things I've ever had to do! And I was lucky to come out of it bruised, disillusioned, but still alive. What matters here? Illusions? Or getting Grandpa back home, free and vindicated?"

"Do you remember how much it cost? Really?" Charles's face was full of tenderness.

Elena saw an emotional nakedness he had never consciously allowed to show. After a moment, she looked away.

"I know it's important to keep dreams alive," she said softly. "I spent a lot of the morning listening to Grandma telling me about when she was young. How she met and loved Grandpa, how sweet he was, how gentle with her. I think he protected her from a lot of things he didn't want her to know. It mattered to him that she saw everything good in him, whether it was really there or not, and I can understand that." She looked back at Charles. "We all want somebody to see us as heroes and not see our faults. But we also need someone who sees our bad sides, the stupid things we do, and loves us anyway. But Grandpa isn't going to be saved from this by idealistic dreams. He needs somebody to look at reality, and then fight for him anyway."

"Are you saying you think he might have done it?" Charles looked startled.

"No, of course not!" she said sharply. "I don't believe it for a moment. I'm saying that if we start lying to the lawyer or the police about small things, we may unintentionally obscure something that really matters, something that could clear him of the bigger thing."

"What are the smaller things?" Charles asked.

"I don't know. Maybe something we think is bad and he thinks is perfectly all right. He admires some of the things Hitler has done."

"Like getting the trains to run on time?" Charles said bitterly.

"I wish somebody would do that for us," she retorted.

"Stick to the point," he told her. "Not many people know as much about the new Germany as you do."

"Yes, I know. And I really believe if he had been there, he would think as we do. But he hasn't. He just sees businesses starting again, and order, and someone who fights against the Bolsheviks, and gypsies and communists. All the people he sees threatening a life he believes in. He wants to keep America free from all that."

"No Jews," Charles said bitterly.

Elena bit her lip. "Yes, I know that. That's everywhere, I suppose, because a lot of the people we think of as threatening our way of life—revolutionaries—are Jewish . . . or we think they are. Right now, that isn't the point. We aren't any better than those we fear and despise if we are only for those people who are like ourselves. That sounds pompous, doesn't it?"

"I can just hear Lucas saying that. Not pompous, but not very realistic," Charles began.

"I disagree. I think he's very realistic indeed," she insisted. "I think he'd say, 'Dream whatever you want, but fight the reality.' We've got to know the truth, so we don't waste time battling the shadows, rather than the substance. Grandfather Wyatt may be a bit to the right for us, but his friends know he is, and they like him anyway. However, they won't forgive him for murdering Lila, crushing her to death with his car! That's a world away from political conservatism, possibly discrimination, and anyway, we're all guilty of that to some degree. Please! The truth may not be perfect—nobody is. For me, the truth has to include all my mistakes." She winced, then added ruefully, "Especially those that I would love to keep private. But we don't always have that choice."

"I want to protect Dorothy, of course," Charles responded. "But mostly I want to protect your mother. She has only happy memories of her father from the past."

She felt her eyes fill with tears. "I know."

"Do you? Do you really understand?"

She looked at his face, then away again. "Yes, I do. I would find it hard indeed if someone told me *you* had done that, deliberately caused a woman's death."

"Could you believe it?" His voice was hoarse.

"No, and I don't believe it of Grandfather. And I'll prove it! But carefully, and only with reality, which may involve conceding that he is not infallible. He may be guilty of ordinary human weaknesses and misjudgments, but nothing worse than that, which we have to prove. For Mother and Grandmother's sakes, as well as his own. And I'd like to put away whoever really killed Lila. You could call that revenge, if you wish. I liked her. A lot. And if she was a spy, and that's why she was killed, then she could have been me!"

"Elena," Charles protested, "don't say that, please!"

"Say it or not, Father, it's still true. I'd like to be as brave as Lila was, even if I'll never be that alluring." She smiled at him, laughing at herself.

He did not reply, but Elena saw both pride and fear in his face.

Elena went upstairs to her bedroom and took out the copies of her photographs that the police had developed. She laid them out on the bed, in the order in which they had been taken. She included the poor ones as well as the good. There were several that were excellent. When this nightmare was over, she would get in touch with the people and offer them those in which they were featured. There were quite a few where the subject had moved, and these were badly blurred. Some were out of focus, and in two or three the light had got in and they were no good at all.

She counted them. They were all here.

But did they tell a story of the evening that was of any help? Or that told her anything she did not already know? A lot of them were taken when she had gone around meeting people with her grandfather beside her. That had been later in the evening, after she had talked with Lila.

Put together, they created a pattern of where people were. Miller must have spoken to all of them and he had copies of those photographs. Was Wyatt really the only one who was unaccounted for, between the time Lila was last seen and the time the waiter came in and said he had found her? Was that just incredibly bad luck?

It seemed so.

harles needed to see three different people, and to speak to them alone, confidentially and possibly at some length. Two full days had passed since Wyatt's arrest. He needed to meet Max Borrodale again, and as soon as possible. Then Captain Miller, to see if they had made any progress. And then he must see Wyatt himself.

He stood at the window overlooking the garden, and tried to plan his day. The meeting with Borrodale would be the easiest to arrange. There were no formalities to overcome, and he was retained by Wyatt, so surely he would make himself available again. And Charles had to assume that the attorney would assist him in whatever ways he could.

Then, even if he had to wait upon Captain Miller's convenience, it was worth it to learn what he had found out so far. The captain had not been back to the Baylors' house since the early morning of the arrest. Who had he questioned since then? The police might have seen any or all of the other guests in the days between, and learned things that jeopardized this case, or strengthened it. Charles would have no way of knowing that, unless he asked, but he was very reluctant to do so without a good reason. How could he request an appointment to see Miller personally, when he had to admit that he had no new evidence? And, of course, he would be seen as biased, being Wyatt's son-in-law. But wasn't that only natural? Charles knew he would have to accept the risk of having any meeting put off at the last minute, but he saw no other way to learn exactly what evidence the police believed they had against Wyatt so far. The question was: Could any of it be politically based?

Lastly, a visit to Wyatt would require the permission of the authorities. Perhaps Borrodale could help with that? Charles was not Wyatt's lawyer, so no confidentiality could be guaranteed. However, the police did acknowledge that Charles represented the family—that is, he was the closest relative who was able to visit. No one wished to subject Dorothy, an elderly woman, to such a devastating emotional experience. Granted, the police cells would be nothing like the harsh and demeaning surroundings of a prison. Please heaven, it would not come to that!

Perhaps he would ask his father-in-law about Free America? There was much he needed to understand in order to move forward in planning a defense.

Katherine had told him about the group after her visit from Mabel Cartwright. It had stirred a fear in her. She imagined it as a powerful organization, more than merely a few like-minded friends. Charles felt her fear. But who were they? People upholding, and perhaps advocating, a certain political view? She seemed to be gripping her courage fiercely, hoping to find some explanation for her father being framed. Charles longed so deeply to discover this as well, and he could hardly bear to look at her. Hers was a fragile courage, taking all the strength she could muster, but courage and hope gave her something, and he could not bear to take it from her. He could offer her so little, except empty words about what people might do to find the truth.

Elena agreed with her mother. She had been present during Mabel's visit, and she had the feeling that this woman knew quite a bit about Free America, although she was very vague about what it might be. But then, Elena judged that vagueness to be deliberate.

Neither Charles nor Elena understood what Free America represented. Did Captain Miller know about them? If so, perhaps he could offer an explanation?

Charles thought of asking Katherine more, but she had become increasingly quiet. The strain was causing a distance to grow between them. Or was that his imagination? They were all exhausted. He also suspected that they were sharing the same growing and unspoken fear that this situation was not going to be as easily resolved as they wanted to believe.

No one could argue that Wyatt had been accused of a crime that aroused deep and violent feelings among the public. His servants had taken the newspapers at the front door and burned them in the kitchen stove, a quick and simple way of ensuring that neither Dorothy nor Katherine could come across any of the articles in them. And they did not ask to see them. Although Charles read only *The New York Times,* and that paper barely touched on the crime, the local papers were blaring the story.

As for bringing Elena along for these visits, Charles was torn. He would have liked to have kept all of this from her, too, but he needed her help, and her honest judgment. He could not afford to protect her from the ugliness of comment and speculation, and she would not be as hurt by it as would Katherine or Dorothy. Reading those articles would not tear apart the fabric of her beliefs. Wyatt was her grandfather, therefore part of her life, but she had met him so few times before her arrival in Washington three and a half days ago. If Charles was counting on her help, she needed to face as much reality as possible.

However, he pushed these thoughts aside. Even if his daughter's impressions were useful, he was certain the authorities would deny her a visit.

Of the three men on his list, he found visiting Wyatt the most difficult prospect to face. Years ago, Wyatt had done his best to welcome Charles into the family, but he had not hidden his, or even Dorothy's, dismay that Katherine had chosen to marry an Englishman. Not only did the marriage wreck all their hopes for her remaining close as she raised her family, but it also required her to live in not just one foreign country, but several. They had missed seeing their only grandson grow up. And then he was killed in the war. It was a wrench that still hurt, and Wyatt did little to hide it. But now the man was in the most appalling trouble. Family loyalty apart, mere decency obliged Charles to do everything he could to help him.

What did he need to do before leaving the house? He requested one of the maids to ask Mrs. Baylor for fresh clothes. Wyatt would certainly appreciate that.

While he waited, he told himself that he needed to assure Wyatt that his family was all right and they believed in him. He must have an honest talk, ask questions and get some answers. Wyatt must be racking his brain to think who had done this to him, what the truth might be. Would he know about Free America? Of course he would! According to Mabel, he was a member.

Charles made the appointment to see Borrodale, then asked Dorothy if he could use one of Wyatt's cars and his chauffeur. "I'll be gone most of the day," he explained. As expected, she told him that everything he needed was there for his taking. He found it interesting, but not surprising, that she did not ask whom he was going to see. He saw hope flicker in her eyes for a moment. Charles was sure she was afraid to ask. If she preferred remaining ignorant of the details, he could respect that. If he had any good news, he would tell her.

It was a pleasant drive out of the suburbs and into the business part of DC, where Borrodale had his offices. At any other time, Charles would have enjoyed the beauty of the trees, especially the delicate white blossoms of the dogwood, which seemed to be all over the place, like stars against the dark green of the pines.

The city itself had far more grace and elegance than he had time to appreciate. It seemed to be full of sunlight. Many of the buildings had a classical look, and it took him a few moments to realize that none of them was high enough to shadow the whole street. Good luck, or a brilliant foresight by someone?

The car dropped him off outside Borrodale's office. Charles thanked the driver and asked him to return in an hour or so.

Borrodale kept him waiting only five minutes before opening his office door and holding out a strong, well-manicured hand. "Good morning, Mr. Standish, how are you, sir? So sorry we have to continue meeting in such difficult circumstances. Tell me, how is Mrs. Baylor? Poor lady. A terrible stress for her, but we are doing everything we can. And your wife? Mrs. Standish is Wyatt's daughter, isn't she?" It was not a question. He stepped back for Charles to come into his lavish office. Charles admired the maple bookcases and the large carved desk with leather-padded chairs on both sides. There were also chairs near a fireplace, which allowed six or seven people to be seated at the same time. He once more noted how the walls were lined with shelves, some of them with small statues on them. And again, he felt there was no time to move closer and inspect them.

Charles remained silent with difficulty. He was sure that Borrodale had expected him to say something, but he wasn't sure what that could be.

"I'm afraid it is as I supposed," Borrodale finally said. "Basically political. Of course, Wyatt is not guilty of this crime. The very thought is absurd. Why on earth would he have anything to do with this wretched woman? But he was circulating around the party, as any good host does. He can remember speaking with almost everyone, but not where or when. You were there. I don't imagine you could account for every moment of your time?" He raised his eyebrows.

"Do they have any idea exactly when she was . . . struck?" Charles asked, sitting down uncomfortably in the chair Borrodale indicated, before he himself took the one opposite.

"Within a quarter of an hour or so, yes." Borrodale nodded. "You haven't grasped the base of this thing, Mr. Standish. Wyatt has always stood by his principles without fear or favor. Such people have enemies. Power has its rewards, and its price."

"Then we have to look at his enemies," Charles said, as if it were obvious.

"There are friends and enemies, and a vast sea of opportunists between them." Borrodale shook his head. "Those are the ones we ought to beware of. People who will say what is of the best advantage to them. To whom do they owe . . . what? Or who can help them get another step up the ladder? Who has debts to pay off . . . or to incur? And to whom? This is something I have to work out. I need a little leverage, too, but—"

"I know politics are complicated, Mr. Borrodale," Charles cut across him. "But very seldom do they lead to the violent murder of a young woman. Surely, there is a limited number of people who had both the opportunity and some benefit sufficiently huge to commit such an act? Are you suggesting it was revenge for something? Or to silence Wyatt in some regard? Or even to take his place?" When should he ask about Free America? Were they an action group? Or just a patriotic society, an excuse to get together?

Borrodale pursed his lips. "Any of those is possible," he answered patiently. "I am excluding people. But I must move with great care. Once a man commits to testify to something, it is very difficult for him to go back on it. Embarrassing, you know . . ."

"For God's sake, man!" Charles had trouble keeping his temper. He should be able to do this! "All you're asking from them is to say that they saw Wyatt, or were speaking to him at this time or that! And usually several people will have seen him. It's—"

"Mr. Standish! It was a good party, plenty of food, and drink," Borrodale said with exaggerated patience. "People don't spend their time looking at the clock, or noting where other people are standing, or with whom. Once I get them to commit to something, they have boxed themselves in, and then they can't go back on it, however awkward or embarrassing it becomes. Nobody is willing to get caught in a lie, or even an unintended error, to the police, or to anyone else."

Except political lies, of course, Charles thought, but he did not interrupt.

"It's an easy conversation," Borrodale went on. *"I say, old fellow, don't you remember the conversation we had? You told me about Woodhouse, and the problem he has . . . Or I promised you I'd speak to Abbott about you, an excellent position, and you are just the man for it."* Borrodale shook his head. *"Must have been close to that time the poor woman was run over. Dreadful to think about it.* In other words, you provide me with an alibi, and I'll provide you with one!" He pursed his lips. "Once I've said it, I can't go back! Catch me in one lie, and everything I say becomes suspect. Refuse a favor, and my next step is blocked, or will it be yours?"

"But Elena took photographs all evening, a record of names and faces. She could say from them who was inside and when," said Charles.

Borrodale put his hand up, as if to stop traffic. "I dare say she can, but I can't call her, Mr. Standish. They'll demolish her."

"For heaven's sake! You're speaking as if she were a child! She was there, she saw . . ."

Borrodale shook his head wearily. "I regret having to say this, but she would be like red meat to a pack of wolves."

Charles was angry. "She's a highly intelligent and brave young woman."

Borrodale leaned forward. "A well-educated, pretty young woman," he corrected. "Gets a job in the Foreign Office, with a little help from her well-placed father. But she throws it all away in a full-blown love affair with a traitor. She actually aids him in escaping. She loses her job and becomes a fashion photographer. Using all those brains, all that education, to take pictures of wealthy women in pretty dresses. Bit difficult to get a responsible job or make a de-

cent marriage. You would really put her through that?" For an instant there was clear mockery in his face.

Charles was so angry he was choking inside. His mind raced to
find a rebuff that would silence Borrodale completely. But even as
he drew breath, the truth twisted inside him: that he could not think
how to fight back. And he certainly could not reveal his daughter's
true work. "Who the hell told you that?"

"Wyatt, obviously," Borrodale answered, with a slight smile. "And
of course I thought of using it! Pretty young woman, loyal to her
grandfather, with photographs to prove it." He lowered his voice a
tone. "Mr. Standish, even if you were prepared to do that to her, I'm
not! Not from any high-minded sentiment, but because it would
blow up in my face. I don't know what else there is. I can't stand
before a jury and say she is . . . what? Honest? Loyal? Tell me, are you
willing for me to do that?"

Charles could not think of an answer. His mind was racing. Who
had told Wyatt about it? And in those terms! That she had betrayed
her country for what? An affair. She had believed in Aiden Strother.
Wrongly. And she had paid for it. But she was now working at something he could not name, risking her life and telling no one. At first,
she had not told him, but now he knew. He thought of how his father, Lucas, had risked his life during the war and after, and told no
one, accepting Charles's criticism without a word. As always, he
blushed with shame for his own blindness to that. Judgment without
any grounds for it.

But who had told Wyatt about Aiden Strother and Elena's disgrace? It must have been Katherine, directly to Wyatt, or indirectly
through Dorothy. Emotion swept through him: fury, and a consum-
ing passion to defend Elena. But no words came that would not
make it even worse. He could not disclose her work with MI6. Doing
so might unintentionally expose Lucas, too. He was helpless. The
most damaging thing he could do was say something that would set
Borrodale off into thinking, perhaps exploring. He wanted to defend

Wyatt, but not at the cost of betraying Elena. And indirectly, perhaps Lucas as well.

Borrodale was staring at him. "Nothing to say? I thought not." Was that sympathy in his face, or satisfaction? "Better you leave her out of this, for everyone's sake," he went on. "I shall keep you informed, as far as news that you can pass on to your wife, or your mother-in-law. You may tell them as much as you think helpful of the difficulties facing us. I suggest you tell Mrs. Baylor as little as possible. She is very dependent on Wyatt, and if it goes badly, she may not survive it well. I can't promise anything, except that I have negotiated that he can await trial released to his own home, and at the price of bail that he can easily afford. He is an old man and his heart is less than perfect. Not serious, you understand, but we will make the most of it."

For the first time, Charles saw a shadow over Borrodale's smooth face, and he realized how much of an act he had to put on for his clients. He still did not like him, but he respected the task he was willing to undertake. Would it have been possible for him to decline it? Or would that have done his reputation, and therefore his income, even more damage than losing?

"Thank you," he said. "That is a big thing, a very big thing. The family will be delighted. May I tell them?"

"You may." Borrodale smiled briefly. "But unless I can come up with some real evidence, he will still have to stand trial."

"Do you think he is guilty?" Charles asked incredulously. "Wyatt Baylor? Guilty of hitting a woman and then, when she lay on the ground, getting into his car and driving over her body?"

Borrodale flushed slightly. "No, of course I don't. But somebody at that party did. And when the chips are down as irrevocably as this, every man's going to fight for himself. The best of them are going to stay loyal to their beliefs."

"Beliefs in what? The law, friendships, debts owed?" Charles asked.

"The best of them, to their political beliefs; position, which might well rest on staying out of other countries' affairs; and putting their own people first," Borrodale answered tartly.

This was the moment. Charles could ask about Free America, which both Katherine and Elena had spoken of. "I did hear that mentioned," he said casually, as if recalling it only at Borrodale's reminder. "Something about . . . Free America? Could Wyatt have offended someone in that group?" He tried to look suitably blank.

Borrodale froze. "Why do you ask that?"

"Because I hadn't thought of it, but I heard Wyatt speak of it a couple of times," he answered. "Who are they?"

Borrodale hesitated only a moment, but it was there. "An . . . isolationist group, I think," he said quite casually.

"That Wyatt belongs to? Or doesn't?"

"Yes." Borrodale was very cautious now. "You are an Englishman, Mr. Standish. I dare say you would not approve of it. You might keep treaties with France or Belgium or Poland, or whoever. We don't. Our first duty is to our own people. To not get drawn into other people's quarrels . . . again."

"You are a member?" Charles asked. Then he saw Borrodale's expression.

"I've heard mention of it," Borrodale replied. "I am not a politician and have no wish to be." His expression changed, a certain tightness in his neck and shoulders. "I practice law, Mr. Standish. I don't inquire into my clients' political or religious beliefs. But I understand the desire to put your own country first."

Charles drew in breath to argue, and realized it was pointless. The landmass of Europe was less than thirty miles from England at the Channel's narrowest point. A long-distance swimmer could do it. Several had! That was not true of America. If you ruled America, you had to do so with America's interests at heart, and people had a right to expect that.

Is that what Wyatt thought? Hunting in his memory for what Wyatt had said in the few hours they had had together, that seemed to be the case.

"And does that include killing Lila Worth?" he asked.

"Of course not!" Borrodale snapped. "If you can find any evidence that points away from him, that would be very useful. But short of that, I advise you to look after your women, most particularly your wife and your mother-in-law, and leave your daughter as far out of this as possible. She might make her photographs available to us, if they are of any use, but nothing more."

"The police already have them," Charles replied. "They developed them at their laboratories, and gave her back the negatives and a set of pictures to keep, in the unlikely case of any of the guests wanting copies."

"This is the least of the guests' problems," Borrodale said witheringly. "If the lack of your picture in some magazine is all you suffer from this affair, you'll be damned lucky!" Borrodale stood. "Good day, Mr. Standish."

Charles ate a solitary lunch nearby, barely tasting it as he turned over in his mind all that Borrodale had said. As a move forward, it amounted to nothing. He had Wyatt's chauffeur drive him to the police station. He did not have to wait more than half an hour for Captain Miller to see him. The man was polite, but he looked tired, and his patience seemed strained to breaking.

"Thank you for sparing me your time," Charles said, sitting down in the chair Miller indicated. "I believe you have agreed to release Mr. Baylor to his own home, to await trial?"

"Yes," Miller agreed. "I'm not sure whether it will be today or tomorrow. In either case, he's to remain in the house. He'll be more comfortable there. He's an old man, although his health is quite good. With sufficient bail, we have no objections . . . for the time being. Now, what can I do for you, Mr. Standish? I'm afraid I have very little to add to what you already know."

"Neither have I," Charles admitted. "Except that I've spoken with Mr. Baylor's lawyer, Borrodale, and he says the matter is far more complicated than it appears. He seems to think there could be political motives behind the murder, and that the intended victim of it all was Mr. Baylor himself. Mrs. Worth's death was the means to ruin him."

Miller gave a wry smile. "It's a theory, Mr. Standish. And if it proves to be so, then the plot is working pretty well. But as to the actual murder: many of the guests we can exclude, simply because they were seen to be in groups nearly all the time. Mr. Baylor, like any good host, moved among them from one to another: much harder to pin down. People don't look at the time very often when they are enjoying themselves."

"What reason is he to have had for killing Mrs. Worth, so suddenly and extremely violently, in his own driveway, with a houseful of guests, including the President and his wife?" Charles asked. "Did anyone see them quarreling? And if so, over what? Not an affair, surely. Was it planned? In the middle of a party?" Charles deliberately kept his voice level. "And if she was having an affair, which you have yet to prove, wouldn't her husband be the most obvious suspect?"

"Yes," Miller agreed wearily. "But no one has suggested an affair. And to the best of my knowledge, Wyatt Baylor is faithful to his wife. No one can connect him to Mrs. Worth."

"Then why on earth would he kill her? And so violently, and in his own home? It doesn't make any sense!" Charles argued, his voice rising. "Except if by framing him, a political enemy is trying to destroy him."

"I agree." Miller smiled briefly. "And that may well be what is happening. He has very well-known right-wing views. He supports the idea of isolationism. He's an advocate for Adolf Hitler and some of his practices, although not all of them: racial hygiene and all that it implies. And, of course, anti-Semitism." He shook his head wearily. "He has a lot of admirers, Mr. Standish, as well as enemies. We have many tensions in our country, as I believe you have in yours. And a wide difference of views. This is healthy, but not when it turns violent." He paused, as if waiting for Charles to respond. When he said nothing, Miller continued, "Mrs. Worth was rather liberal in her views. I'm told she was trying to draw people toward meddling in German and Austrian affairs . . . again. Quite natural, since she was Austrian by birth and upbringing."

Charles shook his head. "You are not suggesting Wyatt killed her over a political difference? There'd be no one left alive in Washington if that were a common practice."

"No, I'm not," Miller said quietly. "We don't know very much about Lila Worth. In truth, the more we look, the less we find. She and Harmon were apparently married in Austria, but there doesn't seem to be any record of that. We don't even know her maiden name."

"Many people change their names when they come to a different country," Charles said patiently, and with a very slight smile. "It doesn't mean they're hiding anything. Could be because English-speaking officials can't pronounce it or can't spell it. Or perhaps it was as a result of the first official who took it down spelling it how he thought it should be. Especially with Czech names, or Polish. They just cut it in half and use a form of it."

"She's Austrian," said Miller. "Or at least that's what she said. And she spoke perfect English. At a guess, I'd say she was well educated. In fact, from all I hear, she was a very clever woman. And she was certainly beautiful." Miller said this with a note of regret. Something good had been lost.

Charles tried a different angle. "Whom did she threaten? Who profited from her death?"

"Financially? No one. And we did look very carefully at Harmon Worth. He seemed genuinely distressed at her death. And more to the point, shocked. You can act shocked, grieved, surprised, all that, but I don't know how anyone can drain all the color from their face in front of you. I thought he was going to faint." There was unmistakable pity in Miller's face.

Charles liked him for that. The man could imagine himself in another's place—empathy, too rare a gift. "Is there any reason to suspect him?" he asked.

"No," Miller answered with a faint smile. "Except that you always look at the husband when a woman is killed. Especially one who's as alive as everyone says she was. And, as I said, very beautiful." He looked down at the papers, and then up again quickly. "I'm sorry, Mr. Standish, I understand you're concerned for your wife and your mother-in-law. I'd think less of you if you were not. But such evidence as I have points to Mr. Baylor. We can't find any witnesses to his whereabouts at the time we know Mrs. Worth must have been killed, that is, between the time she was last seen alive and when the waiter came through the front door and said he had found her body."

"Is Wyatt the only one who can't tell you exactly where they were?" Charles asked with open skepticism.

"No, but when we compare accounts of where everyone was, and who they were with, and we cross-check one with another, he is the only one not accounted for. Of course, there are so many factors to consider when we question people. Some speak out of loyalty, or hold back information if they have hopes for advancement of some kind—money, ambition. So, all those guests who were in various groups—well, it still leaves an area of doubt." He paused for a moment, as if deciding to reveal more. And then he said, "Mr. Standish, in my years of experience, I can share one undeniable fact: people lie for all sorts of reasons." Before Charles could respond, he quickly added, "But we must take into account that it was Mr. Baylor's car."

"Anyone could have driven it!" Charles protested. "The keys were left under the seat, for heaven's sake! Any stranger could have . . ." He stopped, knowing it was futile.

Miller looked intent. He said what Charles already knew. "Mr. Standish, the President was there that night. We knew that. They were very open in telling us. His security was all over the place. They were guarding the entrance and patrolling the boundaries. No strangers could have come in, let alone attacked a woman, hit her, stolen a car to run over her body and killed her, and then replaced the car, put the keys back under the seat, and wandered away!"

"Aren't you saying that's exactly what Baylor did?" Charles demanded.

"No. While the President's security men were at the gates and around the perimeter, as well as in the house, they were not in the parking lot. There was no need, since nobody was able to get in or out of that area. No one could get past them."

Charles thought for a moment, the pieces jagged and ill-fitting in his imagination. "It seems an extraordinary time to kill anyone," he began. "They must have needed to do it very urgently, otherwise they'd have picked a better opportunity. There surely have been dozens. And none of them with armed security guards swarming all over the property. So, yes, there was urgency." He looked directly at Miller. "Lila Worth was going to do something the killer could not allow." The other thought, that it was the most advantageous chance to frame Wyatt Baylor, was at the forefront of his mind.

"Such as what?" Miller asked. "Expose Baylor in some way? Or are you still thinking it was someone else?"

"If it was to throw the blame on Wyatt, then the crime had to happen at an event where the killer knew he would be," Charles reasoned. "And even if this person was Wyatt's friend, there can't have been that many events when they were at the same place, at the same time, and with a hundred other people to offer alibis. And with the President there, too. Perhaps it served him, or them somehow?"

"How?"

"I don't know. But what if their purpose was to have Lila dead and Wyatt Baylor blamed? If so, it worked perfectly!"

Miller thought for a moment or two. "Yes, it did. But why would anyone want that? It must have been a hell of a good reason, to take that risk."

"I'm not sure," Charles admitted. He took a deep breath and then asked the one question that had been burning in his mind. "Do you know anything about Free America?"

Miller's eyes widened. "You know about them? Had you heard about them in England, or did you learn about them in the few days you've been here?"

Charles was surprised by Miller's dramatic response.

"Mrs. Baylor didn't tell you anything," the policeman continued. "I'm pretty sure she doesn't know much. So how did you pick it up? A slip in conversation? Baylor can't have told you anything. Unless you . . ." He stopped.

"Unless I agree with him?" Charles finished for him. "There are plenty of Brits who don't want another war, whatever the cost. The last war revealed so much that no one should ever see, or experience through our loved ones. I lost my only son," he said, his voice dropping. "But no, I am not one of the *never again* group. And I know too much of what's going on today in Germany. If we have another war, it will be far worse than the last. The tanks will be heavier, the guns bigger. And God knows what else." He paused for a moment, and then added, "But I'd rather die fighting than turn into what the Nazis have become. Believe me or not, as you like."

"I agree," Miller admitted gravely. "But we don't all think like that." He looked pale and a little shaken as he said it, as if a memory was still hideously clear in his mind.

Charles drew in breath to mention Elena's photographs again, to ask if they wouldn't present proof, if looked at carefully. And then he remembered Borrodale's words and changed his mind. "You took copies of all my daughter's photographs," he said, deciding on something more general. "Were they of any help?"

Miller jerked himself back to the present, back from what Charles assumed was the man's images of wartime, perhaps the nightmares accompanying it. "Yes, and we asked her about them: when they were taken. Not all of them were clear. As it happens when photographing such a large number of people, sometimes a movement blurs a shot, or a shot is over- or underexposed and the subject isn't recognizable. But a lot of them are very good, some exceptional. And because negatives are in consecutive order, we were able to place the approximate time in which the pictures were taken. Those photographs gave alibis for quite a few people. Unfortunately, Mr. Baylor was not one of them."

"Elena's a very good photographer," said Charles.

"Yes, and it's a pity she won't be able to sell them. At least, in the circumstances, no decent publication would have them."

"And she certainly won't be offering them to some cheap tabloid," said Charles. "But this is hardly important. What we must do is find something definitive to prove the truth."

Miller jumped on his comment. "*We?* May I remind you, Mr. Standish, that this is a police matter?"

Charles offered a little nod of acknowledgment. "Captain, I do believe Wyatt Baylor is innocent. Not only because he is my wife's father, but because his being guilty of this makes no sense. A quarrel, possibly; a difference of political opinion, definitely. But if people kill each other over that, there wouldn't be anyone left alive in Washington. Or London, for that matter."

Miller gave a rueful smile. "Most murders are either robbery-connected or domestic. I've never seen one that was purely political. *Indirectly* is another thing. Money, power, pride, ambition—I don't know which this is, but I do know that it's brutal. And there may be more than one victim."

When Charles requested a visit to Wyatt he was told to return later in the day, after the police had completed their paperwork required to release him.

Charles thanked Captain Miller and left, feeling more confused than before.

It was late in the afternoon when Charles finally met with Wyatt. There was a possibility that he would be released later, but this was uncertain. Charles felt he couldn't wait, that every minute counted, if he was to uncover the truth.

It was not the first time he had visited someone in police custody.

As an ambassador, especially when he had been in a junior position, his job was to visit, counsel, advise, even represent British citizens who found themselves held in police or immigration custody in a foreign country. This was different. This was a member of his own family, his wife's father, his children's grandfather, and the charge was not petty robbery, trespassing, repeated driving offenses, or passport wrongdoings. This was a shocking and brutal murder.

Before being permitted entry to the police station holding cells, he was searched, as was the bag Dorothy had filled with clean clothes. He was then escorted to a small, chilly room where he was told to wait. He sat at the little table, reminding himself that Wyatt had been charged, but had not yet been tried, so he was still presumed to be innocent.

There was one other chair in the room, directly across from where Charles sat.

Wyatt Baylor came through the door, still wearing his suit from the party, but he looked quite different. His clothing was crumpled, and not clean. His thick hair was untidy and, although he had shaved that morning, it had been less than complete, as if he had done it without a mirror.

"Hello, Charles," he said immediately. "You haven't brought Kate, have you?"

"No."

"Thank God." He dropped into the chair. "This can't last. I didn't kill that damn woman. How is Kate? And Dorothy? I hardly dare ask that."

Charles placed the duffel bag on the table, but Wyatt didn't seem to notice. Charles decided to deal only in truth. He wanted to comfort the man, but if he lied now, would Wyatt trust him in the future? Could any of them afford that?

"Charles!" Wyatt's voice cut across his thoughts.

"Katherine's all right," said Charles. "And she's looking after her mother. Dorothy has not really accepted what's happened. It's going to hit her very hard, unless we manage to get on top of this quickly."

Before Wyatt could respond, he rushed forward. "I saw Borrodale this morning, and he's working diligently to get you out of here and home, where you'll be confined to the house until trial. It looks as if you'll be released tonight, or first thing tomorrow."

"And the trial?"

"We're hoping to prove your innocence before that happens."

Wyatt nodded, as if processing all of this. "Be a good man, Charles. Take care of Dorothy. Even when I'm home, this is going to take longer than I thought. It's more complicated. I knew I had enemies: people who stand for anything often do. But it's a battle infinitely worth fighting."

"Of course it is," Charles agreed. There was nothing else he could say. He had no idea what the battle was that Wyatt was referring to. He needed to know that. "But we have to be specific," he insisted. "The identity of the real perpetrator is limited to who was at your party, which means it is someone you know. Many of them have been ruled out." He leaned forward a little. "Think, Wyatt! Who is going to profit from your being ruined, out of the game, even dead?" He felt cruel as he said it, but there was no time to be delicate. And, frankly, there was nothing to be gained by it. He did not know how long he had before the guard interrupted him and escorted him out. And it was not yet guaranteed that Wyatt would be released in the next few hours. "Whose ambitions do you threaten? Actively, not just in principle." Should he mention Free America?

Wyatt was silent for several moments. "I could give you names, but there's nothing you can do about it." His face was bleak. "Some of them are decent enough men, just see things differently. Left wing, full of inappropriate sympathies. Idealists who are not in the real world. Damn dangerous!" He did not add any more. He looked wretched. "I suppose you are always diplomatic. It's your training to be polite. Frankly, I don't know how you do it. I have to speak my mind on some issues. This is a kind of freedom the old world is not accustomed to. I don't mean to insult you, but it's true. We have the chance, and the obligation, to defend the values of decency, honor, a civilization and quality of life that people like the Bolsheviks and their kind are sweeping away." His lips tightened. "We must realize what our freedom is worth, before it, too, is swept away and we are left with only the ashes of all that we knew and treasured. If you've read the newspapers, you'll know what's happening in Europe. The old order is crumbling, because its foundations are giving way. We started again in America, clean and strong. We know what our freedom is worth, and we'll die to protect it, if we have to." There was challenge in his eyes, hot and bright in spite of his exhaustion.

"Freedom," Charles said slowly, as words of an old conversation with Lucas came back to him. "My father used to talk about that when I was young."

Wyatt drew in breath to speak, but Charles ignored him.

"Freedom doesn't stand alone. It's freedom to do something, or from something, such as hunger. But there's no such thing as freedom from the results of our actions. It's a law of physics we can't escape. Action causes equal and opposite reaction, and all that." He saw Wyatt's expression change and ignored it. "Morally, it's the same. You can't escape the consequences of your actions. You may pay, or somebody else may, but the reaction will happen."

"You're waffling, Charles," Wyatt said tartly. "Diplomatic nonsense. We've got to get to the truth, fight for what we value, before it's too late. No time for English politeness, and watching while we sink deeper and deeper into the mud."

"You prefer me to be direct, rather than diplomatic?" he asked. "Fine, so let's start with this: I don't trust your man Borrodale. I think he may have your interests at heart, up to a point, but after that, it's a matter of his survival rather than yours."

"You don't understand!" Wyatt retorted.

"Agreed. But are you sure you do?"

Wyatt smiled again, but more bleakly, and his face lost even more color until he looked waxy, as if a flame would dissolve him altogether. "We're on the same side, ruled by the same goals."

Charles was touched with pity for this complete loss of dignity, as the man's strength faded in front of him. He wished Elena were in the room, but only if Wyatt knew who his granddaughter really was, the role she was playing in trying to clear her grandfather's name. Charles once more wondered who had told Wyatt about Elena's lapse of judgment. He wanted to tell him that she had more than made up for it. If he could reveal what had happened in Berlin, her important and even heroic role, the old man would see to trust her. But revealing this would be the beginning of a betrayal to which there might be no end.

"And your trust of Borrodale?"

"I'm not a fool," Wyatt said urgently. "At the moment, believe me, it is very much in his interest to prove my innocence. I can reward those who help me, and I can ruin those who don't. And anyone who knows me knows that I have a long memory."

Charles had a chilling thought. Was this a veiled threat against him personally? That was absurd. Damage to him would be damage to Katherine and to Dorothy.

A very slow smile spread across Wyatt's face. "You are cleverer than I first believed." Then the moment vanished and the fear came back. "But our enemies are ruthless, Charles. Help me. I'm fighting for my life. Someone at that party murdered Lila Worth. I would like to think she was the intended victim, and I am incidental damage. But I don't. I can't. It would be a luxury for which I would pay a heavy price. I don't think she had enemies of that caliber. She was delightful to look at, enough to turn men's heads and make some of them look like fools, but that's not a reason to kill her. And at my party." He shook his head sharply. "No, she was used to make a dramatic scandal that would destroy me, silence my voice, and perhaps most important, stop my advising Roosevelt to stay out of Europe. And trust me, I know enough to make a very persuasive argument. Perhaps not in England's interests, but in America's." He paused for a moment. "No, possibly England's as well, in the long run. I'm sure the Holy Fox would agree with me."

Charles nodded, in spite of himself. That was the nickname some had for Lord Halifax, a prominent British politician who believed, as many did, that whatever the cost, there must never be another war that was anything like the one that had decimated Europe only twenty years ago. The scars were still there, the wounds still bled.

As if he could read Charles's mind, Wyatt said, "Your only son, and my only grandson. It didn't have to happen, and it certainly doesn't have to happen again. Hitler's got a few rough edges, but he's a civilized man, and our only bulwark against the communists sweeping in from the east, like the damn Huns centuries ago. Nearly swept Europe into the sea, and Christianity with it."

Charles took a few seconds to respond. "Are you suggesting that killing Lila Worth at your anniversary party was a communist plot to get rid of you?"

"No, I'm not!" Wyatt said sharply. "I'm saying I have a lot of enemies, one way or another. That's what you asked me, isn't it?" He lowered his gaze. "Someone killed her, Charles; it wasn't an accident. You might look for her enemies, but that won't help her now. If you look for mine, it might just save my life." He looked up again. "Have you asked that girl of yours about her pictures? If you look at them carefully, can't you prove where I was and who I was with?" After a moment, he added, "If this goes to trial, couldn't she testify on my behalf?"

"I asked Borrodale that very question," Charles said between his teeth, trying to keep his expression unreadable. "He told me that her private and personal mistakes would be used to defame her to the point that nothing she said would be believed. She's your granddaughter. The prosecution would be more than happy to ruin her." He heard the edge of rage in his tone, but he could not control it, and he had his hands clenched because they trembled. "I've got beliefs on right and wrong, too, and family loyalties. And pretty often they're the same thing, because if we change our values when it suits us, we are no use to anyone. My loyalties begin with my wife and daughters, which should be where yours begin as well. But patriotism is pretty universal and has been the justification for some of the

worst acts on earth. I can understand it. That doesn't make it good,
or right."

Wyatt nodded. "I told you, Charles. I've got enemies. I didn't tell
anyone, least of all Borrodale, about Elena. I'm sorry to hear that he
knows. But that means my enemies know, too. Charles, help me."
His face was furrowed, as if the life were draining out of him, and his
eyes held real fear.

Charles exhaled slowly. "Of course."

CHAPTER

12

Peter Howard was sitting in his office. It was an afternoon in the middle of May, and the third full day since Wyatt Baylor had been arrested and charged with murder. Outside, the sun shone fitfully on the windows, as if it, too, were uneasy. He had been waiting for the phone to ring and yet, when it did, it startled him. He hesitated a moment, then leaned forward and picked it up. "Howard," he said simply.

"Report from Wilkerson, sir, in Berlin," said the voice on the other end.

"Bring it in," Howard replied. It would be from the British Embassy there, directly, but ultimately from one of his best agents in Germany, a man who regularly risked his life to get as much as he could of the truth behind the events, the public news, the things anyone could see, if they looked.

A few moments later, a very solemn-faced young man knocked on the door, opening it and coming in before Peter could invite him. He sat down, also uninvited, and his smooth face was furrowed with concern. He was public-school educated, Eton, like his father and grandfather, and then Cambridge, unlike his forebears, who had been officers in the Royal Navy. He had chosen to study modern history, and a certain amount of science. He was John Hastings, the third or fourth generation to bear that name. His parents had an intense feeling of family, and no imagination. Hastings looked ordinary enough: brown hair, fair skin, blue eyes, like a million other young Englishmen. The only thing that marked him as different was an acute sense of the darkness on the eastern horizon.

He began without waiting to be asked. "It's not good news from Berlin, sir. They've definitely opened the camp at Dachau and are rapidly filling it. And that's only the first. There are other camps on the way." His voice was hard-edged and his eyes unexpectedly weary. "It's actually happening: all sorts of people seen as misfits, dealt with as if they were a disease. And the Germans get away with it, because most people simply can't believe it would ever happen to them. It's like a fire that starts at the other end of the street. The fire brigade will put it out before it gets anywhere near us! Except the fire brigade is not coming. It hasn't even been called, nor will it be."

"Is it any worse than the last time you told me that?" Peter asked, although he knew the answer from Hastings's face. Or if he were more honest, he had known it even last summer, when he was in Berlin himself to rescue Elena. Or to attempt it.

"Yes, sir, it is definitely worse." Hastings's voice was hoarse with emotion. "It's not only that more people know about it and look the other way. They don't even pretend not to see it. Either that, or they don't care. Or are afraid to care, because that would mean they would have to do something about it." He looked pale, and his shoulders were rigid under his casual jacket.

Peter frowned. "Do you have family out there, Hastings?" he said, with a sudden leap of concern.

"No, sir. But the Germans are sort of first cousins. If it could happen there, it could happen here."

"They lost the war," Peter said quietly. "That's all the difference in the world. We won. Surely you aren't too young to remember that! It was only sixteen years ago."

"Did we?" Hastings said with a little twist of his mouth. "Doesn't always feel like it. I think the Americans did."

Peter searched Hastings's face for irony, sarcasm, ignorance. He saw only a bitter humor and, underlying it, fear. "You're right," he answered, with his own touch of bitterness. "Or they lost the least, and Germany the most. France and Britain are somewhere in the middle."

"The real winners are those who didn't fight at all," Hastings answered. "And one or two of their lordships have said this, as if they are determined to be among the uninvolved, this time round, if there is a *this time*."

"Talking about this time: What other news have you?" Peter asked. "All you've told me so far is exactly what we've been expecting. You hardly needed to come home to say that."

Hastings's face changed: it was now even more serious. "Sir," he said quietly, "there is something we didn't have last time. Didn't even imagine." He took a quick breath, hesitated, and then went on. "I mean, apart from building new concentration camps, and race hatred, especially against the Jews, the Germans are working hard, and secretly, on splitting the atom. I know that's not new, but they have some of their best scientists concentrating on harnessing the energy so they can control it. Not just for producing electricity and other power, but specifically to create explosive power."

"We know that," Peter said quietly.

Hastings rubbed his brow as if it hurt just beneath the surface. "I know that we are, too, but every indication is that they're far ahead of us. And by us, I mean both Britain and America." He leaned forward. "It's like nothing we have ever imagined. One or two bombs with that kind of power would wipe out most of England. We can't let people know there could be such a thing." He paused for a brief moment, and then rushed forward. "They don't even need to use it—the threat would be enough. Or they might unleash it on some remote country, obliterate it, and then the next country threatened by them will do whatever they're damned well asked."

It was what Peter had been dreading, while still clinging to the hope that it was an exaggeration, an empty threat. That now felt as hopeless as a man clinging to a piece of driftwood in the sea, with no land in sight. Was that black triangle cutting through the water a shark fin? And the answer was yes, of course it was. "I was hoping we were still ahead of them. Apparently not."

"We wish we were." Hastings gave a harsh smile. "That bitter absurdity runs through the whole thing."

Peter was lost. "I don't see any sort of humor at all, bitter or otherwise."

Hastings gave his superior a long look. "Sir, one of the best spies we had working on it is dead. Lila Worth."

Peter put his head in his hands. "Right. The woman murdered in Washington."

"Yes, sir. Her husband is a scientist, working in that field. I don't know how close he is to a result, because it's all pretty secret. Early stages still." He looked desperate, as if knowing enough to be genuinely frightened, but too little to make a difference. "But now is when we need to do something."

Peter looked up. "Thank you, Hastings." He thought for a moment. "Yes, I hear that Harmon Worth is pretty good. And Lila was imaginative . . . even visionary."

"I'm sorry," said Hastings. "I wish I could tell you something different. I can't even say how far along the Germans are. Just that, apparently, they are forging ahead, they can see where they're going. I don't think we can."

"Don't apologize, damn it!" Peter snapped. "Now we have to know who killed Lila, or why. Yes, above all, why. Was it because of what she knew about this? Or she was on the brink of finding out? Or was it something quite different: a domestic row, an affair gone sour.

It could be anything. Even that the German scientists are stuck, and don't want us to know that. What a bloody mess!"

"Yes, sir," Hastings said miserably. "Do you want me to go back there—to Germany, that is—and find out what I can?" There was resignation in his voice, as if he already knew the answer.

"Yes," Peter replied. "But for God's sake, be careful!"

Later in the afternoon came the telephone call he had been waiting for, and dreading. It was just after four o'clock, which meant it was minutes after eleven in the morning in Washington. The embassy would be full of people, and Allenby's presence would not be noticed.

Peter took the call immediately, telling his secretary he was not to be interrupted.

"Yes," he said to the voice at the other end. "What news?"

"Been looking a lot further into Wyatt Baylor, sir. I imagine you know his public record?" Allenby asked.

"Of course—a slow, discreet rise in power. Got one or two senators in his debt, socially or professionally, and possibly financially. Don't know the extent of it. Is it more than usual?" Peter asked quickly.

"I think so. I'm working on it, but I must be careful. I . . ." Allenby stopped.

Peter could only just hear his breathing over the phone.

"I think there could be a lot more to it than there seems at a glance," Allenby went on.

"Like what?" Peter asked. "Political influence? That's almost a given, in his situation."

"I'm trying to get a definite view of Baylor's investments. Not general, but specific."

"Shouldn't be too difficult."

"Not just money," Allenby said patiently. "Influence, favors done, knowledge gained, and debts that are more than a few thousand dollars here and there."

"Meaning what?" Peter asked more slowly. "Insider advice? That's criminal. Blackmail?"

"I don't know, but I think it's far subtler than that. Nothing that's criminal in itself, but collectively it would be worth noting." Allenby sounded less sure of himself now.

"What do you suspect, worst case?" Peter asked. "And stop mincing words. It's a damn irritating habit, and it's not like you."

"Baylor is Charles Standish's father-in-law, sir. He's an adviser to Roosevelt on finances, where to place the money, whose to use long term. Roosevelt is a remarkable man himself—crippled by polio, can barely stand without assistance—and yet the power in him is tangible. There's a lot going on, and much of it may not be what we think it is. Roosevelt has to tread very softly. He has an entire nation to rebuild after the Great Depression. They've barely begun. I don't envy him."

"I know," Peter said quietly. "Not that this has anything to do with Wyatt Baylor, or Lila Worth's death . . . does it?"

"A particularly brutal murder," Allenby reminded him. "And I don't know. It might have. Why was she killed then, and in that place? And is it chance that Wyatt Baylor looks to be guilty? Or was that the intention? If so, why? It could be a set of completely different answers, depending on who I ask."

"Yes, of course," Peter agreed. "And for God's sake be careful! We have a very insecure foothold in Washington at the moment. Any ideas?"

"Honestly, I don't know."

"Guess, man! You've had days already. What are you doing?" His voice was sharper than he had meant it to be.

"Looking more closely at Max Borrodale," Allenby replied.

"Who the hell is he?"

"Baylor's lawyer. Slimy bastard, but clever. At this moment, I'm not sure where his loyalties are."

"Such as?" Peter asked.

"Profit, reputation, money, ambition for higher position. But it's hard to judge where his political loyalties are, short term and long term."

Peter was slightly surprised; this was deeper than he had supposed. Lila's murder was certainly not a crime of passion, as some had suggested. Allenby seemed to be thinking of something more dangerous, perhaps a corrupt conspiracy, or at least one inimical to Britain. "Are you sure?"

"No," Allenby answered. "But it looks more and more likely. And it's what we have to consider. If it's a crime of passion, as some think, betrayal or a jealous woman, then it will all work out, and there's not much we can do about it. If Baylor killed her, he'll have to answer for it. We can't interfere. If it's Harmon Worth in a jealous rage, we can't save him. Which is a pity, because he's a more important scientist than I thought—than any of us thought, I believe. But whatever he is, we can't defend him if he murdered his wife in a violent and particularly disgusting way, and tried to blame someone else. But if it's more nefarious, something to do with national security, then we have an entirely different situation here."

"Could it possibly be the husband, Worth?" Peter asked. How much less complicated if this was personal and there was no need for MI6 involvement.

"I don't think so," Allenby said thoughtfully. "And no one seems to assume that Baylor had any relationship with her." He gave a jerky little laugh. "At least, I have the grace to know that I can't judge who could get caught up in an affair of passion and romantic drama. It obliterates everything else, and even a physical passion can wipe out all common sense. And Lila was certainly a woman who might inspire such madness. But I don't think Wyatt Baylor is vulnerable to that. The things about him that frighten me are his ambition, his fear that racial purity and culture are being swamped, drowned out by inferior, darker-skinned races. To me, these are not the people to fear. If I let my nightmares overtake me, it would be the pale-skinned

Aryan race of Adolf Hitler who are frightening, and a damn sight better organized."

"And that's the route you fear Baylor is taking?" Peter asked.

"It's one possibility," Allenby answered. "Another is that he is of entirely the opposite in his beliefs, but someone wishes to brand him as that."

"Opposite? You mean pro-communist? Bolshevik? Or more moderate, such as socialist? Or international as opposed to isolationist?" Again, Peter's voice was sharper than he had intended, but it was an idea he had not considered before.

"I don't know what I mean," Allenby admitted. "Only that there are a lot of possibilities, and maybe some I haven't thought of. The police seemed to be sure about Baylor on the physical evidence. I'm not certain if they're even looking at anyone else. Charles Standish is about the only person definitely on Baylor's side. But then, he more or less has to be. Baylor is his wife's father. And Charles is a very typical English gentleman, more or less what I pretend to be," he said ruefully, as if to remind himself of his own reality.

Peter knew the reason for that. But this was not the time to discuss it. "He's in a hell of a position," he agreed. "Do you have any idea what Standish really thinks?" He doubted Allenby would be helpful, but it was worth trying.

"No," Allenby replied, "but I'll find out what I can. But to preserve his family, he has to be seen to believe Baylor innocent, and then be shocked if it turns out he is guilty. He can't be such a fool as not to have considered that. Especially with the Baylors' support of Free America."

"That's the group to watch. The more you learn about them, the better. But be careful."

"I'll do my best," said Allenby.

After a long moment, Peter said with a touch of bitterness, "You haven't told us anything I don't already know." Then he asked the question he did not wish to, but it was growing too big to ignore. "And what about Elena?"

"I know who she is, professionally. In relation to Wyatt Baylor, that's a different thing. I need to get to know her better. She's pretending she believes him, but I don't know what she really thinks. You know her better, sir. What do you think?"

That was a question that dug deeper than Allenby could have any idea. At least, Peter hoped so. Please heaven he was not that transparent! Even Lucas, who knew him so very well, had little idea how deeply his feelings went for Elena. He must answer Allenby. The seconds were ticking by. "None of us knows, until we're tested," he began. It was true, but it was also trite, a prepared answer and not what Allenby was asking. It also sounded evasive. "In the past, she has always decided for the truth, however bitter. That is one of the reasons we chose her for the service." That was true; but it needed more. "But it's hard to hurt people who trust you, very hard. She will not do it easily. If you can . . ." he hesitated.

". . . protect her from it?" Allenby filled in for him. "You can't ask her to equivocate. But you can ask me?" Was that amusement in his voice?

"I command it, Allenby!" Peter said sharply. "If you aren't sure of her, don't put her to the test. Isn't that simple enough?"

"Yes, sir."

"Going back to Max Borrodale," said Peter, changing the subject. "Learn what else you can about him. Baylor will be paying him himself, I imagine, but see if you can make sure of that. Who else pays him for services? And for what? Is he greedy? Or has he any kind of debt to anyone? What are his beliefs, if he has any? Who does he owe, or want something from? Everything you can, without arousing suspicion. Now is the time you really need your cover . . . whatever it is you do for the embassy—"

"Not cultural attaché," Allenby interrupted. "That's almost the same as saying 'spy.' I'm part of the Trade Department. Gives me something legitimate to do, and actually useful."

"And cultural attaché is not?" Peter asked sarcastically.

"When you're looking for spies, sir, follow the envoy."

Peter smiled, in spite of himself. "Not romantic, but certainly sensible. But as to Elena . . ."

"You'd rather I didn't use her because it is bound to put her in an extraordinarily painful position," said Allenby. "If Baylor is guilty, it will be agonizing for her, but it will be painful whether she's involved or not. Are you saying to do it if I think it wise, or necessary? And I won't, if I think she's too involved to be safe?"

Peter thought about this. Allenby had said nothing about her belief in Baylor, or what he stood for. Did Allenby know her so well, so soon? He must not betray his own feelings. "Then your judgment had better be as good as you think it is, Allenby," he said levelly. "I can't bring you back now, which you know, and are trading on." And then, to make that sound less like a threat, he added, "If I have to throw you out, you could always try the diplomatic service."

"Yes, sir." Allenby's tone was completely neutral.

Peter caught the seriousness and shifted back into his professional mode. "It matters, Allenby. I'm not interfering because this is far more serious than we expected. We have to move now; there's no time to spare. I've had reports in from Europe, just this afternoon. What's happening on your end may matter far more than we think." He wanted to tell him all of it, about the increasing threat of atomic experiment and discovery in Germany, and about new information leaking from America. But even a secure line was not good enough.

"I do know." Allenby's voice was so soft it was barely audible.

Peter did not question him. "Possibly you do," he conceded. "So, be careful." Small, too-often-used words, but with a meaning too vast for speech at all.

"Yes, sir." Allenby replied, then he hung up.

May days were long in England, and on an almost cloudless day like this, even at nine o'clock in the evening, it was not too late to go for a walk. In some ways, it was the best time. Lucas liked early mornings, hazy afternoons, but evenings were the very best. He could not remember if it had always been that way, or only recently, in the evening time of his own life. A good time, in some ways the best, the most precious. "Come on, Toby," he said. "Walk!"

Toby leaped to his feet as if they were on springs. The only word in the world as good as "walk" was "dinner." Even then, "walk" had it by a slight edge. He started toward the front door.

"Get your lead!" Lucas reminded him. "Just going to take Toby for a walk," he called to Josephine upstairs. He always knew where she was, at least roughly. "I will be a while," he added. He knew she would understand: it was to meet Peter Howard. She would have known because the phone had rung a little earlier.

"I'll hold supper," she answered, then appeared at the top of the stairs. She smiled at him.

He nodded, knowing she understood. A phone call, the dog fetching his own lead, and a walk of indeterminate length always meant the same thing: a call to business. It almost always was with Peter Howard. So many things just from the tone of his voice, the time of day, and whether he took Toby or not. It was comforting that she understood without his having to frame explanations that were neither the truth nor deception. Lies could be avoided.

Toby came back from the kitchen, his lead in his mouth, his tail wagging furiously. Lucas bent down and took the lead from him, then clipped it onto his collar. "Come on," he said quite unnecessarily. Toby was ahead of him anyway. Lucas might have thought he was being discreet, but Toby knew exactly where he was going. Where else but to meet Peter Howard somewhere full of grass and trees, with places to run, and endless little animal smells to follow?

Actually, it was not the woods this time. It was the hour in the evening when many people went for a walk, and he did not wish to be seen. It was better to avoid crowds if possible. Lucas had retired from MI6 years ago, and been invited back just last autumn, when Bradley had left precipitously. Of course, he didn't return to his old position as head, only as an occasional adviser, and only when asked. His knowledge was valuable, and his memory beyond price.

Lucas got into the car, Toby obediently settling himself in the backseat. They set out for the short stretch of ground outside the gate. He would leave the car and walk to the river, where the path wound along its banks for several miles. It was private land, and not so much a river as a stream, but it was beautiful at this hour, with the sun still warm, and well above the horizon. It was not impossible they would meet anyone, but it was unlikely. A man walking with a dog in the evening light needed no explanation.

He went in through the gate that said "Private" and closed it behind him, then bent down and let Toby off the lead. "Not too far!" he said, as if Toby were likely to obey him.

Toby went off at a charge, then swung around and came back, wagging his whole body.

"Yes, very obedient," Lucas said cheerfully. "Don't get lost, Toby!"

Toby sat down, as if to emphasize that he was really listening.

"Don't jump into the river!" Lucas added. He said this every time, and every time Toby forgot. "Off you go!"

Recognizing permission, Toby ran off along the winding path that followed the water's edge. In a moment, he was out of sight.

It was still early evening, sunlight slanting through the trees and dappling the slow-moving water. The river was perhaps fifteen feet wide, the water brown except where it ran over the occasional patch of stones. Then it turned creamy white for a few yards, before losing the energy again. There were tiny flies hovering in the shafts of sunlight, and now and then a fish broke the water briefly, and then slid back again and disappeared. Somewhere above him birds were chattering, telling each other of his intrusion.

A lone willow trailed green streamers in the water, like long chiffon veils. A blossoming tree reflected brilliant light in its white petals, a few drifting down in the motionless air, and some having fallen onto the path, others going as far as the water.

There was a man forty yards along, studying the terrain. It was

Peter Howard. As if aware of Lucas's gaze, he straightened up and started to walk toward him.

There was a commotion in the water. Toby had been swimming and reached the bank. He jumped out, missed his footing and fell in again. Jumped a second time and made it after a little scrambling, then shook himself vigorously until the whole path was scattered over with little pools of water. And then he charged at Peter, reaching him and jumping up.

"Toby, no!" Lucas said exasperatedly, and was totally ignored.

Peter bent and hugged the soaking dog, to Toby's delight, and then stood up again, dripping water himself, and smiling.

Lucas reached him. "I'm sorry." He turned to the dog, who was still wagging his tail happily. He considered disciplining him. Toby knew better than that! But Lucas hadn't the heart. It was only half his fault—Peter was totally complicit. Lucas sighed. "You have news?"

"Not very good, I'm afraid," said Peter. They turned in unison and began to walk along the path in the direction Lucas had been going. The water was dimpled with sunlight, but the air was beginning to cool as the sun faded. The glimpse of the sky they could see through the trees to the west was growing richer in color. Well behind them to the east, it was fading into shadows. Darkness was coming, but the spring twilight was long. It would not be really dark for perhaps another hour. "Not good," Peter repeated. "What do you know of Wyatt Baylor?"

Lucas thought for a moment or two. "I've been looking at his record, as I dare say you have. Comes from an old family, but his wife's family had the real money. Immense wealth from industry. He graduated with honors from Harvard, studied modern history—for cultural purposes, I suppose—and business for practical ones. Started in banking. Adviser for loans, investments, and moved on from there. Nothing you could put a finger on. Invested well. Always came out ahead of the game. Married Dorothy Winyard. Her father was a senator. Heiress to a lot of land, which turned into a lot of money. Had a son, of no particular note, who died quite young—

a railway disaster, I believe. Their only daughter, Katherine, married my son, Charles. As you know, Charles served as ambassador for Great Britain in several European capitals, with some distinction. The Baylors had three grandchildren: my grandson Mike, who died in the last year of the war, and my granddaughters, Margot and Elena, neither of whom the Baylors have met except a couple of times when the girls were very small, and always here, rather than in America."

"Politics?" Peter asked.

Toby came meandering down the path, saw a fish jump in the river, and plunged in after it, sending water in all directions.

Lucas drew in breath to tell him off, then saw Peter's delight and bit it back. "Politics," he repeated. "Opportunism, I would say. Wyatt Baylor knows how to invest money with the least risk and most profit. Plays the stock market. Doesn't always win, but never really loses."

Peter winced. "I don't know why that sounds so bloody cold, but it does. Left or right wing?"

"Right," Lucas answered. "But surely you know that? He makes no secret of it."

"Hedges his bets," Peter replied. "Adviser to the President, who is innovative, to say the least."

"As I said . . ." There was an edge of bitterness in Lucas's voice. "Baylor almost always wins, and he never loses."

"I see." Peter sounded as if he meant that in all interpretations.

Lucas glanced at him. "You don't like him? But you don't like chancers either!"

"I don't like men without principles," Peter elaborated.

"And women?" Lucas asked with a smile.

Peter glanced sideways at him. "Women who can't afford to have principles, that I understand. Women with them terrify me! They cause more emotions, and dump them God knows where!"

"Then watch out for Elena," Lucas said, only half joking.

Peter shot him a swift glance, then looked away. "That's another thing," he said, beginning to walk again. "She is ideally placed to work on this damnable business, and she will do whatever I say. I tried to tell Allenby to leave her out of it, for obvious reasons, but he more or less said he would do as he pleased. And he couldn't keep her out of it, anyway, if she wanted to be in. Which, of course, she will."

"And you won't tell him to use her," Lucas said quickly, turning to face Peter.

"She's there as a private citizen, Lucas. The Baylors are her grandparents, just as much as you are. She'll be involved in caring for her mother, and grandmother, of course. It's only been three days. She'll be starting to learn what she can about Wyatt."

"Rubbish!" Lucas said hotly. He had held her in his arms the day after she was born. He had taught her half the things she knew in life. At least half. "That . . ." he started it again.

Peter was shaking his head. "That's not Baylor's fault," he said. "And if you were to tell Elena that she owed them no loyalty, what do you think she would say?"

Lucas thought of half a dozen answers, and they were all less than even half true, specious arguments. And he thought of Elena, and tried to remember all she had said before she went on this trip. She was anxious about it. Katherine had said little, but she had been nervous, too. It was a long time since Katherine had seen her parents for more than a few days, and that was when they were on holiday. What does one know of a person one meets outside their own environment? A different face, a different reality.

How much had Katherine known of Washington, DC, when she was a girl? Probably only what her parents had wished her to see. She had been young when she had met Charles, and they had not courted for long. Katherine spoke several languages now, and had mixed with all kinds of people. She was a clever and sophisticated woman. How hard was it to go back and see the places of her youth, and the people? It might actually be far more difficult than she had foreseen.

And her father? Lucas tried to imagine it. It was almost forty years since she had lived in Wyatt Baylor's house. Much had to have changed. The entire world had altered completely in that time. War and then the Depression had altered everybody, and everything. She would have to observe them and understand, perhaps forgive, all in days! Most people have the chance to see the changes in each other one at a time, like a slow tide coming in . . . or going out. Perhaps going out was a better simile, to see the water recede and expose an unknown landscape.

The light was fading on the river, the shadows of the trees darker.

What did this accusation expose in Wyatt Baylor? Was even the kindest view of it going to make it bearable for Katherine, so she could forgive him for not being what she had expected, or taken for granted?

And Dorothy Baylor? She had married at nineteen. What had she seen? Or chosen not to see? Her loyalty could well be survival for her, not merely a virtue that was expected, but that was in fact required. If her husband was in any way guilty . . . her entire way of life was tied to his.

As for Katherine protecting her own parents—no amount of time or distance erased that bond. And Elena? Her instinct would be to protect her own mother. Protect her from pain, from disillusion, grief, as Katherine had protected Elena herself, when she could.

Lucas understood that, without even giving it thought. His instinct was to protect, the deepest emotion he had, especially for Elena. It had always been there, from the first day, and continued now, even when she was perfectly safe and impatient with restrictions. It was more than his just being a parent or grandparent: he had a unique link with her, something of the mind as well as the blood.

What would she feel if her other grandfather were threatened? Would she be able to see justice, believe it if it turned out that he was guilty? Would any of them be able to see an obscure truth? And fight, for that matter? Would it be justice, or expediency?

"What about Allenby?" he asked.

"I thought I knew him," Peter said thoughtfully. "I'm beginning to think that perhaps I don't."

They walked a few yards. Toby dashed past them, soaking their trousers where he touched them. He had been in the water again.

Lucas swore under his breath, but it was nothing to do with the dog, who he loved unconditionally, as Toby loved everyone he knew.

Peter was listening. He seemed to know what Lucas was thinking, and why.

"So, are you saying you don't know him?" Lucas asked, referring to his previous question about Allenby.

"It's a different situation," Peter said slowly. "This is family, and two people working together on a case that is intensely personal to one of them, who is the lesser experienced by a long way. I didn't get Elena involved willingly," he reminded Lucas. "She was there, in the middle of things, part of the family, and of the event, whether she wished to be or not!"

Lucas thought about this for a moment. "Even if we wanted to, we couldn't plant anyone inside the Baylor house, or with Wyatt himself," he agreed. "Elena can inquire into the background of all the current events, discreetly. She will be able to find out whatever her grandmother knows about personal enemies. Allenby must appreciate that."

"Don't be naïve, Lucas. She'll be far too emotionally torn in loyalty to her mother and her grandfather. She's useful precisely because she's emotionally tied to the whole issue. She will see it more, understand more, and be more deeply hurt, if we can't save Wyatt."

Lucas stiffened. "Don't you mean, if he's guilty? Or too skillfully framed for anyone to get him out? Or if he has been boxed in, fooled somehow, or blackmailed into something he got into and is unable to get out of?"

"In some cases, we are all prisoners of our own past, and Elena doesn't know what Wyatt Baylor's past is, except that it's different from hers."

"Do you know?" Lucas asked. "Does MI6 have any reason to have looked into him?"

"No."

"What are you going to say to her?"

"Nothing," Peter replied, looking across the water, where the shadows were almost impenetrable now. "I'm not going to jeopardize her by having her come to the embassy where I can get her on the phone. I'll send messages to her through Allenby."

"So, you trust him . . ."

"I trust all the people I work with, or I wouldn't keep them." Peter smiled with profound regret. "Except when I don't trust them, of course. Then I lie to them, as well as you did, I hope."

The light was low over the horizon now, hazy and soft, the fire of sunset fading, blurring the lines between the water and the bank. Toby was running around in circles chasing a smell, tail high in the air.

"Part of me hopes Baylor is just incidental damage," Peter said. "It sounds like an easy answer. But it would mean Lila was careless, and we misjudged her. Harmon Worth was too emotional for the weight of the job we think he has, and Wyatt Baylor is not so much a possible villain as a complete ass! Is it really better he betrayed his wife rather than his country? Most women would forgive misplaced idealism, even when it leads to treason, sooner than the personal betrayal of an affair with another woman."

Lucas sighed. "You're right. But we don't get to choose. We can't afford to let this one take its own course. Too much rests on it, or might do."

"I think Allenby knows that," Peter answered.

Flies danced in a pool of light on the water. A fish broke the surface with a leap, and slid back in again with barely a sound.

Toby stood on the bank, ears cocked.

"Come on," Lucas said quietly. "Home, Toby. You can't catch a fish, and you wouldn't know what to do with it if you did."

Peter laughed softly. "You can't catch it today," he added quietly to the dog, not to Lucas. "There'll be another tomorrow."

"We'd better go, while we can still see the path," Lucas observed. "I'm in no mood to fall in the river. Not literally or metaphorically. Come on, Toby. Home. Dinner!"

Toby came instantly. These were words he understood.

CHAPTER

13

E lena was sitting in the smaller lounge opening onto the garden. It was less formal than the larger room, where visitors were received, and more comfortable in many ways. The big windows faced the early light, and there were French doors that opened onto the lawn, now closed because the morning air was cool. At the end of the lawn were tall evergreen trees, the delicate dogwood blossoms standing out white against them.

The bookshelves were white wood, and filled with volumes all jumbled together, not according to subject or size, but according to how the last person had taken them out, or put them back. A heavy pottery bowl was filled with bright, flame-patterned tulips—reds, yellows, and purples—not arranged, but plopped in together, as if they had grown like that. It was a room at ease with itself.

Katherine came in and closed the door behind her. She looked tired. There was no lift in her smile. She had brushed her hair, but missed several strands, which was so unlike her.

"How's Grandmother?" Elena asked immediately. "Did she sleep?"

"I don't think so," Katherine replied, sitting down in the chair opposite her. "She said she did, but I think she's just wishing . . . trying to pretend there's nothing to worry about, and that it will all pass."

"And you don't think it will?" Elena asked. "It's early, Mother. They can't just brush it away. They have to prove it. And Grandfather has lots of friends. And he'll be home today, even if he's sort of . . . restricted."

"Elena, darling, I know that, and it's important, but it's temporary. Don't try to reassure me with hopes. We all wish it would go away, but I need to have someone to talk to honestly. I know your father is doing everything he can, but he's tiptoeing around me, trying not to say anything negative." She smiled, and yet it was very close to tears. "Like a man dancing on a pavement full of puddles. He leaps over one, only to land in another. He works so hard not to upset me, and I'm working just as hard not to be upset. Let me speak honestly to you, at least."

"Of course," she said gently. This thought frightened her. She feared the truth might be ugly. Not about her grandfather, but about the power of his enemies. They had been overwhelmingly successful so far. Nobody had mentioned them by name, but a man as prominent as Wyatt Baylor was bound to have offended many, even if by no more than succeeding where they had failed.

"I feel so helpless." Katherine stared out of the window. "I've tried to ask Mother about the people closest to him, people who might be his rivals, or who might have lost money through some of his advice, or decisions, but she isn't telling me the truth. I don't know whether it's because she wants to think they're all real friends, or because she doesn't want to sound as if she's gossiping. Especially about Lila, because she's dead, and . . ." She stopped.

"I know," Elena said quickly. "None of the possible answers makes any sense, if it wasn't an accident. Hitting someone could be, but backing up and then running over them isn't. We have to accept that something is going on that's hideous. But it can't be Grandfather, so it's someone else. It could be they never thought he would be blamed, and they can't say anything now without giving themselves away."

"What can we do to help . . . that makes sense?" Katherine said quickly.

"Just be here," Elena replied. "That's all we can do. Except I might be able to think of something. There's another answer, if—"

"Don't get yourself involved!" Katherine said quickly, her hand on Elena's suddenly tightening.

"Why? Do you think I'll make it worse?" Elena asked wryly. "What could possibly do that?"

"If you—" She was cut off by one of the maids coming into the room. "Yes, Elsie, what is it?"

"It's a telephone call for Miss Standish, ma'am." She turned to Elena. "It's a Captain Allenby. He says he'd like to speak with you."

Katherine glanced at Elena, then back at the maid. "Tell him she's unavailable at the moment," she said, impatience in her voice. "Good heavens, hasn't that man any sense! We're in the middle of a family . . ." She could not find a word that fitted, or else she preferred not to use it in front of the girl.

Elena stood up. "Thank you, Elsie. If you show me where the telephone is, I'll take it." She looked at Katherine. "It's not a social call, Mother. He may know something. Please, don't . . ." She wanted to say "interfere," but it sounded so rude.

Elsie appeared as if she did not know what to do. Katherine was the mistress's daughter; Elena was a stranger.

"Thank you, Elsie," Elena repeated with a smile, and began to walk toward the door. "I'll find it." She went into the huge hall with its arched ceiling and splendid staircases. The phone was on a table toward the back, the receiver on a marble-surfaced table beside a notepad and pencil. She picked it up. "Hello."

"Good morning." Allenby's voice sounded purposeful, not in the least tentative. "Will you have lunch with me, if I pick you up at noon?"

"We are . . . not . . ." She was uncertain what she wanted to say.

"I was speaking to your friend Peter," he went on. "He is distressed by the news, of course. I'd like to be able to tell him that you're all right."

She wanted to snap back at him that she wasn't all right, or anything like all right. No one was! Yet she was suddenly overwhelmed with relief. It was a connection with home, with certainty, possibly even something she could do to help. "Yes, yes, of course. That would be a nice idea. I'll be ready, thank you." She heard his reply muffled in the earpiece as she hung up.

Elsie was standing in the hall. Elena smiled at her and thanked her again, then she went back into the sitting room, closing the door behind her. Katherine was sitting almost exactly as she had been when Elena had left: upright, back straight, head high. It brought a sudden lump to Elena's throat. Both she and Margot had their mother to thank for their posture. Katherine had given them constant, patient correction, sometimes with a ruler nudging the back, making straight shoulders a habit, even a subject for taunting at school. "Think you are a duchess?" rang in her ears. How long ago that seemed!

Elena sat down and spoke quietly. "Captain Allenby has invited me to lunch. I can see by your face that you don't approve, and I'm sorry. But I'm going." She ached to be able to tell Katherine why, but it would endanger them both. And if anything did go wrong, Katherine would always blame herself, perhaps rightly. One word of anger could do endless damage, especially if overheard by the wrong person, one who might suspect her already, or twist something she said. It might be too easy to put together her part in getting knowledge, or passing it on, once the suspicion was planted.

Katherine's face darkened. "Really, Elena, this is . . ."

Elena wondered how much she could say. Too little was always better than too much. Her mother was far from stupid; she would put it together so easily. They had never discussed the revelation about Lucas, after she had returned from Berlin. Her mother must know as much as her father! He could never have kept the shattering change in his relationship with Lucas a secret from her, even if he had wanted to.

"Elena . . ." Katherine began again.

Elena smiled, as if it were a slight thing, a casual lack of consideration for her feelings, or Dorothy's. "It's just lunch. And I could learn something. He knows a lot of people. He was at the party, and he could have seen or heard a word, a phrase, that might help. It's worth trying. I won't be long." And before Katherine could argue, she stood, turned, and walked out of the room, through the empty hall, and up the curved staircase.

What should she wear? Something not as plain as the linen dress she had on now. But not striking, either. Not red. She had a floral silk, with irises on it; that would do well.

She started to write to Margot, but she had no idea how much anyone had told her and she was at a loss how frank to be. It seemed cold not to write at all, but if Katherine had not warned her of Wyatt's arrest, mention might only cause her to be even more worried. That was an excuse. She started to write a short letter.

> Dear Margot,
>
> We had a wonderful anniversary party, but tragically a woman was killed in the car park and there has been a horrible mistake made. Because Grandfather's car was used, the police arrested him. Of course, we will sort it all out, but just for the moment, it is rather tense and miserable. If you don't hear from anybody, don't worry. Mother will look after Grandmother, and Father and I will work with Grandfather's lawyer to deal with this. Again, don't worry. We will be all right.
>
> Love, Elena

She put it in an envelope, sealed it, and addressed it. If she put it on the hall table, it would be stamped and put into the mail.

Elena came down the stairs at just before midday. The floral silk was much prettier than she had remembered, and its soft blue-purple shades were very flattering to her fair coloring. The doorbell rang at exactly noon. Nice military timing! She placed the envelope on the table and waited for Elsie to answer the door and show Allenby in.

He behaved very formally, and Elena followed his example. It was not until they were outside, in his car, that he relaxed, became a little calmer. He started the engine, and they moved smoothly along the drive and onto the road.

"You heard from Peter?" she prompted. She felt uncomfortable. Perhaps she was overdressed. She had taken too much care, as if it were personal, even romantic. She could feel the heat well up in her face. Business. She must concentrate on business, not be as light-minded as her mother thought her.

Allenby smiled. "Yes. I called him this morning, from the embassy. I hope you told no one—"

"Of course I told no one," she said sharply. "My mother thinks I'm on a social visit. Romantic. And she disapproves of my selfishness."

He gave a funny, twisted smile, half humorous, half rueful. They were passing under trees and the sunlight was dappled with shadows. "Dressed like that, I'm not surprised. In fact, if I thought it was for me, I'd be flattered."

"I dressed so she would never imagine it was business," Elena replied a little too quickly. "We can't afford mistakes. I feel like a selfish, stupid girl, but that's far better than anyone thinking either of us is . . . professional."

He laughed outright. "You do it very well!"

"What the hell does that mean?"

"I take you very seriously indeed, but no one else will. And if I pay enough attention to you, perhaps they won't take me seriously, either."

She hesitated a moment, then let that go. "What did Peter say?" she asked.

This time it was he who hesitated. "That it's worse than we thought." His voice was very quiet and he was driving slowly, in no hurry to arrive and have the parking valets and waiters inevitably close enough to overhear them. "He said it's very possibly connected with national security, or some political conspiracy. Maybe Lila was on to something, and that's the reason she was killed."

"Oh . . ." This was bitter, but perhaps she had been half expecting it. If she closed her eyes, she could see Lila's face, alive with passion and intelligence. A chill ran through her. This was a different, harsher reality than the grubby affair some people were imagining, painful as that was. This had a vast, dark tide beneath everything she could see or even contemplate. "What are we going to do?"

Allenby was facing the road, intent on following the curves of it, and she could not read his expression. "Try to find the truth," he replied, "and without upsetting too many apple carts along the way. I'm afraid it may not be that your grandfather is entirely innocent. We have to know who killed Lila, but even more than that, why. What did she find, or was on the brink of finding, that was so danger-ous that someone took the risk of killing her and making it look as if it were Wyatt Baylor who did it?"

Her mouth was dry. "Are you sure he didn't?" Why was she ask-ing that? Of course he didn't kill her. He had some views Lila did not like, but that was personal. Possibly he did not know nearly as much as Lila did. But a difference of opinion or politics was a world away from murder.

Allenby turned for a moment and met her eyes. She had thought his were blue, but they were brown. "No," he said quietly. "I'm not sure at all, but I would like to be. But then the question is: Why? How was she a threat to him? He didn't just decide to kill her im-mediately, in a violent and brutal way."

She heard her own voice as if it were far away. "You mean had he needed to do it quickly? Or that he took a chance to do it when he knew she would be there, with a lot of other people who might be blamed? Isn't that a foolish thing to do? Unless he had no choice?" Why was she arguing this way? Her grandfather was innocent.

"Yes," he agreed.

"How well do you know him? I mean, know about him?" Part of her mind was already thinking professionally, running along the lines Peter had taught her, as if it were about people she did not know, did not care about at all. Most of all, people with whom there were no years of trust, or of care. But the care was for Katherine. Elena did not know Wyatt at all, except through her mother.

Allenby was looking at her. Did he see the change in her thought? It did not matter. She repeated the question. "How much do you know about him?"

"Not a great deal," he replied. "He's a man of pride, intelligence, family wealth, although at first it was Dorothy's, and now his own. Charm, but I think it's paper thin, the silk glove over the iron fist is not much thicker than a silk scarf."

"Something close, but not really the truth," she interpreted.

He smiled, but it barely softened his face. "Exactly. We've a lot to learn and not very much time. Can you do this?" For an instant there was something like gentleness, even sorrow in his face; then it was gone. Perhaps it was a trick of the changing light as they drove past a dense stand of trees.

"Of course I can," she replied. "We must." She had believed this was going to be a family holiday. The largest pressures would be how to behave graciously all the time, not just part of it; how to look interested when she was not. Above all, how to get to know her mother's family as she knew her father's, and not to disappoint any of them. She was away from Europe and, she had imagined, away from Europe's problems. In truth, she was only away from the support of those who knew a part of them, and would help her and understand her feelings.

"Elena?"

She realized she had been silent for several moments, and her answer was insufficient. Did she trust Allenby? She knew absolutely nothing about him, except what he had told her. Did he really work for Peter Howard? Anyone could say that.

"Yes . . ." She must play for time, at least until she could make up her mind. No, that was ridiculous. There was no time. She must act as if she believed him, until she actually did. Or did not? How could she call Peter to ask him? Not on any telephone from the house. Anyone could overhear her. And how could Allenby know anything about Peter? Her parents had never heard of him. Only Lucas had.

Allenby's voice cut across her thoughts.

"Lila was working on who-knows-what about the attempt to use the energy derived from splitting the atom, which is beyond our calculations, to create a nuclear bomb. If so, it would be a devastating weapon." He stopped abruptly, as if giving her time to consider the idea.

"Who is doing that?" she asked, trying to delay for a moment the enormity of the thought.

"Everybody," he replied. "We and the Americans are more or less together. At least, that's what we believe. Of course, we may be working separately as well. And the Germans—"

"We are not working with the Germans!" She was appalled.

"Depends on who you ask," he said. "According to our government sources, the Germans aren't very far at all. But according to our scientists, they have some of the best minds in the world. And according to Peter Howard the Germans are definitely forging ahead. That's also according to Lila, and they are very possibly doing this with some help from America, whether their government is aware of it or not. At present, we assume not."

He could not drive and watch her face as well, and she was grateful for that. What he had said was worse than anything she had imagined. She did not wish it to be, but her mind accepted it without question. Her first encounter with the darkest reality had been in Berlin, a year ago. The next that had touched her, where she had imagined herself invulnerable, had been in Trieste, six months ago.

She was forcefully reminded of it recently, when news had come of the attempt to assassinate Chancellor Engelbert Dollfuss of Austria. And Austria was now lurching toward Nazi Germany's widening sphere, possibly even to losing its independence.

They reached the restaurant, left the car with the valet, and went inside. They were soon seated among the other guests, who were glamorous, seemingly carefree in fashionable, late-spring clothes, the linens and silks, the tailored jackets of the men and the bright colors of the women.

They looked so lighthearted, so unconsciously elegant. Were they? There seemed to Elena an underlying tension, and a knowledge, deliberately ignored, of a tragedy not yet passed, of the Great Depression, the war that had seemed to Europe merely to brush past America.

She was aware of Allenby's eyes on her. She brought her attention back to the scene in front of them. "Don't bother to tell me that it would be nice to clear him, but the necessity is to find the truth. I can see that."

Allenby's expression hardly changed. He looked at her exactly the same way as all the young men in the restaurant looked at the women they were with, and a certain tension eased out of his shoulders and his jaw, allowing him to smile very slightly. "I knew that was what Lila was doing," he said quietly. "She knew information was leaking out of here, valuable information about research into weaponizing the power of splitting the atom. But neither Peter nor I knew exactly how far she got."

"Are you suggesting that's the reason she was killed?" Elena asked. "Because she found out who was leaking it, and she would have told someone?"

"That makes sense," he agreed. "Then it would also make sense if it was someone else who killed her. It will be foolish and dangerous to suppose we are the only ones who are interested in her, or in the whole question of atomic energy, and just how far the Germans, or the Americans, have advanced."

"Don't we know where the Americans are with this?" she asked. "If we are part of it?"

"We think we do . . ."

"But we could be wrong," she finished. "And Lila was Austrian, which could mean anything."

"Do you know something about Austria?" He looked at her curiously, and she realized how little he knew about her. Or she about him, for that matter.

"You had better consult Peter about that." She smiled back at him.

"Touché," he murmured.

They were interrupted by the waiter serving their meal of fresh fish, with a light salad.

"What are you going to tell your family?" he asked, when they were alone again.

She was ready for that question, even though she was not sure of the answer. She hesitated, taking a mouthful to give herself more time.

He waited, as if profoundly aware of how she was delaying.

"If my grandfather is innocent, I shall take the credit for helping to clear him. As much as he will guess I did anyway. I won't tell him anything further. Not about you, or Peter, or anybody else."

"And if he is not . . . innocent?" he asked.

"But he is," she insisted.

"But if he had a hand in it? If he thought Lila was selling American secrets to Germany?"

"Could she have been?"

"No."

"You're sure?"

"Yes."

"Then I suppose I will have to appear as shocked as everybody else," she replied.

"You don't think your grandmother has any idea?"

She was about to say that of course she didn't, then it occurred to her that it was an assumption for which she had no base. Elena remembered that she had always assumed that her other grandmother, Josephine, was a wise old lady with a sharp wit, but essentially quiet, a little otherworldly, with her home and her garden, which she knew so well. And then she discovered so very, very differently. That "old lady" had been one of the most brilliant decoders during the war, and knew all sorts of secrets about Allied troop movements and secret agents in France.

"I don't know," she said with a slight shrug. "I really don't. Grandmother Dorothy could be the driving force behind it all!" she added, although she did not believe it for a moment, and did not expect to discover this, either. As for Grandmother Josephine, she belonged to another world, thousands of miles away.

"Aha." Allenby's disbelief was quite undisguised.

"Don't assume!" she said sharply. "The best disguise of all is to look completely harmless."

"You ever tried it?" he asked incredulously, with a flash of humor in his eyes.

"Yes, I have. And it worked very well, because I actually was harmless . . . and stupid!"

For an instant he was surprised, then he studied her more closely. Anyone at another table would have taken it for a young man's increased interest in an unusually attractive young woman.

She laughed, in spite of herself. Although she had not known it then, she had been innocent when she had boarded the train in Amalfi bound for Berlin. But the following few days had changed almost everything.

"Please," Allenby said, bringing her back to the present, "learn what you can about your grandfather, from anyone: your grandmother or your mother. Or if your father knows anything you don't. Tell the others you want to know better, because it's your heritage. But, Elena, tell them anything except the truth. Otherwise, you will be signing your own death warrant, and perhaps mine, if you let them know who you really are."

His face lost all humor for an instant, reminding her that, for all his ease of manner, he knew how deadly serious this was.

"And, of course, this includes Wyatt, when he gets home," he continued. "Be very careful indeed what you say to him. You can't avoid him, unless you are afraid. Then you'll come to bits if you face him and tell him something you shouldn't."

She froze.

"Elena?"

"I know."

"Do you? It won't be easy. But if you don't see him, people will wonder why. Be careful! Be very careful!"

"I will."

"I hope you are as good at this as Peter says you are."

She could not let him see how instinctively she understood his fear. "We all have to hope that he is right about people. What are you going to do?" she asked, then added, "I wish I could talk to Peter myself."

"Too dangerous," he replied.

"You do it," she argued.

"I work at the embassy," he replied levelly. "We all assume you are on your grandfather's side, and expect it." He leaned forward. "Innocence is your best cover. In fact, it's your only one. If Wyatt is guilty—and don't argue with me, it's a possibility—then you are operating in enemy territory. Don't take unnecessary risks to yourself, and everyone else, not just me."

She felt the heat rise up her face. It was a beginner's mistake. She should have known better.

Before she could respond, Allenby said, "*We* are going to start by learning as much more about Lila as we can, beginning with going to her home and expressing our deep regrets to Harmon Worth."

"We are? I . . . I liked her, but I met her only once."

"But you liked her immediately," he replied.

She winced. "But going to her home? That's intrusive!"

"I know," said Allenby. "We'll take flowers, and we'll ask when the funeral is to be, and if we may attend it. Play it from there."

"And why am I coming with you to ask that? Is it not pretty insensitive, since it was my family's house where she was killed, and my grandfather who has been charged with her murder?"

"Yes," Allenby said ruefully. "But you haven't. And you didn't know your grandfather until a few days ago. You can play it any way you like. But awkwardness or embarrassment is not an excuse to let you out of it." There was a finality in his voice that she recognized. She had seen it in Peter Howard's face when he had given her an order he would not have liked to carry out himself, but there were no excuses. Only, very occasionally, reasons. This was not one of those times. Allenby was watching her as if to see whether she was up to it: if she could be a professional, while she was still somewhat of an amateur.

Elena knew what she was going to do: be honest. She grieved for Lila, and was embarrassed that her grandfather was accused of her death. "Right," she said with feeling, and then turned her attention back to lunch. "That was delicious. I would like a dessert, please."

He smiled, and she saw his shoulders relax.

They stopped at a florist and Allenby chose the flowers, merely asking Elena if she agreed. She was loath to say so, but actually it was the perfect choice: half a dozen white lilies. Discreet, blemishless, not too heavily perfumed, beauty as yet unmarked by time. She simply nodded. Nothing needed to be said.

When they arrived at Harmon Worth's home, it felt much more difficult. They had put a card with the flowers, simply stating their names, in case he was not in. If that was the case, they would have to come back another time, the sooner the better. Perhaps a specific excuse would be unnecessary. Allenby might have to come alone, and then report to Elena afterward.

A maid answered the door and left them on the step while Elena inquired whether Mr. Worth would see them. The woman took the flowers, ignoring the tears running down her face.

There were several moments of silence. Allenby did not say anything and Elena was relieved that he did not force her to think of something courteous to say. For those few moments, she would think only of Lila, and how vivid she had been. Elena would have liked so much to have known her better. The maid left them for a moment, and then returned and led them inside.

They found Worth looking slightly confused, standing in his study, sunlight streaming in through the windows and showing the worn patches in a tightly knotted Persian carpet. His face was crumpled, and totally without color. He had brushed his thick hair, but clearly not in front of a mirror.

"It's nice of you to call," he said, as soon as the maid had closed the door behind her. "The flowers are beautiful; Lila would have loved them. She always liked white flowers the most. Did you know that?"

"No, I didn't," Allenby admitted. "They just seemed right."

"Can I offer you—"

"No, thank you," Allenby declined. "We only came to pay our respects. I liked Lila very much. I had occasion to work with her quite often. Two foreigners, you know."

Harmon looked confused. He gestured toward a cluster of chairs and they sat down.

"I work at the British Embassy," Allenby reminded him. "Trade, mostly, but other things now and then. She was helpful. She knew a lot about many other countries."

A faint smile crossed Worth's face and then vanished. He glanced at Elena, trying to place her.

"I only met Lila once, but we liked each other straightaway," she said quietly. "We were going to meet again. Talk about all sorts of things, places we'd been to, people we'd met. My father was an ambassador when I was growing up, mostly in Europe."

"She would have enjoyed that. Sometimes I think she missed Europe."

"Everyone who has traveled misses some of the places they've been," she responded. "It's fun to swap stories with . . ." She saw the pain in his face and instantly regretted the clumsiness of mentioning something so vividly bringing Lila to mind. The memory of her was so close, it was as if she had only just gone out of the room and could be back any moment. "I'm sorry."

"Don't be," he said with difficulty. "I want her remembered alive, not . . ." He was unable to finish.

Allenby left it a moment while Worth regained control of himself, then he spoke quietly. He recalled all sorts of things, and the affection in his voice was obvious. Elena watched Worth's face and saw some of the pain ease in memory. Perhaps it was the knowledge that somebody else had seen Lila as he had: passionate, intelligent, excited, and ready to fight for all the things she saw as valuable.

Elena listened. Allenby seemed so sincere she felt angry at the thought that possibly he was doing all this in order to gain greater knowledge of exactly what Lila had been doing, possibly what her next move would have been. But there was nothing except clear, deep emotion in Allenby's face. Was he calling on grief he had known? If she had been doing this, she would have thought of her brother, Mike, even though his death had been as long ago as 1918. The sharpness of the pain dimmed, a little calmer over time, but she could recall it so easily. The silliest things brought it back: a phrase he had used, a song he had liked, a good joke. Perhaps underneath time and place all grief was the same?

"She knew a lot of the science involved in the atomic work," Worth said. "I think she would have liked to have studied it more. Physics, I mean. On looking back at it now, I realize how much she understood. I never had to explain anything twice."

He went on talking, mainly to Allenby. It became more and more obvious that it was as if, for a little space, he was giving himself a rest from grief.

"I've discovered how much about her I didn't know," Worth said ruefully. "It's ridiculous, isn't it? You learn things from other people, small things, funny things, and realize that you didn't know them. It . . . it makes me want so much to go back and do it better." As if suddenly aware of having ignored her, he turned to Elena. "I'm sorry."

"Don't be," she said immediately. "I know what you mean. I lost my brother."

He looked momentarily confused.

"He died in 1918," she said simply. "In France."

"And you still grieve?"

"He was the sort of person you never forget . . . like Lila." Was that helpful, or only promising that the hurt would never end? She looked at his face, and knew that the fact she understood was, at least for the moment, a comfort.

They sat a little longer together, crowded with memories, in the understanding of loss, and the people they still missed. She did not know who it was for Allenby, but there was someone. She knew that.

They took their leave after having been there over an hour. As soon as they were in the car, she turned and looked at Allenby. She saw an expression in his face that surprised her. It was curiously mixed. There was a gentleness in him, almost a guilt. Was he as aware as she was of their deliberately using Worth's grief to get information? In a sense, they had lied.

He turned away and started the car. Had he lied? She wanted to think that what he felt was real. And if not, whatever the justification, even the necessity . . . so many thoughts filled her mind as they picked up speed along the road.

CHAPTER

14

It was a long day for Charles, full of small duties that Wyatt would normally have attended to himself. One moment Dorothy was fussing about things, the next she wanted nothing to do with them. Not unnaturally, he saw that she was finding it difficult to keep her mind on what she was doing.

"Just do your best," Katherine said, soothing her mother. "People will understand."

Wyatt was due home today, but was still awaiting trial for murder. Charles understood that his father-in-law was unlikely to want to attend to orders for household arrangements, and the other small things he usually controlled, and the enormity of the situation clearly overwhelmed Dorothy.

Charles put his arm around Katherine very gently, not drawing her closer to him; instead, moving a step closer to her. "Don't worry, I'll do it. If there's anything I don't understand, I'll—"

"Don't ask Mother," she said quickly. "She has never dealt with housekeeping money. Everything else, yes. Charles..." She stopped, clearly searching for words. "I know Father won't be able to leave the house or receive visitors, apart from Borrodale, of course. There must be something more we can do than just sit here and . . . worry." She looked away, beyond him into the garden. "Mother hasn't heard much from friends. I suppose they don't know what to say." She resolutely stared past him to the sunlight on the trees. "I'm going to go out to tea, perhaps take Elena with me, exactly as if this were a passing problem. And I know that we need to show that we believe in him, not wait until he's proved innocent, as if we doubted him."

He understood exactly what she meant, and why. But he was afraid that she would be hurt. People were shocked, frightened by seeing something they did not understand and could not have predicted. Old certainties were badly shaken. Some of these friends would not stop and think how they would hurt Katherine or Dorothy, so they would speak first, and perhaps say things for which apologies would not be enough. They might not have the grace or honesty even to admit their error.

"Katherine," he began, and then words again eluded him.

"It will be hard," she filled in the silence. "But to sit here, hiding and waiting, feeling as if we are acquiescing, will be much worse. What happens if it all goes wrong, and they don't prove he's innocent, and we just sat here and did nothing, as if we believed it, or didn't care? How would it be for Mother then?"

He looked at her face, so familiar, but filled with a desperation he had never seen before.

"Charles, do you think he could possibly be guilty?" she asked. Her voice was not angry; it was uncertain, confused. "Is that what you are afraid of?"

"No!" he said vehemently. "Of course not." That was surely true, wasn't it?

"Then what? Are you concerned that we will annoy the police, and anything we do could make it worse?"

Again, he said, "No." After a moment he added, "We may well annoy the police, although I don't see why they should feel that way.

Quite apart from love and loyalty, all the family knows Wyatt could not possibly have done such a thing. And we should not be expected, even for a moment, to imagine he had. But there may be other things that we discover from his friends that we won't like." Deliberately, he drove his memory back. "I heard some pretty ugly feelings expressed at that party. I suppose Wyatt, as a good host, would not openly contradict them, whatever he felt. But, Katherine, they were all very right wing." He felt a knot tighten inside himself. "In fact, distinctly pro-Nazi. I didn't hear much argument for more liberty, more social justice, or equality."

She looked puzzled. "What are you saying?" The harsh morning light had no mercy when it came to softening the exhaustion on her face, the fine lines in her skin. "Political feelings are deep," she said. "You could have wished for a party where everyone would be further to the left, I know, but . . . they aren't."

He could not afford to evade the issue. "How much do you know about your father's political beliefs? Not twenty or thirty years ago, but now?" he asked. "People change."

"Do they? Underneath?" There was confrontation and question in her voice.

"Some do," he said more carefully. He sensed he was treading on dangerous ground. "Don't they say that if you are not to the left in your youth, you have no heart; and if you are not to the right in your age, you have no brain?" He tried to ask it lightly, regretting the honesty with which she had asked the question in the first place.

"Then Father should be to the right," she said. "In the face of the far left coming out of Europe, especially Russia. We all disagree with that."

"Maybe it was a misplaced reference," he admitted. "And perhaps I'm wrong to want to protect you from discussing political views you don't like. It would be worse to try to stop you from discovering the truth that would free him from this suspicion. Maybe Lila's death had nothing political about it. If so, we need to know that. Above all, we have to be able to prove it wasn't Wyatt, no matter who or what the answer turns out to be. You need to remain loyal; we all do."

She searched his eyes, his face. "Are you really afraid I'll uncover political loyalties I can't cope with?"

"Yes." It was an admission he would rather not have had to make, but there could be no retreat from a lie told now.

She smiled very gently. "So am I. But I need Mother to know I'm loyal to Father. And since he's coming home, I need him to know I did everything I could to help. I didn't just sit here and trust that someone else would fight for him."

"Of course," he said immediately. "And let Elena help, too."

"Elena is . . ." Now she looked away, to the side, avoiding his eyes.

How much did Katherine know, or suspect? She was emotionally raw, frightened, and terribly vulnerable, in just the position to betray someone in such a moment, and regret it for the rest of her life. He wanted to protect Elena but would it ease Katherine's worry if she knew her daughter was with MI6? No, that would only make her worry more. "Elena is trying to find out the same things we are," he began again. "Trying to find evidence that points somewhere other than to Wyatt. If we could find—"

Katherine's head came around sharply. "You mean *they*! Elena with Allenby?"

"She can't do it alone, Katherine," he said reasonably. "How would she even begin? She needs to meet people, learn about them, be able to speak reasonably, naturally."

"But with Allenby?" she protested. "Did you even consider how charming he is? And, incidentally, how handsome? And he approached her at the party, long before Lila was killed. Who is he, anyway? What does she know about him? What does anybody know?"

"He's something at the embassy. She's trying to learn all she can, and if she uses Allenby to help her, she may not waste nearly as much time as if she's doing it alone. Don't remember her mistake with Aiden Strother and hold it against her forever. That was seven years ago, so allow her to forget it!" He knew instantly that his voice had been sharper than he had meant it to be.

Katherine answered hotly, "I want to forget it, Charles, I do. Lord knows, she suffered for it. But she isn't a very good judge of men. She hasn't half the sense Margot has. And—"

"And nothing!" he responded. "Let her do what she can to help. If she can find out anything we don't know, about any of the people at the party, especially about Lila Worth and her husband, allow her to do it. Lila may be the real victim in this, and Wyatt just unfortunate enough to be the only one who can't account for his time at the moment she was killed."

"Then who did it?" she asked, her voice harsh with the strain of it.

"Obviously someone we haven't thought about. But if it's true, it has to be faced. And immediately."

"Can I help?"

"Not yet. But ... thank you." He gave a bleak smile.

"Do you know Allenby?" she said curiously. It was a challenge.

"No, I don't. Except he holds a pretty good post at the British Embassy, and he couldn't do that without them investigating him pretty tightly. And before you ask, yes, I did check with them."

She bit her lip. "I had three children by the time I was her age ..." She left the rest of the sentence unspoken.

"Yes, dear, I know. I had the same three. The world was very different then."

Katherine leaned against him. It was a gesture of trust and he put his arm around her and held her more closely. She was strong, a horse rider in her youth, a tennis player, light and fast, and accurate, but now she felt thin in his arms, so fragile, so easily broken.

"He'll be home today. We'll look after him," he said impulsively. "We'll clear his name. And we'll find the truth and prove his innocence to everyone."

She tightened her fingers until she was gripping his arm, but she said nothing.

It was early afternoon when Charles found Elena alone in the garden.

"What are we going to do?" she said before he could speak to her. "We can't just wait and hope. Is Borrodale doing anything? The police might be, but they think they have the right person. Why should they look any further? I've got a lot of questions."

"Such as?" he asked, standing beside her and staring at the dogwood blossoms as if he actually saw them.

She frowned. "Why now? It was a crazy place and time to murder anyone. There were presidential security people at every entrance and exit, waiting staff, guests, all kinds of people. There must have been an urgent reason to do it then! As if it couldn't wait for a more discreet time."

"Or else there was no better time to make it look like Wyatt was guilty," he concluded. "Do you believe that was the purpose, and Lila was lured outside? That seems more likely."

"Yes. And if so, why was she the intended victim?"

"And Wyatt was just unlucky to be suspected? Less likely, don't you think?"

"Yes," she admitted. "Yes. There had to be better chances to kill her, unless it couldn't wait. What was she going to do, if she wasn't stopped?" She stared at him steadily. "There has to be a reason behind all this. If it was Wyatt they meant to destroy, why? What was the result of it? Can we work back from there?"

Charles thought for a moment. "You mean what was Wyatt going to find out, and to do, that was prevented? Do you think it was something to do with Free America?"

"It could be. If he was secretly working against them, this would wipe out any value to whatever he said."

He looked at her steadily. It was a new thought, and for a moment he was awed by it. "Yes . . ." he said slowly.

"Will you ask him?" she said. "Tonight? He may know. Or he may not have considered it before. It's hard to think somebody you trusted betrayed you."

"Hard," he agreed. "But if it's true, it has to be faced. And immediately."

It was soon after that Wyatt arrived home in his own car, driven by his chauffeur. He stepped out to be greeted on the step by Dorothy and Katherine. Charles stood just inside the doorway to offer physical assistance, if it was needed.

Wyatt looked years older than he had at the party, only a matter of days ago. The color had drained from his face, his cheeks looked hollowed and his eye sockets bruised. His hair seemed thinner, scraped across his head. But he held himself upright.

Charles could not help but to admire his courage, knowing what this must cost him.

"Welcome home, Father-in-law," he said quietly as Wyatt passed him in the hallway. He did not offer to give him his arm; Katherine was on his other side.

"Thank you, Charles," Wyatt said with a very slight smile. Then he turned his attention to going up the stairs. They were not steep—the wide curve was too graceful for that—but it was still an effort.

He was going to live in his own room in the east wing. It was provided with everything he might need, and it offered him the privacy he very much desired. More importantly, it gave him refuge from having to accept company he might not want and the chance to see Borrodale, or any other person or business contact, without disturbing the family. He had expressed a wish to be alone, and it would be honored.

He was eighty years old, and perhaps not as well as he had pretended to be. But above all, he was afraid. At least fear was what Charles believed he saw in Wyatt's face. It moved him to an intense pity. This accusation was a terrible thing to have happened to an old man who had been honored and admired all his life. For a moment, Charles was angry at the combined forces of chance that had been visited on Wyatt. Then he renewed his resolve to do everything possible to decipher this, not only for Wyatt, but for Katherine, and for Dorothy, who followed Wyatt up the stairs now, almost like a ghost of the woman she had been a few days ago. Nevertheless, after Wyatt had had an opportunity to relax for a few minutes to collect his thoughts, Charles went to see him.

"Sorry," he said as he pulled up a chair and sat beside Wyatt, where he lay on the bed. "But it's necessary."

"Really?" Wyatt protested.

"Yes," Charles replied. "Unless Borrodale has told you something he has not told us, or the police, we have made very little progress. The charge still stands, and you are still going to trial."

Wyatt drew breath to argue, but the words seemed to have escaped him.

Charles noted again how old and frightened this normally robust man appeared.

"I'm sorry," he said again, and he felt it more acutely than he had expected to. "But there has to be sense behind this, another answer that we haven't thought of. And we need to find it quickly, while people's memories are still fresh."

Wyatt was staring at him. "What is it you think you can do?" he asked.

Charles had it formulated in his mind. He did not intend to mention Elena, because Wyatt was dismissive of her as a young woman with nothing much on her mind but social aspirations and photography, which was exactly how she wished to be seen. "Lila Worth has already been destroyed by this. We want to be sure you are not destroyed as well. We need to know who was the intended victim, and who was incidental damage. Do you know?"

Wyatt stared at him. "Why Lila?" he asked after a moment or two.

"There seem to be several possibilities, but I have no proof of any of them. I am more concerned with you. Here, too, there are several possibilities, but you may know them better than I. You have no state office, but very considerable power and influence, and the office may well come, when the President is more settled in. Who are your enemies? Who stands to lose if you are able to exercise influence, even power? Who are your rivals, possibly less obvious?"

Wyatt sat a little more forward against the pillows. "You've given this a great deal of thought, haven't you?" There was something like respect in his voice.

"Of course," Charles agreed. "I've heard considerable whispers about a group called Free America. Are you for them, or against them? Or maybe I should ask: Are they for you, or against you?"

Wyatt stared at him.

Charles took a deep breath. "Are you one of them?"

Wyatt gave the very faintest of smiles, and there was a bitter edge to it. "Don't you know?"

"No, I don't. But if I have to guess, I would say you are. But whether at heart, or for show, I don't know."

Wyatt gave a slight shrug. "It is for preserving the old values, the ones that made us great, not all this newfangled stuff coming in from the outside. It's a society of like-minded people, not a political power. Don't take it too seriously, Charles."

Charles weighed his answer carefully. "Just in passing," he replied, and hoped Wyatt could not read him well enough to know that was a lie. "Could any of them have heard you say something, perhaps that they misinterpreted?"

"Such as what, for heaven's sake, and who?"

Charles said the first name he could think of, someone who believed fiercely in the Free America principles. "Mabel Cartwright, perhaps? Or her husband, Horace, I think it is?"

Wyatt considered that for a long moment. "I suppose it's not impossible. But are you suggesting one of them killed the Worth woman to implicate me? Isn't that crazy?"

"Somebody did," Charles replied. "At least, if we assume you are the intended victim of all this. And we are, aren't we? Or are we thinking someone chose your party as the time to kill Lila Worth, and you were unfortunate enough to be the one blamed for it?"

Wyatt looked suddenly older, and even more tired. "I see what you mean. It looks like a crime of opportunity. Poor creature was killed because she was outside, and vulnerable. Anyone could have done it, the moment they thought I could not account for myself. A reasonable deduction. Hideously reasonable. I've racked my brains to think who would wish me so much harm, and I can't think of any-one."

"Maybe it isn't personal," Charles suggested. "Maybe it is more about what you stand for . . . or against. Perhaps you are intended to be a warning for others, to show the power these people have. Or, on the other hand, perhaps they want to blame someone for your . . ."

"Downfall," Wyatt finished for him. "Dear God! I wish I could deny it, say that all you are suggesting is rubbish, but it makes too much sense. In fact, it is the only answer I can see in all this." He sighed heavily. "Don't tell Dorothy or Katherine, please. Not until we can see a way out of this. Now, let me get some rest. And thank you, Charles. You're a good man."

Charles rose to his feet. "I'm sorry to push so hard," he said, "but we have no time to spare." And with that, he went quietly out of the room and closed the door behind him.

That evening, before dinner, Charles went for a walk in the garden with Elena. Dorothy was going to have a quiet supper alone with Wyatt. Katherine, Elena, and Charles would take their meal in the dining room. It was still light, still warm, with hazy sunshine, which made the white stars of the dogwood blossom seem almost lumi-nous. He did not waste time by disguising his purpose. "Did you learn anything on your trip with Allenby this morning?" he asked.

"Yes, quite a lot," she replied. "We went to see Harmon Worth."

He stopped walking. "So soon? Isn't that a bit insensitive? What reason could you possibly give? You didn't tell him who you are, did you? Are you even allowed to, never mind the—?"

"No, Father, I didn't. James knew."

"James, is it?"

"Captain Allenby," she amended, glancing away for a moment. "I've got to seek his help, and do it under the guise of something else, however inappropriate anyone thinks it is. And Mother does just that. She thinks I'm behaving selfishly, and like a fool." There was pain in her face as she said it, and in her voice.

"Who is Allenby, Elena?" Charles demanded. "Do you know anything about him, really? What if he knows who killed Lila, and he's protecting them? For that matter, he could have killed her himself."

"Father!" she said sharply. "Stop it! I checked on him."

"With whom? Who do you know?"

"The British Embassy, of course. Who else? Please, I'm doing the best I can, this far from home, and with family involved."

He felt rebuked. He was angry because he was helpless. He was used to being the one who solved things, comforted people, was to some extent in charge.

"I'm sorry," she said softly, interrupting his thoughts. "We've got to find as much of the truth as we can." She carried on reasoning, as if he had asked her for explanations, and she were counting off points on her fingers. "We need to know more about Grandfather, other than what he tells us, which at the moment is very little, except that he is important. He did say that, didn't he?"

"Yes," he agreed wryly, and he told her what he had told Wyatt, and how he had responded.

Not surprisingly, the doctor had prescribed a sedative for Wyatt. After Dorothy dined early with him, she left him to rest and joined her family downstairs.

"Grandma, that's gorgeous!" Elena said, with what seemed to

Charles like very genuine appreciation. Her grandmother was dressed in a very formally styled gown of an unusual dark green, almost black.

"Thank you, my dear." Dorothy accepted the compliment with an attempt at a smile. "I thought you might like it. I'm sorry I have been so defeatist. I should have known we'd get him home. But I do wish it were all over." She looked at Elena as if she hoped for a reply, a reassurance.

Katherine drew breath, as if to answer. And then stopped, as if realizing that the remark had not been addressed to her.

"I think everyone does," Elena said gently. "Except, that is, who-ever did it, of course. It's always humbling to realize we have ene-mies capable of such a thing. No one could blame you for being horrified . . . shocked. But we shall fight back. And then the surprise will be on the other foot!"

Dorothy stared at her for a moment, then gave a wry, faint laugh.

Charles felt a wave of relief. Elena was going to do her best, and Katherine would gain courage from it, and hope.

They went into the dining room where the places were already carefully set out. Wyatt's, always at the head of the table, was also set, as if he were about to join them. The silverware was placed so that, at a glance, there would be soup, salad, fish, and then dessert. Crystal goblets were at each place, and a large jug of iced water with slices of lemon was sitting on a mat at the center. A cut-crystal vase was filled with fresh flowers from the garden. It was the key to every-thing. The evening was going to be family only, casual and intimate. Everything was going to be a little subdued, but only waiting, not with breath held for disaster. Wyatt was at home, even if he was up-stairs in his own room.

They ate the soup and the salad practically in silence. Everyone looked to Charles, as if expecting him to lead any conversation, and he chose to say nothing beyond appreciative comments on the food, and the table in general.

The mood was fragile, and could not last. Charles knew that if he did not break it soon, Elena would. He could see it in her face, in her intense look as he caught her eye.

When the main course was served and the staff withdrew, Elena spoke before he could take charge of the conversation. As was natural to her, she was devastatingly frank. She looked at Dorothy when she spoke. "Grandmother, we all know that Grandfather didn't do this—he wouldn't ever do such a thing—but the police have to go on what they see and hear. Some of his friends will know it couldn't possibly be true, but there will be some who might believe it."

Dorothy drew in her breath, but it was Katherine who spoke, directing her words at Elena. "There are many kinds of friendships, dear, and not all of them are comfortable. Sometimes we disagree with people. But for this party, only people your grandparents know were invited. Some of them are a bit different in their views, but there were no strangers here."

"They thought they knew them," Elena said, speaking quietly, too, but every word was distinct, and she did not take her eyes from Dorothy. "But people change, sometimes for the better, sometimes not." She swallowed. "Grandmother, some of the people you had at that party expressed beliefs I can't think you share. A lot of what people say is just chatter, talk for the sake of it, or to impress other people. Some of it is to draw other people out. Sometimes it's just to fill a silence. But what you really mean is there, too. And if you hear something you truly don't like, you might be wise to remember it."

"Such as what?" Charles asked.

Elena gave a slight shrug. "Oh, things like the assumption that all your opinions are correct, and you shouldn't add to them, or alter them in any way. And also, therefore, other people are mistaken."

"About what?" Charles pressed. He was aware that both Katherine and Dorothy were staring at her. Was that a surprise, or had she looked for this? Turning so he could see the expression on her face, he still had no idea.

"That there's no other correct religion but your own," Elena began.

Dorothy frowned. "Doesn't everybody think that? It's a given, isn't it, if you have a religion?"

"I don't know what any other religions teach," Elena replied. "I'd have to listen to them to know if I agreed or not."

"Which is why religion is one of the things well-bred people don't discuss at other people's parties," Katherine said. "You don't challenge other people's faiths, and you know that."

"But it's fine to question other people's political beliefs?" Elena asked.

"Well, that's . . ." Katherine stopped and smiled back at her.

"Different?" Elena raised her eyebrows. "Not the way I overheard it at the party. Sometimes there was passion in what was said, the expression of fundamental ideas as to how God meant the world to be. There was talk about who was worthy, *chosen,* if you like. And who definitely was not."

Charles knew exactly what she meant. He had overheard some of the same remarks.

"About natural selection?" he asked. "Racial hygiene, and so on? A natural order . . ."

"I think we should avoid that," Katherine began.

"Really?" Charles asked. "Are you so sure it wasn't at the core of what one of our violent adversaries was about? Couldn't he have wanted to silence Wyatt? His is a very powerful voice, you know."

"Yes," Dorothy agreed. "I don't want to think of it. But then, I suppose he did have political enemies."

"Everyone with ideas, and with the will and the power to bring them into being, is bound to have enemies," Elena said quickly. "Somebody killed Lila here, in his home, and saw to it that Grandfather was blamed. That may be the real purpose of it." She turned to her grandmother. "Please, try to remember all the important things Grandfather was connected with, all that he was trying to do. And maybe if he thinks about it now with hindsight, he can remember something, too. Please may I ask him about them?" she implored. "We've got to do everything we can to help."

Dorothy hesitated. "Mr. Borrodale might not like it."

"Who cares more about Grandfather," Elena demanded, "Mr. Borrodale or us?"

"We do, dear. But are you sure?"

"Yes, I'm sure," Elena replied.

Charles looked at her and felt a sudden surge of pride. It was not because of her intelligence or her courage. Rather, it was the belief that she might actually succeed.

CHAPTER
15

The next morning, Elena sat alone on one of the padded seats in the garden. The early sun was soft on her face, and there was barely a breeze moving the flower petals. There was no avoiding it: this morning, she must speak to her grandfather. She had sat with Dorothy quite late into the evening, going over lists of men her grandfather knew, as well as organizations that he supported. Some were outwardly charitable, but in reality they were also political, simply less openly so. Dorothy could not tell her their purposes, but perhaps Allenby would be able to.

She was nervous. Although she had spent a great deal of the evening of the anniversary party with guests, it had been more a matter of hospitality, of outward politeness. She had been in her grandfather's company, but in a sense she had only been beside him. All his attention had been on the guests he was making welcome and comfortable, engaging in easy conversations between them, which included Elena only peripherally. He had trusted her to play her part with grace. It was a compliment, a gracious inclusion announcing that, although they barely knew each other, she was part of his family. She was introduced, of course, but she could not now remember all the names, and certainly not the offices or callings he had included in his welcome and introductions.

It was strange to have a direct blood relationship to someone who, until the day before they arrived in Washington, she had known only through family recollections. The two or three brief meetings years ago, when she was a little girl, were hardly memorable. Such a difference from her other grandfather, Lucas Standish, whom she knew as well as she knew anybody in the world. Her memories of him went as far back as she could recall. He had played with her, talked to her, made little animals out of wire pipe cleaners. Read stories to her. And there had always been a dog. Usually, it was adopted, a mutt that had been lost or injured, or was for some reason in need of a home. For several years now, it had been Toby. Lucas's hands were always gentle with Toby, and he talked to him exactly as if the dog understood everything he said. Lucas would explain ethical questions and mathematical equations, and Toby listened, ears pricked. Most importantly, he understood that Lucas loved him.

Elena remembered sitting beside a different dog and listening to her grandfather discuss complicated subjects. She was perhaps two or three years old, and had no more idea what it meant than the dog did. What she had sensed, however, was that she was being trusted, and involved, and that she was part of it, whatever it was.

She could not think of Wyatt Baylor like that. He was part of her family because she was told he was, not that he was woven into it through years of emotional connections that did not need words to explain. But that was not his fault. There was an ocean between them, and war, and circumstances. Now she had to make up for that. And soon. Before the next crisis, and with fear standing at their elbows.

She got up slowly and walked into the house. She had no excuses left. She was already dressed appropriately, in pale linen with a white collar, pretty but modest. In the kitchen, the maid had a tray of fresh tea brewed and ready to be carried up to her grandfather's room. Elena picked up the tray.

"Are you sure you wouldn't like me to take it up, miss?" the maid asked.

"No, thank you." Elena smiled. "I'll take it." She turned toward the door. She needed to carry it herself so Wyatt would not refuse to let her in. Why did she even think that? She was gripping the tray too hard. She told herself to relax, or she would sabotage her own effort by her attitude.

She tried to remember her grandfather as he had been at the party. He had exuded effortless confidence, even power. He had been kind, affable, and occasionally even funny, the sort of wit at which one smiled, rather than laughed easily. It had made her feel included in the secrets that her family knew, or their society shared.

She reached his door, balanced the tray, and knocked. Wyatt Baylor opened it. He wore a fresh white shirt and light brown slacks. The clothes were clean and pressed, but they looked uncomfortable on him, as if they were a size too big and ill-fitting across the shoulders. He was shaved, and there was a tiny cut on his skin. His hair was combed smoothly. There was fear in his eyes. Elena met them with difficulty, but if she had looked away it would have been an acknowledgment of what she saw, and that it frightened her.

"Hello, Grandfather," she said quietly. "I brought your tea. And a cup for myself, if you don't mind my joining you." She did not ask how he was. The answer was apparent and he would not thank her for dissembling. It would mean she was avoiding the truth, and there was no time for that.

"Hello, Elena, how are you? How is your grandmother today? I have not seen her yet."

"Better," she answered. "Collecting her courage, ready to fight." She gave a tiny smile. "We all are. They send their love, and more importantly right now, their resolution to find the answer to this, so we don't hear any more of it."

"Really?" He looked as if she had made a dry, obvious joke. "And you?" he asked. "Are you the emissary?"

"Exactly. How well put. May I pour your tea?"

"Of course. And your own, since you seem intent on staying." A flicker of amusement crossed his face, and was gone immediately. "Then tell me what you are planning to do."

She poured two cups before she answered. Dorothy had already told her how he liked it. "Ask you questions," she said. "You must have been thinking about this. If you did not kill Lila, that means someone else did. If we can find out who, and prove it, then your name will be cleared." She saw the skepticism in his eyes. "I know! It will not be easy. If it were, you would have done it already, and Borrodale would have put it into effect. Unless, of course, he didn't want to."

Wyatt's intake of breath was sharp. "What on earth do you mean, not want to?"

"We must face it, Grandfather, you have enemies." She passed him his tea. "We don't know who they are, or why. But perhaps you do? And if you don't, then we have to start from the beginning. But I can't believe you haven't considered it. Unless—"

"What?" he snapped, leaning a little forward. Now his eyes were sharp, focused.

"Unless you know, and are doing something about it that you haven't told us?" she explained. "Or you can't?"

"What on earth are you talking about, girl?"

Was he playing for time? Trying to work out how much to tell her? Why? She was imagining he had some sort of secret business, like Grandfather Lucas. She tried to smooth her face of any emotion other than concern. She turned a fraction closer toward him from where she sat. "Grandfather, someone cares very much that your reputation is destroyed, however it is done. Someone killed Lila Worth, on the grounds of your house, while you had your wedding anniversary party. They went to a lot of trouble to blame you. And as far as they are concerned, it worked. If we can figure out who,

then we can stop them from succeeding. One thing to find out is
whether their purpose was to get rid of Lila, and blame whoever fitted into the trap, or to get rid of you, by killing whoever was easiest
to kill, and blaming you."

There was a flash of appreciation in his eyes. Somewhere behind
the shocked and temporarily stunned man there was the will to fight.

She gave him a quick smile. "If we find that out, we are on the
way. You had no reason to kill Lila."

"None!" he said quickly.

"Then we must think who did and—"

"Harmon Worth," he interrupted, his voice hard and edged with
contempt. "He's a fine scientist, you know. No, of course you don't
know." He gave a slight shrug. "But believe me, he is. I've been thinking, too, and I realize she probably used him from the start."

"The start of what?"

"First meeting him, of course," he said sharply. He completely
ignored his tea. "In Vienna. He fell in love with her, married her, and
brought her to America."

It made sense. It fitted neatly all the facts that she knew about
Lila. It just didn't fit the woman she had seemed to be. But if she had
worked for an intelligence service—Austrian, German, British, or
American—she would have been clever enough to hide at least that
part of her activities. Elena thought of herself. What did she appear
to be? A rather spoiled young woman who had squandered an excellent education by falling in love with a man who had never loved
her, but simply used her to further his own betrayal of his country.
She winced at the thought. As foolish as her grandfather Wyatt
thought she was, he might be prepared to love her because she was
his granddaughter, Katherine's child, and not really for herself. And
should she allow him to go on thinking that? Maybe his observations
were more acute than she had supposed.

He was watching her, waiting. She must not arouse his suspicion
by being too astute, or playing at being too foolish. She must seem

totally honest. This was now bigger than family pain, disgrace, even grief. She would take nothing for granted, nothing at all. Not even that Allenby was to be trusted totally. She needed to keep the focus on Lila. "I see," she said slowly. "Of course. For all that, she seemed to fit in so easily, but she could have been quite different underneath. One thing I saw that must be right: she was really very clever. You can't fake that."

He nodded slowly. "So, you noticed that, eh?" What did he mean? Was he referring to Lila, or was he now back to Elena herself?

She sipped her tea. It was still too hot to drink with pleasure. How should she answer? She considered herself bright, but she had been naïve. Those two could go quite easily together. The most sophisticated intelligence could still be blunted by love, the need for human warmth. She, of all people, should know that. "Is that what happened?" she asked. "Lila used him? Made him fall in love with her, and married him so she could get over here, and into the right society? Especially the scientific people Harmon Worth must be working with?"

He nodded slowly. "Interesting you should mention that. We must consider the possibility," he said grimly. "Among others, of course."

Had she made a mistake, mentioning the science? Suddenly, she was cold somewhere in the pit of her stomach. But she could not take it back. Don't try! She would only make it worse.

"Others ... such as ... what?" she asked. "That she was having an affair with someone, and they killed her? Or their wife did? Or Harmon did?"

His eyes were on her face, as if he could read it exactly. He had a peculiarly penetrating gaze, for all his pallor and shocked look. "I've been thinking," he said, with a bitter little smile. "There's not been much else I could do recently, except think. And I won't trust someone else to get me out of this. My enemies may not have thought I would fight, but I will. All the way!"

Elena took a deep breath and let it out slowly. "Who are your enemies?" It was the obvious thing to ask. The one she had been longing to lead toward. She must be obvious, at least most of the time. Never give him cause to think that her intentions were hidden. She must think of her grandfather as a friend, someone who might unwittingly betray her by showing his enemies that he trusted her to be more than she seemed to be. What was it that Peter had said? "Never tell anyone something you don't have to. They may innocently repeat it and it will lead to a disaster ... without ever realizing it. You owe them that protection."

Wyatt was staring at her. "You've thought of something, haven't you?"

This was the time to go forward. She began slowly. "I liked her. She was charming. Could she have been trying to get closer to me, because of you? I don't like being used!" She let anger show in her voice.

He put out one hand and touched hers where it lay on the bedspread. He was very gentle. "My dear, if you have power, or you are close to power, you must always allow for that possibility. She may have liked you for yourself, but that doesn't mean she wouldn't use you if the opportunity presented itself. What did she say to you? Can you remember? Please try."

She hesitated, recalling what they had talked about, and if her grandfather had been mentioned at all. Apart from the truth, what should she say? Something that could be of use, but without being too clever and raising even the slightest whisper of suspicion. "I am trying," she said earnestly. "It was mostly superficial, about gowns and fashion, and what was exotic and what was chic-looking."

"Really? About women's dresses?"

"Yes. And she was funny, and very observant," she answered. The words were hard to say. She must not let him know how much Lila's death meant to her.

He looked puzzled.

She forced her memory back. "She could see how much a dress told about a woman's character."

"Such as?"

"Brave, discreet, self-conscious, tense. What flattered . . . or what didn't."

"I never thought of such a thing," he admitted.

"You may not have been as good at this as she was, Grandfather, but I imagine you can tell a great deal about a man from the cut of his suit, the fabric, the colors he chooses. And a great deal from his tie!" She smiled at him. "Which school, which college."

He relaxed a little. "Of course," he said. "So, Lila Worth was observant. Did she ask about us?" he pressed.

Lila had not, but this was an opportunity she should not waste. "Only to ask if I had been here before," she replied. "I said no, but you had been to England, a long time ago, so I did know you a little. Then she said we should meet again. You were terribly busy, so she offered to take me to the places you had no time for." She smiled. "And, of course, girl shopping, which would bore you stiff."

He gave a polite smile. "I agree with that. Then, of course, that would give her the opportunity to question you more. She would be smart about it. As you say, she was a very clever woman."

"It's pretty frightening," Elena admitted. She identified with Lila, a woman essentially alone, and not who she pretended to be. She had been there herself, not so long ago, both in Italy and in Berlin, trying to learn other people's secrets while hiding her own.

"Tell me about some of the people at your party," she asked earnestly. "We've got to find out who they are, in order to fight them effectively. It isn't enough just to say you would never do such a thing, because somebody did!"

He looked at her long and steadily, as if making up his mind. "I don't want to endanger you," he answered slowly. "You are brave, but not very wise. You don't know these people as I do and—"

"Then help me!" she cut across him. "Tell me! What do they

want? How do they believe that destroying you can possibly do them any good? Or was it really all about Lila, and you are just accidental damage?"

"It's an appalling thought," he said slowly, as though turning it over in his mind for the first time and seeing its brutality. "No, I think not," he added. "I think it was poor Lila who was only a means to an end. What danger could she be to anyone? I grant that she had an appeal, to a certain sort of man. Perhaps she died in the heat of a quarrel, or because she suddenly changed her mind and refused him. Not . . . not something you do at someone else's party."

She drew in her breath sharply to defend Lila, and realized she did not really know her at all. Pieces of Peter's advice came back to her. Apart from rare moments of vulnerability, he never allowed emotion to take over. In fact, he never allowed it to be seen at all. He was the most unreadable person she knew. She wanted to defend Lila, but not if it defeated her purpose. "I think you're right," she said, keeping her voice steady, but only with difficulty. "What are they defending? Help me understand."

"Their beliefs," he answered, sitting a little more upright. "The values in their lives, the things they, and their parents back through the generations, have fought for, worked for, and in many cases died for. Love of liberty and justice, hard work, thrift, everybody working their way, not expecting the labor of others to support idleness, ig-norance, loose morals, and general laxity. You haven't lived here. You don't know how it used to be, and how these other cultures are pouring in, wanting to alter it." He stopped suddenly, his eyes fixed on her face.

"You mean taking from those who work hard, and giving it to the lazy?" she asked. Using those words made it sound all right. She would have said: taking from those who have more than they need, and helping others who are old, or sick, or just bewildered and poor and hungry, but she could not afford to argue with him.

"You think that sounds harsh?" he asked.

How much had he seen in her eyes, or the expression in her features? She must never appear to lie to him. "No," she lied. "Some people will be passengers all their lives, if you are unrealistic enough to let them."

"Good girl! Exactly! Any man is worth the pay for his labor, but nothing is owed those who won't work. And it's more than that. It's at the root of all that we are. American values. Hard work, honesty, decency toward others, doing your share—these are all the key to balance. And civility, modesty, self-control, all the things that make a society great, and always have."

"Always?" The word slipped out, unguarded, in an instant.

"Don't you understand, girl? The white race is different! Blacks, Jews, even some of the Spanish and Italians are uncontrolled. And they breed like rabbits, and then expect us to—" He stopped, looking hard at her face.

She had to keep the emotion out of it, even out of her eyes. She looked up at him. "Rescue them from drowning?"

He sighed. "Exactly. When they overwhelm us, it will be too late. We are only fighting for our own."

"It must be difficult to know what weapons to use," she said. "Some are double-edged." The moment the words were out, she knew they were the right ones.

He had not taken his eyes from her face. "Indeed," he said softly. "I want you to be careful, Elena. Please. You have no idea how deep this is. You are speaking of it easily, as if you understand, but you don't. It's all far away from you, living your safe life in England."

She was about to tell him that she had been to Berlin, and she had seen something far worse than people who were a little different in their tastes, their cultural values. She wished that the terror of what she had seen might move him, but she knew better. "Grandfather." She let the deep emotion fill her mind. "We've got to prove you didn't do this. We must, or they win."

He put his hand on her arm, and the strength of his grip startled her. "Understand me, Elena. This is dangerous. They killed that Worth woman to get to me. Do you think they will hesitate to harm my granddaughter, if it fills their purpose? And you would be surprised whom they will use: people you would not expect. They'll find weaknesses everywhere. For example, Allenby, from the British Embassy. Do you know anything about him, except what he tells you? Just . . . just be careful!"

She stared at him. There was something in his eyes that was violent and very real. No one could pretend the darkness in the mind. He was warning her of something terrible. For an instant, she thought it was a threat. Then sense prevailed, and reality. He was terrified for her. He saw her as young, vulnerable, virtually defenseless, and in very real danger if she continued trying to learn who had so brutally killed Lila. She did not have to pretend to be startled, and aware of what could happen to a woman, even one as prepared and as clever as Lila . . . or herself. "I want to help." She managed to frame harmless words that were real. He must see that she meant them, without the shadow of double intent. "I will," she whispered.

He patted her hand, still holding it hard. "Of course you do, my dear. And you are very sweet and loyal. But these people are fighting for their way of life."

"Then give me their names. Borrodale doesn't seem to be doing much. Anything I can to help . . . please."

"Borrodale will . . ." he began.

"Aren't you on the same side?" she asked. She had to pretend innocence; she did not need to feign fear.

"Yes, I am, but we don't all fight in the same way."

"I see. At least, I think I do. But let me help . . . please?"

"Drink your tea, my dear, before it is cold. And thank you for your loyalty, and your courage. They mean a lot to me. You remind me of your mother, when she was a little younger than you. Bless you."

She smiled through sudden tears. It was the mention of Katherine. This man was Katherine's father! If she could be given one wish, right now, it would be that he was not. It was so much easier when it was someone you barely knew, not a member of your own family, your blood, your heritage.

"Names?" she said again.

"Very well, but be careful!"

She nodded, then picked up her tea and sipped it. It was cold.

Elena found her mother in the sitting room. Katherine must have been watching for her to return after seeing her father, because she turned immediately, her face filled with expectancy. For an instant, Elena thought of telling her all she wanted to hear, then realized the damage it would do. Katherine would not appreciate being protected, as if she were a child, yet Elena knew it was exactly what Katherine would do for her own mother.

"He looks a little better this morning," she answered the silent question. "We had a good conversation." She sat down in one of the chairs opposite Katherine. "I don't think we should tell Grandmother. Not yet, anyway, but he's facing the fact that Lila Worth's killer has to be someone at the party, therefore one of his friends. He helped me put together a list of all of them."

Elena saw how her mother searched her face, as if she was trying to discover something Elena was holding back. "He was very honest," she went on. She thought about their visit, how they were alone. What better time to speak honestly? The colors around them in his room were soft and clear, touched with the warmth of coral. That was her grandmother's choice, understanding how being warm, comfortable, and elegant, always with ease at the heart, made life richer, perhaps calmer.

Ridiculously, Elena felt her eyes fill with tears. She forced herself to speak. "He was very helpful. He's beginning to get over the shock and return his mind to working out who could have done this."

She settled into one of the comfortable chairs. "And he's given me something about each one, and explained why they believe as they do. I can't agree with him, but at least I understand a bit better why they feel that way. Still . . . I think it's wrong." The list was in her pocket, but she did not intend to share it with Katherine. Not yet, at least.

"What sort of thing?" Katherine leaned forward, her face intent. "Elena, be careful."

Elena ran some of the names off from memory. She did not want Katherine to see the notes she had made beside each name, comments underlined and the question marks.

Katherine frowned. "They're all friends, mostly long-time friends," she said slowly. "These are people Mother and Father have known for years."

"Of course," Elena replied gently. "The people you would want to have at your anniversary party. At least, mostly. What about Harmon Worth and Lila? Had they known them so long? Lila was at least a whole generation younger, if not more."

"Yes, Father knows Harmon from working with him. He's a very bright scientist, you know. I mean, brilliant. He doesn't make a display of it, but he's working on something to do with the atom, so Father said." She gave a bleak smile. "Wise people have friends of all ages. It would be terribly dull to know only people just like yourself. You, of all people, should grasp that!"

"I should?" Elena was puzzled.

"Peter Howard must be fifteen years older than you, at least. And Lucas is two generations older, and so is Josephine. Yet there's nobody with whom you are more comfortable," Katherine pointed out.

Elena sat motionless. How much did her mother know about Peter Howard? Yes, definitely, in a strange way she found him easy to talk to about some things. There was a tacit understanding with him. But he was her superior in MI6, and Katherine was not supposed to know that. If Elena had somehow let her know, that in itself would give away too much.

Katherine interrupted her thoughts. "Elena, what is it you're not telling me?" She paused before adding, "Did Father say something to you that you can't tell me? Did someone he trusted betray him?"

"Of course somebody did," Elena said quickly. "And we've got it down to a short list of the most likely. It has to be someone at the party, and that's a very painful thought."

"Can I help?"

"Of course you can." Elena gave a slight smile. "You have a list of all the guests. You can probably tell me something about them. Grandmother can tell you even more, if you ask her carefully. The thought will upset her. But it will upset her a good deal more if she learns that she could have helped, but we didn't trust her."

"I'll get the list," Katherine promised. "Who are your main people?"

"Harmon Worth."

Katherine winced. "Poor man. I hate to think he was the one."

"So do I. I just included him because we shouldn't exclude anyone until we've proven them innocent. And let's not forget Mabel Cartwright."

Katherine's eyes grew wide. "Mabel? Why on earth would she— I can't believe that!"

"Well, I can, so I included her."

"Why, for heaven's sake?"

"Just put her down . . . please."

"All right, if I must," Katherine conceded. "Who else? I don't believe it was either of those two."

"Borrodale."

"His lawyer? Who are you confusing him with?"

"No, I mean Borrodale. I know Grandmother trusts him, but I don't think Father does."

"He doesn't know him!" Katherine protested. "Father's known him for years! Are you suggesting your father can walk in, meet the man a couple of times, and know more than your grandfather does?"

"Mother," Elena said patiently, "it's somebody Grandfather

trusted, because you didn't have anyone he didn't trust at that party! No one wandered in off the road, and up the drive. Don't forget, the President was here, so the place was tighter than a drum, in terms of security."

Elena added reluctantly, "The only other one he mentioned was Captain Allenby. I can't agree with him, but I didn't argue."

"It could be," Katherine said quietly. "We don't know much about him, except that he has taken a lot of notice of you."

"And that makes him potentially a criminal lunatic?" And then she said with sudden tartness, "Grandfather said that, too! Then remarked on my poor taste in men in the past, specifically Aiden Strother, although he didn't name him. I wonder who told him that!" The moment the words were out of her mouth, she regretted them, but it was too late.

Katherine's face went white. She must have felt the blood drain from it, because she made no attempt to deny it. "I'm . . . I'm sorry. We were so upset for you, for the end of your career. And my father was proud of you, as we all were. It was either lie to him or tell him briefly of the truth. I'm sorry. But he is my father, and I trust him as you do your own father."

There was nothing for them to say. Elena wasn't even permitted to tell her own father how that story had ended, although she suspected he knew more than he let on. He was the one she felt she had let down the most. It was he who, very much against his own instincts, had used his personal influence to get her the post at the Foreign Office, from which she had been dismissed in disgrace. Katherine didn't know anything about it, only the shame and the grief afterward. The vindication had come years after. In fact, only this last autumn.

"Don't think about that," she said to Katherine. "It's all over now. But Grandpa might have made his own misjudgments as well, and trusted someone he shouldn't have. It's easy enough to do."

Katherine's eyes searched her face.

Elena waited for the reply, the understanding.

"Yes, of course," Katherine said at last. "If we don't lie, we don't always see when other people do. I'm still sorry."

"Those are the names to begin with," Elena changed the subject back, finally showing her mother the list.

Katherine took it. "I'll see if I can add to it," she said.

Elena gave her a quick hug, then went to look for her father.

When she found him, they went out into the garden to be certain of being unheard.

"Well?" Charles asked. In the sunlight, the strain showed in his face, the fine lines were deeper, the silver in his hair thicker. "How is he?"

Elena hesitated only a moment. "I think he's afraid. But . . ."

"But what?" he pressed.

"He's finding it hard to accept that it was one of his friends. He gave me a list. I gave it to Mother, but I memorized it, too."

"Will it be helpful?"

"I'm not sure," she said honestly. "It's somewhere to begin."

"What makes you say he was afraid?" Charles asked.

She glanced at him. This was the professional side of him, the face she seldom saw. She was familiar with his diplomatic voice, even with its degree of severity. But now, with this deep concentration they were sharing, the kind that looks straight at bitter truths, he was acknowledging that the war was real. She looked at the grass under his feet, bordering the flowerbed. "He mentioned Aiden Strother. Not by name, but he was reminding me of my mistakes, and pretty pointedly."

Charles looked shocked. "Are you sure you weren't reading into—"

"I'm sure," she cut across him. "He was quite specific. When I lost my temper with him, he apologized. But he meant what he had said. The thing is, I was able to see the fear in him. I'm certain he realizes there is no quick, simple answer. He gave me a list of people to look at more closely."

"Who's on that list?"

"Obviously Harmon Worth, Borrodale, Mabel Cartwright, Allenby."

"Why on earth—"

"I don't know, Father. I don't know why he says quite a lot of things. Whether it's fear, or dislike, I'm not sure."

"Fear? Of Allenby? Or is he afraid of not being able to prove his innocence? It must be appalling, sitting there day after day, helplessly. At least now he's home."

"He gave me a lot of notes to work with. Other people to look at, and people who could help . . . perhaps."

"Anything hopeful there?"

He wanted a real answer, not the kind of comfort that comes in promises. "He included a lot of people who seem impossible to me. I can't imagine why Mabel Cartwright would kill Lila, and so violently, but we can look harder. And I don't like Borrodale. If he was part of it, it would explain why he's gotten nowhere in proving Grandfather innocent, as far as we know."

"You don't like him?"

"Neither do you!" she countered.

"And Allenby?" he asked. "Are you sure you can trust him? I can see that he's handsome enough, and charming, but so . . ." He stopped.

"So was Aiden," she said, before he could say it. "Father, please, just believe that I have checked on Allenby."

He looked at her steadily. "Do you really know anything about him, Elena? That is, something that wasn't what he told you, that he wanted you to know?"

She could not tell him the truth: that, apart from checking with the embassy, she was relying on Allenby's knowledge of Peter Howard and, even more, of Lucas.

"There are some people we both know, and they trust him. That's as good as I will get. I can't sit by and do nothing."

"I suppose there are always risks," he conceded reluctantly. "But we have to do what we can." He gave a slight, brief smile. "I would expect you to do all you could, if it were me being accused."

"But it isn't you," she said almost fiercely. "And we've got to prove it isn't Grandpa. I'm going to see what Allenby has found."

"Be careful!"

She did not reply; they had already said it all.

Elena went into the sitting room, and then into the library, where there was a second telephone. She had memorized Allenby's number, and was turning over in her mind exactly what she would say to him.

She dialed the number, but there was no answer.

CHAPTER

16

It seemed far longer than the seventh day since their arrival in Washington to Elena when, the following morning, she was finally able to reach Allenby by telephone. Without any preamble, she asked to see him as soon as possible.

"Of course," he said immediately. "I need to see you, too. Would you like me to pick you up? I can be there in thirty minutes or so."

"Yes, please," she answered, and before he could elaborate, she hung up the receiver. Why had she been so short with him? Was she really so defensive of letting someone outside her family know that she was afraid? Allenby had to know. He could hardly be expected to do his job if she withheld facts, or even impressions. Were the situation reversed, she would have expected honesty from him.

Thirty minutes. She was wearing a very ordinary linen dress of quite casual fit, but she had time to change into a more suitable dress for going out. She went upstairs and chose a slim-fitting navy silk with a gored skirt. It was comfortable, and definitely more flattering. It moved with her. She put on a little makeup, giving herself more color.

"Where are you going?" Katherine said, the moment she saw Elena coming down the stairs. "Somewhere special?"

"No," Elena replied immediately. "Just to get more information, I hope."

Katherine gave her a little smile, brave, as if this were all normal. "If it's a woman, she should be jealous," she said. "If it's a man, he'll be impressed. You've taken a leaf out of Margot's book. She couldn't have done it better!"

Elena could feel herself blushing. "Give me long enough and I'll learn."

It was exactly thirty minutes since she had spoken to Allenby. She would go and wait for him in the sun, outside. Her mother's observation was more astute than she found comfortable.

"Goodbye," she called over her shoulder. She did not hear Katherine's reply.

Allenby drove up within two or three minutes and got out of the car to open the passenger door for her. "Love the dress," he said quietly. "We better go somewhere special. You'd stick out like a sore thumb anywhere ordinary."

She climbed in, leaving him to close the door.

When he was seated, they moved off slowly. "Thank you," she replied, and then added, "I think. Should I really be bandaged?"

"Bandaged? You mean like an Egyptian mummy?"

"Like a sore thumb," she replied. "Isn't that what you said?"

His eyes widened, although he was looking at the road, not at her. As if shaking away the brief side trip into humor, he asked, "So tell me: What happened yesterday?"

It was on the edge of her tongue to say something tart, then she recalled how terribly serious the truth was, and settled for honesty. She was letting her grandfather's responses seep into her mind. Was that what he intended? Or was he only wakening something in her that had been there already, just unacknowledged? Because she liked Allenby, she needed this to be similar to her connection with Peter Howard, someone with whom she could share the whole truth.

"I spent some time with my grandfather. He looks awful."

"I'm sorry, but he was bound to, if he has any perception at all of the truth. I'm afraid it's pretty bad," he answered. "Courage can master the way you move, and the way you hold your head, and the words you choose, but it can't hide everything." He hesitated. "You can't have expected him to be all right, could you? Being at home is better than a police cell, but the truth hangs over him like a darkness everywhere. It has to."

"No, of course I didn't."

"Did you learn anything useful?" He sounded perfectly polite, and it was the obvious question, so why should she be irritated? Because she felt guilty talking about her grandfather's fear, his vulnerability, to someone who was a comparative stranger, and who could possibly use it to harm him. Was that a betrayal? After all, Grandfather Wyatt had given her Allenby's name as a possible suspect for Lila's murder. No, this was not about loyalties; it was about truth!

She was very conscious of his sitting beside her, waiting. Patiently, like a cat outside a mouse hole.

"What is it?" he asked.

"He suggested four specific people he thought could have killed Lila."

"Who?"

"Harmon Worth, which is fairly obvious, I suppose."

"Do you believe that?" He glanced at her briefly.

"No. But he made it sound very reasonable . . . logical. He says Lila married him to get into America, and because he's a top scientist. Is he?"

"In his field, yes. But I think he loved her." His voice held certainty. "Of course, that doesn't mean he didn't kill her. Either because he discovered she was spying on him, or because he thought she had betrayed him with another man."

"Did she?"

They passed under the shade of trees, and out into the sunlight again.

"I've no idea," he answered.

"The spying?" she clarified.

"Oh, yes. But I have no idea whether he knew that, or if he cared."

"If she was spying for the Germans?"

"He couldn't know that, because she wasn't," he pointed out. Then he sighed.

Elena looked at his face as he concentrated on driving, and she saw a deep sadness. It was momentary, there and then gone again. But it had been real.

"At least, I really believe she wasn't," he added. "Who else . . . on that list?"

She liked him for that momentary pain. "Mabel Cartwright," she said.

"A woman?" He sounded incredulous, then he smiled self-consciously. "Sorry. No reason why not. I thought of Mabel as a bit . . . trivial. But if she was jealous, there's no triviality about that. Women can hate as well as anyone."

"You think she has cause to be jealous? Over Horace, that is? You don't kill someone just because they are better-looking than you are, or you should suspect everyone in the room!"

"I do." He gave a real, broad smile. "But some more than others. Did you mean Mabel or Horace?"

"I meant Mabel," she said. "But I could have been wrong. And it doesn't have to be over Horace. It could be someone else."

"I admit, I never thought of Mabel Cartwright having a lover." There was a rueful humor in his voice. "Who else? You said four. That's only two."

"Borrodale. He'd be my favorite."

"The lawyer?" He was surprised. "That would be a bad sign. Not much chance getting a vigorous defense if your lawyer is the real killer." He glanced at her quickly, then kept his eyes on the road again. "You are serious, aren't you." It was a conclusion, rather than a question.

"Oh, yes. How better to defend yourself than to very carefully tighten the noose around the neck of your client? Sorry, they don't hang people in America, do they? Throw a switch on the electric chair, or whatever they do."

"A point well taken," he said quietly. "Poor Wyatt. That's going to be the devil to prove. Who is the fourth suspect?"

It raced through her mind to deny that there was a real fourth one. The unknown? She felt cornered. What if it really was Allenby? He could be MI6 and a traitor as well. It wouldn't be the first time.

"Elena?"

He was pressing her for an answer, and her hesitation would only make it worse. She must do this well. In fact, perfectly. "I'm sorry, but it was you."

"Me? For God's sake . . ." He let out a sigh and his voice was tense when he spoke again. "You didn't deny the possibility, did you?"

"No, of course not. That would tell him either I was an idiot, or else I knew more about you than I could learn during the chance acquaintance made when I arrived here. I thought it might be helpful to know why he thought it could be you."

His face was unreadable. "And? What did he say?" he asked.

"Nothing helpful." She did not want to tell him about Aiden Strother. Perhaps Peter had already done so. And that was an ugly thought. Allenby had no right to know that. Did he?

"Can you remember what?"

His voice sounded on edge now. Why? Was there something Wyatt might know about Allenby that was damaging? Was there even a chance that he would be right? Double agents were possible. In fact, she knew of several. Perhaps something of the truth was safest? She must be careful. This was no time for vanity. "Not about you," she said. "But he reminded me of a particularly painful misjudgment I made of somebody, quite a while ago, and I paid a heavy price for it. I was upset because I didn't know he knew about it."

"Because somebody told him? Was it private?"

Did she hear pity in his voice? He did know. "Yes." Her tone was angry, but she could not help it. "I'm sorry," she said. He looked so genuinely concerned that she was startled. "My mother. I suppose it hurt her, and she told her father. That's natural enough. I would have told my grandfather most things."

"Would have?"

"If I had a secret that was—"

"Lucas. You've been close to him always, haven't you." There was no lift of question in his voice; he was stating a fact.

"Yes."

"It's good to have someone." There was also no condescension, and no self-pity. He was revealing nothing about himself.

They drove in silence for a little while, aware of nothing but the bright sun and the wind. She had no idea where they were going, until he pulled up to a restaurant with outdoor seating.

"All right?" he asked, as he parked the car some distance from the tables.

"Very nice," she accepted.

They chose a table in a sheltered spot, out of the breeze and slightly shaded. A waiter brought them the menu and they ordered.

"I tried to call you yesterday afternoon," she said, when they were alone. "I was going to tell you then. I felt my grandfather was afraid. Not just afraid, but angry, actually facing the probability that he would go to trial. We haven't heard anything more from the police. I don't know if they are even looking for anybody else." She felt again the sudden misery that had swept over her when seated in her grandfather's room. And the pity. Then there was his anger, the lash of his tongue when he reminded her of her fall from grace. It should not still hurt. She had redeemed it, but she could not tell Allenby that! Or anyone. Lucas knew, and Peter, but that was all. Or so she had thought. Until now.

"Then we had better work harder," Allenby replied. "I went to the embassy this morning. Telephoned Peter."

For a moment, she found it hard to swallow. It seemed as if her breath were stuck in her throat.

"It's worse than we thought," he said gravely. "It's not just the question of whatever Lila found out about the science, and that atomic energy can be used in a weapon, and that whoever gets there first has an unbreakable advantage. Ordinary weapons matter, too. Tanks, big guns, armored cars, and conventional rifles. And the means to move them."

"What has that to do with America, or my grandfather?" For a moment she was lost.

"Do you know how much money he has?"

"Exactly? Of course not. A lot, I assume."

"Millions, but it's mostly tied up in steel. Armored cars, for example. Field guns." He stopped.

"Grandpa? For the American army? That's ridiculous. He is against America coming into another European war. No, you have that wrong. Everything I've heard is of isolation of America from European wars. The feelings seem to be pretty strong. I can't entirely blame them, but I wish they were on our side."

"Elena, not for the American army, for the Germans." There was a powerful mix of emotions in his face.

"What? I . . ." She could not think of anything to say that was adequate to her confusion. "He couldn't!" she protested.

"Not openly," he agreed. "It goes as first-class refined steel. He doesn't care what the Germans make with it. And if you asked him, I dare say he would claim it was for cars, passenger railway carriages, anything you like."

"How do you know it isn't?" she demanded.

"I don't, except that I believe Peter. He is the least hysterical man I have ever known. He never lets his emotions rule his thoughts." Now the urgency was plain in his face, even though he was staring straight ahead.

"Is he sure?" She thought of Peter, as much as she knew him. He cared intensely about certain things: great music, the English landscape, infinite gentleness toward animals, the values of friendship, sacrifice, loyalty. His humor was dry, sometimes rueful. Even better, it never mocked the weak, made fun of the disadvantaged. But was there passion in him that could be trusted? Could it also be misled? Perhaps not . . .

"Elena!" Allenby's voice was sharp.

She jerked herself back to the present. "Sorry. I was thinking about Peter. Yes, if he is sure, then I suppose it's possible. Are you certain, beyond any doubt at all, that my grandfather is involved in steel for Germany?"

"No. It's possible he's infiltrating a group of profiteering isolationists, and reporting to Roosevelt. And it could endanger his success if we expose that. Or, on the other hand, perhaps this is their way of getting rid of him."

"Who?"

"The enemy we are looking for," he replied.

"Murdering Lila, and having him blamed? Do you believe it?" she asked.

He hesitated a moment. "No, not really. I just suggested that it's possible."

Another possibility forced itself into her mind. "Or she knew that he was doing it," she suggested, "and that's why she was killed."

"Yes. But the question still remains, by whom? How did they get on the property, and then out, unseen? Or were they part of the security force? Or it was Wyatt himself, or someone on his behalf, to protect him from being exposed by her?"

"I suppose there's no chance you could be wrong about that? Lila couldn't have said that about him . . . to destroy him?" As much as she needed to ask, she hated the thought.

"If he was behind steel exports to Germany? I don't think so. There'd be no point. And apart from that, it's not illegal. America can sell whatever it wants to whomever it wants. There's no crime involved at all."

"So, what is it, other than just information?"

"A lot of money, millions. And if there is a war, or even a full-scale lead-up to war, there will be monumental gains and losses in the stock market," he explained. "A shift in political power, very possibly. It would all come down to money, rather than political ideals on either side. Neutral countries are the only real winners in a war."

She thought about that for a moment. Perhaps it was true. You stood aside and watched your rivals destroy each other. And afterward? You helped to pick up the pieces and aid in the recovery. Maybe both. Surely, you govern the country for its own good? That's the only reason you should have that power—elected, inherited, appointed, or anything else.

Cool-headed, she could follow all the reasoning. But Elena was not cool-headed, which was why she thought and did things that terrified her, and did them largely alone. She acted more on passion, on her deeply held beliefs. She could vividly recall the horror and the burning anger she had felt in Berlin. The fierce pity that had led her to take risks with her own life, and which, in cold blood, she never could have done. Anyone who could not be stirred by such things should still be treated fairly, but she could never respect them. The ability to feel another person's pain had nothing to do with political reasoning or philosophy; it was intensely emotional. That's what drew people to fight for others, long before they had to fight for themselves.

She looked at Allenby's face. Was he anything more than clever? Surely emotion and empathy were the ultimate signs of humanity? She saw humor, but then she knew that was there. Vulnerability? Could one really care, without the ability to be hurt oneself?

She jerked her mind back to the present, and the urgent problems she had no right to try to escape. "So, what did you conclude?" she asked. "What side do you think Borrodale is on?"

"His own," he answered immediately. "And I don't believe Harmon Worth killed her. I don't think he would have, even if she betrayed him, which I have no reason to believe she did. And not so cold-bloodedly."

When she remained quiet, he said, "I think if you kill a woman you love because she betrayed you, either with another man or with another country, you'd use your hands. Strangle her, or hit her several times. But not knock her out and then get into someone else's car and deliberately drive over her, crushing her to death."

"Stop it!" she said fiercely.

A woman at the next table turned to look at them. Allenby put out his hand and covered Elena's where it rested on the table. "You're drawing attention to us," he said quietly, and with a smile that was almost tender.

It was a very good act, and she realized her mistake. "I'm sorry." She meant it, not so much as an apology as a recognition of her error. "What do you know about the Cartwrights?"

"Mabel and Horace? Not enough," he replied, letting her hand go. "But I'll find out more."

"These people with interests in steel, or whatever—Grandfather Wyatt and his friends, his associates—are they out to invest their money where it will get them the best return? Or are they really Nazi sympathizers, and profit is just an added advantage?" She paused before asking the big question, the one she feared asking. "Do they really believe in Hitler's way of practicing racial hygiene? And yes, I have read *Mein Kampf.* Or most of it."

"I don't know if these people have those same beliefs, but they do support his anti-Semitism," Allenby responded. "Aryan as the chosen and superior race. The cry to get rid of communists, Jews, Bolsheviks, dark-skinned people follows soon after, and then homosexuals, the disabled, people they consider damaged and inferior. Less than human. All deemed inferior by them. And then nationalism, my country before all others. Keep women in their place. That's part of it, too. And Christianity, with all its man-made restrictions, but without its virtues." There was a curious, quizzical, and emotional look on his face. "Yes, I think they do support something singularly close to his beliefs. It's a question of which is more important: your belief in yourself, your identity, your need to be superior, or the money in your bank. Poverty can be a temporary state. One can always hope to overcome it. Your identity, however, is at the root of everything. Just ensure that, and the world can be yours. It is by right!"

Is this how her grandfather thought? It was terribly close to an echo of the ideas he had already expressed and brought back the words of people at the party, not quite as frank as that, but in the end, much the same.

Allenby was watching her.

"Do we all think we are nationally superior?" she asked.

"Of course," he replied. "Only we, being English, don't have to say so, because secretly everybody knows we're right."

For an instant, she thought he meant it, then she saw the laughter in his eyes and knew he was joking. But she was touched by a sudden, deep pity for her grandfather. He was uniquely alone in that he did not know which of his supposed friends were, in fact, enemies. A lot of them, it would seem. Could anything be lonelier than that?

"We've got to find the truth," she said, looking at Allenby. "It might be a lot kinder not to know who among your friends are really your enemies, but my grandfather can't afford that."

"No one can," Allenby replied. "Has anybody gone through his papers? Or did the police take them away?"

She had not even thought of that. "No, they seemed to be thinking of it as a crime of passion. They don't appear to have thought of anything political or financial. Of course, everyone knows he is political, but they're not looking at Lila in that light."

"I suppose that was one of her best disguises," he said ruefully. "A woman as beautiful as she was can't be intelligent as well. How damn silly! As if gifts are handed around equally!" He looked at her candidly. "You should keep up the glamour, too. It makes you noticeable, and lots of people won't look any closer than that."

She remembered the scarlet dress she had once worn to draw attention from her face, but she decided to ignore the comment.

"Grandfather's papers," she said. "Could they help us? Do you want me to look for them? As long as I can do it without being caught, which might be hard, now that he's at home."

"Yes, but don't take them. Hide them somewhere, so at least the police don't find them. It might be a good idea if Borrodale didn't have them, either. At least, until we are certain whose side he is on ... other than his own." He hesitated, reluctance plain in his face.

"What?" she demanded.

He said nothing.

"What?" she repeated. "You asked me to trust you because Peter does. Well, how about doing the same in return? Trust me, because Peter does. I lost my job in the Foreign Office because I had an affair with a man who used me. I'm stupid in love, but I'm not stupid otherwise."

He gave a reluctant smile. "I wouldn't like you much if you couldn't make a fool of yourself over something! We all have a weakness. It's good to know what it is. Thinking better of people than we should is a pretty common one. The opposite is worse. But only if carried to extremes." For just a moment, he looked infinitely sad. "I'm sorry you have to discover this in your own family, but it happens. It hurts like hell to find out that those you love worship a different god, one who, stripped of his robes, is hideous. Worse still, if they are of your own blood. And once you know it, you have to choose. I'm sorry if it happens to you. Really, I am." He touched her hand gently. "But yes, read his papers if you have the chance. They may tell us something. But be careful! You know some of your enemies, but not all. Loyalties can surprise us, sometimes."

She looked down at the table. "I will," she promised. "I'll be careful."

CHAPTER 17

Nothing was normal. Charles feared nothing would ever be normal again.

He did all he could to reassure Katherine, and Dorothy also, but his words were hollow, and he knew it. They were polite, as he pretended to believe it would somehow work out. Elena was trying everything she could think of, but she was out of her element. The police were treating this as an entirely grubby and violent domestic murder, and the harder they looked at it, the more it seemed Wyatt had to be guilty, for whatever reason. Charles could think of nothing that would provoke the murder, and also justify it.

Elena was insistent upon talking to her grandmother, although what she hoped to learn he had no idea. Dorothy's idea of Wyatt was tied up with love and pink ribbons of normality. Ripping it apart would destroy Dorothy without helping anything else. Surely Elena realized that?

Charles was doing nothing beyond staring at the garden when the maid interrupted him to say that Captain Miller was here to see him.

"Ask him to come in," Charles said immediately. His heart rose for a moment with the thought of something good, a turn in events. As soon as he saw Miller's face, it died.

"Good morning, Mr. Standish," Miller said politely.

"Good morning, Captain," Charles replied civilly. "Is there any news?" He knew from Miller's face that there was not, at least nothing good.

"I'm afraid I need to see Mr. Baylor again. A few new questions have arisen."

"Of course. I shall telephone Mr. Borrodale and see if he is available."

"If Mr. Baylor insists," said Miller. "But I'm perfectly happy for you to sit in, if Mr. Baylor will allow that."

"I'll go up and ask him." Charles was about to offer Miller tea or coffee, then changed his mind.

He went straight upstairs and knocked on Wyatt's door.

The answer was a rather gruff order to come in. Charles obeyed, and found Wyatt standing beside the bed, still dressed in his pajamas, with a breakfast tray on the side table. By the look of the plates, it was apparent he had finished his meal.

"What do you want?" he asked sharply.

"Captain Miller is here to see you," Charles replied. "I'll call Borrodale, if you wish, but Miller says I may sit in instead so that you have a witness."

"You're hardly impartial," Wyatt said harshly, as if his throat were aching. "At least I hope not?" His face looked haggard. The lines in it all dragged down, and he had not yet shaved. "You're family, damn it!"

"Of course I am," Charles replied, trying to sound reassuring. "Would you prefer to wash, shave, dress, and come down when you are ready?"

"I don't mean to be interviewed by a damn policeman in front of the servants! How the hell am I going to—" He paused, as if gathering his thoughts and his emotions. "Do you realize I was a U.S. senator twenty years ago? A senator! I gave it up. I wasn't beaten! I put my full time into high finance, and I'm damn good at it!"

"Yes, I know. So," asked Charles, "would you like to see him in the study downstairs? You don't want him up here, do you?"

"Of course I damn well don't!" As if hearing himself, Baylor lowered his voice. "Yes. Thank you. I'll come down when I'm ready. Will you please call Borrodale and tell him to come here? I can have you sit in until he gets here, if you'd be so good?" He took a deep breath. "But I think we should wait for Borrodale. It's good of you, Charles. I don't know if you make any difference, but it will ease Dorothy's mind, and Katherine's. And your girl's, of course. This is Elena, the flibbertigibbet one, isn't it? Not Margot."

Charles bit back a reply. "I'll go and ask Miller to wait, and then I'll call Borrodale." He worked to control his temper, reminding himself that the man was very frightened indeed, and almost certainly appallingly embarrassed.

Miller accepted the conditions agreeably enough, and Charles offered him coffee for the probable half hour or more that he would have to wait for Borrodale to come, presuming he was free to come.

Borrodale was willing enough, but he sounded irritable on the other end of the line when Charles spoke to him.

"What on earth has he got to ask now? He had the poor man in his jail cell right next door for days! All right, fine, I'll be there in half an hour. Don't let Wyatt say anything until I get there. I don't mean to insult you, but you are not a lawyer. And anyway, you don't know American law, and that's all that applies here. The crime took place on American soil, and Wyatt is an American citizen. The fact that the victim was born in Austria, if indeed she was, doesn't make any difference whatever."

Before Charles could tell him that he damn well understood all of this and a good deal more, Borrodale hung up.

"He's on his way," he told Wyatt, who was dressed by then. "He should be here in thirty minutes or so. Not in the best temper."

Wyatt did not seem upset. "He's a good man, Borrodale. Done him one or two favors in the past. He'll more than return them now."

The thought that came immediately to Charles's mind was that people who owed you favors were sometimes the last ones to help you. If the favor was big enough, they might be the first to want to get rid of you. That automatically canceled the debt. He did not say so, but he remembered that Elena had told him the lawyer was on the list of suspects Wyatt had given her. What a tangled web of distrust this was.

They went downstairs and sat in the study to wait. Charles admired a couple of the paintings that hung on the spaces between shelves of books. They were pleasant enough, not his taste, but it was better than the heavy silence that would be between them otherwise. It was a matter of taste. They could hardly argue with it. They were architectural. Charles could admire the skill, but he could not feel comfortable with them. He preferred the Dutch school, particularly of seascapes, or at least ships moored in harbor. He found great ease in the cool blues and greens, the fluid lines. Straight lines made him feel ill at ease.

Borrodale was shown in just over half an hour later. He looked weary and a little rumpled. He wore a gray suit that was not cut skillfully enough to hide his extra weight. Or perhaps it was the light color?

Captain Miller was sent for and he arrived almost instantly. Formal greetings were given and Charles sat down. Captain Miller nodded to him. Borrodale turned to Wyatt questioningly, but Wyatt made no comment, and sat down heavily, actually blocking the way Charles would have taken were he to leave.

"What have you to ask me now?" Wyatt said to Miller.

"Every one of your guests and household staff are accounted for, and by one or more other people, sir. All except you."

"You've already said that," Wyatt said wearily. "All I can do is repeat myself."

"If it wasn't one of your guests, or you either," Miller said levelly, "then that leaves only the staff, one of the police, or one of the President's security guard. Or someone who looked like one of them."

Charles swiveled around to face Miller. "You just thought of that?"

"We questioned them all that night, sir. We've only just turned up some discrepancies. Very slight, but worth investigating."

Wyatt looked from one to the other of them, his face suddenly alight. He leaned forward a little. "That must be the answer; it makes sense. No one would notice another guard in the dark outside. He'd look like any of the others." His voice grew firmer, more authoritative. "He could have arrived after the others, killed Mrs. Worth without ever coming into the house, into the light! And then gone again. If he went out of the gate, the guards there would take him for one of themselves, and they wouldn't bother to notice that he never came back. They might think he'd come in another way." He looked from Charles to Borrodale to Miller. "That's the trouble with having two different sets of people doing the same job. They cooperate, but they don't know each other! In the dark, one man in uniform looks like another."

Charles felt a wave of relief. Not total, but a deep easing of the sense of defeat and confusion within him. It was a possible answer. He looked at Borrodale and saw not the lifting of anxiety he had expected, but surprise, quickly replaced by cautious optimism.

"Look at the photographs again," Wyatt urged. "I was inside all evening. And Elena, Charles's girl, will back that up. Max, you're my attorney, try harder. My life depends on it!"

Charles felt a lurch of sympathy that startled him. He turned to Borrodale, and saw fleeting dismay in his face. Then it vanished.

"We will question all the guards again, both police and the President's security guards, and find the discrepancy," Miller replied, meeting Borrodale's gaze with a hard, cold stare of his own. "Somebody killed Lila Worth, and I mean to find out who, and see he pays for it. Your job is to do your best for your client."

Borrodale drew in his breath sharply, and let it out again. "Of course," he agreed. "I'll look at the photographs again. Captain Miller gave me copies of all of them—"

"Are you sure?" Wyatt interrupted him. "All of them? Even the ones that didn't turn out well?"

"Yes," Borrodale assured him. He turned to Miller. "That's correct, isn't it? You didn't withhold any. For any reason at all?"

Miller stared straight back at him. "Of course not, you have all of them. I need the truth, Mr. Borrodale, not just any loose connection. This is far too big a case to afford mistakes. We're talking murder, not a petty robbery or a bar brawl." He looked back at Wyatt. "I want to ask you about your actions that evening, sir: who you spent time with, who you spoke to, and when. If you can remember what you said, that may make it easier to fix your whereabouts."

"Haven't you done that already?" Borrodale demanded.

Miller remained calm, although the emotion on his face suggested it was not as easy as his words made it seem. "Yes, sir, but I'm looking for the direction your conversations took. This can make the difference to the timetable of events, fill in a few blanks."

"So, you fetch up with an impossible crime?" Borrodale snapped. "Very clever! What will you do then? Say it cannot have happened?"

Elena spent the morning at home. She took a breakfast tray up to Dorothy and sat with her, asking about her memories, trying to gain an idea of what Wyatt had been like as a young man. Dorothy's face lit with happiness at some of the memories: the first meeting, their early dates together. Elena had to adjust her ideas radically: the world had changed beyond recognition since the war. Women now held all kinds of jobs, in many ways that were equal to men. They sat on juries, they voted in parliamentary elections. Sixty years ago was 1874! In England, it was the reign of Queen Victoria, before the wit of Oscar Wilde lit up the literary world or Jack the Ripper terrorized the East End of London. Before the Naughty Nineties, the

Paris Exhibition, the turn of the century, and the sinking of the *Titanic*, and with a new king on the throne, the passing of an age. The darkening shadow of the war stretching across Europe, the Spanish flu decimating populations, the Wall Street crash, the Great Depression, and now the rise of Hitler and the Nazis in Germany.

"Tell me more," Elena said earnestly. "This is fascinating." And it was, not only a glimpse of another world, but a glimpse into Dorothy's life, what she remembered, what she cared about, and above all, what she believed . . . and why.

In less than two hours, Elena's views changed absolutely, although the present was still the same: Lila Worth had still been killed. She, too, had cared passionately about the world she knew, and the people.

"Thank you, Grandmother," Elena said sincerely. "That alone was worth coming all the way across the Atlantic to hear. You've given me another side of myself I didn't know about. And of my mother, our heritage." She leaned across and kissed her grandmother on the cheek.

After leaving Dorothy, Elena went straight to her own room and changed from her casual dress of soft linen into a navy silk with a white collar. It had been expensive, but it was of such an excellent cut and simple, heavy silk that it always looked casually elegant. Even Margot would have approved.

Elena knew what she meant to do, and if she was right in both her memory and her assumptions, it was risky, but there was no more time left to play for caution or safety. She had ascertained from Dorothy what were Mabel Cartwright's favorite cakes and biscuits, and she had obtained several of them from Cook, and placed them in a gift box, explaining that Mrs. Cartwright had been generous and loyal to Grandmother, and this was a gracious way of thanking her.

Cook understood completely, acknowledging that flowers were

easier, but no doubt Mrs. Cartwright had plenty of them in her own garden. Something to eat was a far more memorable gift.

The chauffeur had the Cartwrights' address, so there was no need for Elena to look it up in her grandmother's address book. She slipped out without conferring with anyone. This was definitely better done alone.

The drive was not long, and was extremely pleasant. Elena spent it planning and re-planning what she was going to say. They arrived and the chauffeur dropped her at the front door, waited until the door was opened, she spoke to the maid, and then signaled him and went inside. He drove to park the car within sight of the house, but remained within call for when she was ready to leave.

Mabel Cartwright received her in a pleasant sitting room facing the sun and opening onto a tiny lawn, surrounded by flowerbeds. It was very nearly as nice as Dorothy's sitting room. The only noticeable difference was the lack of imagination in the use of color.

Elena glanced at it once, appreciatively and with a smile, then gave all her attention to Mabel Cartwright. "I hope you don't mind my calling?" she said apologetically, offering the brightly wrapped little cakes that Cook had made for her. "This is such a stressful time. I wanted both to thank you for your loyalty to my grandparents and, I'm afraid, to ask your advice. I'm not sure whom else to trust . . ." She stopped, as if there were much more to say, but she dared not say it without encouragement.

"Oh, my dear," Mabel said warmly. "It must be such a shock to you! You cannot possibly be expected to know what to do. Come, sit down." She indicated a large and very comfortable armchair, and Elena obeyed. Mabel sat opposite her, having taken the cakes and masterfully opened the box. "My favorite!" she said with evident pleasure. "How thoughtful of you, especially in the circumstances."

Elena smiled and gave a small gesture of her hand to both accept the cakes and dismiss the kindness as natural.

"How is poor Dorothy?" Mabel said solicitously.

Elena shook her head very slightly. "I'm afraid she's just beginning to realize how serious it is, and that . . . that it's really happening. You know how it is: at first you think it's a bad dream, and you will wake up . . . and after a day or two you slowly realize you aren't going to. It's real, and there is no escape." She looked at Mabel and allowed the fear to show in her eyes. She had learned from Peter to always use a true emotion; people can tell the difference, even if it's attributed to a different cause.

"You poor girl," Mabel said warmly. "It must be terrible for you. It is for us, who are merely his friends. Although we have known him it seems like all our lives."

"That's what Grandmother said. Then you know he could not have done this awful thing! No matter what Lila Worth was like— Grandfather might have deplored her, disagreed with her over everything that mattered, and he had invited her to that party only because of her husband—that's a whole world away from . . ." She stopped, as if she could not bring herself to say the words.

"Of course it is," Mabel agreed. "Wyatt is far too . . . civilized . . . to do anything remotely like . . . killing her. No matter what she said or did . . . or what she stood for."

"What? What did she stand for?"

"Did you not speak to her? I saw you with her several times."

"Oh, we spoke of fashion mostly. You know, what a gorgeous gown someone was wearing, and that she should never wear that color. That sort of thing. Just a way of making a connection. I never saw her before that night." She felt a prickle of tears in her eyes and blinked quickly. "It was all so sudden . . . and so senseless."

Mabel reached out and patted Elena's arm. "I know, my dear. Clearly, she was far more than showed on the surface. I dare say you have never had occasion to meet a woman like her before."

The remark, as Elena thought Mabel meant it, was quite untrue. She had photographed many very beautiful women, and she had known other exotic and dangerous women, but not really one that haunted her as Lila did. "No," she said, modestly lowering her eyes.

"Somebody killed her, and pretty horribly." She looked up at Mabel. "Who do you think it was?"

For an instant, Mabel looked startled, caught off balance.

Elena felt a second of warning. "I'm sorry. Of course you haven't any idea or you would have told the police. We are desperate. I don't think any of us knows whom to turn to. I heard you and Grandmother speak of the society you support. Free America? Do you know them? Would they help? Have they got any power or just . . . wishes?" She looked at Mabel earnestly.

Mabel hesitated.

Had Elena been too precipitate? She looked down again. "It's just that you have been so kind, and I know that my grandmother trusts you." Was she overdoing it? Stop and wait. Allow Mabel to make the next move.

"Your grandfather is greatly respected, even admired," Mabel began.

"Do these Free America people know him?" Elena asked. "If they do, then they know he couldn't possibly have done anything so . . . so vile and stupid as to murder Lila, whoever she is, and in his own driveway!"

"Yes, of course," Mabel agreed. She could hardly say anything less.

"If you ask them," Elena began. "Or perhaps I could, if you would rather—"

"No! Of course I will ask. Or Mr. Cartwright will do so, if I ask him. We will do everything we can. But we cannot draw the President in. I'm sure you understand that."

"Of course! And I was with my grandfather most of the later evening," Elena went on, "so I know he must be innocent. But he is my grandfather, so nobody is going to listen to me."

Mabel blinked. "Did . . . did you tell that to the police?"

Elena looked back at her. The woman's face was unreadable. Was she pleased, angry, hopeful? Her expression conveyed only that she was thinking rapidly . . . and hard. If she stared any longer, it would be an open challenge between them. Elena swallowed hard and lowered her eyes.

Mabel spoke softly. "Whoever killed her, it might have had nothing to do with her affairs, real or imagined."

Elena raised her eyes. "What then? Do you . . . ?" She stopped.

Mabel hesitated only a second, and then leaned forward confidentially. "Lila was Austrian, you know."

"Yes, someone mentioned it. It may have been Grandmother."

"And her husband is a very important scientist," Mabel went on, looking steadily at Elena.

Should Elena acknowledge that she understood all that she meant, or almost all? Would she be overplaying her hand if she pretended not to know? *Be careful.* "She said he was a scientist," she began.

"Very important," Mabel repeated, and then closed her lips tightly for a moment. "And that may be the reason she was killed." Her eyes were bright and unblinking.

Elena took a chance, deciding that not asking would be more revealing. "Was she working for the Germans?"

"Who knows?" Mabel replied. "And, of course, it's not only what she may actually have been doing, but what was suspected of her, perhaps wrongly."

"Oh, yes. That's quite different." Elena tried to look innocent and shocked. She did not need to ask if Mabel believed that. That was why she had mentioned it. Elena had to take it that this was a test of her response. "I never thought of that. If she was a spy, then surely that was why she was killed." Another thing flashed through her mind. Should she say it? Would she be too careful if she did not, and awake Mabel's suspicions? Or not clever enough, if she did not? "That opens up a lot of questions," she said slowly.

"Yes, it does," Mabel agreed. "Be very careful, my dear. You are young, and if I may say so, a little unsophisticated. We will look after your grandfather. He is far, far cleverer than you appreciate. It was most thoughtful of you to bring me the cakes. I thank you for them.

In return, I warn you to keep yourself safe. Look after your mother, and your grandmother. That would be the kindest and most important thing you could do."

Elena lowered her eyes again. She must not let Mabel see into her mind. "Thank you," she murmured.

Soon they had tea, and the cakes Cook had sent, even though it was only midmorning. Half an hour later, Elena left.

It was early evening, and Elena was on her way downstairs when she saw Allenby at the bottom of the stairs. He was watching her. She felt a sudden chill. She increased her speed and almost ran into him as he started up to meet her.

"What's happened?" she said without preamble.

"I need to talk to you," he answered, his voice just above a whisper.

"What? Is it something to do with Grandfather?"

He took her arm and held it tightly enough that she had no choice but to follow him into the main hall. Should she tell him about her visit to Mabel? What did it amount to anyway? She was still turning that over when he spoke.

"It's all to do with him," he answered, "but I don't know whether that's accidental or on purpose." When she said nothing, he rushed ahead. "I still don't know whether he was the intended victim, or if it really was Lila and he's just a convenient scapegoat. The police have got to arrest somebody, and the easiest explanation—the one everybody wants, except Harmon—is that it's Wyatt's fault. He was having an affair with her and got tired of it, or she was blackmailing him, so he had to get rid of her."

She was momentarily confused. "Who does that help? And that's blaming him, anyway, and not her."

"Listen!" he said with increasing sharpness, now leading the way across the hall to the front door, and then out into the sun. "If you want to get rid of a really good spy who's on your tail, quickly and completely, obviously without getting caught yourself, or having that person suspected of being a spy, what would you do?"

Her mind raced. It made a kind of horrible sense. "Kill her, but frame somebody else to make it look like a crime of passion," she replied. "If that were at all believable. Or failing that, a crime of greed. It doesn't matter what anyone thinks of either of them, as long as it's not the truth."

Allenby nodded. "Exactly. Do you think she really was having an affair with him? And just for a moment, think rationally, not as his granddaughter."

"Why would a woman like Lila have an affair with anybody's grandfather?" she asked. Having listened to Dorothy talk about their courtship, and the early days of their marriage, it was even more offensive. But was he still the same man he had been then? Did age make all that much difference? No, not age: time. She had seen him through Dorothy's eyes. Then a totally different picture through Mabel's. But through her own eyes, she saw his true beliefs, and she found them not just offensive, but ugly and dangerous. Not only to her, but to so many of her generation. Age had not mellowed him; it had done the opposite. He was roughly the same age as Lucas, but they were worlds apart. "Maybe we see what we expect to," she said slowly. "Or what we want to?"

"Or what other people want us to," Allenby amended.

"Then who was she working for?" she asked. "The Americans, the Germans, or the British?"

"That's what I was speaking to Peter about."

"Peter? When? Not since this morning. It's the middle of the night in London."

"Midnight, to be exact. That's not so late."

"It's darned late to be at the Foreign Office!" she retorted.

"I have his home number. We spoke an hour ago."

"It's late to be calling someone at home. What's Pamela going to think?" She could feel the knot tightening inside her. They were standing on the pale stone steps in the sun, arguing about things that did not matter at all, and something serious, perhaps disastrous, was hanging over them. "What did he say?" she demanded.

"I'll tell you over dinner."

"Tell me now!" She did not raise her voice. At least she had sense enough not to do that, but her tone was sharp, as if she was on the edge of losing her temper.

"Tell your father you're going out to dinner," he replied. There was authority in his voice and she recognized it with slight surprise. She turned away and walked to the sitting room where her father was reading. Katherine was not there.

Charles looked up.

"I'm going out to dinner," she told him. "I don't know when I'll be back. It's important."

He frowned. "Elena—"

"It's important," she said quickly, this time with more emphasis.

He started to say something, then changed his mind. "Enjoy it," he said instead.

When she was seated in Allenby's car and they were moving, she turned to him. She could see only his profile, but even from that she could judge the gravity inside him. There was not even the hint of a smile. All humor was drained from his face.

"What happened?" she asked.

"Harmon Worth is far more important as a scientist than I thought," he replied, his eyes concentrated on the road. "If they can harness the energy from splitting the atom, it will be one of the greatest boons to mankind. But being the shortsighted, greedy, power-crazy creatures we are, it could also be pretty much the end of life on earth. No halfway: it would give total victory in war to whoever harnessed it first. It would be more than a bomb, it would create radioactive fallout over God knows how much land, perhaps an entire continent. Not a victory worth having, but we'll only know that when it's too late to stop it."

She thought for several moments about what he had said. They came out of the shade of the copse of trees into the sunlight. "Can we stop it?" she asked. "Or, more realistically, can we be the first to have it?"

"That depends on a lot of things," Allenby answered. "One of them is which side Harmon Worth is on. And, of course, which side Lila was on. And, I suppose, who killed her and why. There are several possibilities."

"What are we going to do?" she asked.

"There's nothing we can do about Lila. We have to decide whom we're going to trust."

"Not Wyatt," she began. "At least, not yet."

He turned briefly toward her. "Something new?"

Should she tell him? "Just . . . we need to know more about him," she replied. "I had breakfast with Grandmother. She talked to me a long time, about the past, how they met. All that sort of thing. It sounded lovely, almost innocent, like another world. Was there ever sixty years in which the world changed so much? People can't always change as well, so quickly. We miss our youth, I suppose. Grandmother wants to keep some of those memories. If I had some of them, I'd want to keep them, too."

He smiled very slightly. "With marriage to Wyatt?"

"No," she answered immediately. "Perhaps he's changed. Maybe he once was as she remembers him."

"Or he was never entirely like that? We show only what we think is our best side to those we are in love with," he pointed out.

"She's known him sixty years!" she protested.

"Has she?" The question was not harsh, rather it was gentle, and sad. "Perhaps he cared enough to make sure that she saw only the best in him. We all do that, if we can."

"I don't want only the best of someone," she said immediately. "I want some of the other sides, not to intrude into memory, but at least some of the regrets, the vulnerabilities. They'd know that of me, because I wouldn't be able to hide it. And if I loved them, I'd want them to know the real me, not the sanitized version." He was smiling. She felt self-conscious. "Wouldn't you?" she challenged. "If they didn't, would you wonder if they loved you at all, really? Or just what they imagined you were? That's not—" She stopped. Why was she telling him this?

"If I were in love, I don't know," he answered. "But if I loved them, not fairy-tale stuff, but real, yes, I'd want honesty. But you have to leave some privacy as well."

She needed to change the subject. This was too much truth. She certainly did not want him to know about the worst of her mistakes, what a complete fool she had been about Aiden Strother. He would despise her. "By the way, I went to visit Mabel Cartwright this morning."

He stiffened. "Why? You have to be careful."

"To learn about Free America, of course. I'm sure she knows quite a lot about it. She pretty well told me to keep out of it, that they would look after Grandfather."

He was silent for several moments, long enough for her to find her muscles tightening with tension. Finally, he spoke. "Be careful, Elena. She may be a lot cleverer, and more dangerous, than we think."

"I am careful," she answered firmly, remembering the chill she felt as she left the Cartwright house. "Who else do you need to consider, either to help us or to hurt us?" she asked.

"Harmon," Allenby answered quickly.

"But he might be—You just pointed out that he could be on either side."

"I know, but what else can we do without deciding to trust him? It's a matter of degree. Do we try to use him, without complete trust? Or trust him and hope that he loved Lila, and that he is worthy of the clearance the government gave him?"

She looked at Allenby, but he was watching the road. "Can we get anywhere without trusting him?" she asked.

"Is that what you want to do?"

She could not read the expression in his voice. "I'm not asking about what I want," she replied levelly, as devoid of emotion as she could manage. "I don't think we can get anywhere without trusting him. Who else is there we could ask? Miller won't help us, and I presume he doesn't know anything about the scientific side of it, and we certainly can't tell him. My father? There's nothing he can do. Peter is too far away. There's nobody at the embassy, or you would have mentioned them."

"That's right," he agreed. "But there is a risk. Worth might have killed Lila himself. If he did, he won't hesitate to kill either of us, or both. It will probably be something tidy, like a car crash, from which neither of us will walk away."

She liked Harmon Worth, and she believed he felt real horror and grief at Lila's death. But he could be a German or Austrian sympathizer, and still feel this. Loyalty was a complicated emotion. Family loyalty was powerful. She felt such a deep empathy and liking for Grandmother Dorothy, who had shared her memories and her love, and now it was all threatened. Not only the present and the future, but all the precious days of the past as well. She did not know, beyond doubt, what she would do to protect them, if they could not clear Wyatt.

"There's always the alternative of doing nothing," she said. "Just let Wyatt be executed. We'll all go home at the end of the visit. And maybe my mother will stay and see that Dorothy is all right. For as long as possible. And we can spend the rest of our lives trying to justify why we sat and watched and did nothing."

He gave a slow, strangely sweet smile. "I thought you'd say that."

"Where are we going for dinner?"

"We'll skip dinner. We are going to visit Harmon Worth."

"Whether I come or not! You arrogant, jumped-up . . ." She was lost for the right word.

"Not arrogant," he answered. "I have faith in you. Peter said you took chances, made mistakes, but you never ran away. Or maybe it was Lucas who said it."

"You called Lucas!"

He did not answer, just kept smiling.

Elena was dreading arriving at Harmon Worth's house. It was difficult enough to spend time with Dorothy, but there was at least hope that her husband would come out of this vindicated, perhaps deeply shaken, but alive and maybe even chastened, grateful for his escape, and for the loyalty of his family. Lila was dead. That was final. Nothing would change or redeem that.

Allenby remained silent as they got out of the car and closed the doors. There was no need for words. She knew that he was touched indelibly by the memory of a woman whom they had both liked intensely, and who had been so very alone.

Harmon Worth answered the door himself. Perhaps whatever domestic help he had was gone for the day. He looked exhausted. His skin was drained of color. His hair was dull and tangled. And his shirt was creased.

Elena's heart sank. She ached with pity for him. She had no idea what to say. There was nothing that made any sense. No comfort to offer.

Allenby stepped forward. "We need your help, Harmon. I know it's a bad time, but it can't wait."

"I'm glad you came," Harmon said immediately, stepping back to allow them to enter the house. "I've been looking through Lila's papers and trying to make sense of it. I don't know if I ever will, but I have to try. I want to know what really happened and why. Why Lila? She wasn't having an affair with Wyatt Baylor, for God's sake! There's no reason for it. If . . . no, it doesn't make any sense!" There was desperation in his voice, in his face, the helpless gesture of his hands.

"I agree," Allenby said quickly, walking past him and into the sitting room, gesturing Elena to come as well.

"I've been thinking, perhaps a little chaotically," Worth went on. "I find it difficult to concentrate. I keep expecting to hear her footsteps, her voice." He controlled himself with a visible effort.

Elena felt a twisting wrench of pity inside her. She understood how you could temporarily forget grief, and then remember it again with a wave of pain. You could hear their voices, and remember, and then realize you would never see them again. She thought how we don't treasure things enough while we have them.

"What have you thought?" she asked quickly, before the moment became too painful.

"Lila was a spy, you know that?" Worth glanced at Allenby first, then at Elena. "I'm sure that was why she was killed. You're surprised I know? Or even that that was why she married me? I know that too, but I loved her. And I think she came to love me. Of course, I'm working on nuclear fission, with the possibility of a bomb someday. And that was what brought us together. She understood a lot of it, you know? And that was why she was brilliant." He looked from one of them to the other; neither of them was arguing the issue. "She was on the point of finding out where the information was leaking from, and through whom."

Allenby was tense, his body rigid as he watched Harmon's face.

"She was going to meet someone tomorrow evening," Harmon continued, "and get new information that would lead us to who is the main avenue for this leak."

There was a moment of silence, then Elena spoke. "Do you know what it was? Who? Can you still meet with him, in her place?"

He looked at Elena. "No, but you could."

"I don't look anything like Lila! But more importantly, I don't know anything about atoms."

"They only know that she's beautiful and speaks German. You're beautiful, and didn't you say at the party that you spent some time in Germany?" The brief hope was fading in his eyes, even from his voice.

"Thank you," she said hastily. "You are kind." From him that was an extraordinary compliment that she should even be spoken of in the same breath as Lila. "But it is more generous than true. I suppose beauty might be a matter of opinion. As for my German, it isn't bad. I lived there for a while."

"Does Elena need to know the mathematics?" Allenby interrupted.

"No, she doesn't. It's pretty advanced. But the Germans, of course—"

"She speaks German well enough to pass for one, as long as you don't specify the area," Allenby said.

Worth smiled. "I'll make the contact; I have Lila's information." He excused himself and went out into the hall. They heard him pick up the telephone.

Elena turned to Allenby. "You have no idea whether I speak German or not!" she said sharply. This was getting out of control.

"We have mutual friends who say you can. Several of them, actually," he replied.

"We don't have several mutual friends at all!"

"Peter, Lucas, your father," he said. "What you mean is that it is dangerous, and you'd rather not take a chance. Lila was killed, almost certainly because of this, and you don't want to run that risk."

A wave of anger almost engulfed her. "I don't mean that at all!" she said furiously. "I mean that I don't know what Lila planned to do, so I can't do it. Nobody would mistake me for her, and I don't know anything at all about nuclear fission."

"And you might get killed," Allenby added.

"And I might blow the case wide open!" she snapped.

The telephone clicked in the hall and Worth returned.

Allenby turned to him. "I'm sorry, I can't order her to go as Lila. It's dangerous."

Worth controlled his emotions with difficulty. "Not as Lila. She had a code name, it was Guinevere. But, of course, there's danger." He moved his gaze from Allenby to Elena. "I'm sorry. I shouldn't have tried to—"

"What do they know about Lila . . . Guinevere?" she asked, cutting him off.

"Only her name," he replied. "And that she's beautiful. But not whether she was dark or fair, tall or short, not anything else except that she was intelligent. They know she was extraordinarily intelligent. So, you will do it?"

Elena shut her eyes. She knew this was a mistake, but she could not walk away. "Yes, but you must give me all the help you can."

Harmon appeared to be choking, and then his voice came out in a whisper. "Thank you."

She was relieved that Allenby had the sense to keep silent.

As they drove away, Elena turned to Allenby. "Now we know that Harmon Worth is innocent."

When he nodded, she leaned back and closed her eyes.

18

Elena had not told anyone about the plan. She had come home that evening, as if her excursion with Allenby had been merely a pleasant dinner. She had said good night to Allenby, catching his eye for just a moment longer than usual, then stepped out of the car, without waiting for him to come round to open the door for her. She did not glance back until she heard the engine revving up and the crunch of the wheels on the gravel. And even so, it was only for a moment. Then he was gone and the decision was irrevocable.

No, it was not. She could telephone him later in the evening, or even tomorrow, and say she was afraid to go through with it.

The door was opened by the maid and she thanked her and went inside. Katherine and Charles were in the sitting room. They looked up, Katherine with a slight irritation, Charles with a question on his face.

She longed to be able to tell him, but he would be terrified. He might forbid her to go. Katherine would not even try to understand, and more than that, she might think Elena was lying.

"Did you have a nice dinner?" Katherine asked. Her tone of voice gave no hint as to how she felt about it.

"Very pleasant, thank you. I . . ." She had no idea if they had eaten at all.

Katherine was staring at her.

"We went to see Harmon Worth. People tend to ignore the bereaved, because they don't know what to say." She came in and closed the door behind her. She sat in one of the big armchairs.

Katherine looked puzzled. "Do you?"

"No, not really. Just . . . I didn't want him to think I had ignored Lila, as if she had never been. He looks dreadful. I think some people are exercising great cruelty in their opinion of her, as if pretending she somehow deserved it."

Katherine started to argue, then suddenly stopped. "I'm sorry, that's terrible. I must admit to thinking it, but thank God I didn't say so to anyone, least of all to Harmon."

Elena smiled very slightly. "You wouldn't be so cruel. Whatever you thought of her. If you don't mind, I'll go to bed early. I've got a lot to think about."

"Captain Allenby?" Katherine's eyebrows were raised and there was a slight edge to her voice.

Elena smiled. "No, Mother. Right now, my mind is taken up by Grandfather Wyatt."

Charles looked up sharply.

"No, Father." Elena replied to the question she knew was in his mind. Was Allenby a romantic interest now, of all times, or was he helping her reach for the truth about Wyatt? Whichever it was, she could not afford to tell him the whole truth. It was her sworn oath not to. And anyway, he would consider it his duty to try to stop her, and she couldn't afford that, either. But it would be nice. What an easy way out: *I couldn't come. My father prevented me.*

"Good night," she said with another smile, and went out, closing the door after her.

* * *

She spent the following morning with Dorothy, listening to more memories of the past, people they had known and some of the accomplishments Wyatt had achieved, and how hard he had worked, how wrong anyone was to suspect him. It helped to stiffen her resolve, and banish the fear from her mind that she was risking so much to save someone who, a month ago, even two weeks ago, she could hardly picture in her mind.

At four o'clock that afternoon, Allenby picked her up. Katherine raised her eyebrows, drew in breath to comment, then looked at Elena's face and said simply, "Have a nice evening."

Elena got into Allenby's car and they drove out into the road and then away from the city. He looked at her grimly. "Watch the road," she instructed him.

"Are you all right?" he asked. "I rather pushed you into this. I'm sorry. It's just that there's no one else who can do it. If we don't find the line of connection, exactly who is leaking this information, and how, it will never stop. And you know—"

"Yes, I do," she interrupted. She tried to smile, but it was more of a grimace. "If we don't trace the leak, information will continue to go from here to Germany, until they know as much as we do. I understand. Lila did three-quarters of the job, then was killed. We have to do the last quarter."

"If you want to—"

"Stop now?" she cut him off. "I know that, too, you already told me I can. As long as I don't make any serious mistakes, I'll be all right. And I can come out at any time. You won't blame me for it. We're not in this to avenge Lila, but simply to finish her job, and stop the leak. You told me all that last night. And anyway, I can see it for myself."

"I know you can," he answered quietly.

"Have you got a better idea?" It was said like a challenge, but it was really a hope. She was not at all certain she could carry this off. She knew both Allenby and Harmon Worth would be there, in the restaurant, where she would meet the man Lila had arranged to see, but she was still afraid. Was Lila ever afraid? Elena would like to think that Lila was just as human. Had she been killed by someone she knew was a spy? Had she thought that, at least at Wyatt and Dorothy's home, she would be safe?

Allenby was answering her. "No. If I had another idea at all, I would have used it instead."

She did not reply to that. It gave her no comfort. What did give her comfort was knowing that the press had written about a death without mentioning Lila's name.

They pulled up a discreet distance from Harmon Worth's house and walked the last hundred yards. He must have been watching for them, because he opened the front door before they could knock.

"Come in," he said quietly. "I've got everything ready. Several dresses for you to choose from. I'm afraid you can't carry a weapon. They'd take it."

"Knives—" Allenby started.

"She never carried one," Worth finished. "At least, hardly ever. And, in any of these dresses, it would be visible."

"You knew all about her?" Elena asked, a little surprised.

"Not at first," he answered, leading them into the sitting room. "But I put it together fairly soon. She had an excellent education. She had to use it for something. And she cared passionately about politics. She hated the Nazis. She didn't want Austria to have anything to do with them."

"We know," Allenby said quickly. "Elena understands how important this is. That's why she's prepared to take the risk. What did your wife tell you about this man?"

"Not much," Worth replied. "The name he will use is Weissmann." He pronounced it *Veissmann*, the German way. "He sounds American, unless you listen very carefully indeed. But German is his first language. You will—"

"Will he expect me to speak German?"

"He might. Lila was German-speaking, and he knew that. There are many things you will have to judge for yourself. But try not to appear nervous. Lila never did. She took risks. She . . . cared so much." His voice was hoarse with emotion, and he took a moment or two to regain his self-control. And he did not lose it again as he described what he had learned from Lila's notes. He understood what her code words meant to her.

"Did she know you understood?" Elena asked.

"She may have guessed," said Harmon Worth. "Sometimes, when you trust someone and work with them well, a lot of things are understood, but never said."

Allenby spread out a sheet of paper and drew Elena's attention to it. "This is a plan of the clubhouse. Study it, in case you need to know. Put the picture of it in your mind. This," he said, producing a short list of notes, "is all Lila knew about the man we're calling Weissmann. Better you don't attempt to guess than make a mistake. The idea is that you give him these notes." He indicated the envelope next to a silver evening bag. "They are scientific calculations. You don't need to understand them, only to know that you took them from Harmon, and they are the latest on his work in nuclear fission. These are copies."

"Actually," said Worth, "they are almost accurate, so they won't know the difference until they try the experiment. Then they will realize they are false, deliberately so."

Allenby was watching Elena closely. "That's the point of it. They will realize that someone in their chain of informants is cheating them, lying to them. They will trace it back, and we will be watching. That's how we'll know who is in the chain. We've tried to trace it from their end before and failed. This should make them follow it themselves, which gives us a far better chance of tracing. They'll go more slowly, trying to find the leak."

She looked at the building she was going to. And then, on a separate sheet, the notes she must memorize.

She said nothing, staring at the page until it blurred in front of her.

Harmon Worth touched her arm gently. "It's time you get changed. Choose a dress."

"Which one would Lila have worn?" she asked, getting to her feet slowly.

"It doesn't matter," Allenby said before Worth could reply. "Choose the one you want. The one you feel fabulous in."

She gave him a black look.

He smiled. "The most outrageous . . . and daring!"

"Go to hell!" she said so softly that she assumed he had not heard.

Elena and Allenby went into the spare bedroom, where three dresses were laid out on the bed. Elena was grateful for that. She did not want to try them on in Lila's bedroom, the one she would have shared with her husband. She was not Lila; she never could be.

The first dress was a light red, scarlet rather than crimson. It should suit her coloring very well, but she could see at a glance that it was very low cut at the front. It would have been daring and elegant on Lila, but bordering on the vulgar on Elena.

The second was black, but cut like the gown Lila had worn to the party. She would not wear that. It would be emotionally choking, as if she were thinking in her own mind that Lila was replaceable.

The last one was completely different. It was white silk, very plain, a clinging body with no ornamentation on it at all. No sleeves, and a skirt that would move beautifully when she walked. She would have to walk well, head high, shoulders squared. Still, it was very plain, and there was no jewelry to relieve it that she could see.

"That's the one," Allenby said quietly, but she knew he intended it as instruction.

"Too plain," she said. "It's absolutely unforgiving."

"You don't need forgiving," he replied. "Try it."

"I'd rather—"

"Try it," he insisted, commandment in his voice.

He was insufferably bossy and she wanted to fight with him, but not now. She snatched the dress up and took it to the next room, where she could try it on. It would have to fit. There was no latitude in the design.

She put it on and had difficulty, turning herself into contortions until she got the zip fastened at the back. She must not behave like a spoiled child. They were all three of them frightened. And Harmon Worth must be grieving almost unbearably, except that he had to bear it. The first thing, the only thing, he could do for Lila was to complete her work.

Elena straightened herself up, pulled at the dress to smooth it down, and then walked into the room where the men awaited her.

Harmon Worth was holding out the black wrap that had been lying next to the white dress. Only it was not a wrap, it was a complete overdress of fine black net, with long sleeves and a high neck, except at the front. She slipped it on easily over the white silk, and it fell with elegance all the way to the floor. Was it black, or darkest midnight blue? She was not sure, but it was the most beautiful gown she had ever seen, and it complemented her fair skin and pale hair perfectly. She let out her breath in a wordless sigh.

"She would have been proud of you," Worth said, before his voice choked off.

"Now go and do what she would have done," Allenby added. "You can. You can do anything you want to."

She did not argue. There was no point: he was not going to change his mind, and she knew it.

Allenby and Harmon dropped Elena off at the parking lot of the restaurant and then followed her in. She knew they would, but she affected not to have seen them. She was on her own as she went in through the door and told the receptionist that she was Guinevere, and she was expected by Mr. Weissmann.

"Yes, madame, of course," the young woman replied. "Mr. Weissmann mentioned that he expected you. If you will follow me . . ." It seemed an instruction more than an invitation. Elena decided right then to set the tone of the evening. She walked after the woman, but at her own pace, graceful, head high. The young woman realized she was alone and was obliged to return for her.

Elena saw a man watching her as she moved toward him. He rose to his feet as she reached his table. He was a little above average height, immaculately dressed. His hair was silver at the temples, but otherwise dark, almost black. He was clean shaven, cheekbones showing above strong jaws. It was a hard, clever face. "Good evening, Guinevere." He used her code name as easily as if they were well acquainted.

"Good evening, Mr. Weissmann." She had decided not to imitate Lila's barely discernible Austrian accent. It would be enough to concentrate on the substance of what she was saying, without trying to make sure she did not make a mistake with the accent. Even one error could be fatal.

"Please, sit down, and tell me what you would like to eat."

The waiter pulled out her chair and she thanked him automatically, keeping her eyes on Weissmann. She accepted the menu, remembering that Lila had said she liked fish. She ordered a simple dish, a grilled Dover sole. The waiter suggested wine, and she accepted a mid-priced German white wine. One glass was all she would drink, and possibly not all of that.

Weissmann ordered steak, and an expensive burgundy. "Tell me, do you miss Vienna?" he asked, when the waiter had gone. "It's one of the world's most beautiful cities."

"It used to be," she replied with a rueful, slight grimace. "It is too full of unhappy memories to be so now. At least to me."

"But surely it is rebuilding? And Chancellor Dollfuss cannot remain much longer." He looked at her curiously. Was he testing her?

She knew that Lila had not been back for several years. She had mentioned that in the brief conversation they had had at the anniversary party. It seemed impossible they had met only once! They had learned so much of each other's emotions, memories, impressions. And she had listened hard to Harmon Worth for background information. And, of course, she had with her the envelope she was supposed to give Weissmann. But only after she had learned as much as possible from him. Above all, he must trust her and carry that information onward. That was the whole purpose of this risk.

He was watching her now, almost hungrily. Had she overdone the dress, the hair, the makeup? But then Lila had been truly beautiful, effortlessly so. To be ordinary would have given her away instantly. A woman might change her hair color or even wear a wig, but Lila's kind of beauty would have shown through any disguise. It had a radiance, a grace, a sense of character that could never be concealed.

She smiled at Weissmann slowly, as if thinking back on something hauntingly beautiful. Actually, she had Paris in mind. "I loved it as I remember it," she said quietly. "And that is far back, when I was very young and in love. Then, it was a city of dreams. I prefer to leave it that way, rather than think of war, rebuilding, revived industry, trains that run on time."

"With your husband?"

"Oh, no! Long before that. When I was too young to think of any reality. That is the way to remember a city you love."

"Were you as beautiful then as you are now?" he asked.

She had no idea whether he was joking or not, and for a moment she was robbed of words. She must think quickly. The evening would not be very long. She had to give him the information from Harmon Worth, and between now and then she had to learn all she could about the chain of information from Lila back to Germany. If she could in any way vindicate her grandfather, that would be good—it would be better than good—but it dwindled to an afterthought compared with the seriousness of the secrets of atomic energy passing from Britain and America and ending up in the hands of Germany's scientists, and for them to have that final, immeasurable power of destruction. She remembered the faces of the students dancing around the fires as they burned the books, the ideas and dreams of Western civilization in a bonfire. There was no point at which reason, or beauty, would stop such people from burning up the world.

"I didn't think I was beautiful so long ago," she said. "But then, I don't think so now. But if I had any grace, I would simply say thank you, as if it were a nice compliment, but not one to be taken seriously."

"A well-thought-out and modest reply," he observed. "You are not at all what I expected, Guinevere. Not in any way."

"Good," she said without a smile. "I hate always to be anticipated. Surprise is essential to interest, don't you think?"

"Yes, I suppose it is," he said with a slight shrug. He had been caught on the wrong foot.

The food arrived and for a little while they ate. It was delicious, but her mind was not on it, and she thought Weissmann's was not, either.

"Tell me about yourself," he said, when he was a little more than halfway through his steak. "Interest looks for answers."

So does suspicion, she thought. She smiled at him. "My mother always taught me that a man asked such questions to be polite. The answers are seldom worthy of it, and a lady does not discuss certain subjects, such as politics, religion, or too much about herself."

"But I find you interesting," he protested.

"Thank you." She looked straight into his eyes. "Then let me know what is interesting about you. What do you know that I might understand? I imagine there is much that is secret, or beyond my knowledge, but what is the most important to you, your greatest achievement?"

Clearly, that took him completely by surprise. "Most young women are tired of men who boast, and would far rather talk of themselves." There was a touch of defensiveness in his voice, but his facial expression never moved at all.

"I'm not most young women. Then let us talk about interesting people you know."

"For example?" he asked.

This was the time she must say the right thing, or he would be suspicious. And she must not break his belief that she was Lila—code-named Guinevere—and the only connection to the information he sought.

"People with intelligence," she answered. "Power you would not expect."

His attention was instant, there in the slightly stiffer posture, the sharpened gaze. "Power interests you?" he asked.

"Doesn't it interest everybody?" she asked innocently.

"Examples?" He was being careful now.

But she had no time to back off. "Herr Goebbels. He is very clever, and I think he has far more power than he looks to have. And in England, I would watch Winston Churchill." That was a risk, and she knew it.

"Indeed?" Weissmann said slowly. "He is out of power, and hasn't the nerve to reach for it. He's finished. Or do you know something that I do not?"

She smiled and looked down at her plate. "Probably lots of things, but none of them about Mr. Churchill. I fear you are correct; I just hope not." She looked up again and met his eyes. "What about Wyatt Baylor, who is a new adviser to President Roosevelt? Money is always power, in the right hands. Do you think he has more power than we guess?"

There was a moment of heavy silence, almost as if everyone else had stopped talking, except that they had not. The chatter only moved further away in her mind; words became indistinguishable. Suddenly, she thought of water trickling through stones, as the tide rose inexorably.

Weissmann answered at last. "Then you have not heard? He has been arrested for supposedly murdering a woman who has not been named."

She felt stiff, artificial. Could he see through her pretense? Had he done so right from the beginning and he was playing with her? Perhaps he knew Lila by sight. But she could not take it back now.

"Do you suppose he actually did it?" she asked. "Surely, the police will find someone else to blame. Or has he enemies who need to get rid of him?"

"Why?" Weissmann tried to look innocent, but his clear eyes betrayed him. "What is it to you?"

"Because he has something that someone cannot afford to have him use," she suggested.

"For example?" he asked very quietly.

"Any number of things. It is just a name I have heard in . . . interesting places."

"What places?" he asked, too quickly.

She smiled. "Perhaps I should have said 'people.'"

"And you think they will rescue him? Who, exactly, are these *people?*" he pressed.

"Not President Roosevelt," she answered. "That would be too obvious. Too . . . clumsy." .

"Toward what end?" he asked, a flare of interest in his eyes.

She must take a chance. It was not good, but there may never be a better time. "Someone who is interested in which way America steps, if there is another war. Someone who would like America to side with Britain and France, for example."

"And Baylor is isolationist," he said. He realized his slip a moment too late. He had not made it a question.

"As are a good many men of considerable power," she agreed as calmly as she could. "It would be safer, don't you think, not to get involved? Stand aside and pick up the pieces afterward?"

"Safer for whom, Guinevere?" Now he was tense. It was not in his face, but she could see it in his shoulders, the way it pulled his jacket tight as his arm clenched.

"Everyone," she replied. "New wars bring new weapons. We could destroy practically everything, don't you think?"

Seconds ticked by in silence. Elena could not keep this conversation going much longer without completely exposing her interest. And so, ultimately, her identity. She had to learn where the information was coming from. Hers was coming from Harmon Worth, and he had told her it was false. He had said when it reached Germany, the physicists would know that. Would they trace it back, step by step, to see where the lies began, as Allenby planned? If they did, and Peter knew of it, that should expose the whole chain. Right back to the person who had smuggled the previous information? The person whom Lila had suspected, and who had killed her so she did not expose the source?

She tried to look calm, as if the seconds were not sliding by.

"You exaggerate," Weissmann said at last. "The Germans have excellent tanks, the best in the world, but not as destructive as you suggest. Not at all. Your fears are unfounded."

It was either retreat, or attack. "Are you testing me, Mr. Weissmann?" she asked.

"Testing you?" he replied, raising his eyebrows.

"I'm sure the tanks would be excellent, possibly better than any we have. Cities are not taken by tanks, however excellent their ammunition. It's bombs that level cities, torpedoes that sink boats."

"Torpedoes?" he said with surprise. "The letter you have brought me, Guinevere, have you opened it and read it?"

"No," she said immediately. "But I know what it is about, more or less."

"Indeed? Interesting. I was warned that you were getting a little above yourself."

"Really?" She kept her voice steady with an effort. "By whom?"

"It is not your concern. You will be well advised to stick to your job, and not ask questions that are none of your business."

Should she risk it? Again, it was attack, or retreat. "Wyatt Baylor."

His face froze. "That seems to have been taken care of. And you would be wise to keep your mouth shut. If he knows as much about you as we do . . . Be careful, Guinevere. He was right, whoever he was, to say that you are getting above yourself."

Was it a warning? Was retreat even possible anymore? Or was it too late to go back now, when she could be on the verge of finding the truth? She looked straight at him. "Would you advise me to pretend I do not understand what is going on?" she asked.

"It's a little late to think of that," he answered. "But you don't know nearly as much as you imagine."

"Above myself?" she said with a slightly twisted smile. She meant it to be superior. She must risk a rebuff. "Because I can see that Harmon Worth framed Wyatt Baylor? I just wonder why. Was he simply available? Or is he there when you would like him to be, or need him to be, so you can get rid of him?"

"And why do you care?"

Perhaps she had gone too far?

"I don't," she replied. "But any chain is only as strong as its weakest link."

A small muscle was moving in his jaw. "If a link is broken, it is inconvenient, no more. We can always forge another link."

"So, you will let Wyatt Baylor be executed?"

"Why do you ask? What is it to you?" he countered yet again.

She looked down at her plate. "Nothing."

"You fight for the cause?" It was half a question, no more than that.

She was aware of his eyes on her face. He would notice any movement, every inflection in her voice. But she had gone too far to retreat. And the woman she was pretending to be would never have retreated anyway! She raised her eyes and met his unflinchingly. "I fight for what I believe in."

"At any cost?" he said with slight interest, as if it were of academic concern only, but his eyes said his interest was very real indeed. Unquestionably, she had gone too far.

She made herself smile at him. "I don't know. But I haven't been asked to pay too high a price yet."

"That may come," he replied. "We will not need a second or third course." He took out his wallet and selected several bills. It was far more than the cost of the meal and the wine.

He rose to his feet. "I regret this, but you have left me no choice.

You are altogether too inquisitive. We should leave now. Don't make a scene, or I shall be obliged to hurt you, and very badly. I doubt you came alone. But then, neither did I. We will appear to be together. This is not an association either of us wishes to break. We are useful to each other. And whether you do this for money or not, you will be well paid. It will enable you to continue to dress in the highly expensive and effective way that you do. Added to that, you enjoy being looked at. Every man in the room has had his eye on you, at one time or another. I notice these things. So do you. Come." He took hold of her upper arm so hard it hurt. His fingers dug into her flesh and brought tears to her eyes.

With his free hand he picked up her purse and, as if carelessly, let the catch fall open. He glanced at it long enough to be sure she was not carrying a gun. A knife would have been easier, perhaps disguised as a nail file. But she would never have gotten close enough to use such a thing, even if she had the nerve, or the desperation.

"Don't make a fuss," he warned. "I'm obliged to you for this information." He slipped the envelope out and put it into his inside jacket pocket. "But you must understand that I can't let you just walk away. I think American Intelligence might well be on to you. You are not nearly as clever as you think. I shall let you go . . . later."

She did not believe him. Outside, in the darkness of the parking lot and the trees beyond, it would be so easy to kill her, as someone had killed Lila Worth. She no longer had his trust. Had she slipped? Of course she had!

She pulled very slightly as they walked together toward the back entrance of the dining area. There were cloakrooms beyond, and another way out.

He gripped her arm so tightly she let out a gasp of pain.

"What is your name?" he asked. "And don't tell me it's Guinevere. That means nothing."

"Gabrielle," she answered. It was the name of another woman she had known and liked. She would not name anyone in her family that he could trace.

"Gabrielle," he repeated. "Nice." They were in the passage toward the back door. Only a couple of yards to go and they would be outside. It had worked perfectly so far! Where the hell was Allenby? Surely, she was not expendable after all?

Weissmann reached the back door and opened it, pushing her ahead of him. She slipped on the step and almost fell over, only regaining her balance with difficulty. Weissmann grabbed at her shoulder and missed. Someone else clutched her and took her weight, holding her other wrist. A voice said firmly, "Lila Worth, I arrest you on the charge of treason against the United States." She would have been terrified, had it not been Allenby's voice.

Other figures moved in the dark, not more than shadows. She did not know where Weissmann was, but he had let go of her and had fled.

There was a shot. She had no idea from where. No one cried out, but there was a quick indrawn breath close to her. More men running away. A car door slammed. An engine came to life.

Allenby, gripping her arm, gasped again, then pulled her forward toward his car. "They've clipped me in the arm," he said, pain in his voice.

"Where's Harmon?" Elena asked, fearful for the man's safety.

"Still inside, don't worry about him. Elena, you have to drive."

"Keys?" She held out her hand. "Will you be all right?"

"Yes. Get in and drive!"

She obliged. She understood the necessity. If they did not follow, Weissmann would suspect the plans. He must believe they were desperate to get them back. She opened the car door and slipped into the driver's seat. Allenby went round to the passenger side, and by the time he sat down and closed the door, Elena already had the engine started. She picked up speed swiftly. By the time she was on the street, she could see the other car clearly.

"Follow them," Allenby said quite unnecessarily. She heard the urgency in his voice and the pain.

"I am doing!" She tried to get a feel for the car, how it responded to the accelerator, the steering. And driving on the right-hand side of the road—without the benefit of headlights!

Her eyes became accustomed to the dark and she wove her way around the country road, following the lights ahead. She had been driving for years, but Peter had taught her defensive driving, rapid changes of direction, how to handle ice on the road, or oil; how to weave and turn, how to be aggressive and offensive; how to follow a car and how to lose one following her.

They were on a long road. She increased speed, slowed as she rounded a bend and accelerated again. The lights ahead were closer now.

"Ease up a bit," Allenby cautioned. "We don't want them to think we could have caught them."

"But we want them to think we tried," she argued, gathering speed again. Suddenly, the car ahead vanished. There was nothing but intense darkness.

She took her foot off the accelerator, trying not to panic.

The road curved gently. The lights appeared again, but far closer and getting nearer still.

Allenby stiffened, then lunged for the wheel. "Right!" he shouted at her. "Right side!"

"I'm on the right side!" she shouted back.

"You're not!" He had the wheel out of her hands. "You're on the left! God in heaven! This is America, Elena, we drive on the right side of the road!"

They were slowing. A car shot toward them and disappeared behind on the left, leaving her shaking. "Of course you do." Her voice was hoarse. "Sorry."

It was a moment before he answered, and then his voice was half-choked. "We lost him." He cleared his throat. "Do you think you can drive us home, on the right side of the road? Please."

"I'm sorry," she said again. "Yes, of course I can." She tried to

sound confident, but her voice was shaking. She had stalled the engine. They were sitting on the side of the road, in the dark, but it was
the right side of the road.

"Elena . . ."

"Yes."

"You did a hell of a job."

"Is your arm going to be all right? Is it bleeding? Does it hurt?"

"Yes to all three. But not much. For heaven's sake, get started
again. And don't drive any farther without lights or somebody will
drive into us."

She started the engine, turned on the headlights, checked behind
her, and pulled out onto the highway, her hands slick with sweat on
the wheel and her arm aching where Weissmann had gripped her.

CHAPTER
19

Elena and Allenby pulled up in front of Harmon Worth's house. Elena was relieved to see that his car was there. He must have been watching, because before they could reach the front door, it opened and Harmon stood there, his face flooded with relief. Without words, he stepped back to allow them in. He looked anxiously at the wound on Allenby's arm.

"Needs cleaning," Allenby said with a grimace. "But I don't think it's deep."

"I'll have a look," Harmon said, frowning at it.

"They took the bait." Allenby smiled. "I think we're on the way."

Worth smiled, then turned to Elena. "Lila would have been proud of you. She would have . . ." He stopped, unable to continue.

She smiled at him, understanding. "I'll put the dress on the bed and—"

"Keep it," he interrupted her. "You look wonderful in it. Think of Lila . . . sometimes."

She took a breath to argue, then changed her mind. "Thank you, I will."

An hour later, she was changed back into her own clothes, feeling as if she had awakened from a vivid and dangerous dream, back to a more pedestrian reality.

Allenby was wearing a clean shirt and sporting a heavy bandage around his arm, the shirt sleeve pushed up.

They spoke for a few moments to Harmon, then got back into the car, this time with Allenby at the wheel, wincing as he turned it to go back onto the road.

"I'll drive if you like," Elena offered.

He gave a twisted smile that could have meant anything. "Thank you, but you have a sore arm as well."

"It's not bleeding."

"Neither is mine now. What are you going to do about Wyatt?"

"Look harder for proof that he didn't do it," she answered. "Let me look at all the photographs again. I'll compare notes with my father, and perhaps my mother, too. Together, we might think of something new."

"Haven't the police done that already?" Allenby asked reasonably.

"Yes, of course they have. But they only know what appears within the frame of each shot. And bits of what was around it. That's how they know where each photo was taken." She thought about this for a moment. "If I go over these with my parents and grandparents, memories could be jogged. A memory of someone else being there, nearby but not in the frame. And remember, there are several that didn't come out that well: out of focus, or either over- or underexposed; poor compositions, such as somebody moving, or the faces in poor light. Those are no good as pictures, but they could be evidence. We have to do everything we can!" She knew she sounded desperate.

"The police asked everyone to say where they were and who was with them the first time they questioned them," he said. There was gentleness in his voice, as if he understood her feelings. "Don't you think they would have seen any inconsistencies?"

Allenby was focused on the road, the only illumination coming from the car's headlights.

"Somebody killed her!" Elena said. "Roosevelt's security detail was at the front gate and all around the house. They swore that no one came onto the property around the time Lila was killed. Or at all, for that matter. Miller must have questioned everyone on that security team by now, looking for even the smallest discrepancy."

"That's what the police worked out in the beginning," Allenby said quietly. "Miller is no fool. What else could you find from those prints?"

Elena was trying to think as she looked for words. "An inconsistency," she said. "Someone they thought was above suspicion, and so Miller and his team believed whatever they said, even without proof. It only takes one person to lie, possibly for some reason completely unconnected with Lila or Wyatt, and it alters all the calculations. It's as if you're doing a long mathematical calculation, and you get one number wrong. That's all it takes, just one, and the whole thing is wrong. And I'm sure all of this is wrong. Grandfather did not kill Lila!"

"And you think you'll find this one mistake?"

"Have you a better idea?" she asked.

"No," he admitted, never taking his eyes off the road.

She thought for a moment. "Sometimes we tell the silliest lies, then we can't get out of them without looking stupid. And embarrassed."

"Such as what?" He looked genuinely puzzled.

"Such as watching someone across the room, instead of paying attention to the person you are with."

"Is this relevant?"

"Yes, because if you didn't see or hear something that you would have ... that is, if you had been where you said you were ... it's very relevant. Oh, I don't know!" she added. "Any sort of white lie! You didn't see so-and-so, you didn't notice something, you didn't hear, when you must have, if you were with that person." She heard the desperation in her own voice. "And then when you tell one lie, you have to back it up, and end by saying something ridiculous, or simply saying that you don't remember. You were with so-and-so, when you weren't. That gives you an alibi, and someone else as well. Usually, in the end, it doesn't matter. Even innocent people lie out of fear."

He thought for a moment. "Complicated," he said at last. "And one man in a dinner suit can look a lot like another if they're of similar height or build. Or a waiter, for that matter. But Miller and his team questioned them pretty closely."

"Yes, but the waiters wore cropped jackets, down to the waist, not dinner jackets." She remembered it as she spoke. "You wouldn't mistake one of them. I'm going to check all the photographs and compare them. Especially the ones that weren't good enough to give to the guests, or to a magazine. I'll pay special attention to what's in the background of each one. There's an inconsistency, somewhere! There has to be, and I need to find it."

"Can I help?" he offered.

Elena nearly touched his arm, then remembered his wound. "Thanks, but not yet. I'll go through them all. I'll have my mother help. It will be . . ."

"Hard," he said. "Especially having to relive that night. What are you going to tell her about this evening?"

She thought for a few moments. "I suppose that we had dinner. I've got to account for my sore arm. I slipped on the dance floor. Don't refer to it again, I feel such a fool."

He laughed, but it was a release of tension, not amusement.

After a moment or two she found herself laughing as well, until she could hardly get her breath, then shaking herself quickly, before it turned to tears.

The next morning after breakfast, Elena got out all the photographs of the party, good and bad.

She went to find Katherine, who was in the garden, perhaps to escape company for a few moments, as well as her need to pretend that everything would be all right. Elena saw her from a distance. She looked elegant as always, standing in front of a flowerbed as if considering how to change it next year, when the perennials could be divided and, if she so wished, moved about a little. As if this were her personal garden, and not one on the opposite side of the Atlantic Ocean. Elena wondered if her mother had decided when her annuals could be planted.

Katherine was wearing a pale linen dress and a wide-brimmed hat. The graceful line of it accentuated the angles of her body: the long legs, lean shoulders, and slight bosom: a dancer's body, like Margot's. Elena had envied her sister a few years ago. Now she was happy with herself. It had begun in Berlin, with a red dress. She smiled as she remembered it, and walked over toward her mother.

At first Katherine was not even aware of her. Elena touched her gently and Katherine turned. "Sorry, dear. Did you say something?"

"Not yet, but I'm about to. I need some help going through all the pictures from the party."

Katherine's face clouded. "What point is there now? That time is gone. Surely no one will want to be reminded of it?"

"Mother, the police are blaming Grandfather only because it looks as if he's unaccounted for at exactly the right time, and nobody else seems to be. Well, they're wrong. If we look carefully again at all the pictures, we might be able to see it clearly. And you know all these people."

"Not as well as your grandmother does. It might upset her, but I'm sure she'd try, if you ask her. She's desperate to help."

Elena hesitated.

Katherine smiled with the tight twist of inner amusement. "What could be a far better use to you, dear—and I'm sure you know this—would be the history of all these people. Their relationships with each other, and what they really value. Politically, I mean, and where their money is."

"Do you know?"

"No, but I'll bet Mother does, if she thinks about it."

Elena realized how much they all wanted to help. Even if it was painful, it would make Dorothy feel included, as if she was helping her husband. "If you think she could," she agreed. "Yes, please."

Working together, Elena and her mother and grandmother spread every photograph Elena had taken across the dining-room table. These included those that were sharply focused and those that were not. Some of them were beautiful, and scattered among them were others that were rejected.

Dorothy stared at them in fascination. "Oh, goodness," she said. "I never realized you took so many! What happened?" She was looking at some of the out-of-focus shots. "Why . . . ?" She stopped, as if realizing she sounded critical. "Oh, Elena, I'm sorry."

Elena smiled. "It's all right, Grandmother. There are plenty of good ones. But bad ones happen, people move, the light is not as good as you thought, or the proportion doesn't work. Like this one." She picked out the picture of Mabel Cartwright on the stairs.

"Oh, my dear!" Dorothy said in amazement. "She looks quite beautiful! I've never seen her look so lovely."

Elena laughed. "Neither has anyone else, I'll bet! The light was perfect, and I took several. This one was exactly right." She found the others and put them beside the best.

"Oh! Yes, I see! Yes, the others are quite different proportions. Light on the cheekbones, and there it is on her chin, and on that one her nose looks enormous. It's very clever. It's a matter of angles, color, and light, isn't it?"

"Color, yes, and angles. It's fun, for the one picture that's beautiful. And even better, emotions you catch, something like . . ." she looked for the exact picture she had in mind, ". . . here!"

Dorothy put her hand up to her mouth, her eyes wide. "Oh dear," she declared again. "That's exactly her!" She stared at the picture of a woman wincing as she had bitten into something that was unexpectedly bitter. "How did you catch her doing that? It shows her thoughts exactly!"

"Luck," Elena said. "If we watch people long enough, eventually their faces will betray them. It's there, and then gone again. We don't know what we really saw when it's gone. And the change in the light can make it look quite different: funny in some light, frighteningly sinister in another. Look at these." She spread out a dozen more pictures, and asked Dorothy about the people. And then more again.

Dorothy told them little bits of information, including character, background, political leanings, and now and again a sharp, funny piece of gossip.

"Help me put them in exact order," said Elena, and both Katherine and Dorothy responded.

With the help of a magnifying glass, they spent the next hour arranging the sequence of prints to match the sequence of the shots on the rolls of negatives. So many of the shots were similar, but Elena sensed that the exact order in which they were taken might be important.

"It's there, look!" Katherine stared at them, her face charged with amazement. "That's Father, standing in front of that group of people, then in this picture, too, only moments later."

"How do you know that?" Dorothy asked. "It could be any time."

"No, it couldn't," Katherine replied. "Look, Mother, the light on the floor, the way it strikes the fold of that skirt."

"Yes! Oh, I see. It's exactly the same. She hasn't moved." She turned toward Elena. "Let's take another look."

Five minutes later, Elena saw it. It was there, unmistakable. How could she have missed it before? Because she had looked only at her mistake! It was one of the pictures that was slightly out of focus in one corner. A man's hand. The fingers were blurred, but the signet ring was clear. It was Wyatt Baylor's ring.

Elena ran through another grouping, and found an even sharper shot of the same group: a couple standing before a fireplace. Just behind the man was the ormolu clock on the mantelpiece that said it was twenty-five past ten. Elena remembered this shot very clearly, because it had taken quite a few attempts to get what she considered an acceptable shot. Wyatt had been there, directing them, but he did not show in the photograph. The couple would remember. They could testify, and the photograph showing the time would back them up. This was exactly the time when Lila Worth was reported to be outside, standing on the gravel driveway, meeting the person who killed her.

Elena picked it up, careful to touch only the edges and not leave smudges on the image.

"It's not very good, dear," Dorothy said. "The balance is off. I think it's Freda Hawksley, but her face is blurred. I suppose she moved."

"It's perfect, Grandma," Elena argued, but she couldn't keep the smile from her face, the excitement from her voice. "It shows Grandpa's hand, with his ring. The couple could swear he was there in the room at exactly the time he was supposed to have been outside killing Lila. The police think he had time to do this, and no one else did. But this proves he didn't! He couldn't. They're wrong, and we can prove it!"

Dorothy was wide-eyed with amazement, as if a miracle had happened before her. Her eyes filled with tears, and her smile was radiant. "I knew it! I knew he couldn't have done it! Thank you, God. And thank you, my darling girl, for having found this."

Katherine put her arms around Elena and tried to keep the excitement, the relief, out of her voice. "Then who did it?" she wondered.

"I don't know," Elena replied. "That's not our problem. But it wasn't Grandpa! We can prove it! I'll find Father. We'll take this to Captain Miller."

"Shouldn't you take it to Mr. Borrodale?" Katherine asked. "He can use it to—"

"No," Elena said quickly. "He might come here or he might not. He has an interest in this."

"Yes, to get my father cleared," Katherine said.

Elena paused for a long moment. "Maybe," she said. "Maybe not. Grandpa isn't the only one he represents. We'll take it to Miller. He doesn't want to charge the wrong man. It's the end, Grandma! At least, it's the beginning of the end!"

Dorothy relaxed at last, letting go of her granddaughter's hand, but her face was still showing that beautiful smile. "Thank you, dear. You never gave up on him, did you? I know, and I love you for it!"

Of course, they had to go through the legal procedure. Katherine went with Dorothy to take the news to Wyatt, while Charles took the car, driven by the chauffeur, to see Borrodale and then Captain Miller. Elena, still at the house, made certain to hold tight to the one copy of the photograph. She would not trust anyone, especially Borrodale, with having the power to use it, or destroy it. And she couldn't print a duplicate until she had access to a dark room. As a precaution, however, she took a picture of the picture, and then she called Allenby. He was not at his home, and it took an urgent call to the embassy to find him.

When he spoke, his voice was soft, unusually low.

"Are you all right?" she asked with sudden alarm. "How is your arm? Is it infected?"

"No, I'm fine. It's sore, but I expect it to be. And no, not infected. You've tracked me down here . . . what's happened?"

"We've got it! A photograph that proves my grandfather didn't do it!"

"Where is it?" His voice was urgent. "Don't give it to Borrodale. And whatever you do, keep the negative. Who has the print? You, or the police? We're not playing on a straight table, Elena!"

"I know. I have the print and I've taken a good, clean picture of it, but Miller has a copy of all the photographs, anyway, and—"

"That's not enough," he cut across her. "You can't trust anyone. There's a lot more behind this than just killing Lila. I hate to say it, but I'm beginning to think that Free America may have had another purpose than merely getting rid of her."

"What purpose?" she asked.

When he responded, his voice was low, as if he was afraid of being overheard. Perhaps he shared an office? "I think there might be one person, or a group, taking advantage of another's actions. The more I know about this group, the worse it looks. Please . . . be careful, Elena. Do nothing. Promise me! Let Charles tell Borrodale, and then Miller."

"He's gone to do that. Despite what I think of the man, Borrodale is on Grandfather's side."

"Perhaps. I haven't time to stand around talking. Just hide the pictures and wait there. And for once, do as you're told." He hung up, leaving her standing with the telephone in her hand.

She turned as Katherine came into the room, suddenly looking years younger. Although there were tears on her face, she was smiling. She went straight to Elena and hugged her hard, so hard it hurt. Then Elena hugged her back.

It was ten minutes of laughter and tears before Elena obeyed Allenby's warning. She took the role of film out of her camera and put in a new one, so it would not be empty, if anyone went to look. Then she took the film that had the shot of the photo she had just taken and hid it in a shoe in her closet.

She said nothing to her mother, or to her father when he came back with Captain Miller, nearly three hours later.

Charles looked exhausted, but he could not take the smile off his face. Even Captain Miller looked not displeased, although he now had to begin the case all over again.

Wyatt came downstairs, with Dorothy on his arm. He shook Miller by the hand, smiling.

"Thank you," he said simply. "I don't know how you did it. I always believed they would realize, somehow, that I was innocent. But

I admit I was beginning to fear that the nightmare would go on, perhaps even into an actual trial, before they realized their mistake." He glanced at Charles, and then away again.

Charles was not surprised. Wyatt had been badly frightened. He had pretended not to be, as if he knew his innocence would be proved. But that was not true. Many people have been innocent, and it had not been believed until they had served many years in prison, or even wrongly executed.

But it had not happened. Wyatt was free, and now vindicated.

"Thank you," Wyatt said again, cutting across Charles's thoughts. "I must write a formal letter of thanks to Borrodale."

Charles drew in his breath to speak, then changed his mind and watched his father-in-law walk out of the room.

"Don't be ashamed that you doubted him," Katherine said, putting her arm through his. "I did, too, once or twice. Now, though, my parents can have the party the first one should have been." She pulled away and looked up at him. "And incidentally, it will show everyone that he is alive . . . well, that he's been through a hell of a time but has emerged victorious." She smiled. "And now he'll know his friends from his enemies!"

Charles stared at her. "You've been listening to Lucas too much." He spoke lightly, but he saw by her smile that she meant what she'd said. "I imagine it will be a slightly smaller party!"

"Will Captain Miller go on looking, do you suppose?" she asked.

"I hope so. But at least he won't be looking here. Now come inside, and let's help your parents celebrate."

CHAPTER 20

Peter Howard heard the telephone ringing in his head. It was loud, insistent. He opened his eyes and saw the luminous figures on the clock: just after four in the morning. It was still dark outside, even this close to midsummer. He reached out and fumbled for the receiver, at first knocking it off the cradle, then grasping for it.

Beside him, Pamela stirred.

"Go back to sleep," he said gently. "I'll take it downstairs."

He spoke into the mouthpiece. "Call again in five minutes," he said, then he hung up and replaced the telephone back on its cradle.

"Is it an emergency?" she said anxiously.

"Probably not. Just someone in a different time zone."

She relaxed and curled up again.

Peter stood and reached for his dressing gown, but did not bother with slippers. He went downstairs to his study. When the phone rang again, he answered quickly.

"Yes?" he said.

"Allenby," said the voice on the other end. He sounded tense and extremely tired.

"Are you all right?" Peter asked, alarmed. "Elena?"

"She's fine," Allenby answered. "A few bumps and bruises. I got shot, but it's only a flesh wound. Bled a bit, that's all. But we got them to take the bait."

"What the hell are you talking about?" Peter demanded, trying to scrape his memory together to understand specifically what Allenby had been doing. He came up blank.

"Lila Worth." Allenby said this with an obvious effort to control his emotions. "Over the problem we've already discussed."

Peter's mind began to clear. His agent was referring to the nuclear fission experiment, and the information being leaked to Germany. That was what Lila had been working on. "What exactly are you trying to do?" Peter asked, his voice dangerously level.

"Gather information," said Allenby. "We need to know which one of their top blokes will look at it and will recognize that it's false. Specifically, that it's been interfered with. I'm hoping they'll follow the whole trail back, to find who did that. And then we'll know how it's getting out."

"Follow the trail back to you?"

"Back to a dead end," Allenby replied. "But in that process, we'll find the chain, and that's what we want."

"We?"

"That's what Lila was doing," Allenby amended. "We need to know who the leak is coming from, who's the traitor at this end. There's a real chance that this will work." There was a lift in his voice now.

"How can you do it without Lila?" Peter was skeptical. "You haven't got the knowledge."

"Harmon Worth," Allenby said. "He knew far more about her than we thought. And loved her anyway. She had it set up. We just had to pass over the papers."

"Pass them to whom?" Peter was confused and beginning to get a growing feeling that he was not going to like what he was about to hear. "You aren't making any sense. And who the hell is *we?*"

"They hadn't known Lila, except by a code name."

"Jim!"

After a lengthy pause, Allenby finally spoke. "Elena took her place. It went off just about perfectly."

Peter froze. This was what he had feared. He was clasping the phone so tightly that his hand cramped. He shifted the receiver to the other ear and flexed his fingers to ease the pain. "You sent Elena to meet them? She's not ready for this yet! What the hell are you thinking?" His voice was hard and frightened, even in his own ears.

"She did very well. She even looked the part."

"Damn you!" Peter exploded. "She doesn't know a thing about atomic science, and she looks nothing like Lila."

"They didn't know anything about Lila, except that she was in her thirties and beautiful," Allenby began.

"Elena's an amateur!" Peter almost spat the words.

"She took Lila's place and she did a damn good job of it." Allenby's voice was defensive and angry. "She speaks German perfectly and had enough sense not to volunteer any extra information. I would say she did a thoroughly professional job of it. They got away, and we chased them for several miles. She's one brave and daring driver. Must have scared the hell out of them. It did out of me. Did you teach her?"

Peter felt a moment's pride. "Yes."

"But you forgot to tell her to drive on the right-hand side in America."

"What?"

"We didn't hit anybody, by the grace of God!" Allenby said. "They had to work to get away from her. We were on their tail for quite a distance. They needed to believe we wanted to catch them, as if we were desperate to get the papers back."

Peter breathed out slowly. He really did not want Allenby even to suspect the emotions he was feeling, never mind to be certain of them. "And Worth? Is he all right? Whatever he knew about Lila, it seems that he loved her deeply."

"Harmon Worth will never be all right," Allenby said quietly. "Or, at least, not in the foreseeable future. But he finished Lila's work by helping us in this, and that's something. Also, Elena proved Wyatt Baylor's innocence of killing Lila, and the police have dropped all charges. He's off the hook."

"Elena did that? How? Was he part of this or not?" It was an ugly thought, Elena's other grandfather! It would hurt her unbelievably. But even the worst villains have families who love them. Thank God Elena was spared the misery of her grandfather's guilt. It had not happened to her, and Peter was grateful. "How did she prove it?" he asked.

"With photographs," Allenby replied. "They proved his alibi after all. She had taken several pictures of Wyatt, along with a couple of other people, in front of a very handsome fireplace. They'll swear to that. There's a clock visible behind them on the mantelpiece. A couple of the photos she set aside because of the quality show it very clearly. The police are sure it was exactly the time that Lila was murdered." The pain in his voice was unmistakable.

Peter liked him the better for that. "Then who did kill her?" he asked.

"Unfortunately, we don't know that," Allenby replied. "Probably one of Wyatt's Nazi-leaning friends, and he has several. Whether the time chosen was deliberate or merely opportunistic, I don't know."

"But why?" Peter asked. "What was the purpose in blaming Baylor? A power struggle? Or was he on to them, and actually on our side? Or, at least, on the President's side."

"Not sure what side that is," Allenby admitted. "Wait and see who looks like they're winning, and then join them? Or just sell arms to whoever's buying. At the moment, it's hard to say."

"You are remarkably cynical, Jim."

"Realistic, Peter. You'd be the first to criticize me if I wasn't."

A little smile played on Peter's mouth. "True. Any chance they'll find the guilty party and make an arrest?"

"It's not impossible," Allenby said thoughtfully. "But damned unlikely now. And don't worry, I won't get Elena involved in anything else."

"Sounds to me like she did damn well," Peter said a little testily. But all he heard on the other end was Allenby laughing.

The following noon, Peter went to see Lucas at his home. It was something he hardly ever did, preferring to keep the fiction alive that they barely knew each other. Still, this time, he drove to the street parallel to the one on which Lucas and Josephine lived, parked the car, and five minutes later knocked on their door.

Josephine opened it and her face filled with alarm.

Peter realized immediately that he should have telephoned first. "I've got good news," he said straightaway. "It's complicated. I wanted to tell Lucas myself."

She stepped back and invited him in.

"Thank you," he accepted, following her through the foyer.

"Would you like a cup of tea?" she asked.

"Yes, please." That would give him time to explain to Lucas most of the news that was considered secret. He could answer any of his former boss's questions only because Lucas already knew almost as much as Peter did himself, and he still held a security clearance with MI6.

Lucas was standing in the study, looking at the bookshelves, obviously searching for something. He turned around with surprise when he heard Peter's steps. His immediate reaction was like Josephine's, which was to look as if he feared the worst.

"This is good news," Peter said quickly, as Josephine was closing the door gently and leaving the two men alone.

"What?" Lucas asked. "Why did you come here?" It was not a challenge; it was a simple question.

"Details," Peter answered. "Things I don't want to say over the phone, or write down."

Lucas opened the French doors to the garden and invited Peter to follow him out into the noonday sun. The yellow climbing rose was a mass of flowers. Spires of blue lupins looked like an army marching with banners, and one of the dozen or so gaudy tulips splashed scarlet and purple and gold.

"What's happened?" Lucas asked. "More atomic papers leaked out? You caught someone?"

"Better than that," said Peter. "We planted some information that should expose the whole chain of informants from Washington all the way to Berlin." Peter took a deep breath. "It's a bit early to be certain, but it's got a good start."

"How do you know?" Lucas asked. His face expressed only innocent interest, but Peter knew him better than to accept that as anything but the beginning.

"Lila set it up, before she was murdered," he explained. "Allenby and Harmon Worth, Lila's husband, had Elena follow it through. And before you think the worst, no one died and the whole operation appears to have been a success. They fought hard and the suspects thought they had escaped with a dozen or so papers they stole from Lila. She was using a code name, of course, and they had never met her before."

"Don't tell me her name," said Lucas, holding up a hand. "It doesn't matter. If I don't know her . . ." He looked closely at the younger man. "What else, Peter? And don't spin it out. Why are you telling me all this?"

"Lila was her real name," said Peter. "But there's no danger in your knowing it: she's dead. And I—"

"Are they the ones who killed her?" Lucas interrupted. "What's happened to Wyatt Baylor?" The concern was sharp in his voice.

"Wyatt is free and at home," Peter assured him. "We don't know who killed her, but it was Elena who proved, with her photographs, that it was not Wyatt. Actually, the proof was in a few flawed photos, blurry, but clear enough to see the clock, and Wyatt's hand, with his signet ring, in the corner. The couple being photographed will swear to it. But no, we have no idea who did it. That's a whole different question."

"So, they framed Wyatt? Why?" Lucas asked. "To get rid of him?"

"Probably," Peter admitted, knowing that Lucas would not find this response acceptable. More questions were sure to come.

"Which side is he on?" Lucas asked. "Ours? The Nazis'? The Americans'? Or just whoever he thinks will be the winner?" A brief look of bitterness crossed Lucas's face. "Or is it about whatever profits them the most?"

"Possibly the last," Peter answered, keeping his voice low enough not to carry over the hedges and the flowered walls to the next garden. "But we might be doing him an injustice. The answer is, I don't know."

"But Elena proved him innocent of Lila's murder? Are you satisfied with that?"

"Yes, yes I am. And it's pretty conclusive."

"A loyal granddaughter?" Lucas gave the words no belief, or disbelief.

Peter thought for a few moments. "It was Allenby's impression, I think, that she was more a loyal daughter. After all, Wyatt is Katherine's father. I think she found Wyatt a little condescending." He smiled. "She's quite prickly beneath her good manners."

"Really?" Lucas gave the single word a kaleidoscope of meaning, most of it with a depth of sarcasm.

"She still worked extraordinarily, and at some danger to herself, to prove him innocent."

"She would do," Lucas agreed. He frowned. "But she's all right?"

"Yes. But as you pointed out, if it's not Wyatt who killed Lila, then we don't know who it was. We don't know whether she was the intended victim, or if it was really Wyatt they were after." Peter stopped for a moment, and then added, "Elena's home in a couple more days. She and her parents have spent most of what should have been a holiday working to clear Wyatt. They're going to have a re-peat party, a proper celebration of their sixtieth anniversary, and then two days after that they leave for New York and then home."

"How do you know so much, Peter?" Lucas looked at Peter curi-ously, as if reading something deeper than the answer he had been given. "Are you in touch with Elena?"

Peter could feel the heat rising up his face. He was good at mask-ing his feelings. No one could read him, except Lucas, to whom he was an open book. He had very mixed emotions about being so eas-ily read. It was comfortable to be known, a relief from the blanket isolation, but it also left him vulnerable. "No," he said truthfully. "But Allenby reports to me regularly. More so in this case, both be-cause of its importance and because he's dealing with a family I know, and of course he doesn't."

"And because Elena is concerned," Lucas said. "Which I suspect you knew as soon as her grandfather was arrested."

"Yes."

"Are you going to handle the nuclear fission side of it from now on?"

Peter took a deep breath. "It's too grave to let it rest on the pe-riphery. Our goal is to collect as much information as possible: we need all we can get. It's a terrible thing, Lucas, this knowledge of how to destroy. But the genie is out of the bottle and we can't put it back in."

"Allenby?" Lucas asked. "Does he know enough to head this up? Is he experienced enough? How good is he, really?"

Peter thought hard. "I'm not sure. I think so. He's young, about thirty-five."

"Young enough to be quick, old enough to have some sense," Lucas observed.

Peter stared at him. His instinct was to ask his advice, and yet he knew not to. Lucas would think less of him. He would see it as an attempt to evade responsibility. He would advise, and be shrewd, but the decision was still Peter's.

"Does he speak German?" Lucas asked.

"Yes, and French."

"What's your hesitation? Does he have some flaw that could weaken him? Or is it just your own unwillingness to let go, and let someone else run the show?"

What was it? That he detected in Allenby not only what he said, but the lightness with which he said it? The personal way in which he spoke of Elena? "It's too soon for a decision," he replied.

Lucas said nothing.

"I know," Peter admitted. "It won't wait. And yes, Allenby could be good."

"You hesitate," Lucas pointed out.

"Just thinking," Peter replied.

"About Elena?"

Silence ticked by into more silence. Peter heard no emotion in Lucas's voice, but he knew it was there. Had he any idea how deeply Peter felt about Elena? It was completely inappropriate, in any circumstance, as her superior, her mentor, and, above all, a married man, years older than she. And yet he cared! "She may be in the States, but I'm still responsible for her, for all my people," he replied. "I'll have to ask her what she thinks. Maybe Allenby took risks, but Elena was there, in DC, and it was her grandfather who was in danger. She was going to try to save him, with or without Allenby."

"Yes," Lucas agreed. "Remember, Peter, that Elena will always take risks when it comes to those she loves."

"I will," Peter agreed. "I will."

CHAPTER
21

The following day, Elena helped Katherine and Dorothy send out invitations to all the people who had attended the party at which the tragedy had happened. They knew that some would be unable to come at such short notice, and would send their apologies and good wishes. Perhaps a few would decline because of the previous drama; there was no way to know. As it happened, they would prove to be the minority: nearly everyone accepted with pleasure.

"There were bound to be a few reluctant to attend," Charles said to Elena during a brief break from preparations. They were walking in the garden. It was after the heat of the day had passed, and the sun was casting longer shadows. "And it is a last-minute invitation," he added. "The fact of Wyatt's innocence needs to be celebrated straightaway. It was a terrible time," he added. "And now it's over. At least . . ." He stopped.

"What?" Elena asked, then instantly wished she had not. She knew the answer.

Charles put his arm around her shoulder. It was not something he did normally; he was not instinctively tactile. That was one of the things that had changed over the last week or so: this understanding between them that did not need explanation. "We may not ever find out," he said quietly.

She knew what he was referring to. They had cleared Wyatt, so then who had killed Lila? And why? Was it personal after all? Perhaps someone she had rebuffed, and he had taken it badly? Someone who had a right to expect something from her, and her refusal had enraged him?

"But we know it was someone at the party," she answered. "And there were no uninvited guests. Or it could be one of the staff. There isn't anybody else." She paused for a moment. "It's a pretty awful thought, that some of the people we think we know actually believe something quite differently from us. They value a whole range of things that we find abhorrent." She wanted to address what she was really thinking. "It's not the end that appalled me so much as it was the means considered acceptable in attaining it. They took a life, violently and horribly. Are they blind to how morally wrong that is?"

"Yes, I think they are," Charles replied slowly. "Are you sure there is a difference between the means and the end? Doesn't one determine the other?"

She nodded. "I remember arguing with Lucas a long time ago, when we talked more often," she said. "He told me that he thought the weapons we choose might be hard to pick up, if they are repugnant enough. But we excuse them in the cause, and they gradually become easier and easier to use, until we can't put them down. They become the first resort, instead of the last. It was during the worst part of the war, but there was a lot of truth in what he was saying. It changes you, although you hardly notice it at first."

She thought for a moment. She had always trusted Lucas, from as far back as she could remember. But perhaps he had achieved that balance of moral choices with more difficulty than she had supposed.

"I don't know," Charles admitted. "I've given it a lot of thought, and I still don't know. Perhaps I don't wish to. There are things I have to live with, not knowing or understanding what kind of price was paid for them. There were plenty of decisions I made, as an ambassador, that I would not have made as a private citizen, compromises I would never have come to personally. When it is sanctioned by superiors, you excuse yourself from responsibility."

She thought of that with a new light. "I suppose you pay a certain price for some things. You have to decide whether it was worth it."

"At least we know that Wyatt didn't kill Lila," he said. "And if some of his friends have beliefs we abhor, it's one of the things we have to accept."

"Wyatt's not your blood," she said. "But he's mine. And he's Mother's. I find it so hard that he believes things I can't tolerate. He hasn't seen what I have, which is where the Nazis are going. But what will happen when he does? Does he stay with Free America? Does he support Hitler? All the way?" She looked away for a moment. "Father, can anything on earth be worth that?"

"I don't know," Charles said. "We will be going home in a couple of days. I can hold my tongue until then. And for your mother's sake, you will hold yours as well."

It sounded like a command, but Elena knew it for what it was: her father protecting her mother. "Do you think Borrodale could have got him off?" she asked. "Without the photographs? Or even that he would have tried his best? Or was Grandpa meant to be a sacrifice for someone else?"

Her father's arm tightened a little around her. "It doesn't matter," he answered. "It's finished. You proved him innocent. Whoever was guilty is not our problem. There's a lot of sympathy for Hitler here, but so is there at home. It's human nature, Elena. We can deceive ourselves into excusing almost anything, when we believe the alternative is worse."

"Yes, I've learned that. I don't think people would deceive themselves so quickly, if they knew what they were talking about." She tried to keep the heat out of her voice, but her memories of Berlin were too powerful to put aside. Also, her father was reading her perfectly, indicative of this new bond between them.

"I know you've been closer to Hitler than any of us has," he said. "But many of us have been closer to the trenches." He did not need to say anything else.

She understood the passion of those who swore *never again,* and there was no argument she could muster. How could she, knowing so many people acted out of horror and grief more than reason?

After a few moments of silence, they went back inside and rejoined Katherine and Dorothy, who were making preparations for the party. The same catering company was going to provide all the food and the wine, the extra plates and glasses. And, of course, the waiting staff. There was still plenty to be done.

The next day was equally busy, and by early afternoon everything was ready. Dorothy had gone upstairs for a rest, and Katherine and Elena were alone in the sitting room. There were flowers everywhere, even more than for the original party.

"A bit much," Katherine said, as she looked around the room. "But I like it. I'm not sure that we have more to celebrate, but perhaps we are more grateful for it now. This has made us realize how fragile happiness can be." She smiled at Elena. "I don't expect you to explain to me how you did this, but I'm extraordinarily grateful. Without you, and whatever risks you took, we would still be sitting here alone and frightened, almost certainly looking toward tragedy."

Elena did not know what to say. She felt it would be honest to give Allenby at least half the credit, if not more. And Harmon Worth as well. But she could not do that without betraying them. All the years her own family had thought so little of Lucas, and not hidden it very well, he had never justified himself, or explained what he was really doing. He never even defended himself against unjust charges of weakness, not doing his part. Silence was at the core of protecting himself, but also his family. Now she needed to do the same.

"Well, that tragedy didn't happen," she said with a wide smile. "True, everything conspired against us at first, particularly against Grandfather himself. And then it all fell into place, and we know he's innocent. Let's not talk about it," she suggested. "Or we might accidentally remind him of it, and I'm sure he'd rather put this entire nightmare behind him."

Katherine looked at her steadily. "Do you know who did kill Lila?"

"No," Elena said, "I don't. I wish I did. It would be the proper conclusion to all this, but I really have no idea. I'm sorry. We may never know."

Katherine sat silently for a while.

All sorts of thoughts came to Elena's mind, but they led to the same conclusion, and she did not want to follow it. It raised too many questions about beliefs, the ideas that lay just under the surface of actions, unanswered questions about personal principles and loyalties. What was it anyone really feared? If she were to make a list, at the top would be her wish that Katherine never find out that Wyatt was nothing like the man she had remembered, and thought she knew. How would she get over that?

But it hadn't happened. That is, she had learned nothing appalling during this fiasco. Wyatt Baylor might have Nazi sympathies, but he had not yet seen Nazism close enough to understand its reality. His excuse for his beliefs was that he didn't want another war. But what sane person did?

She looked around the room, with its warmth and its grace, the elegant side tables now piled with flowers, the marble-lined fireplace, the paintings hung on the walls in their ornate gold frames. She turned to her mother. "I'm so glad I saw your home, where you grew up. It's all you said of it."

Katherine smiled back. "Yes, it is. I don't think it has really

changed much." She touched Elena's arm. "And thank you for working so hard this morning. You helped me to accomplish the same
look and feel of the first party. Why don't you go upstairs and rest a
bit? Read a book or something, before it's time to change for the
evening."

Elena smiled in agreement. There was nothing more to say that
mattered. She gave her mother a quick hug and left the room.

Elena did not wear the dress she had worn for the first party, a night
that felt like such a long time ago, in a past that was beginning to feel
almost unreal. Instead, she put on the white silk gown that Harmon
Worth had chosen for her, with the dark net coat-dress that gave it
such a dramatic flair. She had never had anything so gorgeous. In
truth, she had never had anything that was as glamorous or striking,
yet at the same time romantic. It was not black, which she would
have assumed the most elegant shade, but a deep indigo, so dark as
to look black in the shadows. Well, almost black, but for that dramatic whisper of blue. It reminded her of courage, and of Lila. In
her own mind, she was paying tribute to the woman who would have
been her friend, had she lived. She might have hesitated about wearing it, which was something Lila had never had the chance to do, but
Harmon would not be here tonight. Were he coming, she might
have reconsidered.

She took a last look in the glass, turning this way and that. She
was as close to perfect as she was ever going to be. Her eyes were
wide and they looked indigo, like the dress in this light. Her hair was
soft and shining and sleek, as fashion suggested, much shorter than
shoulder length, in deep waves that curved wide at the cheekbones,
accenting the shape of her face.

She went out of the door and along the passage to the head of the
stairs. She looked down, exactly as she had done the night of that
first party, the night Lila had died.

The hall was already filling with people, men in black, women in every color, brilliant and vivid and subtle, dark and pale colors, all the height of fashion. The light glanced off necklaces of pearls and sparkled on so many diamonds draped around women's necks, dangling from their ears, hanging like medals of honor on bosoms.

Even from above, Elena recognized many of the people this time round, people she had merely noted when she had photographed them that first night. Tonight, she had left her camera behind. Memories did not need to be reawakened. She could always run up and get it if it was needed.

Her grandmother came up behind her. "You look marvelous, dear. Quite unique. You are going to be ahead of fashion rather than behind it. I used to like doing that when I was your age. I was married by then, of course, and I think I horrified Wyatt a few times." Dorothy smiled. "He was always very sweet about it, but I wasn't sure he approved."

Elena turned to face her. Her grandmother was wearing a classically draped gown of deep pink silk, and it suited her delicate coloring perfectly. Elena smiled. "It might have been difficult for him to say so, but I'll bet he was fascinated. He might even have been shocked, but never, ever bored!"

Dorothy blushed very slightly, but she could not hide her pleasure. "Thank you, dear. That is one of the nicest compliments I have ever received. Come." She took Elena's arm. "Let's go down and take them by storm!"

"Let's!" Elena agreed, and guided her grandmother as they went slowly, regally, down the steps and into the throng.

They were welcomed immediately. Dorothy introduced Elena to all the groups of people, as if she had never done so before. The last days were not referred to, and everyone was charming.

Conversation buzzed around them. Older memories were brought forth. "Do you remember . . . ?" and then the occasion was mentioned as recollections arose. People, places, events, many of them possibly resembling the original hardly at all, but no one was clumsy enough to make the correction.

For Elena, it all had an air of unreality, as if she had slipped out of the original party and had fallen asleep in a corner, and then stepped back in again. The days between then and now seemed to have vanished. She recognized quite a few of the people from the first party, and their faces, even in many cases the women's gowns, but not always their names.

Among the crowd Elena saw Mabel Cartwright. She was wearing a different dress from the one she'd worn at the first party. It was a different shape, too, but the shade of green was equally vivid. It struck Elena as brave, defiant, but not beautiful. She saw her quite differently now. Mabel was a powerful woman. She had said so only obliquely, but she had let Elena know that she had influence in the Free America society, and she had not disguised the fact that she would use it.

Could she have killed Lila? For personal reasons? Or was she so passionately right wing in her beliefs that she had killed her for political reasons? No, that made no sense. Unless she was not just an admirer of Free America, but an active agent? How far right wing were they? Were they allied to the Nazis in Europe? Nothing suggested this. But if she was any good, she would be clever enough to hide it. As had Lila, or Elena herself!

She looked around for Borrodale. Why would he not come to this celebration of Wyatt's total exoneration? The police had withdrawn the charges.

The house was filling up quickly. Did anybody who was chatting with friends and sharing laughter, and perhaps relief, wonder who had killed Lila, knocked her unconscious, and then crushed her under the wheels of Wyatt's car? Elena saw no evidence on any of their faces. But then, what did we ever see of the person behind the careful, social face of someone with money and power? Come to think of it, she was also playing a part, all the time, but it was not to deceive anyone here as much as it was to be the delightful and welcoming granddaughter of Dorothy and Wyatt Baylor. Still . . . had one of them killed Lila? Elena thought about this for a moment and rephrased the question: Which of them had killed Lila? Because it was almost certain that some guest in this house had done just that.

There was a burst of laughter nearby, reminding Elena that she needed to join the party. This was her family celebration! She attached herself to a group of people standing around her grandfather, all of them raising a glass and toasting him.

"Seems to be going well," a voice said from just behind her.

She knew it was Allenby, without turning around to see him. "I keep looking at everyone and wondering if the person who killed Lila is here," she said, her voice low. "And if so, who is it? Is that wrong?"

"No," he answered immediately. "It's hard to look around for more than a moment or two and not wonder. But this is an occasion that lets you relax. You did a good job, Elena."

"We did," she corrected him. "And we have to include Harmon in that. Poor man. I didn't expect him to come. I'm not even sure if Grandmother Dorothy had the nerve to invite him. How could he want to anyway? And yet, not to invite him would be wrong. At least he needed to know he would be welcome, if he would have liked to have been here. Which, of course he wouldn't." The jumbled explanation made her smile. She turned to face him. "This is a celebration of my grandparents' sixty years together. But don't you think a remembrance of Lila would be appropriate, rather than enjoying ourselves all evening, as if she were never here?"

A flash of pain crossed Allenby's face. "You mean something like making a toast to her? I would, if it were my party. But I doubt Dorothy will do such a thing by herself. It's for Wyatt to do. He's very much in charge."

She heard all the nuances in his voice, and they were there in his face as well. It was the first time she had seen such a nakedness of emotion in him.

"Then we'll have to do it ourselves," she said softly. "But not in public, where her death will be all that will be remembered. She deserves better than that."

He nodded, lips tight, as if he found it too difficult for a moment to speak.

"Perhaps I should get the camera after all," she said. "Not necessarily for any newspaper or magazine, but for the people. And especially for my grandmother."

"Good idea." He nodded. "Lila was one of our own. You and I know that, but we can't tell anybody. These are the times when it hurts not to be able to."

She gave him a brief smile. "Yes," she agreed. Then she turned and went back upstairs to get her camera.

It was where she had left it, in her bedroom, sitting on the dressing table, reminding her that her last-minute decision not to take it was a mistake. But then, why *had* she left it behind? To forget the dreadful first time? Rather than dwell on that, she reminded herself that she should think instead of the picture that had proven her grandfather's innocence.

She stood in the room. What else did she need? She should take her pencil and notebook, as she always did, to note the names of the subjects, in case anyone wanted copies. She checked the point of the pencil: it was still sharp enough. How many pages were left in the notebook? She rifled through the leaves and looked at them. It opened easily to the page noting the photograph in front of the ormolu clock.

Her notes said the picture of Wyatt's friends was taken at ten twenty-five. She had written the time in her notebook, trusting the clock's time to be accurate. The next picture in the sequence, according to her notes, was one that was good enough to use, and she had known it at the time. It was taken just after she photographed Harmon Worth. The time noted was ten-fifteen.

But that was impossible. How could she photograph Wyatt at ten twenty-five, and the next shot was ten-fifteen?

She looked at her notes again. Was her handwriting clear? It was not always! Had she read the clock wrongly?

She flipped to the next page. Her notations read: "Rose Burberry: 10:20," then: "Antony Forsythe: 10:32."

Both names had their home addresses in parentheses. Both photographs were noted as having been taken before the one of Wyatt.

So, what did this mean? The last two shots were taken at the further end of the house, well away from the room where the ormolu clock sat on the mantel.

It made no sense.

She went through her bag and took out the negatives. She had a jeweler's loupe that allowed her to see the negative's fine details. It was not a good photograph, but Wyatt's hand, with its signet ring, was clear, and behind them, the clock. The time was clearly visible: ten twenty-five. And the photo just before that one, in the same room? She unfurled the roll of negatives and found it. It was a family group. The clock said nine-fifty.

A chill ran through her. What had happened to the clock? The only answer that forced its way into her mind, filling it with a slow-dawning horror, was that someone had changed the time. Someone . . . Who else but her grandfather? He had changed the time and then had a picture taken in front of the clock. And there was only one reason to do such a thing: to give himself an alibi.

So many thoughts rushed through her mind. Why wait for her to discover this herself? Why allow Katherine, and above all Dorothy, to suffer all these days in fear, while he grew more and more haggard in jail? Why hadn't he remembered the picture from the beginning?

The answers came after only a few seconds. He had always intended to draw attention to himself. Make sure everyone knew his name. And then what? He would be exonerated? The poor victim? For what purpose? To come out from the shadow of Franklin Roosevelt and run for office himself! A wronged man, falsely charged, emerging victorious! A man owed something by a society that had misjudged him. At the very least, people would know his name. No one would say, "Wyatt who?" He'd played a very dangerous game, perhaps for the very highest stakes! A fighter for lost causes! The man who won it all in the end.

As improbable as it sounded, Elena could not discount it.

It didn't need more explanation than that. Except . . . why had Borrodale not insisted she look at the photographs again? Did he not know? Or a far darker explanation: He planned to let Wyatt stand trial, and then exonerate him, so that he, too, could emerge a hero? That was not hard to believe. Elena had stolen his moment in the limelight. He would not like that.

What should she do now?

Why was she asking? There was only one thing she could do, whatever the cost. She had the proof in her hands. She put the negatives in her small camera case and carried it across the landing to her parents' room. She knew there was no one in it. She opened the door and went in. She searched around for a moment or two, then saw Charles's shaving kit on the dresser, the piece of furniture often called a tallboy. It was a chest of drawers with a wide top, ideal for a man's hairbrushes and combs and personal things. She opened the top drawer and slid the notebook inside, under the socks and underwear, then closed the drawer. Checking that no one was on the landing, she left the room, carrying only the camera in its case.

As quietly as she could, she descended the stairs and went in search of Allenby. Was it fair not to ask Charles first? Or even warn him? Yes, it was. This was not his decision to have to make. And, as it turned out, Charles was nowhere that she could see.

Actually, it was Charles who caught sight of Borrodale and followed him into one of the side rooms, closing the door behind them.

Borrodale heard the click of the latch and turned around, startled, and then, when he saw who it was, became annoyed. "I have a meeting with someone, which is not your concern, Mr. Standish."

"Well, he'll have to wait," Charles said, with uncharacteristic tartness. "Wyatt is free now, proved not guilty. And not by you, but by his family. Tell me, were you ever going to do anything about it? Or just protest a bit and let him go to the electric chair, a martyr to the cause?"

Borrodale smiled slowly. "Really, Ambassador, how can you be so competent, and so stupid? All causes need their martyrs, willingly, if possible. But if not, unwillingly will do."

"So, you would have let him die, and his family be dishonored? Isn't that a bit . . . pointless?" Charles said between his teeth. He was shaking with rage at the man who stood smiling in front of him. Charles was so good with words, but none that came to him were adequate to the emotion that now all but choked him.

"Not indefinitely," Borrodale went on. "We'd have proved him innocent, at an appropriate time. After he was executed, of course, when it was too late to make amends." His lips parted, showing very white teeth.

Charles hit him as hard as he could, right on the jaw. Borrodale's face registered a moment's amazement before the blow landed, then he stumbled backward, fell over the edge of the carpet, and lay still.

Charles checked that he was breathing, loosened the man's tie a little, then stood up and walked out of the room, back into the hallway, smiling. He did not think Borrodale would lay any charge against him. But if he did, what the hell?

CHAPTER 22

Allenby was easy to see, standing taller than most of the men, and Elena walked toward him, smiling at people and nodding. She hoped they might presume she was thinking of photographing someone, and would allow her to pass without drawing her into a conversation.

She approached Allenby and slipped her arm through his. It was a proprietorial gesture she had no right to, but she needed his attention while her nerve held.

He stiffened so imperceptibly that, should she not have been touching him, she would not have known. Did he resent it?

"James," she said, forcing her voice to remain level, "I need to speak to you about a picture."

He broke off the conversation, met her eyes for a moment, and excused himself from the group. He walked with her for a few paces, and then stopped and faced her. "What's happened?"

Elena glanced around, reminding herself to appear calm and relaxed, while making sure their voices would not be heard. "I've been looking at my notebook, where I wrote down all the information about the shots I took. But this one picture—" She stopped. There was still time to change her mind. Would she look like a silly, incompetent creature if she said nothing now, especially when she'd had the answer all this time, but had failed to realize its significance? No, any previous oversight no longer mattered. This wasn't about her; it was about her grandfather . . . and justice.

"You mean the one that proved Wyatt's innocence?" he asked.

"Yes," she said, her voice low with emotion.

"Was it . . . manipulated, somehow?" He looked puzzled.

She could hardly get her breath and her mouth was dry. "Not the photo," she explained. "It's the clock. It's been altered by nearly half an hour."

He gripped her arm, as if to hold her up if she fainted. "Are you certain? How do you know?"

"I found the discrepancy in my notebook. I note times for most of my pictures. The clock in that photo said it was half an hour later than it was."

Allenby said nothing, waiting for her to continue.

"I compared the time with the shots taken before and after. The clock had been changed."

"You're sure?"

"Of course I am! It's the only photo with a clear view of the time. And that picture is out of sequence in the negatives. You can't alter that! If you look at the order of the negatives, and compare that order to my notes, you'll see the error. It's there. Right there. And it can't be wrong."

She paused for a long moment, deciding what to say next. "That's why my grandfather was so insistent on taking a photograph in front of that mantelpiece. He isn't in it, so no one looked at it closely before. But his hand is, with that signet ring. And I can remember it. I would have to swear to it, if I were asked. So would the people in the picture. He must have changed the clock just before he gathered his friends for the shot. There's a key needed to open the glass face of that clock and reset the time."

"And no one noted that the time was wrong?"

"Who would, unless they were focused on learning the exact time, and used that clock to do so. Even then, why look if you're wearing a watch?"

They stood together in silence, as if not sure how to proceed. It was Elena who spoke first.

"Later, he had to reset the clock to the right time. When did he do that?"

Allenby did not respond, as if he knew what she was about to say.

"Perhaps when he was in jail, one of the servants reset the time. Someone with the job of winding the clock every so often. It might have stopped when he was away. And they corrected it when they rewound it. There would be no proof either way. Only someone's word," she said, urgency in her voice. "My God, what if Grandpa did it himself, when he came back into the house?"

Allenby placed his hand on Elena's arm.

"That's why we couldn't find anyone else to blame," she said, the words forced out. "There isn't anyone. He killed her."

Slowly, disbelief faded from Allenby's face, to be replaced by sorrow. "You're right," he said very quietly. "Do you want me to deal with it?"

"No, I don't. Thank you. The proof is in my notebook, which is now in the top drawer of that tallboy in my parents' room. And my memory. It's all there. It can't be a mistake."

"Have you told anyone else?" he asked, a deep line of concern on his brow.

"Not yet. And I wish . . . I wish they didn't have to know. But I can't see any way around it."

Allenby nodded. "He's free to have his political opinions, however offensive they are to us. But if he killed Lila, that's a crime for which there's no excuse. And it was deliberate, planned beforehand. She found out about him and his support of what was going on in Germany. She must have known he had a hand in getting the nuclear fission information out of America and safely into the hands of the Germans. And she would have exposed him for that, if not to the public, then to British Intelligence."

Her mind was whirling. It was the only answer that made sense. Lila had found out, and was prepared to expose not only him, but his Free America friends, too. That was why she had to be silenced, and immediately. Her one mistake was letting him see what she was intending to do. Had she meant to reveal this to him? Imagining he could do nothing? Or even hoping to turn him? Or was it that she hoped to use him for information? And misjudged how he would react? They would probably never know.

She drew in a deep breath. "I wanted you to know. You . . . need to know . . . in case anything happens to me."

"You are not going to face him alone," Allenby began.

"Yes, I am. He's my grandfather."

"Are you hoping there's a way out for him?" He shook his head, his eyes sad, his mouth tight. "There isn't."

"There might be! He must have information that he can—"

Allenby cut her off. "Elena, that's what Lila thought!" Emotion was thick in his voice. "There's no point in arguing with me. His spying is a matter of which side you are loyal to. Murdering Lila is not in that equation." He was holding her arm quite gently, almost as if in affection, but he was very much stronger than she. "This is not a time for heroics, Elena. Nor, however long you hesitate, is there any other choice. We must go now, before we attract everyone's attention, and they come to see what's the matter with us. This is better done privately."

"Yes, it is," she agreed. "It's late. The guests will be going soon. Should I wait until—No, I don't want to. I can't do it in front of his family. It needs to be softer, and cleverer, than that." Now that the moment was upon her, she had no idea what she wanted. Every possible choice was ghastly, and there was no way out.

"I'll ask to see him in his study," Allenby said, the firmness in his voice leaving her no room to argue. "It's a private room. Go there now, and I'll bring him in as soon as I can. Go on, please." He let go of her arm and gave her a very slight push.

She turned and made her way through the room, nodding at guests as she did. She crossed the hall and followed the passage as far as her grandfather's study. The door was not locked. She opened it and went in.

Had she done the right thing? Was Allenby going to bring her grandfather? Or was he going to warn him? Allenby was MI6, wasn't he?

She let her breath out slowly. There was a clock on the mantelpiece. Of course there was. No study was complete without a clock. The second hand moved round the face smoothly, the arc of its progress feeling like a slow step in eternity. It occurred to her that convincing her grandfather to leave his guests, if even for a moment, might not be easy. Was she going to be here all night?

The door opened and Wyatt came in, followed immediately by Allenby, who closed the door behind him. And then, as if quite casually, locked it and put the key in his pocket.

Wyatt glanced at her. "What the hell is going on? I'm grateful, Elena, I already told you that. I don't know what else you expect from me. I've been through hell, and one party doesn't undo that." He looked at her, then at Allenby.

She must put it as plainly as possible. "I presented your alibi to the police, Grandfather, and—"

"I thanked you," he interrupted. "What do you want for it? Payment?"

She looked straight at him, met his eyes and saw anger. Or was that fear?

"I'm going to tell the truth about it," she replied, as levelly as possible. "You insisted on that time and place for the photograph in front of the ormolu clock. Now I know why: you changed the clock."

"What?" His voice was incredulous, but the blood had gone from his face.

"I take notes on all my pictures," she went on. "The time, the subject . . ."

"Your handwriting? That proves nothing!" Wyatt snapped.

"The times of all the other shots were taken from my watch. But the time I wrote down, for that shot of you and your friends, I took from the clock on the mantelpiece. The clock that provided your alibi."

She waited for some response, but the old man said nothing, his eyes narrowed as he waited for more. Allenby, too, was silent. His expression, if she was reading it correctly, was encouraging her to go on.

"When I went back and studied that roll of negatives, that's when I realized that the ormolu clock in the photograph—the photograph that shows your friends, and your hand with your signet ring—was half an hour fast. It's correct now, because either you or one of the servants reset it to the right time."

Wyatt swallowed hard. "That proves nothing."

"It proves you altered the clock to provide an alibi. It gives you half an hour. Plenty of time to meet Lila, hit her, then drive your car over her body and kill her."

Wyatt was breathing heavily. "Why, for God's sake? You—"

"Because she knew that you were feeding information about America's work on nuclear fission to the Germans," Elena cut across him.

He was staring at her as if he saw her for the first time. "And how the hell would you know that?"

She was prepared for the question, and she knew her response must not reveal who she was working for. Or Allenby, either. "I liked Lila," she said. "She told me more than she intended to. And Harmon is not as foolish as you think, nor is he so grieved that he has stopped thinking."

"Lila! She was—"

"In your way," she finished. "But it doesn't matter why. The police were right the first time. You killed her, and I have the proof."

"You won't use it!" he said. "You don't dare!" he added, but his voice was hoarse.

"Yes, I will. I am using it, Grandfather. I'm sorry for both my grandmother and my mother, but it doesn't change anything."

Wyatt gave a burst of laughter, but his face was white. He swayed a little on his feet.

Allenby took a step forward.

Wyatt pulled out the top drawer of his desk.

Allenby lunged and grabbed his wrist before he could get hold of anything that might be hidden there. A weapon of some kind? He couldn't take the chance to find out.

"I'm taking a heart pill, you damn fool!" Wyatt snarled.

Allenby eased his grip a little and looked in the drawer. There was only a half-empty bottle of whiskey and a small bottle of pills. No gun. No weapon of any kind. He let go of Wyatt's wrist.

Wyatt took a step back, breathing hard. He shook pills out of the bottle and into his hand, and then into his mouth, swallowing them down with a mouthful of whiskey. His face turned whiter still. After a very long moment, with silence filling the room, he slumped forward over the desk. Before Elena could reach him, her grandfather slid to the floor.

Elena froze for a second, a beat of the heart, then she reached toward him, kneeling to grasp his wrist and feel for a pulse, but she knew she would not find one.

She felt Allenby's arms around her, lifting her up. He held her tightly, close to him. As if she could not stand alone. It was several moments before he spoke, and when he did, it was gently. "It's better this way," he said. "It will spare him the humiliation, and I expect it will be less hard for Dorothy, and for your mother. They don't need to know the truth. I suppose you could even think of it as a decent exit."

She pulled away from him a little, so she could speak clearly, and gain some control of herself. "Did you know he would do that?"

"No. If I had, I suppose I would have felt the need to try to stop him. Now we can't even trace his contact. Not that, I suppose, that would have been easy to do anyway."

She looked at him steadily. Was that an oversight on his part? Or mercy? She wanted very much, too much, for it to be mercy.

"I'll have to tell my family."

He pulled a clean handkerchief out of his pocket and gave it to her. "I'll tell the household staff, so they can keep order . . . and help people to leave. I think if you can manage it, you should tell your mother and your grandmother. Just say that he was having a heart attack and he took his pills late."

"What were we here for? In this room . . . now?" She wiped her cheeks of tears and blew her nose.

"To see which photographs he would like to have printed. Or perhaps which ones he wanted taken tonight? Which grouping of his friends?" he suggested.

"And you?"

"I was with you at the time. Good manners."

"Of course," she agreed, although she wasn't quite sure what he meant. She straightened up, putting her shoulders back. She had forgotten the beautiful dress. It was, obliquely, a reminder of who she was now, and what she had promised to do. "Thank you."

Allenby did not say anything, as if understanding was sometimes better expressed in silence.

She went out the door, this time ignoring everyone she passed until she met her mother, who was in conversation with one of the guests. "Excuse me," she said, interrupting the man as he was speaking. "I need to talk with my mother." She pulled on her mother's arm and saw the shock in her face. There was no gentle way to do this.

"What is it?" Katherine asked.

"Come with me, please."

"What's the matter? What happened?" There was fear in Katherine's face already.

There was no point in dragging it out. Elena stopped walking. "I'm sorry, I wanted to tell you somewhere more private. Grandfather has had a heart attack. He took his medicine, but it didn't work."

Katherine stood as if frozen, as if a moment of silence would make it disappear.

"I'm sorry," Elena said. "But it was very quick."

"You were there?" Katherine asked.

"Yes. It was very . . . quick," she repeated. "I think the way anyone would want to go." As she spoke, she was looking around the room, hoping to see her father. He would be the support her mother needed most.

Katherine's eyes filled with tears and Elena put her arms around her shoulders and held her as tight as she could, letting her weep.

After a few moments, Katherine straightened up, wiped her cheeks, and gave a little sniff.

"Thank you, dear. I'm so grateful that you cleared his name before he went. At least he knew he was exonerated."

Elena took a deep breath and gritted her teeth. "Mother, do you want me to tell Grandmother?"

"No. No, dear. I'll tell her. But you could tell your father." She looked around. "Where is he?"

"Don't worry, I'll find him."

Katherine touched Elena's cheek and then walked away, avoiding everyone's eyes.

Elena knew that this was not the time to be drawn into polite conversation or say anything before speaking to her father. When she saw him, he looked unusually relaxed, almost buoyant. She wished she did not have to tell him the truth.

She walked toward the group of guests, the dress swirling with her movement. One of the men noticed her and Charles turned to look.

He must have read the emotion in her face, because he excused himself with no more than a word and came toward her. "What's happened?" he asked, as soon as he was close enough to speak to her quietly.

"Grandfather Wyatt is dead," she said, almost choking on her own breath. "He had a heart attack. I was there. He took his medicine, but it was too late."

"There?" Charles asked, holding her arms gently. "Where?"

"His study. And Father . . ."

"What? Elena? What is it?"

"I . . . I'll tell you later. Now you need to say it was just a heart attack, that's all, and everyone should leave. Please."

"But is it all?" he demanded, his face twisted with shock.

Elena felt the tears spilling onto her cheeks and wiped them away. "He . . . he killed Lila. I have proof, but I'll not show it to the police. And I'll not tell Mother or Grandma, not yet. It's all so unbearable."

"But he did die of a heart attack?" Charles insisted, almost holding her up by gripping her arms.

"Yes. He took his heart pills, too many of them. I wasn't quick enough to stop him, but I don't think I would have anyway," she answered.

"Was anybody else there?"

"Captain Allenby."

"You can explain that later. Have you told your mother?"

"Yes, but only that he has died. She's telling Grandma." After a moment, she added, "You must get rid of these people!"

"I will," he said. "I will. Now come with me." He took her hand and led her across the room. He stopped one of the staff and whispered in the man's ear.

Elena saw first surprise and then sadness in his face, and then watched him rush from the room. She was certain he was heading to secure her grandfather's study until help arrived: the police, the family doctor to confirm the death, or someone else—would the man know to call the coroner? She wasn't sure, but she felt relief that

her father was acting on this, and she chastised herself for not having
locked the door before she and Allenby had come to inform the others. Her thoughts were interrupted when her father knocked a silver
spoon hard against an empty crystal goblet.

Slowly, the voices stopped, the room fell quiet. There was anticipation on many of the faces, as if a celebratory toast were about to
be given.

"Ladies and gentlemen, friends. I regret to tell you that my
father-in-law, Wyatt Baylor, suffered a heart attack a few minutes
ago." Before questions could be asked, he added, "I'm so sorry, but
I'm afraid it was fatal."

There were gasps around the room, but no one spoke.

Charles waited a moment, and then spoke again. "But he was in
his home, among friends and family." After another long moment,
he added, "Now, I have to ask you to collect your coats and leave
quietly. We must all mourn his death, and deal with the matters at
hand. Thank you."

Katherine went toward him and took his arm. She did not say
anything, but it was all there, bleak and shocking in her face. Then
she turned and went to Dorothy, putting her arms around her, the
two women standing close together.

Allenby came back to Elena. "Are you all right?" he asked softly.

"Yes, of course," Elena replied. "I . . ." She lost the words.

"You want to speak to Lucas," he said, finishing for her.

"Yes. Please. We can make the call from the sitting room."

She spoke momentarily to the butler, telling him she would be
back shortly, and instructing him to inform her father that she would
be in the sitting room if he needed her.

She and Allenby did not speak until they were alone. She dialed
Lucas's number. A few moments later, she heard her grandfather's
sleepy, anxious voice. "Grandpa? It's Elena. We're all fine, but Grandfather Wyatt has had a heart attack. He's gone."

"I'm sorry," Lucas said quietly. "You . . ."

Allenby put his hand over hers and took the phone away. "Allenby here, sir. Elena solved the murder of Lila Worth. I'm afraid it was Baylor. Definitely. Yes, sir, she has proof. When she faced him with it, he took an overdose of his heart medicine. We're saying that it was a heart attack." He waited a few moments in silence, listening whilst Lucas spoke. "Yes, sir," he said at last. "Very professional. A clean job, and merciful. Yes, sir. The trap is set and they've taken the bait."

He put the telephone back on its cradle and gave Elena a little smile. "He says he's proud of you."

"Thank you." She blinked back tears. She wanted to say more, but the words stuck in her throat. When she nodded, she knew that he understood. Turning, she walked out of the room to join her parents.

For more international intrigue in pre-war Europe,
turn the page to sample

A Truth to Lie For

An Elena Standish Novel

BY ANNE PERRY

CHAPTER

1

"I believe you have been complaining recently that your work is not challenging enough." Peter Howard raised his eyebrows very slightly. In the sunlight through the office window, he looked amused rather than surprised.

Elena drew in a breath, then slowly let it out again. "Yes," she said. She had been recruited to MI6 by Peter just over a year ago, in May 1933. Now, in June 1934, he was her mentor, and her commanding officer. "I'm doing what any halfway competent clerk would do just as well," she added.

A flash of amusement lit his face. "Then you will be pleased that I have a job for you that will require all your talents and abilities. Well, except photography."

Photography was Elena's profession, her art, and her passport to all kinds of places and situations. It was her expertise as a photographer that had resulted in her invitation to a conference in Trieste, where she had also succeeded in her first official MI6 assignment. And more recently, her photographic skills had added so much to her family's celebration in Washington, DC—and ultimately led her to solve two murders.

But she did not want to think about that now. It had been less than two months since the incidents in Washington, which had involved her grandfather, and which had ended so terribly. The pain was still raw for both of her parents, but especially her mother. Elena had hardly known her American grandfather, whereas she had a close and loving relationship with Grandfather Lucas, the former head of MI6.

Peter was talking, and she had not been listening.

". . . Berlin again," he was saying. "You must not be recognized, Elena. This is not an order—the mission is too dangerous for that— but it is a request that you cannot refuse."

The irony of the distinction was not lost on her.

"We're sending another person as well, but you will not meet. Nor will you contact each other unless it is absolutely necessary."

What had she missed? The humor of a few moments ago had vanished. Peter was no longer smiling but squinting as he looked past her, as if he saw something threatening approaching from far off, something that was crowding out everything else.

He must have observed her confusion, because a gentleness appeared in his face. Not just in his eyes, but in his mouth as well. "What is it?" she asked as politely as she could. Now fear brushed by her. She waited, as if for the blow.

"I want you to get someone out of Germany who is currently in Berlin."

She knew he would read the fear in her face, and yet she could not hide it. That first assignment in Berlin had marked the moment she had changed from a naïve—and frankly fairly boring—girl into a young woman of courage and imagination. A woman who expressed a passionate anger against the indifference of those who saw only what they chose to, which was primarily what fitted in their comfortable lives.

Her throat was dry. "Berlin?" She only just managed to get the word out.

"Yes," he said, watching her reactions. "There are two scientists we need to get out of the country."

"Physicists?" she asked, remembering her last mission, also one she had not chosen, but which had been thrust upon her.

"No, this time they are biochemists," he replied. "Two brilliant men. They form a research team, and the work of one depends on the other."

She remained silent, knowing that Peter would tell her only what she needed to know.

"One of them is creating new germs to be used in warfare, while we believe the other is on the brink of finding an antidote to those same germs, which is vital, of course, before using them against anyone."

He was still watching her intently.

"You were a child during the last war," he continued, "but you have learned enough about the use of gas in the trenches to imagine what germ warfare can be. What it can do, not only to armies, but to entire civilian populations, is—"

"Yes," she said sharply, cutting him off. The thought was obscene. "What do I have to do?"

"We're going to get these two men out of Germany. The extraction of one of them is your task. We'll send another agent, Alex Cooper, for the other."

"Why?" The word was out before she thought that perhaps she was asking for more information than she needed.

Peter's smile was bleak and there was a flicker of pain in it. "Because it's vital that we get both of them out. And if they leave separately, there's a better chance that they will survive. It causes less suspicion."

Elena was paying close attention. The last thing they wanted was to allow Germany and Adolf Hitler to have the upper hand in germ warfare!

"The Germans know that we're aware of this research," Peter continued. "And if they discover that we are planning to extract their scientists, they will make every attempt to keep these two men in a secure location, hiding them until their work is done." After a pause, he added, "And then they will kill them so they don't take their knowledge elsewhere. We need to get them out before this happens." He stopped. There was a rigidity in his body, even his face.

Elena knew that he hated having to say this, but he also knew that she needed the truth.

"It will be your job to get Professor Heinrich Hartwig out of Berlin. Cooper will go after the other scientist, Fassler, who, at this time, is not your concern. You need only focus on Hartwig."

She was certain there was more, and she waited. It was not long in coming.

"Elena, you need to understand. Fassler is vital to their germ warfare plans, but he's a Jew. The minute he delivers, he's dead. He knows this." Peter paused. "Both men are prepared to leave Germany immediately. Hartwig and Fassler are research associates, the Germans' top team in their field. They don't work together, or even in the same lab, but their work is complementary. One man's work is incomplete without the other's. Hartwig is developing an antidote to the germ. You can't use this stuff at all until you have a sure protection against it for your own population. If we only get Hartwig out and not Fassler, we will at least have the antidote ourselves. But Germany will still develop the germ. And then they will find someone else who will ultimately develop a vaccine against it."

"And Hartwig is willing to sacrifice his entire life in order to work in tandem with Fassler?" she asked. "Has Fassler no loyalty to humanity, if nothing else? What on earth does he believe in? Hitler?"

"I don't believe either of them cares about politics one way or the other. They care about knowledge, science, and medicine. But it's more than that," Peter explained. "Hartwig is a widower, no children, his life is his work. And he sees where Germany is heading. This is not a sacrifice for him; it's a necessity. Fassler? I know less about him."

"Peter—" she began, but was cut off.

"They both need to get out quickly, while they can," Peter insisted. "The Germans undoubtedly know that any of their enemies will try to lure these men out." His voice was firm, leaving no room for discussion.

"But you said that others would just take their places?" Elena asked.

"For some of the work, of course. Not for the creative genius. That's all you need to know."

Elena saw this as a polite way of reminding her how dangerous this mission would be. If she was caught, as long as she did not have certain knowledge, no threat, no torture in the world, could make her tell.

Peter moved a little toward the window and, in a trick of the light, the shadows vanished from his face. When he spoke, his voice was lower, harsher. "The Nazis are persecuting the Jews even more appallingly than when you were there a year ago."

"Worse than last year?" she asked incredulously, memory scorching her. "I saw a young man on the kitchen table of the people who took me in. The Brownshirts had flayed the skin from half his body. I don't even know if they managed to save him. I can't imagine the persecution being worse than that."

He looked at her steadily. Seconds ticked by. "Do you want me to send someone else?" His voice was not critical, just disappointed.

"No, of course not." She forced herself to say it, before she had time to consider whether it was really what she meant. But what a heavy burden! She was sure there was much he wasn't telling her, but she knew he was protecting her. Her grandfather Lucas would not have told her everything either. He had been protecting her from all sorts of pain for as long as she could remember, far back into childhood. Her memories of him had been of safety, discovery, of long conversations about all kinds of things: the ultimate friendship. She could remember weeding the garden with him, the immeasurable happiness of thinking she was helping. The memory was still so clear, and yet she had been only about three years old.

"Remember, Elena, Fassler is not your responsibility," Peter went on. "Your only goal is to get Hartwig out."

"And if I can't?" It was an unnecessary question, but she asked it anyway.

"Then think of the worst disaster you can imagine. Hemorrhagic fever, or something as dreadful as that. Uncontrolled bleeding, and then death. Entire populations disappearing. Corpses all over the place because there is no time to bury them, and maybe even no one left to do it."

"You don't need to paint that for me!"

"Or bubonic plague," he added. "The Black Death of 1348. It took a quarter of the population of Europe."

"I get the point, Peter. We must get them out."

"Yes, we must," he said sharply. Almost as an afterthought, he added, "You do know that we have our own germ warfare experiments?"

She froze.

"How the hell can we defend ourselves otherwise?" he said quickly, as if he might have said too much. "We don't know what the enemy has, but the more we know about where they are in the development of it, the better chance we have of stopping them." He shook his head fractionally, barely a movement at all. "Elena, if you can bring Hartwig here, he can help us with the antidote. But if you cannot get him out, you must see that the Germans don't arrest him. They must not take him alive. Can you do that?"

She looked at him with intensity. "Kill him? Yes," she said hoarsely. "I suppose there really is no choice."

She looked away. It bothered her that he would assume she would blame . . . and freely. "Is there more?" she asked.

"A lot. You need to know all you can about Hartwig. His life will depend upon you. That means you must learn about his history, his strengths and weaknesses. I will give it to you on paper, which you will memorize, then burn. You will have to contact him first, of course. Introduce yourself, and then say that you can and will help him."

"And who am I?"

"Ellen Stewart. Enough like your own name to recognize or remember it. Ordinary enough. I looked in the telephone book." He gave a very slight, bleak smile. "There are ten in the London telephone directory. I'll give you an address, too. You moved there recently. You will have a British passport, and a driving license. A checkbook as well. I don't expect you'll need it, but it will be attached to a real account. Your father is a schoolteacher of mathematics, and your mother had three children. They lost their son in the war. Their other daughter is a widow, also from the war. We'll stick to the truth as much as possible." Peter looked around the room, his face devoid of expression. "You'll need an explanation for your familiarity with Germany, both its culture and language. I suggest regular holidays, perhaps a childhood friend who came from Germany and wanted you to learn her language. And you studied German in school, and at university. Have it ready in your mind. Never volunteer information, but have it prepared. I think your major problems will be your appearance, your clothes."

She was a little stung by that remark, and then she realized it was not personal, it was strictly professional, and she thought she understood. When she had last gone to Germany, just over a year ago— although it seemed like another lifetime—she had learned that trying to hide was not the best way to disappear. Before Berlin, she had been unintentionally dowdy. She wore inconspicuous colors, soft blues and browns mostly, and dresses that were presentable, but ordinary. Boring, in fact. And no makeup, except a little lipstick to make her fair skin less colorless. When she needed to disappear into the background, her friends persuaded her to dye her hair from what she called "English mouse" to a sort of Nordic blond, which suited her wonderfully. She remembered that well-fitting scarlet dress. It was spectacular! And yet, when she changed into the dress, she disappeared. That was when she learned that people remember the clothing, and not the face of the woman wearing it. If anyone was asked to describe her, it was the dress they would remember.

She had liked the overall effects of these changes so much that she had kept them. Not the dress, which had been destroyed—and in a way she would rather not recall—but she had loved the style. That included the fairer hair, which was much the same as it had been when she was three or four years old.

So, was Peter asking her to become invisibly ordinary again, just like the image of her on the wanted poster that had been all over the streets in Berlin only a year ago? Not the striking blonde she had become, who walked with grace and assurance, as if she were beautiful, and knew it?

She waited for Peter to speak. He was still hesitating, and she wondered what he was thinking.

"Leave your hair as it is," he said finally. "It attracts attention here, but blondes are less unusual in Germany. If the subject arises, your mother was Swedish. And stay with cool, sophisticated colors, possibly even black."

"In June?" she questioned.

"Why not? Or navy. And not a dress. Trousers are very fashionable now, if you can get away with them."

He looked at her carefully and she felt distinctly self-conscious. "Yes, sir," she said obediently.

He did not respond.

Elena guessed that he had known she would say exactly that, and that he had probably known the tone of voice she would use as well. It was the only answer she could give. They both knew the weight of what she was about to do, and the risks as well.

Peter relaxed a little. It was barely perceptible, just an easing of the shoulders. "You will spend the afternoon with Mrs. Smithers," he explained. "She'll see that you have everything you need. That includes money, a map of the Berlin railway system, bus timetables . . . I don't expect you'll need that but it's the sort of thing Ellen

Stewart would carry. You can spend the afternoon however you think most useful, but you will sleep in a hotel tonight. And you will not contact your family. Any member of it! That includes Lucas. I'll tell him later."

She wanted to protest, but remained silent. It would be pointless anyway, and a trifle childish.

"That is an order, Elena," he said. "Disobedience will mean dismissal. And then we'll have to start again to find someone else to rescue Hartwig, before it is too late, which it might already be. Every day counts." He handed her a sealed envelope. "Your information on Hartwig. Memorize it, then destroy it."

There was not even the ghost of a smile on his face. She was quite certain he had not forgotten the scandal when she had worked in the Foreign Office. She had studied for years in Cambridge for her degree. She was good at her work, excellent. Even so, it was her father's post as British Ambassador in Berlin, Madrid, and Paris that had resulted in that position for her. And then she had lost it because of her own stupidity. The disgrace had been deep and awful, especially to her family. For herself, she had deserved it. She was the one who had fallen in love with a traitor, but her family suffered for her, and with her. Peter knew how deeply it had cut, and he worded the warning specifically that way to impress it upon her.

"I trust you to tell them something so that they don't wonder why I don't answer the telephone," she said a little stiffly. "Or why I can't contact them at all."

That he agreed was evident in the softening of the lines on his face. "I might even tell Lucas the truth. Or perhaps not. I might wait until I know you are out again, and safe." His look was almost tender. "Be careful, Elena."

PHOTO: © MELANIE ABRAMS

ANNE PERRY is the *New York Times* bestselling author of two ac-claimed series set in Victorian England: the William Monk novels and the Charlotte and Thomas Pitt novels. She is also the author of a series featuring Thomas and Charlotte Pitt's son, Daniel, in-cluding *Three Debts Paid* and *Death with a Double Edge;* the Elena Standish series, including *A Darker Reality* and *A Question of Betrayal;* five World War I novels; nineteen holiday novels, most recently *A Christmas Deliverance;* and a historical novel, *The Sheen on the Silk,* set in the Byzantine Empire. Anne Perry lives in Los Angeles.

anneperry.us

Facebook.com/AnnePerryAuthor

To inquire about booking Anne Perry for a speaking engagement, please contact the Penguin Random House Speakers Bureau at speakers@penguinrandomhouse.com.

ABOUT THE TYPE

The text of this book was set in Janson, a typeface designed about 1690 by Nicholas Kis (1650–1702), a Hungarian living in Amsterdam, and for many years mistakenly attributed to the Dutch printer Anton Janson. In 1919, the matrices became the property of the Stempel Foundry in Frankfurt. It is an old-style book face of excellent clarity and sharpness. Janson serifs are concave and splayed; the contrast between thick and thin strokes is marked.